MOTHERS

MOTHERS

Jax Peters Lowell

St. Martin's Griffin
New York

 For information, address St. Martin's Press, 175 Fifth Avenue, New York, N.Y. 10010.

Library of Congress Cataloging-in-Publication Data

Lowell, Jax Peters.
Mothers / by Jax Peters Lowell.
p. cm.
ISBN 0-312-14373-7
1. Mothers and sons—New York (N.Y.)—Fiction. 2. Lesbian mothers—New York (N.Y.)—Fiction. 3. Lesbians—New York (N.Y.)—Fiction. I. Title.
[PS3562.0886M67 1996]
813'.54—dc20 96-3326
CIP

First St. Martin's Griffin Edition: May 1996

10 9 8 7 6 5 4 3 2 1

This book is dedicated to my husband, John Lowell,
whose struggle to remember
illuminates in ways unimaginable.

Acknowledgments

Mothers may not have been born at all without my oldest and dearest friend, Jane Krensky, whose life and work and beautiful brood have never ceased to inspire. Nor would it have taken hold so firmly if it were not for my own mother, Catherine Peters, and my late father, John Peters, who rose above their grief to show me courage, unconditional love, and, one last time, what families are made of.

And still, *Mothers* may not have found its voice if not for Sasha Goodman and David Andrew, who encouraged, pushed, praised, and believed before even I; St. Martin's Sally Richardson, who welcomed me with warmth and enthusiasm; my editor, Reagan Arthur, who showered me with a genius many would have reserved for more well-known commodities; Jack Cassidy, whose good heart and wise counsel was my truest compass; Pat Mastandrea, who offered stunning proof that courage need not shout, that generosity of spirit is all; and the small family of cherished friends who gathered around, read, and unreservedly cheered me on.

I will never sufficiently thank these dear people, only honor them by continuing the work.

We shall not cease from exploration
And the end of all our exploring
Will be to arrive where we started
And know the place for the first time.

T. S. Eliot,
Four Quartets

I

Claire never planned on falling in love with Theo, or with anyone for that matter, but that's exactly what happened at the cheese counter at Fraser-Morris one gorgeous fall afternoon. "That's how life is," she said. "One minute you're happily going in one direction, well maybe not so happily, but at least seeing clearly what's ahead of you and then wham—you're on a hairpin turn veering off over a cliff."

It wasn't as though Claire hadn't given romance her best shot. She joked that "The Dating Game" was considering her for a lifetime achievement award; she never could refuse her mother and Aunt Fitzie who fixed her up with an endless supply of sons from their wide circle of prominent friends, luncheon committee acquaintances, and eager would-be mothers-in-law.

"Anyone with a pulse," Claire joked, and according to her own rather exaggerated calculations, she went on thousands of blind dates with boys who never seemed to grow up and leave the rambling Park Avenue and West End Avenue apartments of their privileged childhoods and who, by the tender age of twenty, were already ruined by the belief that an expensive dinner and a ride home in the family limo gave them the right to an after-dinner grope.

Long before Theo, in the odd-job years after film school she referred to as her "starving artist period," she often double-dated with her best friends, Jessica and Baxter, who had just fallen in love, nibbling burgers and drinking Bloody Marys in the hip new places that had begun to bloom all over New York with Peter Max posters, asparagus ferns, and fashionable flower children who came as close to the revolution as their trust funds would allow. But usually before the waiter arrived with the menus, something told her their good intentions would go no further, and most nights, Albert or Charlie or Jeffrey or Gus made their good nights and headed home, leaving the three friends to their nightcaps and the lazy talk of people who are comfortable with one another. Watching her two friends tumble into a taxi always made her sad. It wasn't envy, really. She loved them both; it was just that way down at the bottom of her feelings there was an aching hole that the sight of them heading home to bed always made just a little bigger, a little more jagged.

One summer, she took a half share in a beach house in Quogue which entitled her to a damp room over the windy dunes every other weekend. There she met a nice man named Alan, who she was convinced was Relationship Material, but after two dates he threw her over for someone named Helen who had a full share and an apartment closer to his in the city. He told Claire she was more geographically convenient.

"Can you beat that?" she said. "Dating a girl because she's convenient! Supermarkets are convenient. Dry cleaners are convenient. Love is never convenient. You go out of your way for love. For love, you should be willing to go anywhere . . . to Brooklyn, if necessary!"

When she was being silly, Claire said she was attracted to Theo because as a child she refused to take ballet lessons at Miss Fiona Wills's School of Social Dancing, a decision that left her with a long, flat-out kind of walk she referred to as "the galomph" and a real weakness for good dancers. In more serious moments, she said it was really her brother Roland, who had died in a car crash at the age of nineteen and whose spirit had taken up residence in her body, who had chosen Theo for her. But she was always quick to add that this was long before she was comfortable with the whole idea.

The Hirsh family was more than well-off, which made it even harder for Claire to find true love. Money has a way of generating its own heat, and she never could spot a fortune hunter before he broke her heart, so after a while, she just gave up on dating and borrowed other people's boyfriends the way other people shared umbrellas. Always chummy, always a pal, never a threat, Claire was everyone's friend and no one's love.

Until Theo.

They met on one of those rare and stunning autumn days that

hooks people on New York as irrevocably as any drug. Claire described it as the kind of day that fills a person with the arrogance of living in this shimmering place full of interesting people and abrupt changes in circumstance, and as she walked east through the leafy Village streets toward an uptown cab, she felt every bit as full of possibility as that dazzling afternoon. She was heading toward a dream that was finally coming true, and the power of that simple fact seemed to wash everything in a light even more golden than the glorious day before her. She'd spent years photographing weddings and bar mitzvahs and christenings and shooting public-relations events and not being able to sell her heart's work; one day the owner of the Light Gallery simply looked up from his light box, where Claire's slides were scattered like Scrabble pieces, and asked if she would be interested in their giving her a show.

"Just like that," she had said, snapping her fingers, "after years of drudgery and dreaming, at the age of thirty-three, a little long in the tooth to be considered wunderkind, I became what is known in New York as an overnight sensation."

But even as she walked toward the future she had pictured for so long, excited, confident, and a little bit scared, she sensed something different, something dangerous in the crisp cold breath of that day, and it whispered that everything would change.

Claire had always wanted to be a photographer: not a fashion photographer like so many of her college friends who ran to see *Blow Up* and pursued glamour with every conscious thought, but a real one. Claire wanted to be someone who could see into the souls of people by capturing that split second when all of life is revealed in a glance and all of human experience is written in one ordinary face. She burned to become the next Cartier-Bresson, Stieglitz, Cunningham; to be the Cornell Capa of her generation.

It started the day Aunt Fitzie took her to the Jewish Museum to see W. Eugene Smith's photo essay on war. Claire experienced a transcendent power in the eyes of a young Marine, his face greased against an invisible enemy, one arm holding the lifeless body of a comrade, the other raised in a fist, clenched with hatred for his buddy's killer, his tears carving gullies of sorrow in the fierce blackness of his cheek. A young man and his dead friend leaned against a tree and in that moment of howling loss, a shutter clicked and a photograph recorded all that we know and all that we will ever know about war. A thin, shy girl stood in a cavernous room resonating with the power of that picture, and Claire's dream was born.

"Claire was not the same girl after that show," said Fitzie, who never tired of telling anyone who would listen as she proudly leafed through her niece's photographs. "I'll never forget how afterwards she blinked into the sun just like a shutter opening and closing and said, 'Aunt Fitzie, I'm going to see like that someday.' I knew it right then and there, my little Claire was going to be famous."

Soon after, Claire bought a battered Leica that the man in a gloomy second-hand store on lower Broadway told her had once been used to photograph Paul Robeson. Every click brought her closer to that crazy afternoon when she walked through Greenwich Village saying *"One-woman show one-woman show one-woman show"* over and over like a mantra.

As she walked along West Tenth Street toward Fifth Avenue, she invited a Corgi who was blissfully relieving himself against a tree and laughed out loud when he cocked his head and looked up at her. Smiling at how ridiculous and wonderful all this was, she wondered what Mr. Kimsky and Mrs. Appelbaum, the Russian, and all her new friends in Coney Island, would think of all this.

"Meshugge," Mrs. Stein would say. "Crazy"—shaking her faded curls at the antics of young people today. The Rabbi, what would he make of it? He'd want to put a *"baruch"* on the pictures, bless them, so they would sell for "the nice girl with the camera."

Claire thought of the long winter she had spent with these people, taking the subway every day, hurtling to the tip of Manhattan in the white tiled tube, then inching along Brooklyn's spine, coming up into the clear cold air tinged with salt and the sound of gulls swooping in and out of the great hulking skeleton of a roller coaster and the parachute jump Claire's own mother rode one hot night in 1930, becoming front-page news when it froze and left a young woman with pretty legs dangling in the summer air. How they welcomed her to this strange place warmed by hope, haunted by the shrill laughter of its youth, chilled by the fear of the old Jews who sat on its shore, this grotesque place that remembered its own days in the sun with rusted clowns, condemned rides, and toothache-sweet cotton candy.

She had photographed rows and rows of them, wizened men and gnarled grandmas sitting on ancient wooden folding chairs, studying the ocean, as though a lost relative might suddenly appear from across the years. They kept the vigil day after day in all weather, as though watching the horizon and the deep water that changed from inviting blue to cold black was the only guarantee against a return of the terror that had so brutally stolen their innocence. Claire believed one of them would sound the alarm if anything evil washed up on these shores, something far worse than the used condoms and glittering needles on the wide beach that once had the power to heal the broken, overheated spirits who came from the suffocating tenements of the Lower East Side to breathe a few hours of fresh salt air and to walk barefoot on the powdery sand before going back to the sweatshops.

After a while, they trusted her and looked forward to her visits. As they sat in the fragile warmth of the winter sun, their faces shining, upturned, as though gently cupped in an invisible lover's hand, they spoke of ordinary things, children and grandchildren long gone to subdivisions on Long Island, people who came to visit one Sunday a month, dutiful children who politely listened to their talk of aches and pains, sons and daughters who fought hard to live beyond the smell of cabbage and the old linoleum of their parents' lives.

They spoke to Claire of things that were never whispered in their own families, of sisters and brothers, mothers and fathers gone, all gone to the death camps, husbands and wives torn from them without mercy, things that made the drugs and the violence and the muggings lurking in the doorways of their once peaceful, now decayed neighborhood seem almost innocent.

At first they preened for Claire's Leica, the women smoothing thin, dyed hair, touching lipstick to mouths frayed at the edges like old sweaters, the men standing a little straighter than usual, arthritic fingers running along the invisible crease lines of pants long softened by sitting. But after a while the constant whirring and clicking became just another sound in their lives, punctuating their conversations with the tall blond woman who wanted to hear their stories, the well-mannered girl who showed them respect.

These were her beloved Coney Island people, dark as raisins, looking out from her pictures in silent tribute to the restorative powers of sun and salt air. She could see them now, nestled in coats shiny from years of sitting on rickety folding chairs, playing mah-jongg, lost in the clicking tiles and in the memories of when they were young. Claire had worked on the show all summer and now, as her friends looked down at her from their places on the gallery walls, wiser and more powerful as a group, oddly victorious over something they could not have vanquished in the separate struggles of their lives, Claire hoped they would approve.

As she entered "F-M," as her mother called this Madison Avenue trove of first-pressed Tuscan oils, imported truffles, pâté, porcini mushrooms, endless varieties of caviar and foie gras, foods her old Coney Island friends had rarely seen, much less have easily afforded, Claire could not help thinking they would no more understand the slouching affectation and the ritual wasting of expensive food that attends an opening night than they would the workings of the Vatican.

At that moment, drifting up and down the aisles, propelled by a dream that was close enough to touch, Claire looked more apparitional than real; perhaps she was a trick of the light, perhaps not. She was a tall, slim, interesting-looking woman wearing black, with long pale hair. In the light that poured in from the window, fine cobwebby lines traced eyes of silver-gray and fanned out over porcelain skin, leaving it looking oddly cracked and in need of a good watering. The result was a face that was neither young nor old, attractive nor homely, remote nor accessible, but rather one that found its beauty among its contradictions.

"I'd like to order a selection of cheeses and some pâtés, for an opening party I'm having at the Light Gallery," Claire said to the person behind a counter piled high with cheeses of every imaginable variety, some so ripe that Claire had to restrain herself from casually dipping a finger into a particularly runny Camembert. "Maybe some triple-crème Brie and Pont-l'Eveque?"

"What kind of show is it?" the smiling woman asked, wiping surprisingly well-manicured hands on an apron so smudged with food, it could have been a Jackson Pollack canvas.

"Photographs, actually," Claire answered, a little surprised by the question.

"Yes, I know the gallery. I live downtown. I meant what *kind* of show is it? What's the concept? Who's the artist?" the woman asked.

"Me."

"You?"

"I want everything to be perfect."

The woman smiled. And waited.

"I call it 'Coney Island.' You know, old folks sitting in the sun, Russian bulls charging into the ocean in February, the immigrant thing, Nazi-camp survivors, surrounded by Puerto Ricans and blacks who've moved into the neighborhood, one group living in distrust and begrudging respect of the other, that sort of thing. . . ." The woman closed her eyes, rocked back on her heels, and nodded.

"What's this got to do with cheese?" said Claire abruptly, wondering why she had just given a synopsis of her work to a perfect, or on second thought, maybe not-so-perfect stranger, instantly embarrassed that she had. *I must be practicing for the opening,* Claire thought, surprised at her own candor, so out of character for her, but later she realized it was the unmistakable sincerity of the woman before her, freckles moving as she listened, bread knife tapping the air, head on fire in springy Lucille Ball red curls.

"It's got everything to do with cheese," she was told. "You asked for Brie and Pont-l'Eveque. Nice Jewish ladies in Coney Island don't eat Brie and Pont-l'Eveque. People who go to gallery openings eat Brie and Pont-l'Eveque."

"So?"

"So, you want something Middle European like Liederkranz, Bruder Basil, or Havarti with caraway seeds, with a nice black bread or sour rye."

Before Claire could get in another word, the woman started again, her voice, gaining a strange momentum, at once gentle and determined.

"People should experience art on every level," she declared with a little thump of the knife. "Why not serve what your subjects would eat? Herring would be nice, with some pickled beets, maybe some borscht or Dr. Brown's instead of that ghastly white wine everybody pretends to drink at those things."

She's a little bit nuts, Claire thought, but she couldn't help being mesmerized by this person who talked about food as though it were the love of her life. There was something wonderful about someone who brought such passion to her work, something really compelling.

"Art cannot be appreciated on an empty stomach," the woman continued, eyes blazing now with the conviction of one who believes beyond all else in the rightness of what she is saying. She paused only long enough to offer Claire a sliver of Bruder Basil. "Or on one that's full of the wrong food.

"Think of Proust's madeleines, Colette's delicate blanquette de veau, Dickens's gruel. Food gives art its impact on the senses. For a Coney Island show, hot dogs, at least!"

"You know, I never thought of it that way, but you're absolutely right. Let's do platters of hot dogs, with a nice spicy Dijon, maybe some matzo balls and borscht with sour cream."

She dug in her bag for the details. "Let's see, Tuesday at six-thirty, Light Gallery, 79 Perry Street. We've sent out a hundred and fifty invitations—"

"I couldn't possibly," said the woman, her frown as sudden as a power failure.

"Why not?" asked Claire, stunned.

"We don't do hot dogs like that here."

"What's your name?" Claire asked the flustered woman behind the counter.

"Theo."

"Mine's Claire. Would you mind if I took your picture?"

I GREW UP with that wonderful shot of Theo hanging in the foyer—face flushed, hair flaming against her food-splattered apron, behind the cheese counter at Fraser-Morris; one hand holds a little piece of cheese, and in the other is a bread knife, pointing straight at the camera.

Claire never tired of telling me the story of the day they met and how the two of them ended up driving out to Nathan's Coney Island for hot dogs for the show, dropping in on the Rabbi and Mr. Kimsky, laughing in the golden light, moving toward something neither would have ever predicted, two new friends, one blond, one redheaded, both resisting the attraction for all they were worth, while the radio blared "Baby, It's You" into that glorious, unending day.

Claire and Theo. My mothers.

I see them even now, so young and innocent of life and yet willing to take it on, not so defiantly as the flashing eyes, wide, crooked grins, hands on hips, thumbs hooked into the same bell-bottoms I see again on the narrow hips of a new generation would have you believe. They look determined, I think, not to let anyone know they were afraid.

These images, tattered photographs, some real, some imagined, everything filtered through my own enormous need to remember—I hold them up to the mirror of my own broad face, framed in ginger, sprayed with the buckshot of Theo's freckles, her roundness augmented into manly bulk with a tendency to soften in the name of good food, a face that has seen more than its thirty years around the edges and dutifully wears a summer coat of sunblock in honor of Claire's even paler tendency to burn. In the gathering moments preceding the blinding flash of their combined tempers, the eyes that normally wear the benign indolence of wet moss, gaze back at me in a color that can only be described as cold steel.

My name is William Roland Bouvier-Hirsh, William for my maternal great-grandfather, Roland for my poor lost uncle, Bouvier for the Cajun side of Theo, and Hirsh for the Fifth Avenue side of Claire. But everyone calls me Willy, except my grandmother who always called me Williamdear, even after that no longer seemed appropriate or sincere. There is no question that I am their son, from the tactile joy I derive from my solitary hours stirring and chopping and tasting, filling myself up with the shape and smell and texture and flavor of my own invention in a hopelessly overstocked kitchen worthy of Theo's gifts, to the compulsion I feel to examine and record what I see in the language I have substituted for Claire's ever-present roll of film.

They are with me in every impulse, every reflex, every twitch of memory and muscle, every learned response, and in the idiosyncrasies acquired through the slow unwinding of my own experience. I feel their presence in the time-softened exaggerations of their friends and in the faces of the people I love. They are reflected in the wide-open heart of my wife, Annie, who celebrates those parts of me most like them, who calls me her "woman's man" with real affection. Their names are written in the unfamiliar tug I feel for the two perfect creatures of my own design before me now.

One baby is blond and pale, composed, serious, even in sleep. Fluttering images have already begun their dance behind the veil of golden lashes, brushing infant skin with dreams far older. She considers all faces that come within her tiny range with the practiced eye of a seer. I sense she has taken her first picture of me and I wonder what she will leave in, what part of me she will crop out.

The other reaches for imaginary colors and wears the spark of a bonfire in the making. Her first questions live in her toes and in her fingers, opening and closing around the steady stream of magic that moves around her, that only she can see. Her milky breath stirs the angel who perches on a small boneless shoulder and the ghosts who sit on mine.

Our pediatrician says they're just as strong as you and me, but when Annie is sleeping and I tiptoe along the cold parquet toward their cribs and the amber puddle of the light we have left on in the nursery, the sight of them fills me with awe. Clumsy with love, I am afraid to touch them with my large man's hands. As they slumber through the early-morning scrape of the garbage cans on sidewalks swept clean of danger and the hot blood of the night before, I imagine I can see their dreams, both fragile and fierce, issuing forth into the gray wash of morning, to wait patiently in the universe for their owners to reclaim them. These girls are all fat legs and arms curling like new pieces of paper, stretching in the unfamiliar space, blissfully ignorant of what is to come, twin spirals of life filling the room with their small determination, and I am amazed at having a part in this.

My tiny muses. As I work, writing as I often do in the quiet of the day reserved for housekeepers, retirees, shut-ins, and second-story men, I see their perfection in the stops and starts, words and phrases, then whole sentences that darken the pages scribbled on deadline for strangers who live in my world, but do not share its history. Lately, I race to the end of these responsibilities and by the time the messenger I have hired to carry my words to the magazine arrives in a burst of sound from the revolving door and, like a terrorist with a live grenade, tosses my package at the editor, saving him from the humiliation of yet another empty space, I am already lost in another story. I am luxuriating in the words I will use to explain their lives to them, words not counted in characters and in lines and chunks of copy neatly surrounding a sidebar, but words that will carry the voices of their history and mine as tenderly and as truthfully as I can manage.

I watch my babies, round and shining like spoons on a well-set table, moving to the rhythms of our voices, the light, the memory of a warm amniotic pulse and the beating heart of the clock we have placed near their cradles to ease the sense of loss that has not yet left their muscles. I know I must tell them where they began, why their own hearts might break more easily than others, why one is rooted to the earth, why the other sees faces in the clouds.

I was too young to know, and if I had not been, I nevertheless couldn't know all there was to understand about my mothers. How could I pretend to grasp what they did not? Much of what I will tell my daughters is stitched together, suspended in time—truth, memory, regret, dreams, and bit and pieces. Sentences, whispers, words hurriedly poured into a phone, laughter, conversations overheard and imagined, snapshots and stories outlined in the great, silent longing of children. But I knew more in these fragments, the curve of a cheek, the pressure of a touch, the cadences of our kitchen, the dark heaviness of a sigh long after the lights were turned off, than most who take the fact of their parents for granted.

I don't know where imagination stops and fact takes hold, but I do know I must tell them never to waste precious time looking for this useless place. I must tell them it's not enough to know what happened, but how it changed us all forever. Annie says I must tell them the truth, but I know no one can ever do that. She worries about my tendency to color things.

"It will get you in serious trouble some day," she says and I smile and tell her, "I'm paid to do this."

"Fiction is for liars, not journalists," she replies, "and you are a damn good one."

"Liar or journalist?" I ask.

She beams. When she does this, I imagine I, too, am one of her children, a large unmanageable boy who loves to rattle pots and make a mess in her tidy kitchen. "Both," she answers.

"No," I say. "Isn't belief in what could have happened, what might have happened, truth enough? Isn't imagining just knowing without seeing?"

My wife is able to disagree with her whole body, but there is no energy for that today and the wide beautiful mouth curves down only slightly in its corners. "How could you know these things?" she says. "You were only a child."

"I think we are born knowing everything," I continue, feeling foolish, knowing I sound like Ram Dass, the Great Karmac, and Claire combined. "If we do it right, we just spend the rest of our lives finding out just how much that is." I feel myself color at this, but I stubbornly believe it. I think too many people spend their lives avoiding, denying, afraid of what they know, of what they feel, of what their souls can tell them. I want my babies to grow up looking inside themselves, not to others, for their strength.

Annie has heard all this before. Today, she slips into the nursery, as she often does after she turns toward the warm rut my bulk has made in our bed and knows I am up. They are hungry and she is sleepy and content. She smiles at what I am saying, but I'm never sure whether she is agreeing with me, or indulging me, or just using the sound of my words to lull herself back to the place she has just left. She takes the twins from their cradles, fills surprisingly strong arms with them, looks over her shoulder at me as though I am an older child who has been asked to watch his young siblings, and I imagine she is relieved they have not been drowned or suffocated while she slumbered; now a real grown-up is in charge again. I wince at this thought, and feel the special envy new fathers reserve for their wives, remembering I was warned of this by someone who wanted so much to create miracles, but could only play a small part. In the weak light of this morning, I see that no part is ever that small.

I remember Claire making me promise I would always go out of my way for someone I truly loved, even though we both knew I was too young to know what that could mean, what price it could exact. I can only tell my girls what happened and hope they will begin to understand and trust their own lives to fill in the rest. If I do this right, who knows? Someday they may even go as far as Brooklyn for me.

2

Theo left her little walkup on Barrow Street and moved into Claire's rent-controlled apartment on Central Park West, a soaring space filled with light and wonderful clutter—Claire's collection of hats, antique toys, and ancient cameras, to which Theo added her prized *batterie de cuisine,* vintage clothes, and tribal jewelry. They lived in the greedy symbiosis of new lovers, arising sleepy-eyed from their bed to run all the way to the Thalia for a midnight show of *Casablanca, Sunset Boulevard,* anything Bergman, brazenly stealing kisses in darkened doorways, one never tiring of learning the geography of the other in the purple, pink, and copper bath of their nightly sunsets over the distant water towers and terraces of the East Side, studiously avoiding friends until their fragile bond grew skin enough for what lay outside their apartment door.

They wore each other's clothes as if to become the other—tiny Theo in Claire's black suede baseball jacket, which came down to her knees and lost its severity in the bubble of flame above its collar; Claire, up to her elbows in bangles, trader beads, ivory, and silver as if to claim her lover's music as her own. Theo cooked at all hours as though what was happening between them needed to be stirred constantly. She fired the big kitchen with its black-and-white tiled floor and its wide leaded-glass windows and sweeping view of the park out of the dormancy of an occasional cup of coffee and Mary Hirsh's leftovers into the living, breathing, simmering heart of their happiness. They ate couscous and baked Alaska and moussaka in bed. For Claire, who never quite got the hang of cooking and whose idea of a feast was a bowl of Jiffy Pop and a pint of Rocky Road, life with Theo was like living inside a really good cookbook, written by someone who finally understands that food really *is* love. Claire was sure Theo was the person she had waited for all her life, and the one her mother had dreaded.

"I have to tell my parents," said Claire, when she was positive it was love, that it was serious enough for that.

"No, you don't," said Theo.

"I do," insisted Claire.

"Why?" asked Theo.

"Because it's dishonest not to."

"The truth can be very cruel, Claire. Why not just let them come to it themselves? They will, you know."

"I can't. I'd be living a lie."

"It isn't important to me that you tell them." Theo saw what was ahead.

"I know. But it is to me."

"When?" Theo asked.

"You don't just wake up one morning and say, 'Hey, what a gorgeous day. It's not too cold, not too windy, I think I'll walk over to Fifth Avenue and tell my mother I'm a lesbian.' " Claire tried to make light of her terror at the idea of this.

On a day she hadn't known had arrived until it announced itself as the right one, just as the moment you choose to plunge into cold water does not give a clue until the impulse is upon you, Claire sat in the resounding silence of her mother's dining room, which smelled of expensive wax and overlooked the lush green of Central Park. She took small bites of an English muffin Mrs. Hirsh's housekeeper, Lucy, had spread with strawberry jam and served to mother and daughter on a polished corner of the long, graceful table. Bereft of candlelight, crystal bowls overflowing with freesia, the nightly load of heavy Jensen silver and Limoges on its back, lacking conversation lubricated by good wine and too much perfume in one place, the surface that was as familiar to Claire as the thumb print she always managed to leave somewhere on its gleaming face, showed its age. It was too early in the day for a table that entertained so often. It seemed glacial, cold, already empty of her reflection.

"We could eat in the kitchen," said Claire, trying to buy some time, thinking this felt like eating in a restaurant that had closed. Huddling at the far end of that inhospitable mile of mahogany reminded Claire of standing up in your own living room because the pillows had been freshly plumped for company. *Maybe she won't hate me if I tell her in the kitchen, where daughters are supposed to talk to mothers and mothers are supposed to understand completely and without judgment while they whip up a batch of brownies.*

Lucy set Claire's delicate porcelain cup and saucer and plate on a Battenberg lace mat and stood over her, hand on one bony hip, the other still holding the towel she had been using to dry the Hirsh breakfast dishes when Buddy announced Claire was on her way up.

"Where yah been, dahling girl? You're gettin' t'in. You come ovah dis weekend, ah'll make you some sweet potata pie," teased the old woman. Lucy, who had known Claire all her life, probably had as much right to know as her own mother.

"Lucy, can't you see I'm huge," said Claire, rolling her eyes and blowing out her cheeks. "It's just these shoes making me look skinny," she said, lifting one thick platform sole up in the air with a grin that didn't have her heart in it. "I have to lie down to close my jeans."

"Ya goin' tah break sometin' in those tings," said Lucy in mock disapproval.

"Thank you, Lucy," said Mrs. Hirsh, dismissing her in the way women who have lived with servants all their lives do, marking out the shifting borders of privacy and privilege in the tone of her voice.

Mrs. Hirsh pretended not to see the disappointment in the papery brown face and turned to Claire. "This is fine, darling; your father and I breakfast here every morning."

Claire thought of Barnaby. *Never around when you need him, is he?* She thought of Theo waiting for her at the apartment and what she had said: "If you do this, you can't take it back."

Her mother's knife picked at the English muffin like a scab. *I can't take this back.*

"I'm in love, Mother."

"Darling, that's wonderful!"

She looks so happy. All those years of fixing me up with the offspring of every friend who ever reproduced. All those weak-chinned replicas of the founders of So-and-So & Sons, Blither, Dither, Mather and Schwartz, and Feinberg et Fils. All those mothers hoping for the best, a Bianchi original, the St. Regis Roof.

"Do we know him, dear?"

"No, you don't, actually," Claire said very carefully, feeling the last easy words ever spoken to her mother tumble out and disappear forever. "It's not a him. It's a her."

It's too late now. I've said it. I've killed her. I may as well bury her.

"Mother, she's wonderful. I know this must be very difficult for you right now, but once you get to know her, you'll see why I love her so much." Claire could feel herself gaining momentum, out of control, prattling, but she couldn't help it. While she was talking, something in the stately, silver-haired woman was locking shut, and nothing she could say was going to stop it.

Why don't you shut up and let her talk?

"Her name is Theo Bouvier, we met at Fraser-Morris when I did the food for the Coney Island show. She's beautiful and kind. She's a chef. She's moved in with me. I love her."

"Are you telling me you have become a lesbian?" said Mary finally. She pronounced the last word carefully and with a clarity that would have sounded almost ladylike and brave if Claire hadn't known her mother better. Something twitched in the corner of Mary's eye. Claire shivered in the warm room.

"No. Well, yes. I guess. I mean, it's not something you plan on becoming, like a lawyer or a house painter." Claire knew this was no time for humor.

"Darling, I really see no point in continuing this conversation," said Mary, forgetting Lucy, picking up their plates and Claire's cold, half-eaten muffin. "You'd better leave."

"Mother, please don't do this. Can't we talk about it?" Claire pleaded.

There were no shouts, no threats, no recriminations, none of the maternal angst Claire imagined such a confession would arouse. The apartment door simply closed, and the Hirsh elevator carried Claire away from the sight of Lucy's shock and the sound of her mother's tears.

Afterward Claire told Theo, "It was as though someone had blown out the light behind her eyes."

"Is that all she said?" Theo's green eyes swam with sorrow for the hurt she saw in Claire's.

"She said she had plans for lunch," whispered Claire.

* * *

AFTERWARD, whenever the subject of Theo was raised, my grandmother closed her eyes and released a sound of martyred despair. Claire and Theo nicknamed her Mary, Queen of Sighs to inject a little levity into the heaviness of her silence and all it meant. Mary loved Claire in her own way, and perhaps more deeply than even she herself knew. After all, there had to be something of Mary in Claire's curiosity and sensitivity, in her need to chronicle her own existence, and in the obvious gifts she brought to the camera, the way she looked at life with a cold, unswerving eye. Claire wanted to believe this, and she made a point of drawing mother-and-daughter comparisons whenever the opportunity presented itself, but my grandmother was also the product of her generation and kept her distance, hoping the infatuation would pass.

On the rare occasions when they met—after Theo, Mary never dropped in at the sunny apartment on Central Park West and gave as much notice as she could, even though it was only a brisk walk across the park to Claire's from her own rooms on Seventy-second and Fifth—she was never rude to Theo; was, in fact, gracious to a fault. She simply ignored the real reason for her presence with the intensity of someone who has just let go a stinker in a crowded room—it's there, everybody knows it's there, but it cannot be acknowledged without embarrassment to all concerned. No matter how often Claire brought up the subject of Theo, Mary Hirsh closed it with the finality of a coffin lid.

Claire didn't know many people in her position, and the few she did had been disowned, reviled, abandoned, ignored, disinherited, attacked, and made to feel unclean by their shocked and disappointed parents. Most had cut all ties and drifted in a world of their own creation; some left the city, and others clung to its most remote corners. Claire watched the Age of Aquarius dawn on New York, photographed its often grotesque face, its clownish manners, and understood that even the new dandyish freedom that strutted itself at Freak Fountain and behind the velvet ropes of Shepherd's and Killer Joe's had its own rules. Peace, love, drugs, promiscuity, and protest were fine as long as there was at least one of each sex participating.

Claire continued to push the issue. In her angrier moments, she reminded her mother that if Theo had been a man, any number of flaws would have been overlooked in the name of marrying her daughter off. In desperation, she raised the subject of her mother's own mixed marriage; in *her* day, it was shocking for an Irish Catholic girl to marry a Jewish boy, even if he was from Philadelphia.

My grandmother never took the bait. She simply assured Claire that she loved her very much, no matter that she found her daughter's life a personal disappointment and impossible to accept. We never really knew what my grandfather thought of it all until much later, and by that time no one cared. Like so many men of his generation, he let his wife speak for him on domestic matters; even if he held an opposing view, which I like to think he did, he never let on. He knew better. Barnaby Hirsh was an old-fashioned man, raised with the understanding that his role in life was to make money and provide for his family, not to venture onto the soft ground of his emotions. That was where women walked, and it was where his son Roland had lived, and Barnaby had buried that part of himself with the boy.

Claire's younger brother, Peter, had tried to chisel away at the wall Barnaby had erected in honor of his firstborn and at the solid weight of his mother's private heart. He, too, tried to be both boys, attempting to succeed where Claire had failed, but he was almost ten years younger than the receding image of his older brother, an afterthought who had no taste for his father's well-heeled footsteps, nor for the constant comparisons that left him hollow, believing himself a pale substitute for Roland in his parents' affection.

Peter took the only route a self-respecting, misunderstood young man could at that time. He moved into a railroad flat near Hudson with a gentle soul named Molly who grew small pots of anything green in the few slivers of light that managed to penetrate their long tunnel of an apartment, and he took up poetry with a vengeance not seen since Dylan Thomas supposedly drank himself to death at the White Horse tavern down the street. By the time Claire had dropped the bomb, they had become almost respectable, with talk of babies and a healthy distaste for the psychedelic antics and the grinding bass guitars of their neighbors.

Theo had a tough time understanding the tension between Claire and my grandmother because she was raised by people who believed the only crime in life was being dull. My grandmother Doris and grandfather Roy Bouvier—Roy always like to say he was a distant cousin of Jackie Kennedy's, but not distant enough for her—raised their children in a totally permissive, live-and-let-live atmosphere and believed rules imposed on children before they had a chance to develop their own instincts created neurotics and criminals.

It wasn't unusual to see young Theo, the baby in this boisterous family of seven, toddling around the garden in absolutely nothing at all but freckles and red curls, digging up "yum-yums for dinnie," and Doris, giving the rest of the giggling kids a look that said, "Hush," serving it up on her good Green Stamps china as though it were real food from her own kitchen. When Claire and Theo flew out to the Bouvier family trailer in Broken Arrow, Oklahoma, so Claire could meet the clan, Doris proudly told her she knew Theo was destined to be a great chef the day she found the child cooking a cactus in her new Revere Ware pot.

"What's a few spiny things, Claire honey," drawled Doris proudly as she pulled down the old, pitted saucepan (which she still used), laughing from deep inside her ample bosom, "if it helps put the first woman in the White House kitchen!"

When Theo's brother Buster expressed an interest in Buddhism at the age of twelve, Roy helped him shave his head in their tiny stall shower, and Doris sewed him his own little saffron robe on the Singer. Years later, when Roy Junior decided to enter the priesthood, all the Bouviers went to mass at St. Elmo's on the tribal land down the road and Theo's sister Desi did a special sun dance for the occasion. By the time Theo's oldest brother, Duncan, decided he would be happier as a middle-aged woman, Buster had forsaken Buddhism for the Church of the Macrobiotic and brought his own plum ball to the communion breakfast. The only ordinary Bouvier was Caroline, who moved to Arizona, married a partner in the stuffiest law firm she could find, played tennis, baked cakes, organized barbecues, joined the garden club, the country club, and the golf club, raised money for the reservation without ever actually having seen it, and visited Doris and Ray only when guilt got the best of her. The boys called her Miss Goody Tucson behind her back, but Doris defended her daughter's right to be average.

"Now, you leave your sister alone; bein' bourgeois is just another form of self-expression," said Doris when things got nasty.

The night Theo explained to Doris that her relationship with Claire went beyond friendship, the older woman looked long into her daughter's eyes and, when she saw the truth in them, winked and said, "I guess if you can't love your own kind, who can you love? I don't claim to know about these things, but I do know if somebody makes you happy, darlin', that's the one for you." And she buried her daughter in her arms.

"Every pot's got a lid, right, Mama?" said Theo, mugging Doris's Dust Bowl twang for Claire's benefit, her muffled laugh coming from somewhere inside her mother's good-hearted hug.

Claire loved Theo's crazy family of kissers and huggers, but Theo reminded her that it was just as hard growing up with the Bouvier freedom as it must have been with the Hirsh convention.

"I tell you, Claire, there's not much a thirteen-year-old can do to shock two old Bolsheviks who personally knew Louise Bryant and John Reed himself and just casually mention in passing that you'd look great as a bleached blonde—or that, if you're going to smoke dope, you ought to let them know so they can get you some reefer from a jazz guy they know who might be passing through on a gig," said Theo, explaining the childhood that drove her first to the kitchen, then out the door, and finally, all the way to New York.

Theo liked to say that while most people came to New York to be wild and free and as far away from normal life as possible, she came to New York to be average. But, as Claire liked to point out, there was no fear of that.

Everything about Theo was lush, fragrant, and a little flamboyant. She wore colors no other redhead would dare—fuchsia and melon and fire-engine red—big billowy skirts so long they dusted the floor, dresses from the forties, with Bakelite buttons and kimonos that held untold secrets in the sleeves. When she laughed, joy seemed to bubble up from a spring deep inside her and set her jade and silver bracelets jangling.

When Claire tired of Theo's grass-is-greener approach to the Hirsh family standoff, Claire headed to Serendipity at Sixtieth Street and Third Avenue to meet Suzie, her agent and partner in ice cream since their days at Bryn Mawr, where as roommates and friends-in-the-making, they personally raised the average freshman weight gain from five to a whopping fifteen pounds. Claire used to say Grandma was responsible for at least ten pounds the year she fell in love with Theo.

"C'mon," Claire wheedled a reluctant Suzie one bitter morning not too long after the equally frozen one in the Hirsh dining room. "The cold alone will burn off any calories we might accidentally consume."

"Give me an hour, okay?" a foggy Suzie had agreed.

As was their custom, they got down to business while they waited for their food.

"She's your mommy and you want her to approve of you, never mind that you're a grown woman with a life of your own," said Suzie, who also served as mother, confessor, and proof that heterosexuality wasn't as healthy or even as normal as everyone said it was. Suzie had been married five times, if you counted Duane, the boy she married after her high-school junior prom and kept a secret until the mail-order annulment arrived the same day as her SAT scores. She just couldn't manage to get it right.

"This isn't a lesbian issue, Claire," said Suzie, who was sitting, but still struggling out of her huge Russian greatcoat, which covered a dress the size of the napkin she had unfolded and was now patting down over her knees. "What we're talking about here is the universal need for maternal acceptance."

"Of course it's a lesbian issue, Suzie. My mother can't accept me because I love Theo. She's put terms on her love for me."

"And you expect her to put aside everything she's ever believed, and acknowledge your life without reservation and judgment just because you're her daughter and it's your due?"

"Yes, I do. And I would also appreciate your lowering your voice, Suze. These two at the next table are going to need neck surgery if they lean over any farther."

The women at the next table had stopped eating their salads and both sat upright, forks poised in midair, pretending they weren't listening. Suzie swiveled to see. Her wrought-iron ice-cream chair wobbled on the uneven floor. "Connecticut," she said, staring them down, then turned her back on the stunned women. "Claire, darling, you've just put your tormented little finger on why every psychiatrist in New York can afford to go to Europe for the entire month of August!"

"You know, for someone who dates all the wrong people and wears black leather stockings in the daytime, you're pretty smart," said Claire, suddenly aware of the disgustingly fattening banana split they had been devouring.

"Did I ever tell you what my mother said after Brian and I broke up and I mentioned I was going to Fire Island for the summer?"

"No," said Claire, surprised that she had managed to miss one of the Byzantine twists and turns in Suzie's love life.

"I'll never forget it," started Suzie. "I said, 'Ma, I'm thinking of renting a house in Ocean Beach, you know, a few friends sharing the cost, start dating again, who knows, maybe meet somebody new, somebody nice, somebody heterosexual. . . .' "

"You didn't," said Claire, shocked.

"No, I didn't say 'heterosexual.' I just wanted to give those two something to take home to Westport."

"You're impossible!"

"I know. That's why you love me. Anyway, Claire, she just looked me square in the eye, and do you know what she said?"

"No, I don't, Suzie. Tell me."

"She said, 'All the men out there are divorced.'

"So I said, 'Yeah, Ma, so?' And Claire, you won't believe what she said next," said Suzie, dramatically pausing to blow smoke from her Nat Sherman across the small room.

"Suzie, please don't do that." Claire coughed along with the women at the next table, who were still listening hard.

"She said, 'Suzanne Elizabeth, you don't want to associate with people like that.' "

"People like what? *You're* divorced," said Claire, amazed.

"My point exactly," said Suzie, as she triumphantly ground out the vile-smelling black cigarette Claire tolerated only because she knew Suzie couldn't seem to function without it.

"I said, 'People like who, Ma? I'm divorced, too, remember?' And then do you know what she said? She said, 'That's different.' "

"That's denial," said Claire.

"No, my sweet dumbbell," said Suzie, coming in for the kill, "that's Mother Denial. It's bigger than the iceberg that hit the *Titanic*—and it melts just as fast.

"In the end, it's what's keeping your mother from accepting Theo and will, by virtue of this same perverted Mother Logic, allow her to make an exception of you. Trust me: One day she will wake up and decide other people are lesbians, not her daughter. So if her daughter isn't a lesbian Theo can't be one either. And everyone will live somewhat happily ever after."

Suzie leaned across the rickety table, suddenly a lot older and sadder than the cowboy fringe, ropes of pearls, and rhinestone pins she was wearing that afternoon suggested, and took Claire's hand.

"I envy you two, sweetheart. You have something I've been looking for all my life. Sooner or later your mother will see it and come around. Give her a chance."

Claire wanted to believe Suzie was right, and gave my grandmother every opportunity to conform to her theory, but in the meantime, Theo worked on the Hirsh household the only way she knew how—through their stomachs.

She left Fraser-Morris not long after she met Claire, and opened her own catering business in a little storefront on Seventy-fourth and Second. She and Claire cooked up the name, The Latest Dish, and Claire shot menu covers, business cards, and price stickers, along with an ad for the neighborhood flyer. It was a wonderfully sensuous mouth, caught in a very satisfied smile, a crisp white napkin dabbing at its corner.

From this modest bunker of mouthwatering delights, Theo lobbed great platters of lemon chicken and lasagna and Swedish noodles with caraway seeds, one of Mary's favorites, at the fortress that was 920 Fifth. Buddy, the Hirsh doorman, told her he started drooling the minute he saw her turn the corner; he was always careful to add, "And I don't mean any disrespect by that, miss" in a brogue that went all the way back to Dublin. Theo fought unfairly: with strudel, and Grandpa's favorite lemon cheesecake, and death by chocolate, a dessert that could make even the Rosenbergs talk, but she always took care never to seem too familiar, signing the distinctive card "Bon appetit! Claire."

While Theo cooked, Claire worked hard, trying to make the most of her new celebrity. She had sold most of the Coney Island series, including a framed print of the invitation—disembodied stocking-clad legs in three-inch Betty Grable pumps, dangling from a parachute—which also had been made into a poster. They had fetched the price of a trip to Greece for two, with enough left over to begin saving for the weekend house in the country they both dreamed of owning some day.

"Claire Hirsh has unlocked the last ghetto with an unwavering eye," a critic wrote. Claire had captured a world: Mr. Kimsky playing chess in the park with a shadow; the reflection of Temple Bar El's Star of David in Mrs. Klein's rhinestone cat's-eye glasses as she watched a gang of Puerto Rican street toughs saunter down a windswept boardwalk; the Russian who broodingly accepted his outsider status, frozen in the tender act of buttoning Mrs. Goldstein's coat, hands like plates of meat, eyes sick with love; the Crazy One, lost to everyone including herself, oblivious to Claire and her camera; Mrs. Levkowitz, her bony fingers clutching the frayed sleeve of an Orlon sweater reduced by time to the color of milky tea, offering my mother a leathery arm turned out like a ballerina's leg in first position, no face, no eyes, no hair, no name—just numbers fading into the soft flesh inside her wrist.

Claire described Mrs. Levkowitz as a soft, shy woman whose eyes seemed to hold all the melancholy of Mother Russia, who said she couldn't cry until she saw the horror and the pity written on the face of a young American soldier who could have been her brother as he stepped over the barbed wire and gently held her hand until she could be taken to the field hospital. "Only then did I allow myself to feel what had happened to me," she quietly told my mother.

Claire told the story of Mr. Brodsky, a dapper little man from Warsaw, who sat on a faded deck chair, watching for U-boats in Brooklyn, and bragged about his response to the young fellow from the Coast Guard who tried to get him to evacuate one leaden afternoon when the radio warned of a fierce storm heading for New York's barrier beaches.

"You really should, Mr. Brodsky, they're expecting a twelve-foot tide when that storm rolls in tomorrow," Claire had patiently explained to the proud, stubborn man before rushing home herself.

"I told dat guy," Mr. Brodsky said, his English still as terrible as the day he stepped into the great hall on Ellis Island, "I vas in Dachau, you want I should run away from a little vind?" In the end, Mr. Brodsky sat out one of the worst hurricanes in New York's memory. In the weeks following, he told this story over and over, always getting the same knowing laugh. "I survived Hitler. Now, *dat* vas a storm!" I'll always remember Claire saying how much taller he stood when he said that.

One day in late March the year before my mothers met, when the sting of the wind carried the unmistakable smell of spring and the steely light over the ocean melted into an endless blue-gray, a man with numbers tattooed on his arm summoned the courage to ask Claire if she would take his picture and put it in the newspaper, hoping his sister was still alive to see it.

Now, only a year and half later, critics rhapsodized. Collectors matted Claire's photographs in expensive frames, good track lighting trained on every grainy pore. Important conversation now flowed around them, smug talk of Art, History, and Photography as Investment, while trays of triple-crème Brie and pears were passed under their noses.

These people who ate, slept, got sick, nagged their children, collected Social Security, lost it at bingo and mah-jongg, shuffleboard and pinochle, and also managed to survive the most shameful period in human memory, their psyches forever scarred, their dreams haunted, and their trust in others irrevocably blunted by the accident and the consequences of their Jewishness, were really quite ordinary until Claire came along and made them icons. Suddenly, hanging wasn't good enough for them; they required *installation*—and up there, on the stark white canvas of Serious Art, bathed in hushed respect, they looked like characters out of a Brecht play, bearing stark witness to the Ugliness of Mankind with no time, as Theo loved to joke, "to iron a dress, put on a nice suit."

For her part, Claire was deemed to be in a position to judge things as Right and Wrong, Good and Evil, Moral and Immoral, and Boring and Interesting. She had been launched, adjudged a serious photographer, compared to Margaret Bourke-White, Imogen Cunningham, and Alfred Stieglitz—to whom Theo had laughingly remarked she thought Claire bore a more than passing resemblance—and just before I was born, for the equally compelling images that followed

(Harlem heroin addicts and the forgotten residents of the city's charity wards) was awarded the ultimate prize: a Guggenheim. Which, thanks to Aunt Suzie and her refusal to allow Claire to get a swelled head, I believed was an illegal pitch in softball.

Claire had always been loyal to those who believed in her, and newfound stardom did not change this. People who were not in a financial position to buy art, who had loved her work when she was unknown, now left small amounts of money at the apartment front desk to hold a favorite print, as a sort of cultural layaway. A young, aspiring, and very poor filmmaker bought Mrs. Levkowitz in installments and kept in touch with Claire over the years. He told her he was moved by the eloquence of the cropping, of her decision to leave out what he imagined to be a crooked smile, suitcases full of life under the eyes, a plastic poodle pinned to her collar, a sagging cheek heavy with rouge, all the things that said, 'Look at me! I am not a number!' Later, when he became a not-so-poor, no-longer-aspiring household name, he credited Claire with creating the early stirrings of an idea for a film about the Holocaust that would be his masterpiece.

As Theo chopped, sautéed, boned, pounded, broiled, grilled, baked, simmered, stirred, steamed, and chiffonaded her way to her own growing celebrity, Claire focused on hers in a darkroom of her own design under the stairs that would someday lead to my loft.

When I was a small boy, I believed they were both made of light and magic. I remember watching Claire disappearing into that tiny room with its eerie light, rushing out in her socks, holding an image aloft for Theo's approval; she skidded into the kitchen, eyes shining with the joy of creation. I remember counting Theo's freckles while she whipped soufflés into clouds, studded silken puddings with raisins, and let me lick our blue spongeware bowls of every bit of chocolate and mocha and butterscotch, even before dinner. I remember the big scrapbooks of Claire's notices and Theo's restaurant reviews and Suzie explaining that "kudos" were small chewy candies given out to players who hit "Guggenheims," while my mothers shook their heads behind her back.

Even now, it's difficult to imagine why two such accomplished, ascendant, and thoroughly Bohemian creatures would voluntarily disrupt their lives for a baby, especially an enormous, drooling, moonfaced one like me, but to my eternal amazement, every bubble and squeak, gurgle and goo took front seat to critics, collectors, and customers—food, photography, or otherwise. Back then, I simply accepted their devotion as my due. Today I see how truly extraordinary this was. When she was sure I was old enough to understand, it was Theo who told me how I came to be born.

3

The trouble started when, at the age of thirty-five, Claire ran out of estrogen, which Theo explained, was the stuff necessary to make the eggs that make babies. Claire's heart pounded for no apparent reason, and she picked fights with Theo, who seemed to her young and fertile for spite. She cried for hours on end and suffered soaking sweats that woke her up in the middle of the night, forcing her to sleep on a towel so she wouldn't have to disturb Theo by changing the sheets. Theo sat up with her and infused healing herbs for sleep-inducing tea, holding her hand, drying her wet, matted hair with her own hands, fluffing it and soothing her hot cheeks at the same time, and, more often than not, keeping Claire company as she sat on the cool porcelain edge of the bathtub in the damp T-shirt she wore to bed, making a low, heaving sound that tore Theo's heart.

"How can you love someone who's drying up?" Claire sniffled into Theo's breast.

"You don't drop someone you love just because they're a little sweaty," said Theo.

"Oh, Theo, this isn't just about being sweaty. I really wanted to have a child someday," Claire whispered into the pillow one especially difficult night, and Theo reached across the darkness to stroke her back, murmuring softly, until Claire finally fell into a heavy sleep.

For everyone else, Claire put up a brave front. "Who needs to ruin real silk when you can 'shvitz' in something washable like Qiana and Nyesta—so slimming, so sexy, so synthetic!" Claire wisecracked to Suzie and to Jessica, who followed the details of her symptoms with the morbid fascination of death-row residents.

"Why make jokes?" a puzzled Theo asked. "They're your friends; why don't *you* tell them how you really feel?"

"Would you really like to know how miserable you're going to be in ten or twelve years? Anyway, they depend on me to be funny," explained Claire. Theo was not convinced.

In public, Claire often carried an antique fan, hoping the affectation of a carefully rehearsed snap would divert attention away from the sudden drenchings, which almost always struck when she was saying something clever or important, leaving her face slick, her clothes sodden, and her mood dark. Claire wasn't vain about much, but even Nicholas, who did wonders with color and on whom Claire spent a fortune keeping up her delicate shade of blond, could not reverse the dulling march of receding hormones, causing ugly corkscrew white hairs to rise up in her part. Every morning she plucked a few more and wrapped her head in two feet of gypsy silk.

Despite what Claire called her depressing and premature slide into cronehood, she cheerfully took the pills Theo laid out every morning—E and B_6 for the black moods, C for water retention. She drank papaya juice for digestion. She swallowed a foul-smelling powder called *fo ti* and drank ginseng tea, which the herbalist on West End Avenue near the Transcendental Meditation Institute said couldn't hurt and might even help with the hot flashes. When the weather permitted, Claire played tennis in the park and jogged around the reservoir for her bones; when it didn't, she ran around the tiny treadmill of an indoor running track at the Y. But she worried about losing calcium so early in life, and the threat of osteoporosis hung over her like bad air. She read what literature there was on the subject and weighed the risks of the new estrogen-replacement therapy that was causing much talk and new fears.

"Well, at least I won't get breast cancer," Claire said, looking up from the pamphlet the doctor had given her during one of her all-too-frequent visits and patting her flat chest in the self-deprecating way Theo hated. "You need breasts for that."

Claire's gynecologist was a gentle woman named Collins, whom the suddenly short-tempered Claire labeled smug because she kept photographs of her own babies on her desk where, Claire said, "poor unfortunates like myself can see and have their hearts ripped out."

When Dr. Collins confirmed premature menopause after several soggy months of symptoms, erratic periods, and blood tests that measure hormone levels, Theo said Claire began to see her life as a biological time bomb. She started acting a little crazy, and it showed in her work.

I remember a photograph of what appeared to be a poached egg in a bird's-eye-maple frame; until I was sixteen and Theo explained what it meant, I never understood why anyone would want to hang a picture of a poached egg in their front hall.

At three o'clock in the morning, while cleaning the apartment under the influence of the most horrible bout of PMS Theo had ever seen, Claire found an old diaphragm. It was in the cubbyhole behind her closet, along with some ragged cotton paisley fabric she had once used to transform the ceiling of a St. Mark's Place railroad flat into an Arabian tent, and a turquoise-felt poodle skirt; it was crammed in a dusty shoe box with her old "I Like Ike" button, a pair of ballet slippers said to have been worn by Pavlova, and a Davy Crockett hat that was now home to a family of extremely fat moths.

Theo pulled her robin's-egg-blue chenille robe around her and watched helplessly as Claire rummaged around the kitchen with the cracked diaphragm in her pajama pocket, every now and then taking it out to mutter something unintelligible about the stories the old thing could tell.

Claire fumbled for a while in the refrigerator, unwrapping and rewrapping leftovers, making a terrible mess, until she found a couple of congealing slices of corned beef from one of her solo "duty dinners" at the Hirshes'. A few minutes later, in full view of a very groggy Theo, Claire had warmed the beef in the oven to perk up the color, toasted an English muffin, handed half to Theo, who wasn't even conscious enough to know she wasn't hungry, and carefully centered the other on one of their good cobalt-blue plates. Cackling to herself, she tenderly plopped the diaphragm on top of the corned beef. Claire then whipped up what turned out to be, for her, a pretty decent hollandaise, topped the whole thing off with a sliver of olive meant to pass as a slice of truffle, and, babbling about the injustice of running out of eggs at the tender age of thirty-five, snipped a bit of the asparagus fern, placed it on the plate, and photographed the whole thing. Then she collapsed into bed. But just before she fell asleep, she sat up on one wobbly elbow and said, "I think I'm going to call it 'Eggs Derelict.' "

In the following months, more and more of this strange preoccupation with fertility began to creep into Claire's work, and the haunting images with which she had developed her loyal and paying following were being replaced by what can only be described as a kind of neonatal perspective she couldn't seem to get enough of.

She combed the streets looking for pregnant women and for families out for the day. Claire photographed a woman teetering on swollen feet on the Fifth Avenue bus, her skin shining with the strain of being forced to stand in what looked to be her ninth month, a man sitting in the background, eyes narrowed as if to say, "You wanted to work like a man; well then, stand like a man."

The Leica recorded twins in strollers, triplets in custom-made carriages and identical sweaters that made them look like human three-packs of paper towels. She snapped toddlers waddling along the promenade in Brooklyn Heights, and pampered tots in English prams, their distinctive schooners of navy blue and yellow sailed by stern nannies in starched white, while their mummies shopped for McCardell's and Capezios, worked out the seating for the next benefit ball, and had highlights artfully placed in Baby Jane Holtzer hair.

In grisly contrast, Claire rode up to 125th Street and found mothers whose unborn children kicked and fought and couldn't breathe under their too-tight leather jackets, tiny ones who regularly competed for a vein and almost always lost out to the more compelling habit. Claire carried crisp new twenties to pay these women to allow her to take their pictures, hoping they would use the money to buy food; seeing the speedballs glittering in their eyes, she knew better.

Nothing was safe from Claire and her determination to document her own hunger to breed. It seemed to Theo that Claire just aimed right into New York's reproductive organs and clicked. She mentioned this to Suzie over one of the lunches she had fallen into the habit of having with Claire's oldest friend whenever she, too, needed to talk.

"I suspect even the most revolting fact of urban life, the discovery of a new generation of roaches hatched overnight behind the stove, would somehow strike Claire as tender," Theo had said on one such fattening occasion.

"If that weren't so damn true, it would be funny." An uncharacteristically somber Suzie shared her own distress at this grotesque development in Claire's career. "It wouldn't be so bad," she said blackly, "if Diane Arbus hadn't beaten her to it."

"Things are getting a little tense at home, Suze," said Theo quietly, swirling her butterscotch sauce into a melting puddle of vanilla ice cream.

When a Madison Avenue gallery offered to mount a show of Claire's oddest body of work yet—a series of babies' behinds she called *A Sitting*—instead of enjoying the obvious victory, Claire brooded for weeks over whether she should have held out for La Mama, which, in its own infancy, offered gallery space from time to time.

"It would have been so right, Theo," Claire moaned one night after a frustrating argument with the prissy gallery manager, who called her work "reproductive art" in the brochure.

"And what would we have served, *formula?*" asked Theo a little too sharply, looking up from the living room coffee table. She was sitting on the floor, surrounded by serving notes and recipes for an important engagement party. "No, better still, we'll breast-feed the guests and save all those dirty dishes."

The critics were not entirely unkind, but sales were not brisk. One snide little reporter in obscene suspenders and a bow tie wrote in his review that "one enters the sweeping space and gets the distinct feeling of strolling around inside a giant pair of rubber pants." Another writer, a little more familiar with Claire's earlier work, showed compassion; with tongue in cheek, compared what she called Claire's "nursery period" to Picasso's Blue.

"How ironic. If I *had* a period, I'd have a nursery, wouldn't I?" Claire said ruefully behind the critic's back. "Can you believe people have the nerve to show up at your party after writing drivel like that!" She and Suzie were nervously greeting guests, unused to Madison Avenue and its older, more well-heeled clientele; Claire the nervous artist, Suzie the agent, wineglass in one French-manicured hand, a smoldering Nat Sherman in the other, eyes narrowed, mouth set in what Claire called her twenty percent smile.

"Claire, sweetheart, may I point out that Coca-Cola is probably not going to pay five thousand dollars for the privilege of hanging one of your baby bums in their lobby," said Suzie as she surveyed the crowd for potential buyers. "But Carter's or Gerber's, maybe!" She was always able to see the market potential for anything, always able to cheer Claire out of her darkest moods.

There were thirty-two bottoms in all—tiny black behinds that shone like wet licorice, some white as paper, and some rosy as an English cheek. All the colors of the world hung around the room—yellow, tan, butterscotch, peach, brown, freckled, dimpled, dewy, sunburned, smooth, perfect little moons fat as cream. On the far wall, as though by virtue of its impossible size, it deserved more space than the others, hung the show's centerpiece, a preemie's bottom so small it could fit on the tip of a finger.

Theo stayed home that night, allowing my grandparents to "have the evening with their daughter," as she put it. Theo had a real gift for knowing how other people felt, and understood that it would not be fair to put Claire under any more pressure than the opening party already had by having to also suffer the inevitable and excruciatingly civilized tension between Theo and Claire's parents. So she told Claire she would wait at the apartment and fix a late supper for anyone Claire chose to invite home, and that would be her special gift.

At about eleven, Claire arrived at the apartment, trailing an entourage. Baxter and Jess claimed they could stay for only an hour, otherwise they'd end up owing four years' tuition to the sitter who was watching Jennifer and Brooke, twin angels who had been born that year to the now-married pair. Suzie had several "potential buyers," in tow, who Theo suspected represented potential dates more than anything else. Thad and Alan, Theo's old friends from Barrow Street, arrived with masses of baby's breath for "the muse" and behind them were two delightful elderly Park Avenue matrons; Mrs. Peabody and Mrs. Babcock, who insisted on being called Emmelyn and Mildred and who gushed at everything in the apartment, calling Claire's pictures *très, très formidable.* They were escorted by James, the formerly prissy manager who had so archly called Claire's art "reproductive," but who was now sufficiently softened by many glasses of wine and the prospect of selling the matrons several pieces.

In keeping with the show's theme, Theo charmed everyone with a somewhat eccentric, but entirely welcome buffet of everyone's favorite nursery foods: a crusty meatloaf, baked macaroni with a combination of Cheddar, Gorgonzola, and Brie, pureed vegetables in hollowed tomatoes, and a heaping basket of chocolate brownies. The napkins were diapers, each fanning out from its own pacifier. "Never used!" Theo assured the wary guests.

The door had barely closed on Suzie—who, after what seemed like hours of hovering in the foyer, finally left with one of the "potential buyers," an attractive choreographer of dubious reputation—when Claire embarked on one of those woozy conversations that can change the course of life forever, or at least alter the foreseeable future dramatically.

"Poor Suzie, she never seems to get it right." An exhausted Theo had just melted into their overstuffed sofa, dangling one shoe on her toe while slipping a pillow under her head, when Claire launched the attack.

"Every thirty seconds, people are having babies they don't want. Every time I pick up a newspaper, another baby is found in a garbage can or beaten senseless or stuffed into a pillowcase and left on the Cross-Bronx Expressway. Women are out there burning bras and demanding the right to have a say over what happens to their bodies. 'Get on the Pill,' they say, 'choose your own fate,' but what about me? I have no say. I can't choose. I've run out of choices. What's reproductive freedom, if you can't reproduce?"

Claire looked like a broken doll, her careful eye makeup smeared by tears that had now begun to fall freely, her delicate skin turning a mottled red.

Theo leaned over to touch her cheek. "Claire, it's late, sweetie, you've had a tough night. I'll clean up; why don't you go to bed?"

"Theo, do you think we could have a baby?"

"Excuse me?"

"I said, let's have a baby!"

"I don't think we can do that, Claire. We're women, remember?" said Theo evenly, beginning to gather herself up, feeling the retreat moving into her muscles.

"What I really mean is, do you think you could have a baby and we could raise it together?"

"Are you completely nuts, Claire?" shouted Theo. She sprang from the sofa as if it were on fire and stormed into the kitchen, one perilously high heel off, the other still on. She began to hack away at a brownie.

"Can't we talk about this, Theo?"

"Oh, sure. Nice party, let's have a baby."

"I'm sorry, honey. It really was a nice party," said Claire, suddenly contrite.

"About a day late and a dollar short," muttered Theo. "Claire, have you any idea what a responsibility a baby is? You can't just put it in a camera bag or make a nest for it in a bureau drawer or put it down for a nap in your fur coat." Theo emptied leftovers into storage containers and tore plastic wrap in short ugly bursts. "And just when the light is perfect for your series on 'Carhops, a Disappearing Breed,' it will not wait for you to get the perfect shot of a bubble hairdo, it will spit up on your shoes."

"Aren't you overreacting a little, Theo?" Claire stood in the doorway, afraid to come all the way in, her heart seizing up at the ferocity of the words coming from Theo, usually so serene.

"Overreacting?" Theo continued blindly wrapping food and slicing the brownies, her hands beginning to shake. "May I remind you that we are lesbians, Claire—gorgeous, lovable, and smart, but lesbians nevertheless. Do you want your child to hear the bad names the world calls women like us—butch, dyke, deviant, fill in the blank, Claire!"

"Theo, stop it!" shouted Claire. At this, Theo paused, dropped the knife, pulled off her earrings, and rubbed the deep lines they had carved in her lobes. Claire reached over to rub her neck, but the thunderheads gathering in the green eyes said this was not the time.

"Oh, sweetie," Theo continued in a low, even voice, "it's one thing to live in New York surrounded by our permissive, liberal friends and another to raise a normal child in the real world. Claire, your own parents haven't been able to make peace with us, and they love you more than life itself. Isn't this hard enough?"

Exhausted from the evening and from the force of her feelings, Theo collapsed like an old sofa whose springs had suddenly given up. With a whoosh and a kind of thumping sound, she caved in on herself as though she had been shot. Sitting there on the kitchen stool as the mess she had been making of the brownies came into focus, she looked a little dazed.

"Well, you don't have to be so polite about it, Theo, you can say what you really feel." Claire tried to cover her own hurt.

"Why does everything have to be so funny with you, Claire?" Theo straightened up on the stool as though bracing herself for another round, auburn brows knitting themselves into a solid line. But instead of coming around for a second attack, she just said, "Never mind," and slid off the stool, as though going to bed were the easier solution.

"Everything is funny because if it isn't, the pain will swallow me up," muttered Claire, more to herself than to Theo, laying her cheek on the cold tile of the countertop. "If I could, I'd have a baby right now, but I can't. And you can. You can, Theo."

"Let's talk about it tomorrow, kiddo," Theo said softly as she turned out the lights and kissed Claire's damp brow. "It's been a long day, we're both beat."

They didn't talk about it that next day or the day after that or the one after that. In fact, after that night in the kitchen, when each had said more than she intended, they carefully avoided the subject.

Claire still used her camera to express the "baby thing," as Theo diplomatically put it, and in spite of a dwindling number of deposits left at the lobby desk, the Leica would not be stilled. In the downstairs darkroom, ever-increasing numbers of babies were born out of the dark and ghastly-smelling fluid and whisked up to dry, still damp, like so many diapers on the line of her growing disappointment.

One gloomy Sunday afternoon with a dull rain beating on the huge studio windows, Theo looked up from the *Times* crossword puzzle and picked up one of the contact sheets Claire had laid out on the floor, where she was organizing her next show. Very slowly, eyes hard as glass, Theo said: "You know Claire, they've never been able to pigeonhole you as a feminist artist, but it's beginning to look as though your view of the world extends no farther than your own vagina. That's a little narrow, don't you think? Where are those riveting images, those universal, non-gender-dependent works of art you once created?" Theo demanded, waving the contact sheet like a summons, her cruelty deliberate, out of character, cutting.

"Speaking of stereotypes, you know you really ought to stick to catering," said Claire lamely. The sting of Theo's words followed her out of the room and into the darkroom, where she sat on an apple crate and wept until Theo went to bed.

Doors slammed and words dangled in the air that winter in the Bouvier-Hirsh household. Always, there were apologies, but they began to sound the same, balm applied to a scab that wouldn't heal, the residue of what could not be taken back building up like toxic material in drinking water. A tense truce settled over them, but the air in the apartment was thick with their separateness and all that was unsaid.

Theo closed the shop for a few weeks in February and went home to Broken Arrow, "to do some thinking," she had said. Claire spent more time with Molly and her brother Peter in the old apartment they were quickly outgrowing, and with Jessica and Baxter, whose lives seemed to be as solid and as permanent as the walls of the brownstone they were restoring, already full of oddities brought home from their travels and the giddy sound of their two small girls, Jennifer and Brooke. She went to Coney Island for a long-overdue visit with her old friends. Mrs. Levkowitz patted her face and said, "If he loves you, he'll come around eventually," when Claire told her everything but the truth.

This was the winter of 1963. Dark, silent, unusually cold.

In March, the days began to soften and so did Theo and Claire. Slowly, almost imperceptibly, they were swept into the rhythm of forgiveness that comes when love loses its innocence and concessions must be made if it is to endure.

Claire was shooting new work on babies with Down's syndrome, who in those days bore the terrible scar of the word "mongoloid" and were hidden in the deepest corners of places like Creedmore and Willowbrook. It was a compelling series that had all the signs of her earlier and more powerful images. Theo's catering business was showing signs of becoming a hit. *Gourmet*'s editor in chief himself wrote the magazine's review; he said, "Theo Bouvier's 'Latest Dish' is the word on everyone's lips." There was talk of a cookbook and a line of products.

Theo now came home flushed from the stove and full of tales of near-disasters in her tiny shop's kitchen. She carried shopping bags brimming with divine-smelling leftovers. The apartment simmered in the constant heat of creation. Theo's mistakes, as well as her triumphs, found their way to the red-lacquered Parsons table. They ate chocolate mousse Theo had chilled without whipped cream to cut its sweetness. They devoured brioche that had lost their heads, nibbled muffins that had spilled over their tins, lopsided cakes that couldn't be used, and chocolate cookies that fell apart in mouthwatering chunks. Claire had resumed the habit of leaving her darkroom in time to help Theo close the store and walk back home through the gathering dusk and that endless, melting spring.

"Good God, Theo, what have you done?" said Claire one warm evening in early May, rolling her eyes at the corn tortillas Theo had layered with chilies, grilled chicken, avocado, salsa, and sour cream. "Is the world ready for this?"

"I call it Mexican lasagna," said Theo, grinning at her latest creation. "I'm thinking of doing it with corn muffins and a green salad for the Friedlander brunch. Taste test starts in about twenty minutes." She slid the casserole into the oven.

Claire set the table near the window overlooking the street lamps now coming on in the park. Theo changed out of her food-spattered work clothes; when she sat down to their Mexican feast, Claire had placed a frosty margarita next to her plate. Claire couldn't help thinking how happy Theo looked, sitting there in a voluminous white poet shirt, happily licking the salt off the rim of her glass. A young Shakespeare relaxing after a hard day on a sonnet.

"You really are good at what you do, you know," said Claire, taking Theo's hand in hers between bites.

"You are too, toots," smiled Theo, turning Claire's hand over in hers for a quick kiss that tasted of lime and something called cilantro. "Ready for dessert?"

"What did you have in mind?" said Claire, happily watching Theo clear the table.

"I still can't figure out how you can cook and eat like this every day and not get fat," groaned Claire, tugging at her jeans.

"Large clothes," shouted Theo back into the dining room as she reached up into the cupboard for two taxicab-yellow dessert plates. Three huge strawberries and a scoop of raspberry sorbet went on each one, then a large dollop of what looked like apricot purée.

"Oh, thank God," Claire said when Theo slid the plate in front of her, "something dietetic for a change!" Then, licking fruit sauce off the handle of her spoon: "Mmmm, this is fabulous. What is it?"

"Claire, I've been doing some serious thinking," said Theo, her tone suddenly grave.

"Thinking about what?" asked Claire, trying to ignore the alarm bell going off at this abrupt change of mood.

"I thought we'd try," said Theo.

"Try what?" A warning was now reaching up to squeeze Claire's heart.

"It's baby food, Claire," said Theo slowly, letting the words sink in. "I figured since we're going to have so much of it around, we ought to get used to the taste."

4

For most people, the search for the perfect mate is an arduous process that takes many years, sometimes as long as a lifetime. And we all have an Aunt Suzie for whom even that much time isn't enough. Just as an apparently ideal candidate moves into sight, some quality which he or she does not possess—insight, sensitivity, courage, a good sense of humor, a love of small animals, concern for the environment—surfaces in another person, leaving the current object of desire pale and disqualified by comparison, and the whole game of getting-to-know-you starts over.

The subtle unraveling of character, as each trait conspires to sum up the whole, can be as painful as slowly peeling an onion from the wrong end, which any cook will tell you involves a good deal of crying. All too often, the end result is shattered hopes, broken engagements, divorce, disillusionment and inevitably, a return to square one, leaving the seeker older, wiser and better equipped to handle the next round.

Claire and Theo did not have that kind of time. Even though, at thirty-four, Theo had enough eggs to last as long as it took to find me a father, plus some to spare for my sister (a thought she would keep to herself until the right moment), she envisioned the process in terms of months, not years. Once she decided she really wanted a child—not for Claire, but for herself and all that she could bring to its creation—she rose to the idea with every ounce of energy she had.

Claire did not say how much the idea of Theo with a man troubled her, even though such an encounter couldn't exactly be described as making love, more like coupling for a good cause. Deep down, the thought chilled her. She remembered how she felt when she watched Jessica and Baxter tumble into a cab and home to bed, their heads together in the back window as they waved good night. She thought of Suzie telling her about Brian and the woman she'd found with him in their bed, how her face still crumpled at the memory of this. She remembered all the starving actors and stage managers, stand-up comics and independent filmmakers moonlighting as cab drivers and furniture movers she had dated, all of whom lived in what might as well have been the same roach-infested, rent-controlled walk-up anywhere on St. Mark's Place, in the barren precincts below Houston Street, or on wind-ravaged Hudson. They all had green mold in their toilets; after a spaghetti dinner and a bottle of Chianti that offered a money-back guarantee on a bad headache, their hands were not as clean, but were just as greedy, as those of the sons of her mother's uptown friends. She thought of her dead brother. Roland: What would he have been like? Would he have had children? Would we have been close? Why do I miss him so much now?

She remembered the night she and Theo played true confessions, when Claire admitted that she once went out with a guy she met on the Third Avenue bus, who turned out to be a fry man in a fish house somewhere around Wall Street and never quite managed to get the smell off his hands, and that she dated one of the family chauffeurs, Rocky was his name, but did not find him quite so appealing out of uniform. When the laughter had died down and it was her turn, Theo said very quietly that she had been married once.

"I was very young and it didn't last." Theo's voice was dreamy. "I'm sure I did it to prove something to Doris and Roy, but I can't imagine what. David was his name."

Claire remembered how Theo had said this from somewhere far away, and she worried that a part of her might still be there. Theo said the marriage was, in many ways, the beginning of her attraction to women; she laughed about poor David dragging the legacy of that into the bedroom all his life, but Claire was acutely aware of the fact that Theo was still very much the object of male attention whenever they went out. *If only she weren't so beautiful.*

I suppose way down at the bottom of her own insecurity, Claire was afraid that Theo would meet a man who made love like a man, but loved like a woman. To make matters worse, the man they were looking for was no ordinary man—he had to be perfect, and looking for him brought her closer and closer to her terror. *What if she has our child and I lose them both?*

It was she who wanted to have a baby, not Theo. How could she admit to something as petty as the jealousy she was feeling now? Cold feet.

Theo knew. One morning, when Claire's downcast eyes gave her away and she left the table to try and suffocate the fear in the airless concentration she brought to her work, Theo followed her into the darkroom, kissed her tenderly on the back of the neck, and said, "You know, I'm not sure I can carry this off, either. I think I'll feel like some tramp in a sleazy motel."

They avoided talking about how it would happen, instead, they talked about who. For weeks, they assessed every man they knew and ones they didn't. They discussed character, looks, intelligence, predisposition to disease, moral fiber, athletic prowess, artistic versus analytical leanings, left brain versus right, fullness of hair, the Wassermann test, and table manners.

Every evening when Theo closed The Latest Dish, Claire sat at one of the tiny tables, which encouraged nothing more than a coffee and a comfortable wait for an order. Her Leica slung over one shoulder, she'd nibble at a small plate of smoked bluefish or a sliver of pâté Theo usually popped on a plate to take the edge off Claire's appetite while she cleaned up and packed their evening meal. Theo wiped down burners, moved platters of chicken, Swedish meatballs, pink lobster, fat shrimp, and honey-baked ham burnished with her secret marinade out of the display case and into a neat row of bowls and platters in the huge stainless-steel walk-in refrigerator. One night, as Theo lined up the ingredients she would need for the next morning's baking, assessed the dishes that would and would not hold for another day, and mentally made lists for the dawn foray she would make to the wholesale market, they began to ponder the delicate question that carried them home each evening.

"Well, you can't exactly sidle up to Baxter, let's assume he's a candidate, and say, 'Listen, Bax, we're considering you for the job of fathering our child, so, in twenty words or less, could you sum up your medical history? You know: heart disease, cancer, diabetes, phobias, allergies, baldness, hernia, insanity, the clap, that sort of thing," said Theo, juggling their dinner while securing the gate over the front door.

" 'And by the way, Bax, photocopies of your degrees and scholarships, and the results of any psychological or intelligence-related tests you might have taken would be real helpful, too,' " added Claire.

"Good point," Theo agreed, as they entered the park and felt its lush green slow their steps. "We have to be pretty sure about our man before we pop—no pun intended—the big question. It would put a strain on a friendship if we had to reject someone we love and care about just because bad genes or a sloppy past disqualified him from fatherhood."

It was a warm evening, and the tennis courts were full. They stopped to watch a fast doubles game, played by four trim men somewhere in their mid-fifties.

"Eye-to-hand coordination," Claire mused, admiring a high-speed volley that split the quiet like gunfire. "You never notice it until it's too late then, twenty years and thousands of dollars later, the kid's still taking cha-cha lessons."

"Uh-huh." Theo was watching a couple who had been playing singles and noticed the man congratulating the woman for a game well played. She listened hard for the patronizing words men often use to cover defeat, the gestures that would belittle the woman's performance, but heard no such thing, just genuine respect for the victor and honest irritation at having lost.

"C'mon," the man said, toweling off his sweaty face. "O'Neal's. I'm buying." Theo smiled at them; realizing they were being observed, they acknowledged her appreciation with the kind of nod that says, "Yes, we *are* unusual; how astute of you to notice."

"I don't know whether it's learned behavior or genetic, but I think it's critical for our candidate to like women. I mean *really* like them, not just long enough to get them into the sack," said Theo, watching the couple zip their racquets into plastic covers and swing them in the direction of well-earned refreshment.

Claire laughed. "You mean a man who understands why a woman caught in the grip of pre-period tension is beautiful even when she's ripping his face off."

"Exactly. A man who can feel the pain of water retention and feel puffy, too!" Theo rolled her eyes and blew out her cheeks.

"No allergies, either," said Claire. "I can't stand children who sniffle."

"Absolutely. What about baldness? If we have a boy, I wouldn't want him to grow up bald." Theo had lost interest in the tennis players and resumed strolling.

"Well, it wouldn't be so attractive for our daughter to grow up looking like Zero Mostel, either. Anyway, I think the baldness gene is on the mother's side, so no matter what we have, it'll be your fault," answered Claire.

"I don't feel strongly about whether the donor's a vegetarian, do you?" asked Theo suddenly serious about her favorite subject. "That should be a conscious decision later on, don't you think?

"We could ask *him,*" said Claire, eyeing the attractive, well-muscled thirtyish specimen in very brief gym shorts who was now loping toward them on the path.

"Don't you dare!" gasped Theo.

Just as the man passed, lost in thought and the rhythm of his pace, Claire grinned maniacally, did an exaggerated backwards twirl, and fell into step with him.

"You there! Yes, you, sir." As he struggled to hear her over the loud argument between a large German shepherd and the feisty poodle in his path, Claire kept talking. "You look like a healthy fellow. Could you lend us your, ah, equipment for a day or two?"

Slowing down, the man touched his ears, pointed to the barking dogs, and strained to hear what Claire was saying.

"Certainly. We understand. You would require a deposit and some identification—a driver's license, or a Bloomingdale's charge, perhaps," said Claire for Theo's benefit.

The man came to a full stop and stood directly in front of Claire. He raised his palms up, as if to say, "Okay, you've got my attention. You've ruined my jog. What?"

"I said," said Claire, pointing to his shorts and drawing out every word dramatically for Theo who was now red to the roots with embarrassment, "do you know where we could get similar sporting equipment?"

For a few seconds, he just stared at them, eyes narrowed as if to squeeze some deeper meaning out of what he had just been asked, knowing he was being made a fool of, but not quite sure how. No New Yorker, except maybe a mugger—and even muggers had standards—would intentionally interrupt a person's evening exercise to ask a stupid question like that. He wiped his face with his shirt, looked over his shoulder while a number of responses formed in his face but did not materialize, then shook his head at Claire and said, "You're nuts, like everybody else in this rotten city."

"Nice day at the office, dear?" said Claire, hands on hips, biting her cheeks as they watched him trot away. "Don't you think a well-developed butt is an asset?" she asked.

Theo groaned, but she couldn't stop laughing at Claire's nerve.

"Sure, if you like the sensation of being followed around by a basketball," she snorted, wiping mascara tears from her cheek.

On Seventy-second and Central Park West, just across the street from their building, a distinguished-looking silver-haired man read a newspaper in the back of a midnight-blue Rolls stopped at the light. "Do you think the ability to amass large sums of money is passed on by the father or by the mother?" Claire asked Theo, who nodded as though she might have been wondering the same thing.

As the light turned green, a pretty butterscotch woman in a minidress and nosebleed-high platform shoes fell into step with them, and Theo wondered whether ruling out "color" was racist or not. At the same moment, Claire said, "He's got to be white, don't you think? Life is going to be tough enough with two mothers without having to face life as a blond, red-haired, freckle-faced mulatto photographer chef."

"Oh, I think we're going to have to approach this more scientifically, my darling one," said Theo, loving the fact that they had begun to think alike. *Just like an old married couple.*

When things got tough and I searched for reasons to feel special, I remembered their stories of how hard it was to decide who would be perfect enough to help them create me. Whenever I felt angry at them for making me live outside the world of fathers and sons, fishing trips and Little League games, I remember how much they wanted me and the pains they took to make sure I would be whole and healthy and there would be not only as few bad surprises, but as many advantages in my life as was humanly possible.

The party was an elegant ruse designed to narrow the field of potential fathers without causing any suspicion among the candidates. On the pretext of creating a family tree of friends and of sharing personal histories, questions that would be considered rude under any other circumstances could be asked in the spirit of the evening. It was entirely Theo's idea.

The First Annual Hirsh-Bouvier Family Tree Trimming
An Evening of Forefathers, Foremothers,
Skeletons, Feuds, Family Secrets,
Ethnic Food, and Ancestral Dish
All in the relative comfort of
115 Central Park West, Apartment 6D
Saturday, August 23, at 8 o'clock
Come as you were!
RSVP 629-4955

The air was close on the night of the party, heavy and hot, and Theo pushed open the tall casement windows to let in whatever breeze had risen on the steamy darkness. She wore a long tiered skirt of tissue-thin peach cotton which came from Grandma Doris, who was part Cherokee on her father's side—which was why, she told Theo, she was always so comfortable raising a family in a trailer. "It made me feel as though I could pull up stakes and move on with the seasons like my ancestors. Never did, but I like to think I could have if the feeling ever came over me." The skirt was caught at the waist with the silver and turquoise conchas Doris had given her when she moved to New York. "There's no sky in Greenwich Village," she had said, handing her daughter the talisman that held all the wild dreams running in her tribal blood and reflected them back in a brilliant shade of blue. "That's why I left."

A small silver crucifix flashed at Theo's throat for the Bouvier side of the family. It had once belonged to her aunt Aimée Cassard, who claimed direct descendancy from Captain Jean Lafitte, and who was said to be as unpredictable as any pirate when riled. Roy's people were Huguenots who fled persecution by French Catholics and scattered, some to Germany, others to South America, and a handful all the way to America, burying themselves in the deep bayou country of Louisiana. Over the generations, Cajun cadences softened the Bouvier speech and imbued it with the music of ghosts long gone, they were clannish people who had their reasons to be suspicious of outsiders, people who are still a little wild. One of them left a wife, children, and a thriving New Orleans medical practice to fight in the Mexican War of Independence. They called him El Rojo, not merely for the flaming crop of red hair Theo and I inherited, but for his fierce and rather undoctorly ability to spill Spanish blood.

Claire stood behind the beveled glass of the French doors that stood open, glittering like arms full of diamonds, and watched Theo move about the room, now flickering in the light of the hurricane candles she had placed on the long refectory table that would be the scene of one of her famous suppers, on the oversized coffee table, and on the wide windowsills overlooking the park. As she neatly refolded napkins, squinting as an artist would to ensure their symmetry, and rearranged silver bowls of salty almonds and long lacquered trays of chèvre, salmon mousse, and vitello tonnato, her jewelry tinkled in the sultry air like a living wind chime. Claire could not help thinking that no matter what Theo wore, it merged with her violent coloring and became spectacular. As Theo bent over the tables and bowls of flowers she had so carefully placed around the room, Claire was filled with wonder at the woman who would soon wear the weight of their child with the proud bearing of an Indian princess, Theo who had planned this evening with the cunning of a spider. She also thought of her visit to Broken Arrow and of how Doris had craned her neck over the row of cacti crowding the narrow trailer sill. "Look at that sky," Theo's mother had said, "always rushin' off somewhere. Sometimes I'd like to know where it's going." She remembered the quiet pleasure Roy had taken in his wife's restlessness, and imagined it quickened his own. At that moment of shimmering happiness, Claire prayed Theo was not entirely her parents' daughter.

"The family trees were an ingenious touch," said Claire, sweeping into the room in her own combination of Celtic and Jewish roots, a silver Claddagh pin caught at the throat of the black Irish-linen blouse, a black-and-white shawl to signify her Semitic side draped around one hip of the matching, almost transparent sweeping linen skirt, the pale-blond hair drawn up off her neck and away from the little drops of perspiration that had begun to gather along its length. The Leica, as always, was in the black camera bag discreetly within reach.

"What a beautiful license to snoop on our friends!"

"They'll forgive us when they find out why," said Theo, gathering stray rose petals that had wilted and drifted onto the table, leaving some where they fell to reflect in the crystal bowl above them.

"Only if we tell them," said Claire, gazing out at the sleeping park. Theo had drawn whimsical family trees for everyone to fill out, funny little stylized apple trees, miniature cherry, weeping willows, cedars, sycamores, redwoods, black oaks, cypresses, eucalyptus, and the gnarled baobab of Africa's Serengeti. Each bore the name of a special guest; when everyone was gathered, Theo told them that the information contained on each would be collected to inform the special friendship tree she would create and send out as a memento of the party and of their unique bond in this family of their own design.

They chose him that night. Or at least that's what I believed. I imagined they phoned and asked to meet him for coffee or invited him over for dinner. Alone. After the first awkward conversation, which probably included incredulity, suspicion, and the dawning realization of the request's seriousness, they talked about it many more times. I can't imagine him agreeing to something like that right off, or even understanding it fully, not in the way we take the idea of sperm donors, artificial insemination, and in-vitro fertilization for granted now.

It was just fatherhood then, plain and simple, no fancy words for it, no cold legalese blurring what was in the blood, no lawful and binding contracts telling the parties what they could and could not expect from the agreement, what rights they were signing away. Custody and visitation had no bearing on those early conversations. These were fighting words reserved for married couples only, along with others like alimony and child support.

At the time, I'm sure my mothers didn't consider themselves advanced or even brave, just hungry for something they couldn't have, and I think once he understood that Claire and Theo intended to have a child whether he agreed to have a part in it or not, my father relented. Maybe he had his own reasons, too, beyond his affection for them and their absolute faith in him.

For years, I would not ask his name. I believed it was better not to know the answer, which would lead to more questions and inevitably, to disappointment. I kept my suspicions to myself. When I did finally learn who he was, I understood much more, but I imagined him for far longer than I knew him, in fragments of dreams, in the faces of strangers and of friends, and that's how I see him still—young and handsome, but in shadow, one of a group of young people raising their glasses in a basement restaurant that is small, dark and full of itself like so many on narrow crooked streets like Carmine, Waverly, MacDougal. Or maybe they are outdoors, slouching toward the shaft of sun that has penetrated the dark cool of the avenue and has pooled on the sidewalk around their chairs, celebrating their pact and wondering if any of the passersby have such grand plans. My mothers are suddenly shy in his presence; their eyes glitter with wine. The woman with him is proud of what he is doing, but more afraid than she will let on, caught up in the spirit of the moment. They refill their glasses; this helps them avoid the conversational shallows that might lead to any discussion of the darker side of their decision, and they do not look back.

A FEW WEEKS LATER, on what should have been another warm afternoon in a long succession of steamy Indian-summer days, Claire found herself shivering in a Checker cab inching uptown on Eighth Avenue, which was a solid wall of cabs, cars, grimy trucks, and Con Edison vehicles, waves of brisk Canadian air breaking over their backs on one of the most unseasonably cold October days in memory, begging the driver to turn on the heater.

Claire remembered how reluctantly Dr. Collins had advised them that if they were determined to persist in such a risky enterprise as do-it-yourself artificial insemination, there wasn't much she could do to stop them (actually there was much she could do in 1964 when such things were illegal, but her only request was that they not compromise her by asking her to participate); but that it might actually work if they kept the specimen as warm as possible and used it within two hours of ejaculation. "I wouldn't vouch for its motility after that," she had added firmly, drawing the visit to a close.

Claire imagined tiny sperm teeth chattering in the jar next to her and persisted. "I *said,* do you think we could have some heat back here? I really am cold," Claire asked the dazed hippie behind the wheel, who swiveled around and smiled dumbly.

He muttered something unintelligible, and pulled on the joint he had going in the ashtray. Claire watched a long, matted clump of hair rearrange itself under a grimy headband in a blast of air from the river. "Could you at least close the window?"

"You want a hit?" he asked, sucking up all the warmth that was left in the cab, sounding like someone who had blown up too many balloons.

"No. I don't want a hit. I want heat. H-e-a-t and for you to go faster."

"Hey, I'm doin' my best, man."

"All I want to do is get somewhere in under two hours and I get the one on slow acid," whispered Claire through clenched teeth, wondering how druggies could get hack licenses from the police department without the cops noticing anything suspicious, while normal people have trouble renting an apartment without an investigation.

"Please don't die! We're almost there," she begged the thick wool sock on the cracked leather seat next to her. "C'mon you guys, what's a little cold?"

Two bleary eyes stared at her in the rearview mirror as she squeezed the sock under her arm and feigned shivering. "You comin' down from a real bummer, ain't ya?" said the driver, putting the cab in neutral, throwing his arm over the seat.

She had wanted to be part of this in some small way, and delivering "the goods" was as close as she could get. "Neither rain, nor snow, nor dark of night . . ." she had chirped when she left that morning, sounding like a cross between the Merry Mailman and Jimmy, the Pall Mall bellhop, snapping Theo a crooked salute as she disappeared into their elevator.

It was more than a bit awkward at "Chickpoint Charlie," as Claire, in what was becoming a manic determination to cover her nervousness with humor, had dubbed my father's apartment. It was in the black-and-white art deco tiled bathroom where she had powdered her nose, taken a million pees, a bath or two and once, after having had several balloon glasses of wine too many, placed her cheek on that cool surface and slept until she was discovered and they put her to bed under the familiar chocolate-brown duvet cover that my father was trying to think about anything but the empty jar in his hand.

She remembered how she'd needed some breathing room when she and Theo were suffering their "winter of discontent" and she had come here to sleep fitfully in their tiny guest room. They had served her a breakfast of coffee and croissants and a tangy strawberry yogurt they said was imported from France, on a tray that held a tiny framed photograph of Theo and herself smiling into the sun of a happier day.

Now she felt like an intruder in this place as familiar as her own, while the makings of her son were being ejaculated into an empty jar of baby-food peaches.

"We wanted to get apricots," said the nervous young woman, motioning Claire into the kitchen, "but the A&P was out."

"Oh," said Claire, almost forgetting she had told them about the night Theo announced her change of heart with baby food. She smiled at this kindness. "As long as it's sterilized, it doesn't matter what flavor."

"Would you like something to drink? Juice, iced coffee, tea?" She wiped the counter for the third time.

"No thanks." Claire thought *Somebody really ought to be recording this for posterity.*

"Is it getting cold in here?"

"It's always warmer in the bathroom," said my father's wife, still hovering. "No cross-ventilation."

"I hope he's doing those visualization exercises I taught him," said Claire, staring at a spot above the stove. "I think it's important to see a healthy, whole person right from the beginning, don't you?"

"I'm sure he's visualizing something," she said, finally smiling at the thought of her dear and generous husband behind the bathroom door. "I just hope it's me." They were both grateful for a genuine laugh.

Three hours later, Claire and the acid king rolled to a stop on Central Park West, and even though Claire sprinted through the lobby and up the stairs, where a nervous Theo waited to do her part for me, Claire knew she was carrying duds.

"I don't think the boys are in the mood today," announced an exhausted Claire, seeing disappointment eclipse the eagerness in Theo's face. "Between the traffic backed up all the way to the George Washington bridge, a damn gale wind blowing right on them, and the fact that they are a full hour past swimming time, not to mention the stress of having to drive with someone who is so stoned he thinks neutral is a political position, these guys are way past deadline. I think they've lost that lovin' feeling, if you know what I mean."

"You know, I could just go with you next time," said an exasperated Theo. "I'm sure they'd let us do it there."

"That's not very romantic."

"Neither is dead sperm in a tennis sock."

Most people wonder what they'd be like with a different father, but I used to wonder what I would have been like if one hardy individual from that first chilly batch had, with its last dying shudder, managed to swim past the dead and dying bodies of his comrades and do the job. I could have been soft in the head, missing fingers or toes, or at very least, one of those people who can't take the heat and faint at barbecues. Natural selection probably would have taken care of the result, but that would have caused too much grief; and, who knows, they might have gotten cold feet after a miscarriage and called the whole thing off. Of course, I might have been fearless, like the little sperm that could—an adventurer, an astronaut, a climber of mountains, a race-car driver, a general; or maybe I'd have been just a little stronger and more persistent, a little better at knowing the blind spots in the road and seeing around them.

Claire was prepared the next time. Leaving nothing to chance, she rented a bicycle with a basket, packed it with her warmest cashmere sweater, wrapped her bell-bottoms in Theo's old bicycle clips, and headed downtown. It was sixty-five degrees. The weather was on our side.

"Special Stork-o-Gram for Theo Bouvier!" a soaking-wet Claire sang to Theo when she burst through their bedroom door less than an hour after the donor "did his thing," as she tactfully put it.

After Claire presented Theo with the rose and the leftover Valentine's Day heart she had managed to find in the marked-down section of D'Agostino's, she followed her into the bedroom, where the sterilized instrument of my delivery was wrapped in a freshly laundered and lint-free linen towel.

This part was entirely Claire's idea, discovered in the library, where she had spent hours poring over almanacs and farm journals and horse-breeding books and fat dusty tomes on animal husbandry to find out how prize stallions and bulls and Irish setters managed to sire whole families out of state. "People have been doing this for years. Well, not exactly *people*," she had explained.

"You realize I'm never going to feel the same way about Thanksgiving again," said Theo, unwrapping the bulb baster while Claire clutched the small jar still wrapped in her sweater.

"Be careful now—there's only a tiny bit in here," said Claire. "Not a whole lot to make such a big-deal wet spot on the sheets, is there?"

"Isn't it supposed to be cloudy?" said Theo, ignoring the joke and staring at the scant teaspoon of liquid at the bottom of the jar.

"It's okay. Dr. Collins says it turns clear after twenty minutes or so."

"Well, I guess that's not something you notice when you do it the other way, is it?" said Theo, eyeing the jar on the edge of the dresser. The baster was in her hand. She gripped the bulb and gave it a good squeeze, then let out a yelp.

"Claire, it's gone!"

Theo had just sucked the sperm right into the bulb.

"It can't be gone. It's got to be in there somewhere!" Claire could feel the panic rising. She couldn't go through this again.

Theo pulled the bulb off the baster and peered into it. Before she realized what she was doing, it was too late.

She felt the drop. "Oh, my God, I just got our child in my eye."

"Stay there. Don't move!" ordered Claire and Theo felt the Leica's flash go off in her good eye.

"Claire, do you mind!"

Theo staggered a little, still off balance from the flash, squinted at the baster with one eye, considered the physics of the problem, and realized if she was going to make good use of the last bit of semen that somehow, miraculously, managed to cling to the inside of the bulb, some acrobatics would be required. Determined that what went up would not, in this case, come back down, she sat on the floor and opened her robe.

"This reminds me of my first tampon," said Claire. "My mother couldn't get the words out, so she just said, 'Why don't you run along to your room and install this.' " She was on the floor next to Theo, whose legs were on the bed to keep her from falling over from an extremely precarious head-and-shoulder stand.

" 'Insert,' 'push,' 'stick up,' or even 'shove' might have been a better choice of words," said Theo into her own chest.

"I read the instructions six times," said Claire, trying to distract Theo and keep her from toppling, "then I took the paper off and stuck the whole thing in, applicator and all."

"You didn't." Theo was starting to shake.

"I did, and it hurt like hell. I kept it up there for two hours until I finally couldn't stand it and told my mother the thing wasn't exactly as comfortable as she had promised."

"Claire, that's really dumb."

"No dumber than getting sperm in your eye."

"How long do I have to stay like this?" said Theo, who looked dangerously close to exploding.

"I don't know. A little longer," Claire hoped there was enough natural light to record this special moment.

"Could we at least lower the lights, maybe put on some romantic music?" pleaded Theo. She was trying very hard to be a sport in spite of all the blood rushing into her head.

5

Theodora Bouvier and Claire Hirsh
announce the arrival of their son,
William Roland Bouvier-Hirsh,
10 pounds, 2 ounces, on June 8, 1965.
To share their joy with those less fortunate,
the mothers request that gifts of toys and clothing be donated to
the Elizabeth Blackwell Shelter for Children
in New York City

If my birth announcement had been widely distributed to include neighborhood police officers, postal workers, and grocery clerks, it would have surely caused a scandal and perhaps even a criminal investigation, which may well have resulted in my permanent residence in a foster home. But it was sent only to family and trusted friends who understood the precarious nature of its admission, those people for whom it was, or should have been, second nature to protect my mothers' privacy, as well as their joy, from the censure of strangers. It bore Theo's beautiful script and a photograph of a fat-faced cherub in a tiny sweatshirt that said "Boy!" For as long as I can remember happiness, the announcement hung in a place of honor in our growing hall gallery.

If it were not for my somewhat untimely arrival on a rainy Tuesday night in that exceptionally wet spring, Grandma Hirsh might never have made peace with my mothers; but, as I know now, the deepest feelings live in a place far beyond the clear boundaries of right and wrong, should and shouldn't, yes and no, and the unspoken terms of social behavior. Nothing happens without a good reason, and new life gives everyone an excuse to start over.

Positive that Theo would deliver no sooner than the fourth of July, and reassured of this daily by Dr. Collins, Claire had flown to Las Vegas for a weekend of shooting.

"Let's put it this way: You have enough time to fly around the world and back before the baby is ready to be born," the patient doctor had said after Claire's fifth call.

Claire had been working on a new concept and was anxious to finish the series before "B Day," before her undivided attention was required and while she could still be away from home for long stretches. She liked to say this new work looked at "life as a repetitive disorder"; she was fascinated by the curious, self-destructive, and often deadly things people did to avoid the reality and the adversity of their lives. While Theo cooked, packed, made arrangements with another chef to keep the store open while she was recuperating, and suffered the last indignities of what turned out to be a very large pregnancy, Claire shot the hookers, hustlers, and heroin addicts on Times Square and along the dark side of Central Park West. When she was sure Theo would be all right for a few hours, she shot drag balls up in Spanish Harlem, the contestants sweaty with nerves, showing the shadows of beards no amount of Pan-Cake could camouflage, ballroom dancers at Roseland drifting out of Brooklyn and the Bronx on an ocean of sequins, moustache wax, and tuxedos worn in the seat, and bingo nights in hissing, overheated church basements in Astoria and Flatbush, the women who, night after night after night, abandon family and the quiet hours of conversation to hunch over dog-eared cards, squinting up through cigarette smoke, ears tuned to the numbers that will set them free. They all had one thing in common, she told the extraordinarily uncomfortable Theo, who welcomed hearing anything that would still what she swore was the sound of her own skin stretching—a moth-like drive to batter themselves against the brick wall of their own circumstances.

The plan was to cap off the series with a trip to Las Vegas to shoot the "grinders," as the casinos called them. This was a special breed of repetitive disorder, the pensioners and the drifters and the waitresses and disabled Korean War vets, people who needed every penny they played and yet fed the nickel slots in what could only be described as a drugged, almost dreamlike state, mechanically pulling the levers until one arm grew larger than the other, in the vain hope that one day, they would hit the big one, which would transport them out of their misery and into an affluence they were sure they could handle.

"Are you sure it's okay?" Claire had asked twenty times while packing for the trip.

"It's fine," Theo assured her while she iced a cake she was testing for the store. "I'll just sit here and eat this cake until you come back. It's really okay." Theo handed Claire her camera bag.

They agreed that Claire would finish up on Sunday morning, when only the truly addicted filled the casino floor, their clothes a little seedier, their faces a little more worn, their determination all the more naked in the cruel early light. Then, having gotten the last of the photographs, she would hop a flight to Broken Arrow and spend a few days with the Bouviers, then fly on to New York with Doris and Roy midweek. Doris was elated at the prospect of Theo's first child and her newest grandchild and the idea that Claire and Theo had both wanted her with them to help out filled her with a sentimentality Claire would not have predicted. Roy didn't say much, never did, but Claire saw his excitement in the suitcase that was already packed for New York when she arrived.

"She was an amazing baby, our Theo," said Doris proudly. She passed Claire seconds of the gumbo she had cooked all day in honor of Claire's visit and Roy's taste for his Southern roots. "No'leans," he called it.

"She'd tie her diaper around her little shoulders like a cape and waddle and strut around like the Queen of the Nile. Everyone fell in love with her, Claire. It's no surprise you did."

After dinner, Roy stood up, nodded at the seated women, and headed for the BarcaLounger he had set up in the small yard behind the trailer to catch a breeze. "Give you girls a little time together," he said into the metal hatch they called their front door. Doris followed him with a broad smile. "There's a little Jimmy Stewart in him, don't you think?"

Before Roy was settled in for a "sit," as he called the times he gave himself over to the evening and his own thoughts, Doris got up, waved away Claire's offer to clear the table, and went to the tiny bedroom, motioning Claire to follow. "Want to show you something, Mama."

Doris snapped open an old cracked leather suitcase with reinforced corners. It bore the faded remnants of stickers from "iagra Fa" and the "rand Can." Inside were the neatly folded and labeled baby clothes of all the Bouvier children; one after another, she offered them to Claire, who fingered the soft flannel of Theo's tiny kimonos and diminutive undershirts, even softer now with age. She couldn't imagine a Theo so small, especially now with the enormous belly that held their child.

"I know Theo would love to see them again, but I really don't think you need to bring these to New York, Doris," Claire said, trying to be diplomatic, knowing they already had more baby clothes than I'd ever have time to wear. Between them, they had cornered the market on coveralls, sleepers, jaunty caps, and tie-dyed T-shirts; what they hadn't bought themselves arrived daily in the arms of Suzie, Jess, Molly, Peter, Alan, Thad, or Bax, including a miniature pair of high-button shoes and a string of baby love beads.

"Wait till you see the nursery, Doris," Claire said, remembering the day she and Theo, Bax and Jess and Suzie put on their painting clothes—Suzie's painting clothes were something other women would wear to the opera—and converted the loft she and Theo had been using as a library into the most perfect nursery a child could have. She went to her bag and got the photos, which she fanned onto Doris and Roy's black-and-pink chenille bedspread: Claire in bib overalls, a blob of sunflower yellow on her nose, a ballooning Theo in shorts and her chef's apron, Bax and Jessica always correct in white painter's caps, and Suzie in high heels, defiantly holding a paintbrush in one hand, her Nat Sherman in the other.

"We painted an Oklahoma night sky right over your grandbaby's bed," Claire said, smiling at the happiness of that day. They all painted till they dropped. Then Theo served them chili in Mexican pottery bowls set on the brightly splattered tarp she had thrown on the living room floor, and they all told stories of their own childhoods, most telling the versions they preferred. When the nursery was finished, it was more like a nest or a treehouse than a real room, with a ceiling of star decals from the Hayden Planetarium, butter-yellow walls, a cradle of robin's-egg blue (later a real bed with a bright red quilt printed with Peanuts characters), and no door to keep their baby from being lulled to sleep by the steady hum of the adults downstairs.

"I used to weave little strips of colored fabric for her wrists, so she could wear bracelets and learn her colors," said Doris wistfully, letting Claire's happy chatter wash over her, thinking of her beloved Theo about to become a mother.

Claire hugged the older woman, touched by the gift of light and texture and form she had given her daughter, thinking how gracefully Theo had carried it from childhood into adulthood, how she used it to nurture everyone who came into her life, and now, in the time they had spent together and in the baby she had conceived because of her, had given it so freely and with so much love to Claire. Claire smiled at the thought of the layers of amber and trade beads and silver and ivory Theo always wore up to her elbows. They were her grown-up versions of the baby bracelets Claire held now.

"You love her very much, don't you?" said Claire, overcome by the sight of a miniature anklet hung with a silver moon and a star. Doris, surrounded by her memories, filled up with her own feeling of mortality and the love of mother for daughter, eyes brimming with happiness, just nodded.

"I love her, too," Claire said quietly, when the phone rang.

THEO WAS TRYING very hard to remember everything she learned in the Lamaze class, trying not to panic in the empty apartment without Claire to help. No pillow, no jokes, no Claire razzing the man who was helping his wife on the mat next to them.

"You must be a very good friend. Is her husband away?" he had asked Claire politely in between his wife's and Theo's rehearsed grunts.

"I'm no friend," Claire had deadpanned. "I'm the father."

No nervous laughter, louder and full of real mirth when the man told himself she was only teasing. None of that now. Now there was only pain, and it was tearing her insides. She dialed the doctor first.

"How far apart are the contractions?" the woman asked.

"They're coming every three minutes," Theo gasped, a new one plowing into her like a truck.

"Get in a cab and meet me at Lenox Hill," ordered Dr. Collins before she hung up, grabbed her bag, and asked her family to keep dinner warm.

Theo hung onto the back of the front door and lifted the ancient intercom. "Andy, the baby's coming!" she panted into the receiver. "Have a cab waiting for me when I get downstairs. Lenox Hill."

"Jesus, Mary, and Joseph," replied the stunned doorman, with a whistle.

"Jesus, Mary, and Joseph." "Jesus, Mary, and Joseph!" What is that? Doorman for "Right away, ma'am"? Another contraction hit. *Why isn't Claire here?*

A few moments later, Andy was at the front door, blushing and brimming over with an odd kind of pride Theo could only figure had something to do with babies born in his building.

"I've got five of my own, Miss Bouvier, you're in goods hands now," said Andy. He had knocked once, as he was taught to do, but let himself into the apartment with the house key he had remembered to put in his pocket as he raced past the office, tapping the snoozing janitor and pointing to the door. "Watch the door, *amigo.* We've got an emergency up in 6D! And get a cab. *Ahora!*"

Theo was dialing again when Andy rushed in and stopped short, a little surprised at seeing her on the phone. Another fierce contraction kicked in and it took her breath away, but she waited for Lucy to summon Claire's mother. She could hear the housekeeper shouting, "Miz Hirsh, Miz Hirsh! We're havin' a baby!"

"Is there anything we can do, dear?" Mary Hirsh said stiffly, sounding as though she might be talking to Barnaby's secretary or the young girl who shampooed her hair.

"No, not really," answered Theo, hanging on to the table in the grip of a contraction. "I'm on my way to Lenox Hill Hospital, and Claire and my mother and father are getting the next flight here. I just wanted you to know."

Another one. Theo pointed to the red canvas bag on the floor under the hall table. They called it the emergency kid kit; it had been packed and ready for weeks. As Andy slung it over his shoulder, Theo's swollen legs began to buckle, and he caught her with a muscled strength his doorman's coat had never revealed.

"Off to the hospital with you, miss!" Andy said this loudly, the way he shouted greetings to the tenants over the blare of traffic and jackhammers, not meaning anything by it, filling the empty sidewalk with words the wind blew back unanswered. Just then Theo remembered the little automatic camera Claire had tucked into a side pocket, summoned up the strength to reach around Andy for the bag and patted the place she wanted him to open.

"Claire would have wanted a picture of me on the way to the hospital," said a now-ashen Theo. While Andy nervously fiddled with the camera, Theo hung the bag around her neck, put one hand on the place that used to be a hip, held on to the doorknob for dear life and attempted to smile through the most violent contraction yet.

"Andy, hurry up!"

"Okay, Miss Bouvier. That's it. Give me a nice smile. Could you move a little to your left? No, *my* left."

"Andy!"

Apparently, my head was in the wrong place. That hasn't changed much over the years, but that night, my inability to be in the right place at the right time did not make it easy for Theo.

"It hurt like hell. If I had been given a choice, my darling boy, I would have run like a cowardly dog," Theo had explained when, years later, I asked her about the scar that peeked out from the top of her bikini bottom.

When Dr. Collins arrived, Theo was prepped, breathing hard, and terrified. The tall, silver-haired woman in an expensive suit who was holding her hand said, in the clipped tone of someone who does not suffer delays: "Where have you been, Doctor? My grandchild is coming and my daughter-in-law is in great pain."

By the time Claire, Roy and Grandma Doris landed at Kennedy, threw their luggage into a cab, drove what seemed like hours on a deserted parkway through the sleeping borough of Queens, and finally burst through the hospital doors, bleary-eyed and manic, I was sleeping peacefully in the nursery, a little red but clean and sweet-smelling after a grueling battle with a pair of forceps and an umbilical cord that had turned deadly. Theo was sleeping off the epidural Dr. Collins injected to dull the pain of the Caesarean that in one swift and merciful moment of oblivion made Lamaze out to be the monster he really was. Grandpa Barnaby was nodding off in a plastic chair in the fathers' waiting room, accompanied by a life-sized teddy bear with the F.A.O. Schwarz tag still around its neck; Baxter and Jess had arrived with cigars and champagne; Peter was in a pair of khakis and a pajama top; Thad and Alan had Suzie in tow. Grandma Hirsh sat wide awake, ramrod straight, Claire's automatic camera in her hand, ghastly-green hospital scrubs over a soft bouclé jacket that should have been worn to the Palm Court; not to witness the blood and curses of a woman in the agony of a hard and dangerous birth.

Claire tiptoed into Theo's room, saw the slight trace of a smile on her pale face, in spite of the long tube that stuck out of the back of her hand and snaked up to the IV bottle high above her head. She smiled at the small framed photographs that she had packed in the emergency bag to make things feel more like home, remembering how Theo had laughed, saying "I'm not moving in, I'm just going there to have a baby." As Claire placed a single apricot rose and the tiny silver teething ring on the pillow next to Theo, the pale red lashes fluttered and through slits of sleepy luminous green, a voice thicker than Theo's drifted up from the sheet and murmured, "He's so beautiful."

When Claire saw me for the first time, taking in my toes, counting my fingers, gasping at the amount of shocking carrot hair on my large, old man's head, smiling tenderly at the bracelets of fat encircling my wrists and padding my ankles, gazing into eyes that could not be a cross between her own silver-gray and Theo's green, but miraculously were, Grandma Hirsh had stood quietly watching the joy and the amazement and the love and the tears gather in her daughter's face. After a while, she stepped softly up to the glass, never taking her eyes off me, and gently took her daughter's hand.

They watched me for several minutes and then Grandma's arm slowly moved up along Claire's shoulder, and Claire met it by turning her body in to Grandma's, and they stood holding one another like this for a long time.

"Did you feel this way when you saw me?" asked Claire, suddenly shy in the presence of her mother.

"I still do," said Grandma through tears of her own. "I love you very much, darling."

No one, not even the boisterously happy young father standing next to Claire, could make out her answer or hear her whisper "I never meant to hurt you," to the older woman at her side. Nor did the graceful cadences of my grandmother's cultivated voice disguise the pleading in her question.

"Are you going to call him Roland?" she asked.

I WAS TO BECOME the subject of many photographs in my young life—not the grinning arrangements found in most family albums, but stunning black-and-white compositions, beautifully matted in row upon row of blond museum frames. There I am in the requisite pony cart in Central Park, on the carousel with Aunt Suzie and one of her besotted companions none of us remembers, in a bright-colored sling on Theo's back, with Jessica and Baxter and the twins, with Peter and Molly and a scarecrow at the farm they'd bought just after I was born. In one I'm surrounded by all the basketballs, volleyballs, baseballs, footballs, golf balls, and beach balls my grandpa Barnaby made sure found their way into my "real" boy's life, my own round baby face a new pink Spalding among them.

Most of these show an infant, and later a toddler who takes the warmth and cosseting of female flesh as his birthright and who might even be shocked to learn that others were raised by hard-muscled people who did not encourage the expression of feelings, the playing of make-believe, singing in bed, or the unabashed enjoyment of a softly pulsing breast.

But there is something else in this the earliest of photographs, taken from the other side of the nursery viewing window. I am only a few hours old, wrapped to bursting in hospital swaddling, and I cannot see beyond the tip of my nose, much less smile for a camera.

Nevertheless, I am aiming a big, goofy, toothless grin directly at Claire and Grandma Hirsh, the two women who would determine so much about my future beyond that moment. All the baby books say an early smile like this is more likely a bubble of gas, and it would have been impossible for me to distinguish anything beyond shadows and blurry shapes at that point, and even if I could I would not have known what I was seeing—but I know better. And I like to think they did, too.

It's impossible, but whenever I see that photo I get the feeling that at the moment it was taken, I knew something had changed irrevocably, and that it had happened because of me.

6

My infancy was hard on Claire. When the mountains of pre- and post-natal reading material she and Theo amassed on their groaning coffee table described the natural phenomenon of bonding, including the period of abject misery visited on most fathers in the months when neither mother nor child seem to have any use for him, Claire had been either out of town shooting Norman's House of Toast for her "Silly Billboards" series, or in such a heightened state of denial that she convinced herself that she would be the first non–birth parent in the history of mammals to transcend this biological fact of life. After all, wasn't she the one who'd wanted me in the first place? Shouldn't I have known this and divided my time accordingly?

It was, she said, the loneliest time of her life. Only when the shock of this staggering primal blow had moved out from under her solar plexus and into words that always seemed to require apologies, did she admit to envying Theo her exalted position as my "natural" mother with an intensity that could have crossed the line to murder at the drop of a nursing bra—or at the very least, seriously damaged what had become an increasingly fragile bond between them. Claire had had no idea how much the sight of Theo as sleepy Madonna snuggling her child would hurt.

At about four o'clock one morning, an exhausted and not completely recovered Theo had just slipped back into bed after an hour of humming, murmuring, patting, walking, and gentle stroking, which had only succeeded in quieting me down, not in lulling me to sleep; Theo was sufficiently worn down to have decided to let me nestle with her in the comfort of her own bed.

"He can't breathe. He can't breathe!" Claire panted, eyes wide with alarm as she fought to close the space between sleep and the dim safety of the bedroom, still reeling from the hands of her subconscious on her throat.

Theo shifted me to her other arm and reached over and massaged her back. "It's okay, honey. It's only a dream."

"I dreamed I puréed you and passed you off as crème brûlée for the Marmelstein brunch," murmured Claire. She was sweaty and obviously shaken from what she would later describe as a "textbook rejection dream." Predictable, but no less terrible.

"No wonder you're upset. You're in the wrong dream. I'm the one who has cooking dreams. You can't cook, remember?" said Theo, who was not too sleepy herself to notice that Claire did not smile at this.

"You were emptying the refrigerator into a suitcase that had no bottom," said Claire, shivering a little, still very much in its grip. "Everything disappeared into a lid lined with sharpened teeth. The more I begged, the more you laughed. You picked up the kitchen table with one hand and threw that in too, then you dragged Willy out of his crib and put him in and sat on the whole thing because the suitcase was bulging and wouldn't close and he was crying to get out."

Instinct told Theo this was not the time to analyze, but to respond only to the dream's humor; Claire was swimming too close to the surface of her fears for truth.

"Was I good as crème brûlée?" she said.

"Delicious," said Claire, who had regained enough equilibrium to notice my feet sticking out from the other side of Theo, and had begun to bite my toes. "But not as good as this little one," she teased, now wide awake, flinging her resentment into the toothless gurgle of my laughter and Theo's good-natured chagrin at knowing she would have to quiet me down all over again.

Some mornings, lazy and protected from the world, Theo soundlessly slid out of bed to whip up one of her wonderful breakfasts, leaving Claire and me to the noisy beginning of a bond that would eventually grow as deep between us as the blood between Theo and me. When she came back, loaded with berries and muffins and coffee, floating in her big silk kimono printed all over with the palm trees I later came to imagine would gently sway to life and drop coconuts in the perfumed darkness of her closet, the tension was gone and we were a family again.

Sometimes we stayed in bed for hours, slipping in and out of sleep, tumbling back into play, eating berries dusted with sugar, a jumble of arms and legs, large and small. One morning Claire set the timer and hopped back into bed for a portrait that gave them the look of two lionesses, one tawny, one fiery red, both sleepy but alert to any danger that might overtake the tiny cub wobbling between them on big clumsy paws, ready to take aim at anything that might shatter the illusions held by what looked to be an extraordinarily happy child shining out from that photograph.

"People do terrible things in the grip of postpartum depression, Willy Wonka, and I suppose Claire was the first woman to suffer *post* without ever actually having experienced *partum,*" explained Theo one afternoon a few weeks after I became a father myself and was convinced my sweet-natured beautiful Annie had been spirited away in the middle of the night and replaced by a vicious wolf-mother who bared her teeth and foamed at the mouth whenever I approached.

"Don't worry, you're just jealous, and Annie's being held hostage by her hormones, that's all," said Theo, when I confessed my anger and puzzlement at this. "She'll come around . . . just like I did," she added quietly.

For her part, Theo was kind to Claire; she instinctively understood the isolation of fathers who stand helplessly by, forsaken by their own progeny for the powerful magic of nourishment and the all-consuming need to climb back into the warm red-velvet hammock that rocked their days before that wrenching moment of bloody hands and impossibly bright light.

She studiously avoided the smugness of new mothers, that pained, mysterious, superior look that says, "I have suffered, I have lost my figure, but I have done something far more important than anything you could possibly imagine, than you could ever do."

Maybe it was the tenderness Theo felt for her own father, left stranded in the maternal wake of Doris, marshalling her ducklings and dispensing what he could not to the Bouvier brood, or maybe it was simply the look on Claire's face when I nestled at her breast, snug and content with the idea that while I couldn't exactly crawl back inside, I would always be as close as a button's breadth to mother love and my next meal.

I cried if Theo so much as left the room. I wailed when she returned to the shop for a few hours a day, and when I heard the familiar sound of her key in the door I grabbed the soft red curls that matched my own, smelled her own wonderful mixture of milk and carnations and warm skin as she picked me up, and I sang with the happiness and relief of every infant who knows his mother has not left him forever.

Claire winced her way through these first few months; once, while Theo stole a few hours at the shop to work on a new menu, she tried to give me her own skinny nipple, which left me howling and even hungrier for Theo.

"Helloooo! Is anybody home?" Theo called into the strangely quiet apartment. "Where is everybody?" she called again, feeling her step quicken, the rolling sensation of fear, then a strange lightness in her legs at the sight of Claire tightly coiled in the rocking chair in the nursery.

"I tried to nurse him," said a miserable Claire, who had kept her eyes closed until Theo was upon her, grimacing at the rising wail that greeted the reappearance of nourishment.

"Oh, Claire," said Theo, still clutching the Latest Dish bag she had brought home, chest slamming with relief, not knowing whether to laugh or cry.

"What happened?"

"It hurt like hell is what happened. We're both a little cranky from the experience. I can't speak for Willy, but I, for one, feel a little foolish."

I think Claire really believed nature would make an exception of her. The realization that our enlightened and alternative notion of family had affected nothing in the grand biological scheme exhausted her. To the unseen hand that had drawn this ancient pattern, designed the pull of the moon and the planets and duplicated it in perfect symmetry in every single cell, we were just an odd little family of salmon swimming in the wrong direction to get to the same place, slapping and flailing against what always was and always would be, and Claire believed the universe had gently chided her for this overblown sense of self-importance. It humbled her with the sight of tiny fingers walking contours already familiar from a floating dream, eyes blind to everything but the shape and smell of mother love, food, shelter, safety, and a dry diaper.

She watched Theo unbutton her blouse and settle in to nurse her frustrated child; she realized then that the Cosmos did not give a rap how much she yearned to switch places with Theo and was telling her so with the perfect cupid's-bow mouth of a little boy seeking his mother.

It seems ironic now that it was really Claire who prepared me for the shock and the resentment I felt at my own uselessness in the wake of my babies' urgent need for no one but Annie; that it was she who reached into the future to teach me this lesson in fatherhood through Theo's telling.

Apart from my impossible clinging to Theo, especially around feeding times, Theo and Claire shared everything equally, carving up their time with me as carefully as they would a rich pudding, every minute fairly dispensed and blissfully savored, along with those not so sweet, neatly divided.

They put a sign on the apartment door that read "Shhh, Baby Sleeping! Do Not Ring Bell!" Theo, a better juggler than Claire, was able to see friends, cook, grow a business, and care for a baby, a lover, and a home simultaneously. Claire would not even answer the phone during her time with me. Instead, she phoned Pearl, her favorite operator at our answering service, and instructed that she give the following message to anyone who called: *Claire would love to talk to you, but knowing how much you hate to be interrupted by His Nibs, you'd probably rather she call you back during his nap which will be in about seven minutes.* Claire actually alerted the service to the approximate time of my nap every day.

Tina, Pearl's nighttime counterpart, who knew all our friends, and who loved to straighten out snarled dinner dates and movie plans, decipher garbled instructions, and figure out who was waiting for who and where, once told Jessica who had called to confirm the time of a lunch set for the following day that I had a little colic, nothing to worry about, but that she should probably go ahead and start serving without Claire.

"I'm telling you, honey, with Theo doin' that party way up on

Riverside and Claire on her own, it's gonna be a while before she gets that baby and herself dressed and settled down, then all the way to you."

They agreed that whoever wheeled the carriage into the park would say, if asked, that she was the mother, which more than confused the women lining the benches up and down the paths around the sailboat pond and under the stony pigeon-splattered gaze of Hans Christian Andersen. Claire enjoyed watching doubt, suspicion, then outright envy move among them as they first took in my miniature heavyweight status and then eyed the lean length of her in the skinniest clothes she could find for these parades around the park.

On one of our outings, she innocently smiled into the collective narrowing of eyes and, as she sat deliberately on the sunny row of benches reserved for the regulars, said: "I don't know what all the fuss is about. I had a very easy time." Then, winking at my bracelets of fat, she added, "It's amazing how quickly a person can lose ten and a half pounds.

"I can hear them now, desperately trying to figure out how I lost all that baby fat," she bragged to Theo, who patted her still-zaftig behind and said, "Let's hope I don't run into the same group."

"Serves them right," Claire said defiantly, flushed from her victory but feeling a little dumb at just how shallow it was. "Let them all diet till they drop."

Theo knew it was Claire's jealousy talking, but laughed with her anyway, never letting on that during those early days she often looked at Claire as though she were another child going through a difficult stage, loving her more for her vulnerability, for trusting Theo enough to let it show.

I attended my first formal brunch at Cafe des Artiste at three months and my first slide presentation at the Hunter College auditorium at four. The meal went smoothly and I slept undisturbed through the mimosas and the asparagus frittatas with smoked trout, right up to the blueberry cobblers and cappuccino, snoozing in the sling Theo had designed for such occasions. But the shadows of the photographs on the ceiling, and the droning sound of the lecture, became too much for me; somewhere between slides of wild dogs of the Third World and the painful, time-lapsed unfolding of yet another calla lily, I pierced the pindrop hush of the cavernous space with the youthful protest of someone who has not yet learned to suffer the pretensions of the art world in respectful silence.

When I was six months old we dropped in on Grandma Doris and Grandpa Roy in Broken Arrow. This required that I take my first ride in an airplane, which, I did not altogether enjoy—nor did the flight crew—once my delicate ears experienced the new and painful sensation of popping, which could not be relieved with a yawn no matter how much Claire opened and closed her mouth to get me to mimic her own wide yapping. My grandparents had not seen me since that first night at Lenox Hill, where they slept on hard hospital chairs while waiting for a proper introduction, and the two hectic weeks that followed could hardly be considered a visit; over all too soon. Until my arrival in Broken Arrow, they had been content to follow my progress via a steady flow of gray manila envelopes marked "Photographs! Do Not Bend!" in red grease pencil.

Alternative lifestyles, same-sex unions, relationship-defining contracts, palimony, galimony, life partners, pre- and post-nuptual agreements—these were all concepts my mothers helped pioneer, but nevertheless would have hated had they been exposed to them in the numbing, politically correct jargon that makes so much that is out of the ordinary, exotic, and self-expressive seem colorless today. Acknowledgment of their relationship in anything more than the criminal sense in 1965 was unheard of. But that was also the time when bearded hippies and achingly young girls who wore flowers in Rapunzel hair were pretty much celebrating anything they pleased in meadows and on mountaintops and in the communes that were springing up around a definition of peace, love, and anti-war sentiment. Claire and Theo watched all this with great interest from the distance of their years, feeling that they had established a counterculture of sorts all their own; they, too, wanted to celebrate their union and the bond of family in some special way.

They decided to get married.

A few days before we left for Broken Arrow, Claire secretly went to Cartier's and bought matching rings of six connected bands of pink, yellow, and white gold, and hid them in her cosmetic bag to surprise Theo during the ceremony my uncle the Reverend Roy Junior had arranged and dubbed, in the spirit of the times, "A Happening of God, Peace, Love, and Family Unity." It was to be held on the tribal land, which was the only place that would allow it, and it got him in plenty of hot water with the church management, which didn't stop him from telling them he'd "do it again tomorrow."

Baxter and Jess, Suzie, and my "uncles" Thad and Alan, had all flown out to surprise them.

Uncle Peter came without Aunt Molly because they had decided that my cousin Charlotte, who was only four, was too small to be left alone with a sitter for more than a few hours at a time.

"Are they coming?" Claire had asked him in a private moment before the ceremony.

Peter shuffled a bit and said, "Her arthritis has been kicking up lately, and you know Dad doesn't go anywhere without Mother."

"Arthritis doesn't keep her off those damn committees of hers, and she moves all right when one of her friends throws a charity ball."

"You know she loves Willy," said Peter, with the unmistakable discomfort of one who is caught between loyalty and a lie.

"It's her daughter she has a problem with." *He's still trying to get something from them, still trying not to take a side, hoping they'll wake up and love him as much as Roland,* Claire thought. But he had flown all this way to be at her wedding, and he looked tired. She had the decency not to pursue it.

Getting married is never without its complications, but back then there were more than a few hurdles for Theo and Claire, not the least of which was the fact that their union was recognized by no one except our little family and even that approval was not unanimous, painfully apparent in the calculated absence of Mary and Barnaby Hirsh. To further complicate matters, those were the years when people who gave birth or threatened to do so before saying "I do" forever bore the stigma of being "easy." But even rumors of marrying for the sake of a child held the implication that, however unsuitable the person was, one married a member of the opposite sex. My presence in the stroller they wheeled straight down the middle of an old sweat lodge they had transformed into a chapel for the occasion put an interesting twist on their already-thorny problem.

Claire, Theo, and I all wore white. "Otherwise, we'll just fight over who gets to be the bride," Claire had decided. Suzie, who could manage only the basic guitar chords, gave "Amazing Grace" her best shot for our odd processional, and during the vows, when Uncle Roy asked Claire and Theo if they would follow the requirement given by Jesus to the woman in the Gospel of St. John and simply "love one another," Suzie plunged into a lurching rendition of "Both Sides Now," practically drowning out their answers, my wailed agreement, and the sentimental sniffling of our family and friends.

Afterward, everybody piled into cars and went back to the Bee-Line for one of Grandma Doris's barbecue suppers.

Even though we've got our backs to the camera, the shot of Claire and Theo standing before Uncle Father Roy, who is asking them if they will love and honor and cherish each other and me forever while I listen and play with their rings from the carriage between them is the one I love the most.

When I showed it to Annie in the months preceding our own wedding, she grinned wickedly. "I knew your mothers weren't exactly traditional, but I didn't realize they *had* to get married."

I am told that somewhere around the two-year mark, I began to call Theo Mama and Claire Mommy. Claire used to joke that I called her Moma for the Museum of Modern Art, but I think she invented this to make me sound precocious.

As far back as I can remember, most Sundays Theo cooked a big potluck dinner and opened our apartment to as many members of our extended family as were in town and hungry. Everyone knew they could change their minds and drop by even if they'd said they wouldn't; Theo always managed to coax something wonderful out of our big kitchen and produce another place for stragglers and strays and friends of friends.

Of all my memories of Theo, this is how I remember her the happiest, beaming as the people she loved most enjoyed her food, closing her eyes and nodding at their compliments, refilling their plates, urging them to eat, touching their shoulders as she passed their chairs, inserting a comment here and there, telling a joke, finishing a sentence for Claire before moving on, orchestrating, encouraging, appreciating, welcoming, urging newcomers back, pressing gifts of food along with her kisses good-bye.

Happily deluded into the notion that the world was filled with good-smelling foods, loving hands, and doting aunts and uncles, I learned that love has its own language, its own smell, and even a taste that leaves an indelible mark on the memory.

On one such languorous afternoon in late fall, everyone was admiring a rocker she and Claire had discovered during a weekend visit to the farm Uncle Peter and Aunt Molly had just leased (and would later buy) in the sleepy Long Island village of South Neck.

Baxter gave it a long and appraising look and said it looked like the work of Gustave Stickley to him. "If it is, there should be a brass tag somewhere underneath that says, "Craftsman Workshops, Eastwood, New York," but even if there isn't, luv, it's a nice example of the early Crafts movement." Bax always encouraged enjoyment over investment, even in the acquisition of the far older and more valuable antiquities and architectural oddities he found in remote corners of the world and sold in his antique shops, a series of connecting street-level front parlors in the row of ancient and crooked mews houses on MacDougal Street.

Uncle Bax said "luv" the way a Cockney says "guv"; the ghost of his London childhood lingered in his broad A's and in the faintly aristocratic way his cigarette floated between long slender fingers as though someone else had put it there to surprise him. Baxter had just taken off his soft suede moccasins, touched the edges of his Sergeant Pepper handlebar mustache and assumed his own lanky version of a half-lotus, and was about to inspect the chair's oak underside when Peter and Molly arrived.

"Stickley, hell. More like 'Stick it to the city slickers' to me," drawled Peter in his exaggerated country-bumpkin voice. "I'm learning those farm boys don't give away too many bargains."

"Oh, here he is now, the Fifth Avenue hayseed," Claire teased.

"Well," Peter said, eyeing his sister and beaming an appraising smile at Theo's billowing sleeves. "You two don't exactly have 'local' written all over you."

"I'm sure there isn't much call for floor-length batik and toe rings on a potato farm," said Jessica from inside her shining black curtain of bobbed hair. She had been enjoying the exchange from the vantage point of her favorite chair, in front of the huge windows. The light was dropping fast. Against that backdrop, coiled among the cushions, she looked more like a figure from a twenties bas-relief than a young woman living in the Age of Aquarius.

When Aunt Jessica wasn't teaching the twins Italian or French, or how to recognize the dressmaker details that define the subtle difference between couture and ready-to-wear, she entertained her friends with stories, many of which featured a plug ugly fashion editor who made ridiculous pronouncements like *Never wear dancing shoes on the street!* and *A good suit can be worn inside out!* She loved to say the editor did this so people wouldn't notice her resemblance to J. Edgar Hoover. When not redecorating the English country house–cum–brownstone on West Twelfth Street that was always being photographed for interior design books, Jess wrote gloppy stuff about clothes in fashion magazines and was often away in a place called Location.

She drifted away from things, Aunt Jess, preferring the world of imagination to the mundane, albeit elegant, one she and Uncle Bax inhabited. Fabrics like chiffon, charmeuse, and cashmere were not *worn,* according to Jessica—*mais non!* They *floated,* they *clung,* they *poured* like thick cream from the masterful hands of Hubert, Oscar, and Yves, whoever they were.

I remember once watching her work. She smiled at the blank white pages filling up with words, her lips moved constantly in an imaginary conversation, and she smoked nothing but air through a silver cigarette holder, while her hands gestured extravagantly, gathering her power around her. Theo showed me the neat printed columns signed Jessica McClain Baxter, for which, Claire said, Jess was paid "tons of money."

Claire never took pictures for Aunt Jess's magazine because, she said it taught people to value the wrong things, and sometimes there was tension between them, but not that day. That day, Jess sat next to my grandmother, who was never completely comfortable at our house but adored Jessica and always asked after "that darling girl with the English husband."

Molly's hands always flew into action before she got as far as the living room, and that Sunday was no exception. She offered me a set of antique blocks found in an old trunk in the farm's attic; gave several pots of her own black-currant jam to Theo, who had promised to try it out in the store; and handed Claire an herb wreath she had dried and wired for our kitchen door and some old photographs found in the same trunk—all this before she was halfway across the living room. As usual, Peter followed close behind, waiting to help peel away the coat he knew she would only manage to get half off before it became hopelessly entangled in her enthusiasm.

"You really must stop coming here empty-handed," said Jessica. She was faintly dismissive of Molly, but never mean to Claire's unsophisticated Midwestern sister-in-law, who always smelled vaguely of apple pie. I don't think she understood Molly's total disregard for fashion, her peasant's enjoyment of the earth and simple country pleasures, and her refusal to compete with her fast-talking New York family.

"Somebody's got to listen," Molly once said when Suzie and Jess and Claire were all laughing and talking, interrupting and stepping all over each other's lines in their manic version of conversation. "Mercy, how else would any of you know what you've been talking about?"

"You have to love someone who says 'mercy,' " Jessica had said.

Peter had finally given up living in Roland's shadow, rejecting the life Barnaby had so desperately wanted him to embrace, along with the muggers he was convinced waited for him on every street corner now that he was a father with responsibilities. Molly hated the idea of raising Charlotte and my two-year-old cousin Harry, who would be my lifelong friend, in the cramped, soot-encrusted apartment they had once loved with the fierce loyalty and superiority of city dwellers.

"They'll wither," Molly had said, always finding her words in the garden she longed to grow.

Tired of the "bohemian" life and the odd writing jobs he had once loved and which he now understood meant irregular paychecks, Peter was going to try his hand at growing potatoes and corn, running South Neck's small newspaper, and raising a family in relative peace and quiet with a minimum of summer people, who for the most part preferred the trendier precincts of the island—the Hamptons, and the island's Atlantic gold coast.

He and Molly had come alone that day, having left my cousins with Molly's parents, who were visiting from Ohio and were as thrilled at the prospect of having their grandchildren all to themselves for the day as Peter and Molly were at the idea of one of Theo's "afternoons."

"I love the country on weekends, of course," Jessica said in answer to Molly's gushing descriptions of the farm and their decision to move, "but really, isn't this taking things a little too far?"

"Why don't we all make ourselves a plate of something?" Theo interrupted, afraid someone would fall from the high wire that always seemed to stretch a little tighter when Mary Hirsh was present. "Thinnest first," she announced, looking directly at Jessica and Mary.

Apropos of nothing, which is the way she started most conversations, Jessica began, "Do you remember how you told us about Theo, Claire?" Jessica never waited for an answer.

"Well, Bax and I were in St. Thomas or Aruba or somewhere," she said, settling into her story. "I was doing swimsuits, which were ghastly in 'sixty-three, those tiny crocheted things that got soggy and fell off when wet, leaving absolutely nothing to the imagination. Bax was working too, scouting the island for good examples of the Dutch colonial period, anything that hadn't gone completely off in that insufferable heat, and I think he was having lunch in a mill or a plantation or a castle, I can't recall. It was a ruin, anyway, and the owners were anxious to sell off their collection. It was just before Christmas. No, actually, it might have been the day after, Boxing Day as Baxter calls it," she said, imitating her husband's clipped English accent. She sounded like the italics in her magazine.

"Sweetheart, you're drifting," Baxter said encouragingly from across the room.

Jessica smiled sweetly at the husband who knew her too well.

"The plan was to stay on for a little holiday with the girls when one of those awful 'dear friends' Christmas letters arrived at the hotel from guess who?" Jessica nodded dramatically, shivering the curtain of silky black hair, which closed dramatically over one large almond eye.

"It wasn't an awful letter," interrupted Claire, feigning hurt.

"Of course, it was, but that's perfectly all right. You're a famous photographer and you're not expected to write compelling letters.

"Well, there it was," continued Jessica, "buried somewhere between the weather in New York and how many cigarettes Suzie smoked at the Coney Island show: 'I've fallen in love with someone named Theo and he's a she!' "

The lining of my grandmother's pale pink suit rustled softly and the soles of her crocodile pumps made a small slippery sound as she recrossed her ankles and shifted slightly in her chair.

Peter shook his head at Molly, who slid a furtive glance at her mother-in-law.

"Well, I did what any best friend would do under the circumstances. I wrote an immediate reply."

"Opening with 'Oh my God, have you told your mother?' " said Claire, who had not seen Mary shift again in the soft chair.

"No, it was 'Darling Claire, colon, Oh my God, have you told your mother?' "

In the kitchen, Theo shook her head and prayed Mary Hirsh had a strong heart, but Claire and Jessica were beyond noticing or caring. This was their ritual, a story they would repeat until they both believed their friendship had not been diminished or damaged by this drastic development in Claire's life.

"You weren't exactly sure how you'd fare either, asking if I would think you and Baxter boring heterosexuals, now that I was a lesbian, which of course, you had to type in all caps." Claire remembered feeling oddly disloyal to her friend when she read that part.

"I suppose it was a little silly to feel threatened by Theo of all people." Jessica continued, interjecting another "Oh my God, have you told your mother?" which brought up Grandma Hirsh's color. Claire, blotchy from so much laughing, finally came up for air. "Do you remember how you signed off?"

"I think the complimentary close was entirely appropriate given the circumstances," said Jessica: " 'Well, good-bye, you old dyke!' " Which drew fresh laughter from Thad and Alan who had arrived mid-story.

"Are you all right, Mother?" Peter asked as Mary passed his chair.

"Fine, dear. I'm just going to see if Theo needs help in the kitchen," said Mary, clearly uncomfortable in the lap of such unbridled honesty.

At our house, no one needed to be called to dinner twice. After a while, Theo stood near the French doors and smiled, which was the signal to rise and move toward our red Parson's table set with Molly's gift of homemade bread, a baked ham cut into a perfect pink spiral accompanied by a piquant mustard and horseradish sauce, bubbling Lyonnaise potatoes, and a large tureen of smoky lentil and andouille sausage soup. As people drifted out of the living room toward the fragrant, homey food, Jessica linked arms with Claire and, making sure Mary was out of the room, paused just long enough to let the moment settle. She tilted her head in Claire's direction and winked. "I guess we can all be grateful she didn't send pictures."

On her way to the kitchen my grandmother wandered into the foyer, which still carried the sweetness of the armload of freesias and tea roses Thad and Alan had handed to Claire along with their coats, covering their generosity with a lie about not wanting to leave them to die unsold.

Uncle Thad, a soft-spoken chef, and Uncle Alan, a lover of exotic flowers, were Theo's friends from the Barrow Street years when they all met for coffee every Wednesday afternoon or had dinner in Theo's floor-through, which was narrow and ordinary, except for the huge old-fashioned kitchen with its working fireplace across from the stove, which made it the most coveted and most welcoming apartment in New York. They had banded together while learning their way around this often inhospitable city with its strange customs and its hard lessons for people who didn't yet know the ropes.

Mary thought about these young people she did not understand, and she looked up at the letter from Jess that Claire had framed along with the rest of the mementos and photographs that lined the wall. Between the lines of its dashed-off spontaneity and total, if not brutal, honesty, on pale blue paper spotted with something that might have been sun lotion just under the stamp of its clubby hotel crest, it revealed much about love and trust and taboo and perhaps more than Jessica intended about its author's fear of being left behind in her friend's new life.

Listening to the voices rise and fall in the living room, shifting to other topics with the arrival of fresh faces, Mary wondered what was best—showing the world such bare-faced reaction or allowing the passage of time to temper one's response, letting it pass through the filter of judgment before putting such strong feelings into words, waiting it out and letting the rigors of life decide and in the end, finding no need to comment at all.

When she slipped back into the room, the talk had turned to the time, when just after my first birthday, Theo had closed the store, Claire had loaded her camera, and they parked me with Baxter and Jess to take what they called their second honeymoon trip to Paris, where they stayed at a place on the Left Bank called L'Hôtel.

"Our cab driver had a small dog in the front seat that stood on its hind legs and stared suspiciously over the seat at us every time its owner said, *'Quelle hôtel, mesdames?'* Each time the man repeated the question, the dog barked and growled more menacingly," said Theo, bending over to refill Baxter's plate, which was under the coffee table while he still fiddled with the new chair.

"The cab driver closed his eyes and made the *puh* sound Parisians always make when they think you're crazy. Well, we finally found it and it was a lovely trip, but when we got home and went straight to you-know-who's from the airport to collect our darling boy," she said, ruffling Baxter's hair, "Jess answered the door with a face full of chalky white powder. She looked like some bizarre Kabuki player and, of course, she couldn't imagine why we were staring at her."

"I thought she was trying on some new look for the magazine," said Claire, jumping into the space she always found in Theo's conversation to make it her own. "Or making pancakes," said Theo, deftly jumping back.

"Well, I certainly didn't know what all the fuss was about," said Jessica. "It was just baby powder. I invented it with the twins. Whenever a little baby bottom needed changing, I'd dust a bit on my face first. I, for one, would rather smell *poudre* than poo," she said, pointing to my fat diapered bottom as I waddled by.

"That's my girl," said Bax.

"All this talk makes me think of Fitzie," said my grandmother primly, enjoying but not really listening to the talk around her, thinking of the sister who was always trying to make a match for Claire and who had passed away suddenly a few months before I was born.

Fitzie had gone to Bergdorf's one afternoon for her weekly styling. While she stood at the salon's elegant desk to pay, her heart failed, and she died in the ambulance on the way to Lenox Hill.

"Poor Aunt Fitzie would never have dreamed of dying before her comb-out," said Claire to cover the gaping hole her favorite aunt had left in her own life. Fitzie had never abandoned her and had often dropped in on Claire and Theo, as Claire put it, "when it was not the correct thing to do in the Hirsh family."

It wasn't unusual, during the quiet part of Sunday, when the fading afternoon light drew its magic around sleeping children and wistful adults, softening the edges of their memories, to hear Grandma Hirsh and Claire tell stories about their beloved Fitzie, who herself had never married and who was, in many ways, the real mother of the family.

Sometimes, they laughed so hard they snorted, remembering the time Fitzie, whose real name was Margaret, had decided to give little Claire a home permanent, then locked herself out of the apartment while the developing solution turned Claire's fine blond hair into something that resembled felt. At other times they fell into a reverential silence, as when they talked of the man named Fitzpatrick who had promised to love her forever just before he was killed on that terrible day at Pearl Harbor.

Grandma always said the stories were for me, so I would know our family history and my aunt Fitzie's place in it, but I suspected that this was her own way of grieving, of keeping her little sister alive a little while longer, or maybe of holding on to something she and Claire could be comfortable sharing.

There was no such reflection that day. The front door buzzed and Aunt Suzie swooped into the room.

"Everyone say *bon jour* to Philippe," she announced, then promptly abandoned the poor fellow to the others and made a beeline for me, murmuring "Hello, *mon petit* cuteness, my adorable boy," swallowing me up in a flash of rhinestones and the unlikely swoosh of taffeta and leather. To my utter delight, she never failed to take off her hat or her pearls or whatever shiny object she happened to be wearing and hand it right over to me, as though everything about her was merely a prop for my pleasure. That day, I happily munched a felt flower from her hat, slowly chewing every bit and smiling a mouthful of purple petals for Claire, who immortalized the moment in a photograph she called "Late-Blooming Flower Child."

Suzie's friends always pretended to blend in with the family but followed her every move the way an inmate watches a guard, never overtly enough to draw attention, but always aware of the other's position. They usually ended up talking with Barnaby, who was always there but never said much, watching his wife's reactions, measuring the distance he needed to keep from his own feelings about those Sundays.

I grew up believing I was the natural heart of these people, who hadn't really known each other before I was born—and, in Grandma and Grandpa Hirsh's case, hadn't wanted to—and I carried my responsibility for their happiness on my tiny shoulders. I cooed in the awkward silences, I kept the conversation going with the antics of a small comedian doing pratfalls on fat legs. I screeched my pleasure at the slightest attention and, like every creature still small enough not to be misled by words that do not match intention and who operates purely on sensation, I always curled up with the one who needed me most.

On one of these Sundays that now seem part of the same childish blur, when Thad came to dinner without Alan and everyone was unearthly still, I climbed into his lap and clung to his sweater and was the only person who could make him smile that day—and all the other days that followed, when he came to sit in the corner of our apartment just to hear our laughter and to be in the company of people who loved him unconditionally, people who did not ask to see the part of him that was broken by the endless round of meals served in teaspoons, the constant ministrations and indignities suffered by his beloved Alan, who could no longer open the dark shop and pick flowers for Theo and Claire and their boy.

I became his belief in the future simply because I was at the beginning. I had no concept of death or of the cruel disease called Amyotrophic Lateral Sclerosis that was taking Alan away from us muscle by dying muscle. First to give way were his strong arms, which once cut through bundles of thick stems from the wholesale market in a single slice; then the legs, which could stand all day in the tiny shop, dance, run, walk in great long strides all the way up from the Village to our apartment, could no longer support his own weight and forced him to sit in the humiliating lap of a chair until finally he could no longer speak or swallow and every labored breath brought him closer to the final gasp. Nor could I fathom the bitter irony of this illness's association with the great Lou Gehrig and the manly sport Alan had no idea how to play.

I had no understanding of this, only the headlong interest in life enjoyed by those still close to its source, and I did not fear the hand that held a warm cloth to Alan's crusted lips, pulled out thick ropes of mucous from lungs that could no longer cough and trembled in the face of his lover's harsh sentence or offer comment on how he was handling it. I simply gave him proof that life goes on, and he gave me the security of thinking all families were thus.

There would be many Sundays, filled with the reassuring jingle of Theo's bracelets, the click of Claire's Leica, the easy laughter, loving arms, and the soft laps of friends and family, each one unique as a snowflake in its particular cacophony of footsteps, doors opening and closing, in its choreography of arms picking me up and gently putting me down, in the waves of laughter washing over me, and in the singular combination of voices rising and falling on fragrant gusts from the kitchen.

The advancing light of each of those afternoons moved as though an unseen hand ushered the memory of it into a kind of emotional bank account, toting up a balance against the inevitable rainy day when I would first hear the word "dyke," a word I would always remember as not spoken, but spat, like something viscous and foul caught in the throat.

7

If Claire and Theo's life together was hard, I never noticed. If the world received them with less than open arms, reserving its harshest judgment for their decision to live openly as a family, that was not my concern. I was the child and like all children, regardless of their parents' peculiar genetic combination, racial, religious, sexual, or political tendency, or even geographical situation, I squeezed all experience through the fine sieve of my own needs. But I was not blind to the choices made on my behalf.

Although it did not come as easily or as naturally to her as it did to Theo, Claire tempered her artist's life and all its implicit creative and personal freedom in the name of motherhood. Instead of rushing down to Washington to chronicle the sprawling protest of squatters' tents called Freedom City, the explosions of rage in Harlem and Newark and other cities incinerating in the name of civil rights, shooting the camera-shy police ringing the Monument, protesters and press people running before their horses like jackrabbits, she changed diapers. She cheerfully attended school conferences and doctor and orthodontist appointments, chauffeured me to school, and imposed the time constraints of family on the compelling images she continued to coax out of the bath in her darkroom. There are photographs to prove her dedication to something that did not always come naturally to her, compositions taken just as carefully as the ones she and Suzie discussed in important whispers during my nap—Claire sitting in a tiny school chair, taken by me; Claire and me at the bus stop, taken by the driver, and every single bruise, scrape, bang and bump, Easter, Christmas, Passover, every childish scribble, smile, and pout dutifully noted for posterity with cryptic remarks on the back, like "First tooth!" "Today kindergarten, tomorrow Columbia!" and "Willy's first diaper." This she actually photographed before throwing it into the diaper service's pickup bag.

I was accustomed to announcing my arrival home from school with the details of my day—graded tests, pictures drawn in art class, Pilgrim hats made of kraft paper, crudely drawn maps full of bits of cotton from the tops of medicine bottles, matted clumps of grass from the park, gluey slivers of wood, and the odd invitation to a birthday party or class outing—regardless of what was going on when I got there. And indeed, everything stopped, even the hollow-eyed insanity of putting a show together, phone ringing off the hook, dozens of conferences with Suzie, who paced the apartment, smoking the awful black cigarettes Theo tried to outlaw in the name of my developing lungs.

"When Baxter does it, it's elegant; when I do it, it's air pollution," complained Suzie, who had spent one such afternoon filling our living room with her peculiar brand of fog while Claire pored over contact sheets. "I'll give you a lollipop if you don't tell your mama," she said, kissing the top of my head. I never told, and even though I never smoked myself, I still love the bitter smell of Suzie's cigarettes.

When she heard me come in, Claire dropped her grease pencil and the loupe she was using to examine the tiny squares on each slippery page in the stack in front of her and padded down the hall in her socks to meet me halfway.

"I missed you!" she said between kisses planted in my collar. "What wonderful things have you been up to today?" She only pretended to scoop me up, because I was now too heavy for the real thing, but I went along with the game as she folded her legs yoga-style on our deep pillows, patted her lap, and invited me to present the day's accomplishments. She took my doodles seriously and critiqued them as carefully as she did the efforts of the eager students who gathered in our apartment in steadily increasing numbers.

"Why did you choose green for the sky?" she asked, gazing long and seriously into my second-grade splatter.

"Because when I stand on my head, the grass is where the sky should be," I answered with the absolute confidence of one who has not yet learned the boundaries of scientific impossibility.

Claire grinned broadly and squeezed me hard. "Don't ever forget that, Willy Wonder. Anybody can see, but only special people can draw what they feel."

I showed her a paper my teacher had marked with a big red F, scrawled across the top like an angry incision. "She said I made it up and I was supposed to say what really happened," I offered, shame reddening cheeks already inflamed from the cold bus ride home as I waited for what I was convinced would be her profound disappointment in me.

"Great! Wonderful! That's my baby!" she exclaimed, as she scanned my wobbly letters on the wrinkled paper. "Any fool can see what happened here," said Claire, thrusting my composition at Suzie. "The teacher has no imagination."

"Are we going to have another artist in the family?" said Suzie, her laugh setting off a chain reaction in her bracelets. She grabbed for the place under my arms where I loved and hated to be tickled. "You'd better grow up faster than this, otherwise the art world newest enfant terrible is going to have the world's oldest agent."

It never occurred to me that there might be issues on the table more serious and profound than my incessant pondering of important questions. Nor could I imagine other children growing up another way, waiting in the silent apartments of our neighbors for attention that was not given so generously.

Theo's burgeoning business had not yet grown into the mail-order and cookbook empire it would become. Claire's decision to work closer to home, combined with Theo's unbusinesslike refusal to keep the shop open on Sundays even though that meant doing brunches far into Saturday night because we needed one day a week together as a family, were the facts of my life. Like all children who see, but choose to ignore, the small cracks that become the deep fissures that will one day sunder their parents, I felt no guilt pressing hard on my shoulder.

When I was old enough to walk four avenues over to the store, I did not think it at all unusual for Theo to rush out from behind the counter or from the kitchen to greet me, nod appreciatively at a painting or read a composition aloud to all gathered on the premises, her voice full of praise and quivering pride. I often found my artwork tacked to the menu board that announced the daily specials, and once I received applause from customers and staff alike for my poem on Mother's Day, which had described my life as doubly blessed, a reaction that was all the more surprising for the lack of attention, beyond the odd snicker, the poem had received at school.

It wasn't until I became a man myself and became aware of my own sexual needs and learned how other aspects of my life competed for that pleasure, that I began to wonder how my mothers even had time for the lurid and unnatural acts they would be accused of. When my own children were born, I saw firsthand how little time there is for love and what a cruel joke society plays when it marks people for life according to how they might have conducted themselves in the unbearably short season of passion before life presses in and bed becomes a place to be dead for a few hours. As a child, and especially as a curious young boy full of half-truths and with dangerously little to go on in the way of carnal knowledge, I assumed Theo and Claire made love all the time in a dark, mysterious way I could not imagine and could not hear, even though I strained to, in the creak and rattle and the distant siren wail of our sleeping apartment.

It never occurred to me that they collapsed after a grueling day in a small kitchen, a foul-smelling darkroom, an exhausting round of errands, ministrations, and the endless details of a household that includes a growing boy. It never occurred to me until I did the very same thing, grateful for the sound of Annie's gentle snoring telling me that she, too, found sleep as irresistible as she had once found me.

I never realized that their relationship, because of its outsider status, needed the special nourishment of time alone and time spent with people with whom careful presentation of themselves was not a requirement. Nor did I think they could ever be prey to the problems that beset the mothers and fathers of my schoolmates, mainly because I saw them as heroines who had declared their love to the world and having done that, could only be loved back. I suppose this is the fantasy in which every child lives, and in spite of my growing distance from the other kids, in spite of the disapproving looks from their parents and the increasing uneasiness of the truce between my grandmother and Claire, I held on to it for as long as I could. Seeing our parents as human is seeing the real terror of the world we are about to enter; I suppose, like every child before me, I dragged my feet.

Ignorant of the details of my mothers' intimate lives, I would have been further surprised to learn that every little boy is not as happily embraced as I was by our family and friends.

Most of my weekends were spent rutting in the soft ground of Peter and Molly's farm with my cousin Harry and Bartie and Blisset, their eternally muddy black Labs; I had countless overnights at Jess and Baxter's brownstone with its secret back staircase, its ballroom-sized pantry full of old bottles and foreign-looking tins, and a musty attic that came as close as a boy could imagine to living in a haunted house. The idea that any of this might have been arranged for anything other than my exclusive pleasure was inconceivable.

How could I have known that it was highly unusual, if not entirely unheard of, for little boys to regularly attend their parents' friends' soirees, especially those held in one of the most beautiful brownstones in Greenwich Village? All I knew was that I never tired of sitting at the top of the long curving stairs, where Jennifer and Brooke and I were allowed to observe the festivities. I loved following my mothers in the room below, watching them carve separate paths in the swirling party.

On one such evening, I remember observing the proceedings with particular concentration. I watched Theo touch shoulders, arms, cheeks as she talked with people, smiling broadly—always moving, her eyes, her head, her hands, nodding as she'd say, "How wonderful it is to see you . . . Aren't you sweet to say that . . . Of course, we've love to . . . Claire is around here somewhere . . ."

I watched Claire, standing in her favorite spot, just to the left of the blazing fire Baxter had set in the massive carved hearth, the drink she pretended to sip balanced above her on the wide mantel. She looked uncomfortable and muttered something I could not hear to a man who wore a velvet jacket and had mutton chops that reached his chin. "I saw your show at the Witkin," he blustered. "Bravo, my dear, bravo."

He tried to draw Claire out, but after a few moments, he moved on to someone more receptive, while she remained a quiet distance away from the small knots of people flirting with conversation, tall and cool and unapproachable, slightly above it all as only shy people can be when they don't want you to know they're shy.

Two more attempts were made before Jessica took matters in hand.

"Claire dahling," Jessica said, echoing Brooke's perfect imitation of her mother rescuing mine, "have you met Fernando? He's doing wonderful things with flatware!" I pretended to enjoy the twins' incessant giggling at the guests, but from my hideout at the top of the stairs I watched very carefully that night, missing nothing, believing that sooner or later, the distance would tell me something being close never could. I was waiting for them to become dykes. I figured if I watched long enough when they thought I wasn't looking, I would understand why other people didn't like them; and even though I wasn't exactly sure what a dyke was, I was convinced I'd know it when they did it.

Angel, a fat kid from Buenos Aires in my second-grade class, had said a dyke was a woman who hated men and wouldn't talk to them, but liked to wear their clothes. But that night, as I sat on the stairs and saw Theo give Uncle Baxter a hug and a big kiss on the lips, and when I heard people say, "You look fabulous" and ask, "Where did you find that gorgeous skirt?" as she whooshed by in tangerine taffeta that grazed her ankles, I knew he couldn't have been right.

A tall woman with silver bracelets, masses of white hair, and sunken cheeks that hinted of fashionable starvation, asked Theo how she managed "to create all that gorgeous food and not get fat?" And I laughed to myself, knowing how much she hated that question, inevitable when someone discovered she had founded The Latest Dish. Theo really believed she was fat, no matter what Claire said to the contrary.

"Wonderful pâté, don't you think?" Theo said, ignoring the question, winking in Jess's direction, then shooting the woman a conspiratorial look as she picked up a bite-sized square of toast. "I don't know where she finds the time."

Everyone was attracted to Theo and flirted shamelessly with her: I think she enjoyed it immensely. That night, one of Baxter's friends smiled at her and she winked at him. Claire looked pained and distant as she watched the man approach, the tiny lines around her mouth becoming more pronounced as she clung to the edge of the room, determined not to let anyone see her discomfort. Seeing this, I felt something flatten in my stomach, something that felt like I was on the bottom of a roller coaster just before it starts climbing.

Theo saw it, too, and moved in Claire's direction, but before she could get there and murmur what I imagined were soft, reassuring words, a large woman Jess had just introduced to all gathered as "the new Dr. Spock" steamed over, interrupting them. "I understand you are raising a son together."

"We are," Claire said warily.

"I can't imagine how you're handling the absence of a father," the woman continued. "Is he someone you know?"

As Claire fumbled for her composure, Theo was there. "If you don't mind," she said, eyes glittering dangerously, "when my son asks that question, I'd rather not have to say I told a rude stranger first." As they walked out of my line of sight, I heard Claire ask, "Why did you say *my* son, Theo? He's *our* son." They were gone before I heard the answer.

Angel said dykes *did stuff* with other women that was against the law, but he didn't know exactly what. Later that night, when I could barely keep my eyes open and rested my head on the cool banister, after all the other guests had left and it was just family, Uncle Bax put on a Van Morrison album and Theo and Claire and Aunt Jess and Aunt Suzie held hands and danced with each other to "Brown-Eyed Girl," while Baxter pretended to play the drums on the back of the chair and Suzie's date sang along and watched her with sad brown cow eyes that said he wouldn't last long, much less require a trip to Brooklyn, but I couldn't imagine anyone calling the police because of that.

There were no such revelations in South Neck. There was only Harry and I and the slam bang of small boys egging one another on with an energy unknown to anyone over the age of twelve. There was Charlotte, who despised us with the loathing of older sisters, and Aunt Molly and Uncle Peter, who lived calmly in the eye of storm and who did not believe in overthinking the actions of their brood.

I loved the open pastures, the smell of earth, the stereophonic creak of the front and back porches, and the apparent disregard for our safety on the parts of these gentle grown-ups as we skidded around the property in the company of galloping dogs, pausing long enough to race the Jeep up the driveway at lunchtime and at suppertime. I loved the freedom out there, no thick plaster, no elevator, no lobby, no doorman between me and the wind and sun on my face, no shoes to keep the sand from between my toes. But it was out there that I also learned about boundaries, so necessary to people who lived out in the open for all their neighbors to see.

Of all the crazy things I loved about the farm, I suppose that's why I remember the fence the most. It rolled up the hill behind the house, past the barn where owls nested in the rafters and dust motes hung on the thousand needles of light that pierced its rickety slats and pointed to the ghosts of dairy cows lowing in the dark empty stalls. The fence followed the slippery sound of the brook down alongside Aunt Molly's potting shed, where she spent most afternoons up to her elbows in life, teasing tender shoots out of their small pots and gently transplanting the more mature seedlings, settling them into roomier quarters in rich loamy soil that felt good under her gardener's hands.

The pickets rolled past the pool and grazed the back of the old bomb shelter that Uncle Peter had converted into a writing studio. There he said a different sort of war was raging, between himself and the old Smith-Corona, which did not give up its secrets easily; he struggled to find the right way to say something so everyone would understand, not to show off for the few people who were willing to work at his meaning, but so everyone would feel they were being addressed directly and with no condescension, so everyone in the small town of South Neck could slap their foreheads and say, "Right!"

The fence wasn't imposing or impenetrable like the ones you see around prisons or zoos or around the polished darkness of Uncle Baxter and Aunt Jessica's.

Uncle Peter's fence had no signs that said "Keep Out!" or "Beware of Dogs!" even though Bartie and Blisset, the black Labs (who pee with delight at the first sight of me in the family Jeep) would tear the limbs off anyone who tried to sneak behind its enveloping whiteness. That fence was about as standoffish as it got in the farming community I liked to think of as my second home. When I was a small boy I believed my weekend visits had more to do with my love of the place than with my mothers' need for a little privacy.

Theo usually closed the store for several weeks in August, when we'd go somewhere special like Martha's Vineyard, or Maine, or one year, the Grand Canyon with a stop in Broken Arrow. But there was always a separate month for me at the farm. Most Friday nights during my stay, Claire and Theo would arrive tired and stiff after a long evening fighting traffic on the Long Island Expressway just so they could be there when I woke up. When the store was too busy for Theo to get away, Claire would make the trip alone, even though she hated to drive.

No matter how late, I listened over the buzz of the cicadas for the car door to slam, the crunch of footsteps on gravel—sometimes two sets, sometimes only Claire's—Bartie and Blisset thumping out their greeting on the legs of chairs. Then the screen door would slap, Molly and Peter kissed them hello, and everyone tiptoed into the kitchen, where they thought Harry and I couldn't hear them from our summer beds on the sleeping porch.

"Look who's here," teased Uncle Peter in the morning, winking at Claire and Theo hiding in plain slight behind him. No matter how often they did this, I always pretended to be surprised to see them. As I got older, this became sillier, but it was our ritual, our family greeting. As Molly dispensed her "energy cocktail"—tomato juice, brewer's yeast, and a banana—to tired-looking Theo, clucking about "the cobbler's daughter," we told the stories we'd saved up all week.

If you squinted through the slats in Uncle Peter's fence, you could see everything on the other side, the way you can see if Christmas lights are balanced before you decorate the rest of the tree, and when we drove past the farm on the rutted lane that ran alongside it, down the hill to the front gate, I imagined we got a glimpse of our own lives the way strangers saw it, flashing like a deck of picture cards, like the faces of people you'll never know flickering in the windows of a speeding train. Claire and I fiddling with a camera while Harry and Blisset posed with Bartie in Aunt Molly's gardening hat. Theo ringing the triangle, shouting "Chow time!" in the direction of a squirming pup tent. Two stacks of inner tubes with heads and feet. City kid and country cousin discovering the grass is greener wherever they're together.

I imagined being watched by a stranger, a big man with kind eyes, hair that once might have been four-alarm red before the sun baked it to brick, one brown bicep caressing the side of a Ford pickup loaded with lobster pots, the other gently holding the road with one finger hooked into the steering wheel, kicking up the dust at the edge of our fence, turning his head in time to see a face as familiar as his own on the other side of those slats and thinking he, too, had imagined this.

Park Road, a one-lane blacktop that ran past the front gate, was the only town road considered important enough for the South Neck public works department to paint with a fresh dotted line every year after winter and the town plow ruined it. The mailbox there, which Uncle Peter had ordered from Vermont, bore no number but simply said "Sound View Farm" in the same neat script as on the jeep's driver-side door, only a little bolder so Whistlin' Bill could see it. Harry and I called the postman, whose real name was Mr. Milowski, Whistlin' Bill because he never delivered a letter without a song or a pocketful of biscuits for all the dogs on his route, who set up a Pavlovian racket, howling at his approach the minute they could see his Estate Wagon inching its way down the familiar path. Below the mailbox, at a place on the road's shoulder where only a car making a U-turn could see it, a small sign on a stake barely two feet tall said "Private Drive," in the same understated hand, which was all that was necessary to let people know where you stood with respect to unexpected company.

I think what I loved most about the fence, which stood a discreet distance behind this quiet declaration of family privacy, was the fact that it always held its ground politely without ever having to get ugly and lose its loopy up-and-down grace. I know it was just my imagination, but I always got the feeling that its gate swung open a little wider for me and that in the squeaking hinges, in the pebbles scraping its bottom, it sang, "Slit slat, slit slat, Willy's here, how 'bout that!"

While people in South Neck believed in fencing off their land, nobody ever locked their doors, and every now and then, on Saturdays mostly, when Harry and I got home from the beach (or, when we got older, back from prowling the town for girls to ignore), we'd find a pie or a jar of homemade apple butter or a big bunch of lilacs twisted in tinfoil on the front porch or waiting for us on the big worktable in the kitchen. There was never a note, but we always figured out who'd left the treat. As Aunt Molly said, "People always tell you an awful lot about themselves in the presents they give."

If someone left an anonymous gift on our doorstep in the city, we'd eye it suspiciously and buzz down to Andy for a description of the caller. On Central Park West, if someone looked directly at you on the street and did not avert their eyes the second you met their gaze, you'd look around for a cop if you were smart, but even though Baxter and Jess and Suzie and sometimes even Grandpa and Grandma Hirsh teased Molly and Peter about their decision to forgo sophistication for South Neck, I didn't see the big deal about being sophisticated. My mothers were about as sophisticated as it got, and as I was to discover, not everyone liked them.

I loved the way people looked in your eyes and said how do, period, no question mark, in South Neck. When we were old enough, Harry and I liked to strut down Main Street. First past the Beehive, where the high school kids came to drink root beer floats and dance to the jukebox in the back, and we gagged on the pack of Camels we'd pilfered for the occasion,trying to blend in and pass for freshmen instead of the nerdy eighth-graders we were. Then came Kooperman's Beer and Soda, and on down to the very end of the business district, to Abediah's Lunch and Antiques, which was really a delicatessen decorated with some old junk—trunks, a few prints, and some ratty old porch furniture from old man Abediah's attic, arranged near the tables to appeal to the "impulse buyer," as his daughter Emily called the overdressed people who occasionally turned up for one of her BLTs, looking for relief from the fancy new restaurants that opened and closed every summer like fireflies on a hedge.

On rainy days, Harry and I watched summer people stand in line at Saugatuck Farm, their MGs and Jags parked one on top of the other, for the privilege of paying too much money for the fresh peach and strawberry-rhubarb pies Aunt Molly gave away for the pure pleasure of it.

"How do." We tipped our invisible hats to Mrs. Henrietta Ott, the last survivor of the old whaling families who built the big white clapboard houses along the wide, leafy streets on the residential side of Main Street. They looked like birthday cakes to us, with their turrets and gingerbread and tiny gazebos out back, widow's walks up top, where we would imagine the wives of sea captains and sailors watching for months and sometimes years for the ships that would bring their husbands home with fresh supplies of candle oil, ivory, and silk, with bits of bone and scrimshaw tinkered during the long months at sea. For some, the only reward for waiting was a visit from a respectful ship's officer, delivering news of a dark and grizzly death and perhaps a letter penned in a quiet moment before the sea turned oily and hellish. It was hard to believe the gnarled old woman in tennis shoes and a faded old dress who smiled back at Harry and me remembered all that *Moby-Dick* stuff.

A little farther on, we often ran into one of the Roses, who sold my uncle the farm and who still owned practically every acre from Main Street down to the bluffs where neat rows of potatoes and broccoli and corn fell away to wheeling gulls and whitecaps on the choppy sound below. I liked to nod my head and close my eyes in acknowledgment the way I'd see them do at the 7-Eleven when one pickup pulls out and another takes its place in the dusty lot.

If Uncle Peter's neighbors in South Neck knew my mothers were lesbians, they didn't say much for it or against it. In fact, they didn't say much about it, period. I was Peter's sister Claire's boy, Charlotte and Harry Hirsh's cousin, their neighbor Molly's nephew, and that was all they wanted to know. They couldn't have been nicer to Theo, passing the time of day, asking her about table settings and new recipes, dying to find out what city people ate at their parties, what famous ones she knew, and trying to wheedle her trade secrets away from her in the good-natured way I mistakenly took for acceptance.

The fence around my uncle's farm didn't teach me to keep my distance—I already knew how to do that—but it eventually taught me that you don't have to be unfriendly about it and that you don't have to slam a door to have a little privacy. I liked the fence because it stood in plain sight, unlike the one deep inside of people that never gives a warning before it closes around the heart, the one you never know is there until, when you least expect it to, it slams shut, catching you hard.

8

"Willy, Willy, poor little tyke, he's gotta be a fag, 'cause his mothers are dykes!"

In 1972, there were no picture books entitled *Heather Has Two Mommies* or *Daddy's Roommate.* No one had written *Gloria Goes to Gay Pride.* There was just Claire or Theo, anger spilling over the sides of the small school chairs from which they lodged endless complaints. And there was my seven-year-old's belief in the benign nature of the world and the fact that my mere presence in it conferred immediate acceptance, love, friendship, and understanding.

Every day another of these illusions fell hard and lay at my feet, glittering in the sunlight like so many dangerous shards of glass on the asphalt of the McCall School yard. It was a sunless, fenced-in lot taken over by the school when the townhouse next door was torn down, where boys like me learned to defend the delicate manhood fiercely budding inside their pounding hearts and angry fists, where conformity equaled acceptance and all differences were pummeled into the sameness mistaken for strength. At any age, a boy with two mothers is a threat, an aberration to be dealt with harshly. In the second grade, it is a serious liability.

"Willy, Willy, poor little tyke, he's gotta be a fag, 'cause his mothers are dykes!"

One day, just as the final bell signaled the rush for the exits, Theo had swooped into my classroom to demand an explanation of how I came to know this word, which was not part of any civilized curriculum.

"Maybe you'd like to tell me why my son has a black eye?"

"It would have been so much better, uh, Mrs. . . . Miss Hirsh

. . . if you and your uh, . . . had agreed to present a more conventional relationship—well, I mean, for Willy's sake. You know how boys can be in the formative years," my teacher stammered.

"No, I don't, actually, and perhaps you'd define 'conventional' for me, Mrs. Langelotti," snapped Theo, eyes blazing with fury, humiliation, and hurt enough for both of us. "I seem to be having trouble understanding."

Sleet battered the tall window while we waited for my teacher's reply. The radiator knocked.

"Well, I just meant—you could have told him something that would have been more acceptable here at school," said the uncomfortable young woman. Mrs. Langelotti sat behind a scarred wooden desk that seemed too big for her. It looked as though it contained the ghosts of all the teachers who had ever intimidated a roomful of school children. Theo imagined Mrs. Langelotti casting about from the safety of its bulk, searching for what her teacher's intuition told her would be the one small victim who did not know the answer to the question dangling in the air, her search punctuated by the lowering of heads and the sound of feet nervously shuffling under desks. In the edgy silence of the universal mantra—"Don't pick me, don't pick me"—swirling in the chalk dust above the top of her desk, this aircraft carrier for broken books with stained covers, Theo knew a teacher's cruelty always landed on the one who least expected it, who least deserved it.

I waited at a safe distance, the pain in my eye receding in the wake of this fresh embarrassment. It was three-thirty, but I listened hard for the sound of a witness who might have lingered on the empty linoleum outside the battered classroom door.

My teacher looked across her desk and down at my mother sitting in the small student chair next to her, and I think she understood that Theo's shining anger could not be avoided, that she was not safe behind that desk or her authority as my teacher. Did she know she had pushed her open purse between them, a brown leather barricade raised against what? Mrs. Langelotti kept it there the whole time as if it could protect her, not only from what my mother had to say, but from what my mother was.

"Are you suggesting we should have drawn straws to see which one of us would pretend she was his maiden aunt?" Theo continued. "Or maybe you think we should have told him we were roommates; then, when he saw us kissing and hugging, or barged in on us in bed, he could see our relationship as something nice and dirty, something he could spend his whole life trying to hide. Or maybe he could develop a really sick attitude toward women and grow up to be a rapist or a mass murderer. Is that what you mean by 'more acceptable,' Mrs. Langelotti? Maybe you should think about what's right for Willy instead of what's comfortable for you. You know, you have no idea how dangerous you are, Mrs. Langelotti."

Theo drew out the "Mrs." as though it were something obscene, as though by virtue of that appellation my teacher was in some way defective, as though marriage and an unseen man had somehow allowed her to abdicate all responsibility for integrity and independent thought.

"Do you understand," hissed Theo, coming in for the kill, "that I pay this snooty private school the ridiculous amount they charge for tuition so that *it* can pay *you* to teach my son his lessons and to keep him out of harm's way until he's old enough to make his own decisions about what's bad or good, right or wrong? Do you understand, Mrs. Langelotti, that your personal bias toward me or toward my partner has no place in your classroom?"

My teacher sat still behind her big teacher's desk.

"Good," said Theo, arising from that tiny piece of furniture like an heiress from a priceless antique. "See that you remember it," she ordered the stunned woman from over her shoulder, without waiting for a response, as though Mrs. Langelotti were dog dirt stuck to her shoe. "And see to it you keep those little savages from hurting my son again."

"Willy darling," said Theo, turning her back on my teacher, softening at the sight of me standing as close to the classroom door as I dared. "Claire is going to meet us somewhere special for a surprise." Her voice was suddenly too warm, too loving, too full of her lack of regard for the opinions and judgments of others; the rest of her raged, every muscle struggling to contain the fury.

"Miss Bouvier . . ."

Theo turned and stared coldly at the small woman behind the big desk, dwarfed even more by Theo's distance.

"I *am* thinking about what's right for Willy," said Mrs. Langelotti quietly.

"That's *my* job," said Theo, just before she slammed the door hard and sent up a cloud of chalk dust, which left a silky film on the pitted school desks, the parched Boston fern on the windowsill, and the two stick figures I had dressed in the brightest Crayola skirts I could find when we were asked to draw our family portraits, and which now wore a wad of Bazooka bubble gum and the mark of the class graffiti artist, the word "dyke" scrawled across my mothers' names in a mean shade of magenta.

Later that evening, while I was looking for a picture of a cow to paste on Argentina, it started. "There's one in the blue cookbook in the basket under the table, sweetie," said Theo, absently pointing to the kitchen. "I don't need it."

"It was bound to happen," said Claire.

"Knowing that doesn't make it any better," snapped Theo.

"I know," said Claire, looking up from her contact sheets, grease pencil in one hand, loupe in the other.

All evening Theo had tried to concentrate on the Metropolitan Museum party. It was her biggest, most visible catering assignment yet. If she could carry it off, she would have all the "ladies who lunch" eating out of her hand. As she whirred and stirred and chopped, brushing the glaze on a test duck that would be lacquered as richly as a Fifth Avenue living room but would go unappreciated in my lunchbox the next day, Theo tasted a bit of the sauce from the back of her hand and I heard her chuckle. "What irony. A caterer whose success rests entirely on people who never eat!"

But just as this small amusement released a bit of the day's tension, the events came rushing back. Mrs. Langelotti's pinched young face rose before her and she marched into the living room again, pastry brush in hand, pouncing on her anger from another angle, attempting to rid herself of her confrontation with my teacher, the bitter aftertaste of which no amount of cooking could cancel out. Talking was the only thing that helped. Talking to Claire.

"You should have heard that officious bitch, telling me we should have made up a story for Willy. Practically telling me we've ruined him, with her damn purse sitting open between us like Harridan's Wall," huffed Theo.

"Hadrian's Wall," corrected Claire, without looking up.

"My version is more accurate. God, I hate stupid, intolerant people who pick on little kids because they don't have enough guts to pick on people their own size."

Without waiting for Claire's response, Theo stomped back into the kitchen, only to return in less than a minute.

"The nerve of her, calling you my 'friend.' "

"I am your friend, sweetie. I'm your best friend."

Claire reached for Theo as she paced close to her chair, but missed.

"Don't be simple, Claire. And don't try to calm me down. I'm really furious."

"Okay."

It was still going on when I brushed my teeth and kissed them good night.

Whenever Theo got really mad, which was almost never, she cooked, even if it was three o'clock in the morning. She also became clumsy, which was very unusual for her, so Claire got up and followed her into the kitchen many times that night just to make sure she was chopping only the food and not her fingers. This little problem of Theo's could be a real liability for someone in her line of work; once, when some junkie had attempted to hold up the store, the anger that had replaced Theo's initial terror had engulfed her so completely, she cut off the tip of her pinkie.

Curled in my Peanuts quilt, acutely aware of the fact that I was the reason for all the trouble, I floated above their voices under the painted clouds of my sleeping loft, listening to the sounds below me, sharp and crackling like violent bursts of gunfire, then receding as I strained to follow their muffled words into the kitchen.

Theo stood in the kitchen doorway watching Claire work, completely absorbed in the images around her. *They're all strangers,* Theo thought. *Just pictures of damn strangers.*

"Maybe she's right," Theo whispered to the back of Claire's head. "I think this is the part that gets harder on us, so it can be easier on him," she said when Claire finally looked up and realized she was there.

"What do you mean?" asked Claire, bracing for wherever this was going next.

"You should have seen him standing there today, Claire," her voice very small now. "He wanted to disappear. He wanted *me* to disappear."

"Don't be ridiculous, he worships you. You're his *mother,*" said Claire, surprised by the bite of this unalterable fact.

"I know. That's the point." Theo moved across the room to rest on the arm of Claire's chair, the pastry brush still in hand, forgotten for the moment.

"He doesn't love us because we're lesbians and we're doing this swell thing and aren't we just a couple of rebellious modern women. He loves us because we're his mothers. End of story."

"But we are, sweetie," said Claire.

"What?"

"Lesbians. We're lesbians, Theo."

"Do you have any idea how selfish we've been?"

"No. But I have a feeling you're going to tell me." Claire uncurled her legs, rearranging herself in the chair, as though finding her balance would keep her from being knocked over by this.

"We've been so busy demanding our rights as parents, shoving our lives in everybody's face, forcing people to accept us, we're forgetting Willy's feelings. He's just a little boy who is different from the other kids, and I think we ought to start biting our tongues with his teachers and thinking about how we can make it easier, not worse, for him, don't you?"

Something angry and raw appeared in Claire's face, but Theo continued.

"Claire, I know how it feels to be different all the time, to have crazy parents who live in a broken-down trailer, talk to trees, and sing labor songs, and to wish you were just like the other kids." Theo had spent her anger in great heaving gulps and in the physical exertion of cooking and now the force of her own memories rekindled a dangerous ember, but the sight of a solitary tear rolling down Claire's cheek filled her with an uncomfortable mixture of guilt and tenderness as she gently wiped it away. "Don't you think we should give him the chance to choose us, the way we chose him?"

Something inside of Claire rose up and pushed Theo's hand away. "I'm not going to pretend to be your roommate or your old-maid cousin, if that's what you mean." She stared at the faces of people on the floor looking up at her, not seeing them, just feeling Theo at her back, pushing her out of the picture. Her witnesses.

"It's not going to stop at Willy's teacher or some classroom bullies, Claire. It's going to get worse."

"It is not. All kids go through this in some way or another, especially boys. They tortured my brother at this age, and his parents were perfectly normal—well, for them," Claire said, tired of Theo's determination to make this more than it was, trying to return her attention to her work.

"This isn't art, Claire. This is life. You can't crop out what you don't like," Theo said just before she slammed the kitchen door.

PEOPLE with a small amount of power over others are very dangerous. This is especially true at free clinics, unemployment offices, military installations, and, of course, in schools, where a certain kind of sadism always finds a captive audience and lives just under the surface of things.

This was something I always felt, but never could articulate until after I'd smashed my legs in a skiing accident and the orderly who was supposed to wheel me down to the physical therapy department at Lenox Hill deliberately smoked a cigarette in my doorway, with every languid puff relishing the fact that I needed him, loving the idea of keeping me waiting.

His eyes said, "Who do you think you are? Don't you think I know you wouldn't talk to me if you weren't here? I will make you pay for being special. I will make you pay for the fact that I am not."

The knowing of a child is such that whenever his parent takes on his teacher, he understands he will be made to pay, as I knew I inevitably would in the silences between her words, in the nuance of her questions, in the bright light of an afternoon I would never see coming. But that day, listening to Theo cutting my teacher off at the knees, I could only think: *You don't want to mess with my mother.*

I'm sure Mrs. Langelotti would have been shocked to learn that she was making me pay for her discomfort at my unusual family situation. But she picked on me with a vengeance usually reserved for people who are more equally matched. She started the day after Theo's visit.

"Did everyone have fun during winter vacation?"

"Yes, Ms. Langelotti!"

"Will someone tell us what they did?" she asked, scanning the room, looking away from me, lulling me into thinking she would call on someone else, waiting until the very last second . . .

"Willy, how about you?"

I was too young to know how to tell a story without mentioning the key characters, how to invent a version that was more acceptable. I learned to do that much later.

I stood on wobbly legs and looked into the smug faces of my classmates, the small eyes of the one who defaced my picture, seeing no damage on the fat lids or the pig snout on which I was sure I had landed a punch, and told a hostile audience about New Year's Eve. Theo had taught Claire and me to wrap little balls of dough around a list of all the things we didn't like anymore and wished would go away, and throw them into the fireplace.

"My mothers let me have a sip of champagne and stay up with them to throw another little pile of dough into the fire at midnight with all the things we wanted Baby New Year to bring, and in the morning our living room smelled like a brand-new loaf of bread," I said.

Somebody giggled and Mrs. Langelotti said, "Be polite, girls!" I remember not telling them, but thinking of how I wished Claire would go to sleep and turn into a real father, but still be Claire and how I didn't tell my mothers that either; that I just balled up my dough and wished it with all my might.

Nobody heard me when I said, "We visited my uncle Peter and aunt Molly on New Year's Day and Harry and I played in the barn until dinner, and we had a picnic on the front porch so we could watch the snow," because they were twisting in their chairs, smirking at one another. No one noticed that I deliberately left out the part about not ever wanting to go home, wanting to live with Harry and Charlotte and pretend I was their brother.

My face burned hotter every time I mentioned my mothers and I heard more snickering, each time a little more brazen, and the tapping of paper on wood sounded like the mice scurrying in the thick walls of my bedroom at Uncle Peter's, as notes were being passed. Mrs. Langelotti said nothing to stop them and I hurried to tell about the snowman we built so I could sit back down on the tip of my spine and appear smaller than the big carrot-haired kid with a swollen eye I was, who wished he were invisible.

"Red, Red, your father's dead! They made a mistake. You got two mothers instead!"

Just before recess that morning, as everyone got ready to tear down the stairs for lunch, Mrs. Langelotti said: "Don't forget to remind your parents that tomorrow is Parents' Day and they can come early and watch you in class." She saved the zinger for last.

"Willy," she said, rounding her eyes with innocence, "that means your mothers, too."

She delivered this parting shot with impeccable timing, winking at me, turning her back for a moment, allowing the snickers to reach a climax, a spitball to reach my collar, and the promise of renewed hostility on the battlefield that was lunchtime to reach my ears. "Hey Willy, Willy, got no dad. Just two mothers, now ain't that sad."

I dreaded the morning and the jeering bus trip across the park to the place where Claire and Theo paid hundreds each semester to have me tortured. I would have run away, out to Uncle Peter's farm, if it had not been for Carl.

He was small for his age, dark and solemn, all eyes, like a drawing in one of my picture books. He swayed a little while Mrs. Langelotti introduced him to the class that day, but he didn't seem to mind that he was the focus of all the attention. He didn't smile and he peered out from under black lashes that kept us from seeing he was really looking at a point in the middle of our foreheads, a technique I would later borrow to calm my nervousness in front of large groups.

"This is Carl Jacoby from Chicago," she announced with one hand clamped firmly on his shoulder. Did she think he was going to run away? Or faint? I wondered, but didn't really care. They had forgotten about me for the moment.

"What do we say, class?"

Thirty angelic faces gave no sign of their capacity for cruelty.

"Welcome, Carl!" they sang.

The sleet had given way to a cold so chilling, the drawings Ms. Langelotti had taped to the big casement windows were stiff with frost. The schoolyard was dangerously slick, determined unsafe for children by the headmaster who almost broke his neck on it but caught himself on the fence a few minutes before the lunch bell. So we filed down to the dark cafeteria, where no matter what was being cooked, nothing ever tasted the way it did at home. Down there, all food became one big lunch smell; even pizza and hot dogs took on the same stale odor of the steam table. Everything tasted a little chalky and I always lost my appetite, especially on the days mashed potatoes were on the menu and Mrs. Ryan, our school dietician, who always wore a greasy hairnet and had wet patches of gray kitchen sweat under the arms of her pink uniform, plopped lumpy balls of the glop on each plate with an ice cream scoop. By the time my vocabulary had grown enough to describe that sound as clammy thighs slapping together, I had sworn off mashed potatoes completely.

Outside, we were free to eat lunch from home in relative anonymity and Theo always packed something wonderful—cold homemade pizza, hand-ground peanut butter, French raspberry jam on crusty bread, a cup of thick soup in the thermos—and I enjoyed it unmolested. But inside, people who did not buy cafeteria food were sissies.

I didn't see Carl Jacoby quietly standing behind me as I slipped my lunch into the trash can outside the noisy lunchroom.

"What are you doing?" he asked.

"Nothing," I said, emptying the sturdy paper sack into the can's huge, gaping mouth.

"Could I have your banana before you throw it away?" Carl said, ignoring my answer.

I handed him the banana while continuing to dispose of the remaining contents of the Latest Dish bag, careful to keep my distance from the can's foul smell, eyeing the smaller boy beside me.

"Cool bag," he said.

"My mother's store," I answered.

"Wow." Carl's mouth was now full of banana.

"You know I've got two mothers," I said, warning him off, wondering why he was still standing there, why he hadn't joined the noisy group now pushing through the cafeteria's swinging door.

"I've got a grandmother," he said hopefully, missing my point.

"Where are your parents?" I asked.

"Dead."

"Yeah?"

"They were in a plane crash, and after the funeral I had to move here to live with my grandmother. She said they shouldn't have been sitting on the wing, but I don't think it was their fault," Carl explained, his solemn eyes darkening at the memory.

"Are you an orphan?" I asked.

Carl shrugged.

"Maybe I could borrow one of your mothers some time," he said.

WARY OF EACH OTHER at first, Carl and I spent the next few weeks and all the precious minutes we were not rendered silent by the stern looks of our teacher, tiptoeing around the edges of our lives, each time filling in a little more as our trust in each other grew. I began to dream of lost parents, dead people in picture frames who cannot touch you, cannot tear you in half, people who sit in shining perfection on the lids of grand pianos in dark apartment buildings with cool tiled lobbies and doormen who treat schoolboys like gentlemen.

I dreamed of people who died in grisly plane wrecks, strapped to fiery wings, or in the backs of highway emergency vehicles, their red lights and sirens screaming "Move, move, move, move over, now!" behind the cars of the living, people on their way to work, to the movies, to the beach.

I was haunted by people who withered away slowly in stale shuttered rooms, one following the other a few sad months later, poor lost souls whose best and happiest moments were forever frozen in heavy silver—a strong-jawed dad, a pretty mom, a smiling boy between them, reaching up to hold their hands.

I dreamed of a parakeet named Jimmy who slid down a slippery rubber mat into the kitchen sink, chirping "Jimmy's bath, Jimmy's bath" as he showered under the tap and performed other equally amazing feats for an old lady with skin that rustled like the tissue paper in Bergdorf boxes, a woman who doted on her lonely grandson from Chicago.

I dreamed of the way the boy lowered his eyes when the teacher announced Parents' Day, how he might look wistfully toward the sky when the Scout leader talked of merit badges and sleep-away camp, and how the other kids would draw him back, telling him their dads said it was okay for him to come along with them and how he acquiesced, accepting their gift without eagerness, as his due.

I dreamed of playing shortstop in the McCall Junior Little League without having to endure Claire and Theo flipping a coin to see who would pinch-hit in the father-and-son game because Uncle Peter lived too far away or Uncle Bax was in Bermuda or Burundi or somewhere buying stuff for his store and Thad didn't know how and Grandpa Barnaby's knees were too old to slide into home plate.

In my dream, Claire did not win the toss (or lose it, depending on how you looked at the matter) and get her period right before the game and miss every ball because she had such cramps. She wasn't out there slipping on the grass, acting like she was my father, while all the real fathers laughed at her behind her back and Theo sat in the stands, hollering her head off, taking us out for pizza afterward. In my dream, Claire and I weren't dirty and depressed and we weren't the only family not invited to go to the Flick and have banana splits.

Dead parents can't embarrass you.

I suppose that's why Carl Jacoby and I became best friends.

9

So many photographs. Frozen images. Acid-free. Double-matted in frames of museum-quality bird's-eye maple. Rows of them line the long corridor of our lives. They lead the visitor from our hall buzzer with its strong door, sturdy Medeco lock, ancient intercom, and peephole thick with paint to the faded and slightly tipsy-looking wooden figure of Jiggs, who hands us our mail from the tray glued to his gloved mitts, keeps our keys and sunglasses handy, and longs for Maggie, who was not cut out for such work.

These pictures illuminate the path from our front door in clean pools of light from invisible ceiling tracks, instructing the potential friend, the honored guest, the newcomer, in our secrets and ushers them up to the French doors that separate carefully chosen illusion from the plain truth of the family living beyond its beveled-glass panes.

I called it the Great Wall of Normalcy, the crash course in Claire and Theo and me that was a prerequisite to settling in on one of the soft, overstuffed couches, chairs, hassocks, poufs, and pillows dotting our large sunny living room, furniture that says, "Please, be comfortable with us." One after the other, the photos speak: "See, we are just like you. We are a family, too. Our knees get skinned. We graduate. We marry. We mourn. We have a son and he is the food Theo hungers for in her search for the perfect recipe. He is the truth Claire seeks in Mr. Kimsky's battered leather bag of a face, in the heartbeat before the eye registers the camera and the soul goes into hiding." Our wall says, "Park your assumptions at the door." It warns, "We are not responsible for any baggage left unattended."

And that especially means that invisible trunk you're dragging around with you, the one that's so full of 'should's and 'mustn't's and 'bad's and 'good's and rights and wrongs and judgments handed down from the beginning, that you can't lift it, you have to sit on it to keep it closed, but it always bursts open eventually, spilling your dirty underwear all over everybody. That one. That's the one that's not welcome here."

For Grandma Doris and Roy, Suzie, Jess, Baxter, Thad, Uncle Peter and Aunt Molly, people who already knew us and loved us, but sometimes forgot exactly how much, and especially for Grandma Hirsh, who loved us with as much begrudging affection as someone of her generation and social standing allowed, but was very quick to point out that love should never be construed as approval, our wall was a reminder that life is not as racy as imagination will lead you to believe and children quickly grow where there was once only enough room for rebellion.

"We are just like you. Only different."

Our pictures were pieces of the puzzle offered up as introduction. They were the gauntlet we had thrown down. Make no mistake. They were a test.

My childhood toddled along that wall; if the evidence can be believed, my progression from grinning Buddha to small boy to wary teenager to man, to artist, to husband, to healer of wounds was measured in smiles, party hats, and ponies, never far from my mothers' steadying hands.

My mothers are guarded in these pictures, these two women squinting into the future with questions knitted into their eyebrows. They see disappointment—mine? theirs?—lurking in every stranger's smile, and this burden shows in tight lines around the mouth, in the proud thrust of a chin. They gamely push their faces into the camera as if to say, "Look! We are young, we are beautiful, we have a son, we are in love and we own the world." Something in their eyes says they do not always believe this.

My mothers primp. They mug. They wrap themselves around images of friends and family the way protesters lock on to street lamps when it's time for the police to drive up in the van and drag them away. Theo sweeps a stray lock away from Claire's forehead and, in the seconds before the click, proves the eye is not always quicker than the hand. They say *"Fromage"* instead of "Cheese." It is their joke and the reason they always seem to be pouting about something.

I am a fat, freckled child in a snowsuit, a thatch of orange hovering over me like the fiery tongue of a Zippo lighter, a small flame reaching for the sky over a huddled knot of mourners. It was taken the day we all climbed into long black cars and drove over the Queensboro Bridge to say good-bye to Uncle Alan in Calvary Cemetery, a place I will always remember as an endless field of loose teeth. I'm holding my aunt Jessica's beautifully manicured hand, and I remember how it shook inside her soft kid gloves as I peered out from under hooded eyes, hands curling and uncurling into perpetual fists, always ready, even then, to throw the first punch.

I am the boy who towers over Theo at twelve, the young man in a mortarboard who pretends not to see maternal pride beaming in the third row. When I see the groom who is quietly weeping for the joy of seeing Annie floating toward him on the arm of her father, so beautiful, so happy, I see so much more. In that nervous young man's face I also see misty Aunt Molly and proud Theo, her pale skin ashy with fatigue despite the bittersweet happiness blossoming on her cheeks. She stands in the pew reserved for parents, which Uncle Thad had festooned with a white satin bow and blush-pink freesias. There is Carl at my back (having reappeared in my life as suddenly as he had come, his dark eyes older, but still sad, peering out from behind a copy of Plato's *Republic* in the Princeton stacks, as willing to begin the slow rewinding of our friendship as he had been the day he asked for my banana). Harry is at my side, buoying me up like a strong wind.

Among our family pictures, there are people I do not know, grinning into the years before I was born. There is what looks to be an all-female soccer team in front of the Parthenon, with Claire and Theo down in front wearing shorts and sneakers and sunglasses, the Leica dangling between them. Claire's blond hair is ironed flat, parted in the middle, Theo's a fiery Afro. Their arms are around each other and their neighbors, and their smiles hint of having begun to invent the details of the story they would tell me one day.

"When we arrived in Patmos, all the tour guides and the old women in black in the markets crossed themselves at the sight of us," Theo began. "They thought all our husbands were dead and we were traveling together to get over our grief."

"So they sent all the men in the village to the taverna to dance with us, to cheer us up," Claire finished for her.

"And by the time they found out we were a planeload of lesbians on vacation"—Theo was grinning—"they were stuck."

"They already liked us!" They recited this last part together, laughing for the sharp memory of that time, while I joined their laughter more for the feeling of closeness it gave me than because I understood this story that had nothing and everything to do with me.

For me, meaning lived in these frozen moments; I would carry that one a long way, looking hard into it, trying it out on various people in my life, before I cherished it as they had.

There are other images not on the wall. These flicker in the sepia light of my memory. Two women slow-dancing in the kitchen with the radio on. A tumble of red and blond hair on a pillow. Theo sleeping in the crook of Claire's arm. Claire's pale skin mottled red and swollen in grief. Theo boning a chicken with the strength of a butcher. The hard sound of ice thrown into a glass. The metallic click of a lighter in the dark. The long, graceful fingers of an artist turning the pages of a bedtime story, the short stubby ones of a chef, wearing every new nick and ping, scratch and puncture like a Purple Heart, the sound of a Band-Aid scratching the page, two pairs of hands wearing the same pink-and-yellow gold and platinum wedding bands woven together; inseparable. Claire reads *Robinson Crusoe,* Theo *Black Beauty.* One cries for a horse, the other laughs at the idea of a servant in a place with no dust bunnies and no one to invite for dinner. A chapter a night before lights out for Mr. Baby. Quiet laughter. Sighing in the dark.

I remember strangers, faces coming to life on dark, wet paper floating in the sink as Claire plucked them out of the basin with her tongs and strong slender arms, always at the perfect moment of creation, giving a little whistle when she was pleased, the sound of a tire with a slow leak when she was not. I remember her face, taut as bone, the white-blond hair caught up in a comb to keep the thick curtain of it from closing on her work, the way she pushed out her lower lip in the Martian light of her room under the stairs in which I was always a welcome, if not bumbling, assistant. I remember how much I wanted to be one of those pictures, able to touch the place in her that could weep for joy as she lifted them out of their bath and proudly carried them to Aunt Suzie.

Flashes of things darker and more disturbing. The set of a jaw. Muffled voices. The strangled sound of disappointment. An elderly woman in a bright pink raincoat who came to blow out the sun.

CARL JACOBY lived in the magic kingdom called Tudor City, and it was the scene of our blood brotherhood for one unforgettably giddy year. Set high above the FDR Drive like some turreted medieval town, it was just far enough from the blare and rush of First Avenue to be as close to suburbia as two city kids could get. It was better. It was our castle in summer, a cool, ivy-covered lair transformed in winter into a silent gray fort, a stony outpost in the frozen wilderness, buffeted by icy blasts off the river we imagined was our private moat.

Like Gramercy Park, its rich relative a mile farther downtown, this warren of buildings, stone paths, and steep steps, built in 1928 for working-class New Yorkers, had its own commons, with grass a bright green that bore no relation to the dun clumps that pass for lawns in most other parts of town. We called it the Emerald City. It nestled between the buildings and was enclosed by a huge black wrought-iron fence with curved bars on top just like the bear cages in Central Park; only, these were not to keep the danger in, these were to keep it out. Inside were trees and benches, monkey bars and seesaws, swings and secret paths and unscarred grass that was soft under our bare feet. It was a wild Marlin Perkins jungle full of danger and adventure behind a huge gate that scraped the cement when it swung open to our boyish imagining. Carl had his own key and wore it on a chain under his flannel shirt, hidden away from the greedy eyes of older boys who would mug a little kid for less.

On Saturdays and Sundays and sometimes on school holidays, when Carl's grandmother allowed him to visit me, making sure his bus money was safely tied in the clean white handkerchief she gave him every day, we played "Where's Papa?" in the park. The best places for this, we discovered, were at the zoo or the carousel or the

Wollman Rink, where divorced fathers and their pretty girlfriends spent the weekend with his kids from the marriage. "They have to," said Zachary Rifken (a weasely-looking kid in our class whose own parents had been divorced twice each, which left him with eight guilty grown-ups, all of whom wanted to buy him stuff), "otherwise the girlfriend goes."

These groups were easy to spot because the fathers always looked tense, the girlfriends smiled too much and wore too much makeup to be real mothers in the park, and the kids, always sullen and overdressed, looked like they wished they were somewhere else, especially when the father made it a point to hold his girlfriend's hand and they averted their eyes, embarrassed at all that was implicit in this public display that did not include their mother. Aunt Suzie told us once that when parents fight, the court always gives the children to the mother, even if she doesn't deserve them. "The court gave me to my grandmother," Carl had answered, and I asked her what it would do in my case. But she just smiled and said, "Don't worry, my sweet boy, that will never happen to you."

Each of us looked for faces in the crowd and whoever picked the person who most resembled his father or, in my case, the one who most resembled me, and therefore could most likely be my father, won.

Some days even the Emerald City was off-limits and we had to make our own fun in Mrs. Jacoby's gloomy apartment.

"I see a color and it is . . . blue!"

We bobbed at either end of the heavy cut-velvet sofa in the dark sunken living room where plastic runners led the way to the exits, and antimacassars and doilies protected every surface. We were bookends with energy to burn. Mrs. Jacoby's apartment was our playground on days the rain kept us from our castle, and we transformed its silent rooms with our games. The heavy smell of lemon wax and clove, the sharp tang of Jimmy's birdseed, and an oddly stale but not unpleasant odor I would always associate with old age clung to thick drapes that discouraged light.

Carl's parents, peering out from silver frames carefully arranged on the sleek piano nobody ever played and which we secretly called the Runway because that's where they were headed when Carl last saw them, waving good-bye from tiny airplane windows like the hula dolls in the back windows of some cars as their plane taxied away from the windy gate, would have laughed at our antics had they not been laughing already, blindly smiling into a future that did not include them.

"Onetwothreefourfivesixseveneightnineten!"

A steady rain poured shadows on the wallpaper as I skidded on Mrs. J's freshly waxed parquet, breathlessly looking for a hiding place before Carl came up for air and raced after me. Jimmy came in low, dive-bombing the coffee table, a bright blue warplane packed with steaming white death pellets, aiming for my hair, screaming "Hello! Hello!" I crouched and swallowed hard to cover the sound of my pounding heart, panting under the dining room table. An old woman's feet shuffled by, puffy and shining in their carpet slippers, attached to legs that had outlived their reason to run. She had no idea I was there. Maybe Carl would miss me, too. The overhang of the musty Quaker lace cloth kept my secret, screening the light like the dark confessional at St. Pat's Grandma Hirsh insisted we visit one Saturday on the way home from Rockefeller Center. *Bless me, Father, for I have two mothers. I have two and Carl has none.*

Sometimes we played stagecoach on Mrs. Jacoby's delicate vanity table. Pushing aside dusty bottles of Ma Griffe, Je Reviens, and Shalimar and a man's tortoiseshell brush-and-comb set, we sat on the glass-topped surface, resting our feet in the small depression that contained secret drawers (which, I imagined, held love letters from Mr. Jacoby, who had disappeared into the merchant marine the week Carl's father was born). We pretended we were in the driver's box; the tiny matching chair was our team of shining black stallions carrying us through dangerous Apache territory with our pouches full of gold and mail for the settlers. Of course, I am part Cherokee on Grandma Doris's side, so if we were attacked, and we always were, I would say, "I am Willy Two Squaws," and they let us pass. The stagecoach got through and saved the town. "Yahoo! Eeeeeiiii! Rollin' rollin' rollin' Rawhide!"

Most days we were sent to Carl's room to do homework until the Latest Dish van picked me up and delivered me to the shop, where I helped Theo clean up and nibbled cookies. We waited for Claire to arrive for our walk home through Central Park, which has been a family tradition since before I was born. Once we became friends, I was allowed to ride home on the school bus with Carl and stay with him until dinnertime, when the van made its rounds and I was returned, like so much left over coq au vin, to Theo's kitchen.

Sometimes when Claire was away making pictures and Theo was cooking for a big party, I was allowed to stay for Mrs. Jacoby's sauerbraten with gingersnap gravy and potato pancakes (which Theo would die before cooking), or for an A&P pot pie and ice cream dinner, which we never had at home. I loved this heavy, homey food so much, I didn't even care that I had to sit politely while Mrs. Jacoby smiled at us and took tiny bites and made awful sucking noises. I didn't even care that sometimes she farted and didn't hear it and we bit the insides of our cheeks until they bled to keep from laughing as it rumbled through her.

Sometimes, we invited Carl to our house and he hopped in the van with me. We were allowed to pick our dinner from anything in the store and Carl almost always ate a fudge brownie before dinner after we all swore never to tell his grandmother. We helped Theo clean up and wait on the stragglers who begged her to stay open one more minute, which she always did because she couldn't stand the face of a hungry person.

It was April and we had just come in from mucking around on the muddy lawn downstairs. Carl's grandmother had made us take our shoes off in the hall and held up our filthy jackets like two dead animals, between the tips of her fingers and as far away from her frilly white blouse as possible. She pointed down the hall and I washed my hands and face in the Jacobys' avocado green–tiled bathroom, then dried them defiantly with the dainty guest towels I was told never to use; if I was not a guest, who was?

For some long forgotten reason, school had let out early and we waited in Carl's room to be called to lunch.

"Do you miss them?" I couldn't help thinking about Carl's parents sitting on the wing.

"I miss them on Saturdays," Carl said.

"How come?"

"That's the day parents aren't allowed to go to work or talk on the phone with people from the office," answered Carl from the other side of his Wild West bedspread.

"Oh." I wondered if Claire and Theo knew this.

"Maybe Claire and Theo aren't really parents," I said, thinking this is the only reason they would break this rule.

"My grandmother says some kids just have mothers and some just have fathers and some have to spend a little time with each one because they live in different houses and some are dead like mine, but I think she said you had to have one of each to have parents."

I DON'T REMEMBER whose idea it was, only that we were too restless for homework and it was a day that seemed too far from our final exams, which for those of us in the third grade at McCall School could not have been terribly difficult or stress-inducing, only an annoying disruption of our games, more than anything else. It was also Wednesday, the day Mrs. Jacoby put on her good coat and took her patent-leather bag out of its dust cover, then left for the crosstown bus she rode to have tea with her friends at Lord & Taylor, allowing us to play in the apartment alone. As soon as the door had closed, we decided to hold the séance on the baby grand piano, because none of Carl's grandmother's tables were black and spooky enough.

We found the candles in the emergency drawer in Mrs. J's narrow kitchen and I contributed the pilot's wings I always wore pinned to my shirt because Carl's parents were sitting right over the wing when they were last seen alive. Carl laid the ratty piece of flannel, all that was left of the old baby blanket he always kept in his pocket, out on the piano's inky-black mirror, so they'd know it was him.

"I feel funny calling them Edgar and Marilyn," he said, working up the nerve to summon them.

"If you don't, how are all the dead people going to know who you want?" I asked with the perfect logic and superiority of a boy who is about to be nine, thinking we'd sound like babies calling for Mommy and Daddy in a séance and how stupid we'd feel if somebody else's parents showed up because we weren't specific.

After draping rosary beads around our necks because we'd heard you could accidentally wake up the devil if you didn't, we dragged Mrs. Jacoby's kitchen stools into the living room and sat at opposite sides of the piano, fingers touching, eyes closed, lights out. In the flickering candle glow, we urged the photographs to come to life. Just for a minute. Just to make Carl feel better.

"Eeeedgar. Marrrrrrrilyn. This is your son Carllllll and his friend Willeeeee. Where arrrrre youuuuuu?" We elongated our syllables, hurling them into eerie tunnels that distorted our words for the dead.

We heard something shift in the shadowy corners of the living room and the silky hairs on our arms and on the back of our necks stood away from flesh. There was a creaking sound, the air was suddenly cooler and we felt something, a presence.

We barked orders into the gloom—"Eeeeeeedgar. Marrrrrrilyn. Speeeaaak to us"—pretending we weren't scared stiff.

In the dark, we didn't see what the dripping wax was doing to the glossy surface of the piano Mrs. Jacoby told us Carl's father had played every Saturday morning for his patient and blessedly stone-deaf teacher, Mr. Gilchrist from the Settlement School. Nor did we hear her key in the lock. We didn't see her fists aiming at us until we felt the first blows, superstition and fear pummeling us senseless.

"Leave them alone. Let them rest. My poor Edgar!" she screamed, throwing her shopping bags down on the couch, blowing out the candles, rubbing at the wax with her coat sleeve, and hitting us, all at the same time. "Look at this piano!"

I did not identify the heat that rose to my face that day as shame until many years later when I saw Mrs. Jacoby's look in someone else's eyes and I recognized the rising flush of my skin and the flutter in the pit of my stomach. That look went down to the core of things. It said, "You are damaged and evil, the product of something perverse, and you will always screw up, and here is proof I am right."

"You made my Carl do this, you, you . . . devil!"

Shame is a cumulative thing. If you feel it enough, you believe it.

CLAIRE HAD JUST come home from a shoot in Atlantic City and was showering off the casino muck, as she jokingly called the grime that rises up from the dark edges of the rug daylight never reaches and attaches itself to money that is prayed over, spat on, and moved hand to hand. Theo and I were in the park playing tennis. Actually, Theo was playing tennis and I was clumsily learning to return her serve, which was more dangerous than her stature and her delicacy would lead you to expect.

Andy had seen Claire go up, so he let the intercom buzz while Claire found a towel and her terry robe, grabbed her hairbrush, and squeezed a covered rubber band around her hair, which was dripping uncomfortably down her back.

"I need this?" she muttered as she mopped up her own wet footprints on the rug, cursing her timing.

"There's a Mrs. Jacoby to see you, ma'am," Andy said, sounding the deeply resonant tone he affected in the presence of strangers.

"Give me two minutes, then send her up, will you, Andy?"

When Claire opened the door, Carl's grandmother was wearing the most awful pink coat she had ever seen. She looked like a hopelessly wrinkled Kewpie doll.

"I won't be long," said Mrs. Jacoby, clutching her lurid top button, refusing to give up her oversized bubble-gum wrapper to the hanger Claire offered.

"Please, come in and sit down. Willy has told us so much about you and your grandson, Mrs. Jacoby. Theo and I are so grateful—"

"My son was a good boy."

"I'm sure he was, Mrs. Jacoby. I'm so sorry. It must be very difficult for you. I lost someone. My brother. My parents . . ."

My parents, what? Claire thought. *I don't know what my parents felt. They never told me. They never shared it. Here I am pretending I know how this woman feels.*

". . . miss him."

"My son and daughter-in-law were not modern," Mrs. Jacoby said, flatly ignoring Claire's small talk. She held on to an exceedingly shiny handbag, strap coiled around her wrist, fingers splayed over the clasp, as though someone might try to grab it.

"I'm sure they were wonderful parents," replied Claire diplomatically, giving herself time to grasp the old woman's point.

"I can't afford private school on my pension, but I send Carl to McCall to keep him away from the undesirable element." Here Mrs. Jacoby paused, as though realizing she had made a bad start, and Claire rushed to fill the silence that swirled around it.

"You can't be too careful in New York," said Claire. "That's why we send Willy there, too."

"I'm an old-fashioned woman, Miss Hirsh," said the old woman, gathering her purpose around her, "and I would rather have my son dead than live the way you do. Willy is a nice boy. I don't know how you could raise him in such an evil household."

It's one thing to know you are in the presence of an enemy, quite another when someone you know, someone you've trusted with your child, throws a punch into your solar plexus. Claire struggled for air.

"My personal life is none of your business, Mrs. Jacoby," Claire managed to say just before she felt her throat begin to close.

"My business is Carl. It's better Willy don't see him anymore."

"But, Mrs. Jacoby, Carl and Willy are best friends! Think whatever you like of Theo and me, but don't make the kids pay for that," said Claire hoarsely.

"Your son tried to call my son and daughter-in-law back from the dead this afternoon. You can live any way you want, but I'm not going to let him turn my grandson into a godless queer."

Mrs. Jacoby had been hovering just outside the French doors as though she could not say what she had come to say in the intimacy of our living room. She did not want to see the Claire and Theo who concerned themselves with the comfort of their guests, who offered a cool drink, a chocolate, a soft chair. She already knew all she cared to know about us. She was gone before Claire could collect her breath, which had become a pounding, corrosive lump in her sternum.

When Theo and I got back from tennis, noisy and sweaty and fresh from my first contact with Theo's serve, eager to give Claire the blow-by-blow, the shower was still running, and it kept running for a long time. Claire sat through dinner looking scalded, as though she had scrubbed her delicate skin with steel wool. She wore a blank smile, the kind you paste on when you come in second and the camera records tears as brightness around the eyes. She nodded vacantly when Theo said, "Say hello to the future Mr. Forest Hills," bragging about my deadly two-handed forehand, and she barely noticed when Theo changed the subject and boasted that she had sold out her Tuscan salad with bruschetta before noon.

"What do people do in heaven?" I asked Claire, my small-boy mind still wondering what Edgar and Marilyn were doing when their son called, why they didn't hear the phone ring. Maybe we had the wrong area code, like how we sometimes forgot to dial 516 for Uncle Peter.

"I think they do whatever made them happiest here. I like to think your uncle Alan is making corsages for the angels," said Theo with one eye on Claire, who looked as though I'd asked how to get to the moon.

"If somebody calls you up there, can you hear it and come back and visit?"

"Well, honey, I think being in heaven means you know everything that's going on, even if your friends can't see you or hear you. It's not like being in a place, exactly. You can't get phone calls, but I think you know when people you love think about you."

"How?"

"It's like blowing out your birthday candles and making a wish. If you really concentrate and see what you wish for on the little TV screen behind your eyes, it will come true. If you do that when you want to talk to someone in heaven, they'll hear you," Theo looked sideways at Claire when she said this.

"Like a dream?" I asked.

"Yes, my darling, just like a dream."

"Will they answer?"

"I think so. But only you will hear it." Theo smiled as though remembering something she had forgotten, something wonderful.

With a strangled sound, Claire suddenly dropped her fork. She pushed away her plate and slid it back with such force that the legs scraped the kitchen floor making Theo and me jump.

"Think it was something we said?" Theo lamely joked, looking stunned, as we watched Claire stalk out of the room.

"Maybe she misses Uncle Roland," I ventured.

"Maybe," said Theo, staring at the kitchen door with its regulation restaurant porthole Claire had put in for her birthday one year. I got the feeling Theo wasn't surprised by whatever it was that just happened; she just sat there, looking at the door still vibrating with Claire's shove. She sat there for a long time glaring at it, as though blaming it for being too flimsy, too open, too trusting.

I heard them talking long into that night. The bedroom door slammed, a toilet flushed, water ran, and the light in the kitchen went on again just before dawn. I couldn't make out what they were saying, but the heaviness of their footsteps on the bare floors, the random pattern of the sound, the unfamiliar smell of a cigarette burning, and the weight that was sitting on my chest told me once again it had something to do with me.

Grandma Hirsh had once said I made enough noise to wake the dead, but I didn't see the harm. How could it be hard to go back to sleep in heaven?

10

The day after Mrs. Jacoby came to our apartment, Claire refused to get up. The clock radio clicked on at six-thirty, right in the middle of Imus in the Morning, who was saying something about a front and flooding on the East River Drive, a steady April rain slashed our tall windows and in the gloom, a fine mist clung to the budding outlines of trees in the park below. As she did every morning on her way to the kitchen, Theo wound up Tweety Bird, our mechanical canary, and held up its cage at the foot of my stairs to wake me with the tinny song I liked better than my crocodile alarm clock. Without fully opening her eyes, she ground the coffee beans, started the pot brewing, and padded back into the bedroom to start her shower and to rouse Claire, who, at the first sound of their favorite morning host, had muttered something dark and threatening and kicked the radio across the room.

"C'mon, kiddo, there's art to be made," Theo prodded, as she gave Claire's behind a gentle swat on the way to the bathroom, but Claire pulled the blanket over her head and wouldn't budge. I stood at their bedroom door; when Theo saw me, she tickled Claire's feet and said, for my benefit, "Last one in the kitchen is a poached egg." Then I saw her lean over the lump that was Claire, whisper something, and rub the lump's back, but it did no good. Claire burrowed deeper into the duvet until all we saw was her elbow sticking out from under the covers and I thought: *All alone like that, without a body, when you're not sure exactly where it fits, an elbow is an ugly thing.*

The phone rang. "C'mon, Claire, that's Suzie calling to remind you you're going to Brassaï today. Remember him? Photographer,

Paris, the twenties, cafés with mirrors?" said Theo, hoping the prospect of this busman's holiday would get a rise out of Claire.

"I'm not getting it," called Theo over her shoulder as she headed for the kitchen.

A pale foot slithered out from under the covers and kicked the phone across the room in mid-ring.

"That's really mean, Claire," Theo hollered over a blast of peanuts in the grinder. "She got up early for you."

I once heard Theo say Suzie was an insomniac, and that that was why she never phoned before noon, but for the longest time I confused this with kleptomaniac, which Suzie herself explained was someone who couldn't help shoplifting, so I thought she dressed oddly because she never got a chance to try anything on. I suppose I wasn't far off, considering all those rhinestones and pins and sequins were enough to keep anybody up all night.

The phone rang again, but this time it was a bit more subdued, as though chastened by its sudden flight.

"I'm still not answering it," called Theo, moving back down the hall toward their bedroom, straightening pictures as she went.

"Claire, for God's sake, answer the phone," said Theo, slipping into her kitchen clogs and pulling a long flowered skirt over her head.

"It's still ringing, Claire," Theo announced, buttoning the brilliant white embroidered shirt she wore instead of a chef's jacket.

"Please, Theo, please . . ." Claire had come out from under the covers and begun jabbing wildly at the phone with her finger at the sound of our tape recorder. *Click.* "You have reached the Bouvier-Hirsh household—" She tilted her head in its direction and rolled her eyes. "Theeeeohhh!" —"and Claire and Theo and Willy are not able"— Until Theo finally relented and plucked the phone out of the basket of socks in which it had landed.

"Hello, Suze," said Theo flatly.

"Tell her I have the flu," whispered Claire, covering her head with her pillow as though Suzie were in the room and could see she was perfectly well.

"Claire told me to tell you she has the flu," said Theo, staring down at Claire, who glowered out from under the pillow's soft linen flap. Theo hated to lie because she said it only put off the inevitable moment you had to tell someone what was really the matter and by that time, whatever it was, it was always worse.

"Tell her we're going to Madame Romaine's for omelets after," said Suzie, "something full of Stilton and pears."

Theo stood over Claire as she talked to Suzie, never once taking her eyes off Claire, who had disappeared again into the twisted blankets. She frowned down at the lump under the covers while she smiled into the phone with her voice, the way she did when she called school to say I was running a slight fever and thought it best I stay home.

"Suzie says you're going to Madame Romaine's after . . ."

Claire peeked out and shook her head.

"Tell her I didn't get to sleep until four," pleaded Suzie, worry now fighting for space with annoyance.

"I don't think that's going to work this morning, Suzie. She's upset about something that happened yesterday. Go back to sleep, she'll call you later."

Theo and I ate our cereal with blueberries and slathered thick English muffins with butter and strawberry jam and tried to pretend everything was okay, but whenever one of us wasn't watching, the other would slide a look toward the kitchen door and listen for the familiar slap of bare feet on cold tile. When I was almost ready for school and stood at the door for our family hug, "Three for one and one for three, Mommy One, Mama Two, and Willy," Theo said, "Mommy is feeling sad today, sport."

I kept working my arms into the sleeves of my slicker, which was grabbing my school blazer, making it bunch up where I couldn't reach. When Theo, seeing me struggle, slid her hand up the back to pull it down for me, she didn't surprise me with a quick tickle, which is what she always did, and that was how I knew it wasn't just Claire who was feeling sad.

"She's mad at Carl's grandma for being so mean to you," Theo explained with both hands on my shoulders, bending to touch my forehead with hers, speaking without talking.

Later, when we were gone and the apartment was empty, Claire wandered its rooms, tidying up the brightly colored plates and bowls that had fallen to Theo's breakfast whirlwind, picking up my toys and putting them back into the old sea chest Uncle Bax had found in an estate sale and had lovingly refinished, painted, and lacquered with Lucy and Linus and Charlie Brown decals. She smoothed my sheets over and over as though ironing something out—as though they needed consoling, not she.

Claire examined the easy comfort of our home, once her solitary haven, meticulous in its carefully composed clutter, quiet and unchanging from day to day, year to year, the rooms now rumpled and alive with the push and shove of a family, and felt as though someone had broken in during the night and gone through our things with a stranger's dirty hands. As she picked up the evidence of our haste, she thought, *Everything looks exactly as it did yesterday, but nothing is, or ever will be, the same.* And when she bent down to retrieve the slipper I had left under the kitchen table, the reason rose before her in the form of a large red circle around Friday on the big weekly planner pinned to the back of the open pantry door. The matching scribble in the margin in Theo's enthusiastic hand said, "Peter's this weekend with Carl and Willy!" Claire stared at it for a long time, struggling with the vain hope that this time would be different, that this time she would get what she so badly needed, before she gave up and called her mother.

"I'M NOT ALLOWED to talk to you anymore."

Carl stood on the sidewalk outside the red brick building, which had once been owned by an Astor or a Rockefeller or somebody like that and had been cut up into a dark warren of classrooms for kids who cabbed, walked, bused, or were dropped off in long, black cars, like special-delivery packages, into its privileged mustiness. It was still raining and the sidewalk was slippery as parents rushed the building with golf umbrellas, briefcases, and children in blue blazers, a telltale pajama leg peeking out from under a soggy mink coat here and there. Vehicles double- and triple-parked, discharging my schoolmates into the expensive hush of East Seventy-Fourth Street, which if not for the howling mob surrounding the McCall School and the vacant lot it called a schoolyard would have been just another row of consulates, mansions, maisonettes, and doormen standing guard in the polished-brass and wrought-iron arteries between Park and Madison. The Latest Dish was only three and a half blocks away in the blare and bustle of Second Avenue and as was her custom, Theo had dropped me off in the van on her way to the store. I waited for Carl's bus so I could say I was sorry for bothering Edgar and Marilyn in heaven, which was how Theo explained the problem to me.

"Carl's grandmother is just getting used to them being in heaven," she said as we turned off Madison and double-parked. "She was angry because if they heard you and came back, she'd have to say good-bye and feel sad all over again. Can you understand that?" she asked as she handed over my lunch bag, which had been on the seat between us.

"I guess."

I didn't understand. I knew that if Grandma Hirsh saw Roland again, she'd be happy. I know because when I asked her what he looked like and she showed me the photographs and the baby book, the tiny tooth, but not the yellowed newspaper clippings about the accident she kept in a rosewood box in the locked bottom drawer of her armoire, she said, "I would give anything to see him again, William dear, even for a moment."

"I didn't mean to wake up your mom and dad," I said, edging closer to Carl, who silently held an umbrella open for both of us.

"My grandmother says what your mothers do is against the law," Carl said solemnly.

I was aware of heat building up inside my slicker; the white button-down shirt Theo had ironed that morning was beginning to stick to my skin.

"She says they do stuff with other women and don't believe in God."

"So? Your grandmother goes to Lord & Taylor every Wednesday with a whole bunch of ladies. Is that against the law?" I did not understand and wondered if the police would arrest me, too.

"That's different. Anyway, we go to synagogue on the holidays." Carl shifted uncomfortably, looking beyond me to a group of boys disappearing into the front door. "My grandmother says your mothers aren't real parents." His dark eyes focused on a spot above my head.

I felt the tears stinging the undersides of my eyelids and I squeezed as hard as I could to keep them from spilling over. I moved closer to Carl and something very hot moved up from my shirt to my head and down into my hands and I heard myself shout, "I hate your grandmother and I hate you and my mothers do *so* believe in God and you can't come with us to my uncle Peter's farm on Friday—" The rest of the words were lost in the buzzing in my ears and the blood pumping in my arms.

Carl was crying when somebody's father pulled me off him and the rain was running bright red down the front of my slicker like the poster paints in Mrs. Flynn's art class.

Not far away, in the store's cramped kitchen, Theo was cutting butter into pie dough. As she dipped the knife in and out of the jar of ice water and deftly worked the floured board with a certain absentminded skill, she could imagine Mrs. Jacoby's frayed mouth hissing the words "godless queer, godless queer" over and over again; she did not realize she was bleeding until she saw the same sticky-looking stain repeated on every pie shell on her work table and the water reddened a deeper shade with every pass of the knife.

CLAIRE HATED TO DRIVE, especially all the way out to South Neck on a Friday night, but Theo's hand, with six stitches in it, was wrapped in a big white glove of gauze and she had taken some Percodan for the pain. So Claire was forced to get behind the wheel of our broken-down VW Beetle, which neither of them had the heart to sell. Grandma and Grandpa Hirsh kept it in their building's lot for us. By the time we'd cabbed over to the East Side, rung the night bell, walked down the steep hill into the garage, and packed the car, until I jumped out of the car to push open the gate to Sound View Farm, it was very late. Aunt Molly gently steered a groggy Theo, who had fallen asleep before we hit the Long Island Expressway into the guest room.

Claire stayed up with Peter long after Molly settled me into Harry's small room under the eaves, then tiptoed downstairs to sit up against her own pillows, listening to the familiar sighing of her house, before sliding down into sleep.

The darkened kitchen was lit only by a pale moon and the small lamp that teetered on the ledge of an ancient hutch that filled the wall with trivets, old muffin tins, odd plates and china cups, cookbooks, gardening notes, clippings, photos, and the small triumphs of children. Peter and Claire sat at the table, and the long, prayerful sweep of their arms, the way their bodies gave the impression of leaning in and holding something back, in their long, slender faces, all angles and seriousness, suspended in a halo of blond made even more luminous by moonlight, they were brother and sister down to the bone. They lowered their voices when they spoke of the history that ran in their blood, and of things that did not include me, or Theo, or Molly or Charlotte or Harry or the slumbering beasts that rested large sorrowful heads on their feet.

Peter entered the silence, which until now had been broken only by the occasional thump of a tail and the knocking of a gust rising up from the Sound.

"Why did you call her?"

"I should know better by now, shouldn't I?" Claire peered into the dark edges of the quiet kitchen, feeling a cold nose on her foot.

"What did she say?" asked Peter, not because he really wanted to know, but because he knew his sister needed to talk about it.

"She said, 'I was just having a cup of tea' in that the-queen-will-see-you-now voice she always uses when, God forbid, any of us need to talk," Claire's skin began to mottle at the memory. "And, of course, the minute she says that, it's Dad's clue to slump deeper into his chair and pretend he's napping. For once, I'd really like to know what Barnaby thinks, if he has any balls, any backbone at all."

Claire fell silent for a moment; then her voice rose again. "He answered the phone and I, fool that I am, thought he would actually have an opinion, some fatherly advice."

"Did he?" said Peter, knowing the answer.

"Are you kidding? He said, 'Let me get your mother.' " Claire snickered.

Peter had his own thoughts on Barnaby, but kept them to himself, sipped his brandy and let Claire play this out. She would come back to the question. She always did.

"Why can't she, just for once, take my side? Why can't she say, 'Dammit, you're my daughter and I don't care if you're a lesbian, that woman was out of line,' instead of saying in that hasn't-anybody-taught-you-anything voice, 'How did you expect the poor woman to react, dear?' "

"Because she can't, Sis. And she does care, you know that. So why is it so important that she bless everything you do? She loves you. She adores Willy. She'd give her life for him—"

"No, Peter," Claire interrupted, "she'd give *my* life for him."

He paused, ignoring this. "In her own repressed way, she loves Theo, too. She just can't pretend she approves. You know that."

Claire looked deep into the brandy bottle between them, ran a finger around its sticky wax seal, and edged it closer to her glass, offering its dark neck to Peter, who lowered his eyes and covered his snifter with his palm.

"And what do you know, little brother? Do you know that no matter what you do, they will never notice you, no matter how you twist yourself inside out for them, try to understand their pain and to forgive their silence, that they will never do the same for you? Do you know that your little newspaper could win a damn Pulitzer Prize and you would not be any different in his eyes because you're not Roland?"

Peter bowed his head, but Claire could not stop herself.

"And you can explain them and defend them and make excuses for them, but she's still going to lower her eyes and say, 'We lost our son,' while you're standing right there. Do you know that?" Claire flashed the anger she had been holding all day.

"I do, but thank you so much for pointing it out," said Peter coldly. "I also know that inflicting pain on somebody else when you're feeling it yourself seems to be a trait not restricted to our parents."

"Well, you know the Hirsh family motto, 'No kindness unpunished,' " said Claire, taking her brother's hand in what he understood was as close to an apology as she would give.

"I poured out my heart to her, Petey," Claire continued in a murky whisper, replenishing the amber liquid in her glass until it swirled dangerously close to the rim. "I told her how Willy was ripped away from his best friend because of a stupid, superstitious old woman who was afraid he might touch something in her house, and what? What could this innocent little boy do to hurt her, get queer germs on her precious piano? I told her about the look on Willy's face when Theo told him he couldn't go to Carl's anymore and how he wanted to call and apologize for contributing his United

Airline wings and waking up dead people who are trying to get some sleep in heaven." Claire winced at the memory of my childish confusion.

"You know, Petey, sometimes I think she's sorry it wasn't me."

"C'mon Claire, you know better than that," said Peter, reaching for her hand. "She's sees him in you, that's all."

Claire had held back the tears all day. After Theo and I left the apartment, she tried to work in the darkroom, but the images in the pan swam in bitter salt. When the school called to tell her I had beaten up a boy half my size, and when Theo called from Lenox Hill's emergency room to say she had severed some nerves in her hand, and even when she had to drive and her own hands shook on the steering wheel because she forgot to take the detour that would avoid the little clump of trees just beyond the peach orchard where it took three hours for police to pry a blond teenage boy from behind the wheel of what once was a Chevy Impala convertible, she did not cry. She just held the wheel tighter and hardened herself against the memory of what had happened in that spot when she watched them pull a blanket over Roland's face, a face so like her own, and she felt ripped in half and they told Barnaby and he locked shut, his grief becoming a hungry, howling thing that fed on silence and ink from behind the curtain of *The Wall Street Journal.*

Now, she cried. Here in her brother's kitchen, where she finally felt safe, where she could say anything and still be loved, the tears came.

"I'm so afraid," said Claire between sobs.

"Afraid of what, honey?"

"Afraid I'll screw it up. Afraid Willy will hate me for giving him this life. Afraid Theo will get sick of me and leave and take him with her. Afraid I'll be alone, one of those sad, interesting woman in trousers with a strong face and a tragic past. Somebody who pretended she was a mother once."

Peter reached over to smooth his sister's hair, he was touched by the trust that prompted her to show him her fear.

"I love him too, you know," Peter said.

"I know you do, Petey," said Claire, blowing her nose.

Peter thought about how his sister had used this wounded perspective to inform her pictures with a kind of emotional baffle, how her images jumped from the wall to say hello with one hand and pushed you away with the other, and he wondered if she knew how appealing she was, how lovable and how impossible to leave she was when she let this show, not just in her work, but in herself. He wondered how she, who was so good at looking, could not see that same wound in their mother.

"I asked her to tell me how to be a good mother."

"What did she say?"

"She said I should have thought of that when I went to bed with Theo. She said I was lucky the woman didn't have me arrested."

"You know," said Peter, thinking of the chill that had settled over their parents after Roland's death, when he was too small to understand why he was no longer the center of their world and wondered what he had done to cause it, "I don't think kids are ever too young for the truth. You'd be surprised what they can handle if given the opportunity. I think a good mother would do that. And you know what?" he asked, taking her hand.

"What?" she said into her arms, now folded on the table.

"You're a very good mother, better than Willy will ever know," said Peter softly into her ear. "And Theo adores you."

Claire's eyes were closing, but she forced them open and smiled at this.

"Why don't you tell her what you're afraid of and trust her with it?" said Peter quietly and with a love that did not need to be spoken.

THEO DID NOT wake up when Claire stepped softly into the guest room, undressed, slid under Aunt Molly's blue-and-white star quilt, careful to stay clear of the bulky bandage lying awkwardly on the sheet, and touched Theo's bare shoulder with just enough pressure to cause her to sigh deeply, which meant she would roll over and let Claire snuggle at her back. Claire turned her face toward the pillow and into the warm curve of Theo's neck and raced the advancing light to sleep.

11

In the dream, he is a big man with large, gentle hands. His hair is a warm reddish-brown, quite long and curly, a sturdier version of the soft down on his chest that shows, when he moves, inside his denim cowboy shirt. It is my own hair with the flame turned down to Low. His words start somewhere deep inside him and rumble up to a wide, generous mouth, creased by what I imagine is an easy laugh. Deep bass notes hang in the air long after they are spoken. I try to make him speak to me, but he is too tall and cannot see me at his side. I tap the hard muscle of his thigh, but he cannot feel it. I call up to him, but he cannot hear me. He is holding Theo's hand and she is smiling. Claire is sitting on a bed full of potato chips and offers a bag to Theo, but she won't accept it and puts her hands in her pockets when Claire insists. Claire begins to cry and Carl comes out from under the covers and wraps his thin arms around her neck. He fixes his dark eyes on her and calls her Mommy, but she pushes him away and calls after Theo and the man with silver-gray eyes. I run after them and just as I reach them, I wake up.

"I'M GONNA PEE. Wanna come?"

"No thanks, I've already had one."

It was a Saturday afternoon, a few weeks before school let out for the summer, and I was spending the day with Uncle Baxter, one of the last before my month at the farm. We were eating bologna sandwiches with mustard, pickles, and potato chips on disgusting white bread, the kind you can use to hang wallpaper if you run out of glue.

Aunt Jessica was in the dining room arranging the table for one of her "little suppers," as she called the parties she gave on Saturday evenings when they weren't on location in London or in Morocco or any of the other places named on the collection of postcards in my dresser drawer addressed to "Cher Willy . . ." "Mon Enfant Squeezable . . ." "Monsieur Bébé . . ." "Willito . . ." "Dear Gorgeous One . . ." During these suppers Uncle Baxter held forth on his latest coup for the antiques shop and Aunt Jess stirred new people into the evening as easily as the exotic-sounding spices she carried home in bits of colored tissue paper and knotted cotton handkerchiefs for the dishes she always gamely tried, but never quite carried off the way Theo could.

That night, they were having something called tagine, but that afternoon Uncle Baxter said, "We need to provide Mr. Willy Bouvier Hirsh with some perspective on what manly men eat for lunch on Saturdays when there are no women around," and fixed bologna sandwiches for the two of us, despite Jessica's horror at the sight of them on our plates. "Next you'll be taking him to a poker game," she had sniffed.

Aunt Jess looked up from the army of silver candlesticks she had been amassing in the center of the huge table. Its base was really a pair of richly veined black marble pedestals that had once held up a mirror in J. P. Morgan's bedroom, and on top a slab of beveled glass floated dramatically and ran the length of the room. Alongside it sat a church pew they had unearthed one summer in a dusty attic down near St. Ives when they drove England's winding Cornwall coast, the same summer they found my antique rocking horse and the cache of royal livery buttons—onyx for Claire, said to have been worn for Queen Victoria's mourning, and silver greyhounds for Theo's green velvet waistcoat. The long Gothic bench, with its pocket for prayer books and the hymn sheets for what Uncle Baxter called Gregorian sing-alongs, was now used to store their vast collection of placemats and napkins and table runners. It was polished smooth, its patina arising from centuries of devout behinds sliding out of the slightly canted seat designed to encourage unwilling souls into the kneeling position, but now it was buried under a pile of fat cushions in an inky-blue toile depicting Napoleon's victory over what looked to me like a flock of geese.

Aunt Jess shook her silky black Louise Brooks hair from somewhere inside one of the enormous gilt mirrors cantilevered on each end of the room.

"Willy Nilly, it's amazing you survived all that bathroom business. I remember your mommy being so scared you'd never see a penis and grow up thinking you were some kind of defective girl, she made Uncle Bax drag you into the loo every time he had to tinkle."

"Poodles tinkle, Jess love. Real men pee," said Uncle Bax, brushing the crumbs off his handlebar mustache and curling up the edges, so I could see the lumberjack face he was making for me.

"Whatever," said the huge almond eyes in the mirror.

My aunt Jessica was the kind of person who couldn't say "pee" if her life depended on it. I couldn't imagine her peeling off her Levi's, swiping down her underpants, sitting and talking to me or to Theo in the next room in the absentminded way Claire left the bathroom door open and attended to this annoying interruption of anatomy without missing a word in the conversation.

The mood was not so lighthearted when Theo and I arrived that morning. The day had started out uneventfully, all three of us walking through the park to Fifth Avenue, idley chatting about Aunt Molly's peach chutney for the store, Uncle Peter's latest and most brilliant editorial on land-hungry developers, Suzie's newest adventure in dating (the owner of a discothèque that boasted a tank of live snakes and scorpions), Harry's case of poison ivy and how we would have to remember to pack calamine lotion for my vacation.

We talked about how much Baxter and Jess would miss me when I was at the farm, and what he and I would do that day while Theo worked on a new menu and Claire walked over to St. Mark's Place, where she was observing the odd mixture of Hell's Angels and hippies, natural-born enemies that seemed to have joined forces in the battle for space with uptown boutiques and newly sprouted fern bars. What time they should reconvene for dinner, who might be there—it was easy, nonsense family talk and it carried us through the muddy, rain-slicked park, which was beginning to show signs of an early summer. We covered everything except why this was another Saturday that would not be spent with Carl and why a morning like this could turn ugly for no reason an eight-year-old could see.

As we stepped onto Fifth Avenue, we found ourselves nose to

nose with Grandma's doorman, who was banishing a pile of leaves to the gutter.

"Hi, Buddy," we all sang.

"So your father don't slip," said Buddy, touching his cap to Claire as we marched past the building, returning his salute in unison.

"How's the grandlad?"

I smiled from beneath my Grange cap, which I hadn't taken off since Uncle Peter had explained it was what real farmers wore on their tractors.

"Buzz up a hug up to Barnaby," Theo called over her shoulder.

Two very thin women in short plaid skirts and Capezio flats walked by, wheeling identical blue strollers.

"Did you know that twinsets cause cancer in laboratory rats?" said Claire, smirking at them.

"You should probably warn your mother," said Theo, stiffening a bit, unsure of what might be next. I felt my own muscles follow suit.

"For your information, I could have had a pre-war, park view, twinset kind of life, too, you know," Claire said, while I silently mouthed the words to the rest of a conversation which I had heard more than once since Mrs. Jacoby had come to our apartment.

Theo's eyes narrowed and I saw that she was about to say something but had thought better of it. I wondered if she was going to remind Claire that she could not have had me by herself because she was not my birth mother, but only my "family mother," as they explained when I was too little to know any better and asked if they both carried me in their stomachs. But the moment passed.

"I could be picking up Willy from Brearley—calling him Wills, of course—skiing in Gstaad, driving out to the polo matches in the Range Rover, planning a benefit for the preservation of crown molding," Claire continued, oblivious to the color rising in Theo. "Claire Hirsh of the Manhattan and Long Island Hirshes has nuptials held against her will and will heretofore be addressed as Mrs. Spunky Danforth, Three Sticks. Jess could write the announcement. I'm sure she could write something absolutely ridiculous about what we'll wear."

"That's really mean, Claire. Jess is your best friend, and you don't exactly have a corner on the market for self-expression. Why can't you appreciate that she loves beautiful things and has a gift for describing them, instead of picking on her for not being a serious artist. Art is made in different ways by different people," Theo said, quickening her pace as if to outdistance Claire's dangerous mood.

"It's *fashion,* for God's sake," said Claire.

"Just like that big, black, ridiculously expensive Italian bag you simply must have for your precious Leica and spare rolls of film," Theo shot back.

"You're not exactly the butch-haircut-and-Birkenstocks type yourself, darling," Claire said evenly, and I imagined these things were not very pretty because I had learned to understand sarcasm, which was Claire's favorite way to fight without raising her voice.

Earlier that winter, when Claire eyed a group of elderly women and said they looked like escapees from a mink farm, little alligator shoes scratching the pavement like claws scurrying along under their ankle-length fur, Theo laughed. We made a game of spotting them, disappearing into Gristede's or Greenberg's Desserts, popping out of the Met, swarming out of the boutiques and little restaurants that line the side streets between Park and Lexington. Extra points were given for matching hats and handbags.

On another such day, Claire slipped the Leica out of her bag and pretended to shoot us grinning at her from inside our mufflers, but she had really aimed between us at a woman who was standing near a fire hydrant waiting for what looked like a rat on the end of a rhinestone leash to relieve itself. Both were wearing mink coats.

"I wonder what Jess would say about this," Claire had teased, happy with what she knew was a great picture of wealth not necessarily insulated against bad taste. "What would the caption say?" she asked, starting the game. "'You look like a dog; why not dress like one?' No. Jessica would be subtle. How about 'Matching minks and diamond collars bring out the animal in both of you'?"

"Why not something simple and direct," Theo had offered. "All you have to do is learn to lift your leg!"

"We need something more socially conscious." Claire had walked along, entertaining herself with captions for her picture, forgetting we were there.

"I've got it," she shouted triumphantly into the gentle snow flurry that had begun as we walked. 'Does an animal have to die so you can dress to kill?' "

"Your mother, the artist," Theo had said to me, shaking her head with mock disapproval, eyes full of love.

Now, only a few months later, there was no laughter and her eyes were cold. I got the feeling that even though I fought my natural instincts as a New Yorker and waited patiently at each corner for the light to change ("Cross at the green, not in between") and even though I looked both ways, I was going to get hit by a truck I would never see coming.

"Why do you always make fun of people who are different from you and expect the same people to respect the fact that you're a little different from them?" demanded Theo, crossing away from A La Vieille Russie, taking a shortcut between the bored horses waiting to pull a line of hansom cabs, ignoring their irritated snorts as she pushed through them. "Claire, this is not about Jess," she said, stopping in front of the statue of Abundance across from the Plaza, refusing to go any farther.

"No, it isn't," answered Claire.

"What, then?" said Theo, holding her ground.

"It's about your insistence on keeping our son in that damn snooty school with all those vain, shallow, and bigoted people," said Claire. "It's about us and how you're changing. It's about Willy and how he's going to have nothing but heartache if we don't get him out of there."

We watched her disappear into the crowd that hungrily pressed itself against the windows at Tiffany's and Bergdorf's, Rizzoli and Charles Jourdan. It swallowed her up like the feeling that came over me the first time Carl turned away and I realized I no longer had a best friend.

It was only ten-thirty when Theo and I arrived and Aunt Jess was hard at work on one of her columns. She sat at the lipstick-red typewriter perched on a cluttered satinwood table full of clippings, sketches, photographs, hair clips, swatches of silk, tweed, herringbone, satin, buttery suede, a large basket full of scarves and bracelets. This particular morning, a lone shoe of aubergine velvet fit for a lord sat atop a pile of soft wool of the same rich hue. As she worked, waves of Puccini crashed over her and out into the garden beyond her cozy study. When Theo, Uncle Baxter, and I passed her open door, I noticed she was typing with her eyes closed.

"Hi, Aunt Jess."

"Willy, darling. You're here!" She looked startled, as though she was surprised to find she was not in the atelier of some as-yet-undiscovered dressmaker toiling in destitution and lonely anticipation of Jessica's footsteps on the stair. In the slightly breathless way she had when she was on to something really interesting, she blew us a kiss, then leaned over, touched the fabric coiled on the desk next to her, and said from somewhere in the world she had been inventing, "Isn't it ironic that something as luxurious and as perfect and as outrageously expensive as cashmere could possibly contain the word *'mere'*?"

"Nothing short of stunning," Uncle Baxter said, raising a bushy eyebrow at his wife, who was, in his opinion, well on her way to becoming the world's youngest eccentric. "Completely incongruous. You should really mention that to someone, darling," he said, smiling fondly at his dotty wife. Aunt Jess had a way of turning these minor revelations into compelling fashion copy that urged readers to rush away from the mundane details of their lives and join the swarm of cabs heading to Saks or Bergdorf's or Bendel's in the frenzy of acquisition that made the sacrificial lunches of lettuce leaves and poached chicken seem worthwhile.

Aunt Jess loved losing herself in her work, and Baxter knew better than to try to summon her back (it would be hours before she needed to see to the preparations for that night's dinner), but that morning an uncharacteristically tense Theo in need of a talk waited patiently for her, while Uncle Bax did his best to entertain me.

"YOU WANT to walk to the park?" Baxter applied a gentle pressure at my back, nudging me away from the study.

"Nah, we just walked here," I said, remembering Theo's angry steps swallowing long blocks, lights turning green in her path, fueling her march, my own steps quickening with her escalating mood, trying to keep up with her, afraid to ask why Claire had suddenly turned away and disappeared into a westbound block.

"We could have an exciting round of you-know-what," Uncle Baxter suggested, seeing my mood was low.

"Where's Papa?" wasn't as much fun with Uncle Bax as it was with Carl, because I knew he was playing the game just for me, even though he explained his father was lost, too, somewhere off the coast of Bermuda when I asked him if the elder Baxter ever came to America and visited him in New York.

"Old Dad got hit by a flying cricket bat and died of a cerebral hemorrhage a week later," Baxter had explained. "Mother remarried ten years later, a decent chap named Cuthbert, but when the old bloke looked up at the mantel and saw the silver art deco cocktail shaker with Dad's remains—Dad loved his martinis, he did," said Baxter, laughing in spite of himself, "all he could do was wonder what sort of container he'd end up in.

"The poor man became so distraught at the idea of his remains in an egg coddler or a pickle jar or tucked in the toe of his patent-leather evening pumps, he suggested they take a cruise and give his predecessor a decent burial at sea. So one night, my old dad had his ashes hauled right up on the top deck in a full moon."

"Was he a sailor?" I had asked.

"The funny thing is, he never liked the water. Didn't swim. Hated boats. But Mother's husband feels much better."

True or not, Baxter's stories had a way of shaking me out of the small tragedies that beset growing boys, so I soon learned not to ask too many questions or spoil the gift; but that day I sensed something going on. I noticed how Theo let Jessica hug her for a long time before they moved into the study and Aunt Jess softly closed the door behind them.

"C'mon, let's go play store," said Uncle Bax, determined to amuse me. "It's too early," I said. "C'mom, we'll eat afterward, when the coast is clear," he insisted.

Our Saturday custom was to have lunch, walk over to MacDougal and the shops, where he'd let me sit on the furniture while he spoke respectfully to the handsome young couples who wandered in and out of the rooms, pretending they knew what they were looking at, pretending they could afford his prices. Baxter knew he really didn't have to open up for these people, because they rarely bought anything, but he told me browsing was part of what they did on weekends after brunch and he couldn't disappoint them.

In New York on Saturdays and Sundays, doing the galleries, flea markets, boutiques, and antique shops like Uncle Peter's was a kind of mating ritual. They played at furnishing imagined apartments. They seduced each other with their knowledge of the postmodernists, the performance artists, and the new graffiti kings. They slouched in and out of the galleries, stood before my mother's own work, and in reverent tones discussed the deep emotional issues of the day. They used the word "resonate." They carried bags that proclaimed their familiarity with the shifting moods of fashion and rattled with trinkets and found objects as they moved from store to store.

It was, Uncle Baxter had explained, a kind of courtship that was fueled by the consumption and admiration of the same things, a kind of visual shorthand that tells people who do not yet have the wisdom or the courage to look into the heart for what they have in common; to see that they come from the same place; that they are safe with each other. In a city as enormous and as isolating as New York, unlike London with its suffocating rules designed to sort out these and even more important matters and with nothing but appearances to recommend strangers to one another, Uncle Baxter pointed out that this behavior was quite common. "None of that 'Not our kind, dearie' rubbish over here, old sport." He was always quick to favorably compare his adopted city to "old blighty."

As we walked to the store, Baxter and I usually made a game of pointing these couples out where they lounged in the charming little cafés that line the crooked Village streets, sipping cappuccino and espresso, feeding each other little bites of cheesecake and cannoli, their eyes drinking each other in, the day's packages tumbling around them, discarded like so many articles of clothing and as Jessica might have put it, "melting into each other like good cashmere."

Uncle Baxter did not enjoy the browsers that day, nor did he flirt with the women and wink at the men and tell long, outrageous stories about the beautiful things in the store, elaborating pedigrees, generously offering the box of After Six mints he called digestives and kept on his Jacobean desk even though he knew the browsers would leave with nothing of consequence—a modest silk dresser tassel that might turn up around a pretty neck, or one of the small silver frames he had had reproduced from their Georgian ancestors.

Baxter did not say that this repartee brought back good memories for him as he often did and told me no stories of his own crazy courtship of Jessica, not that morning. Instead, he focused on me as though he were seeing me for the first time, as though there were a hairline fracture somewhere inside me and he was assessing the damage, trying to figure out where it was so he could reinforce it without destroying my lines, the way I saw him fix the curve of an armchair, stabilize the ball and claw of a prized table.

I did not have much heart for watching the people who would surely wander in and out of the rooms and ask for the prices listed in the book near my special chair, or for listening to the banter that always put them at their ease. Sensing this, Uncle Baxter did not flip the "Closed" sign when he unlocked the shop's creaking door.

"Let's just putter today," he said, as his keys found their mark in the ornate silver temple bowl on his desk.

We headed towards the back room to look for the ivory chessmen for the seventeenth-century tournament board Uncle Baxter had set up on the gateleg table near the front door.

"Harry says Grandma Hirsh called last weekend while they were playing badminton on the front lawn and Uncle Peter got really mad and hung up on her." I said this into a deep container full of packing popcorn near the delivery entrance.

"You must have been pretty mad yourself, to pop Carl like that," Baxter said into his own crate and there was a mixture of pride and maybe even a little amusement in the question, as though he were seeing a new side of me, a side he liked.

"I guess," I said, remembering Carl's face, how ugly and small he seemed the second just before I punched him and how scared he looked when he realized the blood spurting on his sweater was his own. I did not say how much I missed him.

"Can you keep a secret?"

I nodded. "Sure."

"Promise not to tell Jess or your moms."

"Okay."

"I think he deserved it." Uncle Baxter grinned his evil grin, the one that always made Jess's eyes roll dramatically before she said, "Bax, for goodness' sake, be attractive!"

"If somebody says something bad about you or your moms, it's okay to haul off and show 'em what you've got. That's what your old Bax thinks. I'm not telling you to solve everything that way, kiddo, but I think there's too damn many women in the family, telling us how to behave."

"Uncle Bax."

"Right here."

"Are they fighting because of me?"

"Nah," said Uncle Bax, unconvincingly.

"Are they going to get a divorce?"

"I wish I knew, sport," he said, pretending he was frowning at the empty carton, which did not contain the chessmen we were looking for.

12

I believe that forgiveness given prematurely is its own form of punishment. When the hand is offered before the heart says it's time, judgment lurks behind every smile (the way a speck of blood clings to the gap between tooth and gum, and tells you there is something wrong beneath the toothpaste pink brightness.) When forgiveness is coerced or offered for the wrong reasons, every incident adds to the bulging case of evidence mounting in the silences between words. Every gesture, every conversation, every glance carries an unbearable weight, until the pressure can no longer be contained and one event forces the one who has not forgiven into an action that comes as a shock to everyone but the one who knows it as another escalation in a battle that has never stopped raging in one-sided, long-suffering silence.

Claire said this is the moment the camera records when it sees the subject before its presence is noted, before the lip has had time to curl out of the grimace worn by people who are too quick to please, before the eyes brighten and mask malice, when a trick of light reveals the lie.

I've seen this myself with drunks when they feign sweet temper and spite rises up higher and higher out of each successive glass until the very thing they work so hard to hide strangles them in such a familiar way its appearance is loudly celebrated and the truth shouts in whiskey's coarse voice.

Forgiveness is never the dramatic end of things we've all seen on the big screen, the instant cleansing of hurts, but the only beginning of a slow rewinding of trust. Often it is a tactic when one sees the other is unwilling to risk a staggering loss rather than strike a compromise, forcing the issue to retreat into a manageable, yet pernicious, silence. There in the shadows, the wound crusts over, infects, and feeds on every slight.

Theo told me some people eat, growing large with their secret. Some slide into the mosquito net of drugs, while others wear a perpetual look of pained sweetness. Still more turn to prayer, good deeds, philanthropy, and the protection of orphaned children and animals while they wait for their moment.

In my own boyish experience, I saw what happened in school when the teacher made us apologize for words and deeds we were not yet ready to accept as cause for contrition, when we were forced to lose something of ourselves in the name of peace. We could only lie in wait, harboring thoughts of gruesome revenge while we played alongside our prey without tipping our hands.

I know now that real forgiveness is a lot like being tall. It sneaks up on you in small doses. You never see it until all at once you see people from a more sympathetic perspective and you know you're there. You sense it in the generosity of your actions, in the softening of the heart, and in hundreds of small acts of genuine kindness and you realize no other course was ever an option, much less more desirable. You no longer give too much to hide your guilt, and you no longer believe the word "no" holds the power to lay bare the coldness of your heart.

Claire was not the first person Mary Hirsh had pretended to forgive. She had never forgiven my grandfather Barnaby for shutting her out after Roland's death. He had chosen a silent grief that did not include her, and he kept to himself the empty place that had once been filled by my uncle, the flaxen-haired boy named after Barnaby's own father, the son who would inherit the Hirsh instinct for business and make him proud. That place was now occupied with business deals and meetings with other men who never spoke of their own scarred hopes, and who appeared promptly and in appropriate attire for their wives' constant round of dinner parties and benefit galas. Like Barnaby, they attended to their social responsibilities with silken charm, revealing nothing of themselves in the rapt interest they paid their dinner companions, first to the left, then to the right.

Mary suffered this loss because it wasn't in her nature or in her upbringing to do otherwise. It would never have occurred to her to plumb her own emotional depths, nor would she have known what to do with the feelings she found. She could not simply ask her husband to share his grief, nor could she give him the kind of comfort he would never have solicited, only accepted with unspoken gratitude. Mary did not question her husband's distance because it covered the deeper wound of seeing Roland every time she looked at her daughter. She did not grieve with her daughter or try to understand Claire's special loss—the loss of self that always comes with the death of a twin—because she did not know how. Mary hid behind her belief that adults who acknowledge the feelings of children, even those ungainly swans in the making who show signs of impending adulthood, are courting disaster in their pandering to unchecked adolescent emotion. Mary simply assumed Claire would leave these feelings behind with her sophomoric crushes and the dreadful poetry she penned onto the thick pages of an artist's sketchbook.

In a family that understood such things, Claire showed all the signs of survivor's guilt and bore the full brunt of her parents' grief. She affected the tapping of Roland's fingers on a table, the wink that took the sting out of the truth as he saw it, and when these gestures were greeted not with kindness and understanding, but with shock and stern reprimands, as though she had trodden on the velvet cord that sealed off his room, she retreated in small ways and the woman I knew as my mother was slowly formed, not unlike the tree in California that grew in spite of the hole in its trunk you could drive a Greyhound bus through.

It never occurred to my grandmother that twins are bound by a cord that cannot be severed at birth, during life, or even in death, and that Claire had not merely lost a brother, but a large piece of herself. Once while in her daughter's room, Mary slid her arm into a sweater pocket to turn it right side out and found a sheet of paper that had been balled up and thrust in its deepest corner. In turquoise ink and Claire's crabbed hand, it said: "How can I deny my will to eat? I ate your flesh to succor mine long before it was time to leave our mother. I left you behind, but I carry you within. You are my dark side, my will to win, my other."

Mary folded the piece of paper and slipped it into her daughter's desk drawer where Claire would find it with her journal and other evidence of a budding diarist and not remember that it had been any place but there. It was too late, Mary decided; the scab was beyond picking. Pounds melted away from Claire's naturally slim frame the year Roland died; during a particular gaunt period, Mary almost mentioned the poem, but decided to let nature take its course. *Girls that age are always dieting,* reasoned my grandmother. But Claire did remember—how Mary averted her eyes when they came in to clear away Claire's untouched plate. She remembered a pink sweater with empty pockets.

When I told Annie the story of my mother's lost twin, it was she who made the connection between Claire's guilt about eating, her determination to take up less than her allotted space in the world, and her love for round, ripe Theo who would feed a parking meter if it stood at the table long enough. But that was years later, when many things were understood in the clear light of retrospect.

Mary never forgot that Roland came first after a hard night of labor that ripped her open and drenched her bed and caused her to curse Barnaby, who was waiting it out at his club. There, men of his generation and standing accepted cigars and brandy for their progeny, while at home their exhausted wives were given a touch of rouge and cleaned up for appraisal. Mary cursed the kind, yeasty-smelling woman who held cold cloths to her wrists and temples and murmured a constant stream of comfort. In the last painful minutes the boisterous baby boy was joined by a screaming infant girl who echoed his cries and his image.

When my grandmother looked at Claire and later at Theo and me, I believe she always saw that loss, never her gain.

AUNT MOLLY RUMMAGED in the cedar chest for sweaters that had not yet been aired of their mothballs. Harry and I felt the late August chill in the earliness of dusk and in the growing distance we put between ourselves in preparation for the inevitable separation of the new school term that would reunite him with his classmates and remind me of the one who had chosen not to be my friend. As we readied ourselves for this annual separation, I felt the clammy skin of this kind of slow death forming around my mothers.

They no longer fought with any passion. Their disagreements

seemed to have lost the energy they once had—and with it, perhaps, the belief that enough conviction could really change anything. There were no more stormy scenes on Fifth Avenue, no more tearful reconciliations at the urging of loving friends. Forgiveness came too easily. But on its heels, the signs of a deeper loss—a slight incline of the head, a dull look in the eye, resignation and defeat in the line of a shoulder, a door that closed too softly.

Theo and Claire became wary of each other, as though one false word might destroy their carefully constructed truce. They avoided words that had to do with the private time between them, words like "honey," "sweetheart," "Boovie," and "bug," words that were once spoken in rounded laughing tones, filling the house with their mischief and filling me with a sense of peace. They avoided any discussion of how we should present ourselves to the world, what kind of school I should attend, where we should live, Mrs. Jacoby and Carl.

Claire wanted us to make friends with other mothers who lived in similar circumstances and to move away, if necessary, to where there were no Mrs. Jacobys and Mrs. Langelottis and people down the hall who warned their sons away from us.

Theo had begun to make new friends, friends she said would provide a more balanced view of the world than Claire was willing to provide.

"Can't you just pretend we're a traditional family?" I heard Theo whisper one night. "I know what I am and what you mean to me. I don't care. If it means Willy is accepted by his teachers and the kids in school, why do you have to care so much about what people think about us?"

Their voices became more shrill, and I pulled the pillow over my head to block out the cruel sound of Theo hissing, "I am his real mother and I will do whatever is right for *him*—not *us,* Claire, him!" I kept it there as the strangled sound of sobbing filled Claire's tiny darkroom and drifted out into the sleeping apartment; Theo kicked a door shut to keep it out of their big bed, where her own heart succumbed to the gasping shock of having found itself torn so agonizingly between two people she loved more than life.

After that, I tried to stay out of their way as much as possible.

One of Theo's new friends was a recently divorced woman named

Bitsie Clark whom she had met while catering a brunch to benefit the Preservation Society.

"Please. Call me Bitsie," she had said when Theo had looked down at the name tag that read MRS. CARTER LEIGH CLARK, JR., "everyone does." Bitsie had been filling all her time with charity work to staunch the flow of blood from a deep gash recently inflicted by her husband's decision to leave her for his young legal assistant. "I don't know which he found more attractive," she had said over the small steaks and oysters Theo had provided to capture the taste of the grand and copious food served at New York's Victorian tables, "her legs or her family lineage."

Theo had seen the thin line of bitterness around Bitsie's mouth, heard the sense of betrayal in her voice, but when she found out Bitsie also had a son in the fourth grade, she decided to bolster her confidence in forming new relationships and promptly invited her to lunch at the store.

I suspect Theo liked Bitsie mostly for the freedom she allowed in her ignorance of our family situation, but I also think she felt a sisterly sense of pride in the halting and often perilous progress "Bits in Pieces," as Theo jokingly called her, was making in her attempts to remake her life and replace her errant husband with someone equally *comfortable.* We all knew it didn't hurt that Bitsie had a son, Drew, also in the fourth grade at the Goodwin School, a little farther up on Fifth Avenue.

"I'm sure there are lots of men from good families who are comfortable *and* believe in monogamy; I just don't happen to know any of them," the determined Bitsie said one day after Theo forced her to laugh at the dating disaster that had befallen her the night before. It amused Theo that no one in Bitsie's crowd ever used the word "rich" except to describe the nouveau riche. Like "those awful people who own cabs," who were buying pop art, giving parties to which they had the audacity to invite Bitsie, who had no idea who they were or where they went to school—or even "*if* they went to school," as the befuddled Junior Leaguer pointed out the day she showed Theo the gaudy yellow invitation with its awful checkered border.

"I suppose this is what is meant by having a checkered past," quipped Theo, knowing exactly how to play this game but not really enjoying it. Whenever Bitsie said, "I'm as democratic as the next person, but . . ." Theo knew she was about to learn something she did not necessarily want to know about the habits of this inbred group of New Yorkers. Deep down, Theo wondered what Bitsie saw in her at all. Maybe that earth mother Claire used to find so damned attractive, she thought ruefully.

Theo brought selective bits of information and observation home to Claire. "Isn't it odd that in certain quarters, 'comfortable' is always understood to mean 'moneyed,' and in other neighborhoods it just means someone you can hang out with—go to a Mets game, read the Sunday papers, watch Archie Bunker, cook, have kids with. . . ."

Claire never took the bait or the peace offerings. All she needed to know was that Theo's friend preferred to be called by her childhood name, Bitsie.

"Ever wonder why there's no such thing as the *Senior* League?" said Claire coldly. "Because they couldn't call themselves Bitsie and Bopsie and Missy and Muffin, that's why. What do they call Drew—Poo?"

Open hostilities resumed one night when a sleepy and apologetic Bitsie called close to midnight to say she was sending me home in a cab after I had refused to sleep in one of the pup tents that had mushroomed on her living room floor for the Carnegie Hill version of sleep-away camp for Drew and a pack of howling boys from Goodwin.

"I don't know why he went down to the lobby in his pajamas like that, Theo, but I suspect all the other boys were bragging about their dads—you know, pup tents and camp and all that father-and-son business that is so important at this age," Bitsie had whispered as Claire rushed to dress so she could go down to our lobby to wait for me.

"Yes, he really misses his father," said Theo—as softly as she could, but not softly enough for Claire to miss it.

"You're a big brave boy, aren't you?" Mrs. Carter Leigh Clark, Jr., had said, trailing a good six inches of nightgown under a hastily donned trench coat, her naturally curly hair twisted, flattened and clipped around several large blue rollers that bobbed as she handed me the clothes I had not put back on in my haste to get out of the apartment and out of earshot of the snickers that caused the Abercrombie & Fitch pup tents to jiggle in the dark.

"Yes, ma'am," I said, wishing I could disappear into the swirling pattern of the carpet.

Theo had explained that Drew's father still loved him and would still be his father even though he was going to marry someone else, but as Drew's mother fiddled with my overnight bag, explained that she couldn't come with me and leave the rest of the boys alone, and looked ridiculous, I had a feeling that if she hadn't gone to bed every night with those stupid things on her head just to have long straight hair like everybody's else, he would not have run away with somebody else.

I did not cry until after the Clarks' doorman gave the cabbie our address and I sat in the stale-smelling darkness of the taxi's backseat as we plunged through the sleeping park.

Claire was on the sidewalk when I arrived. Upstairs, they both fussed over me and Theo told me Drew was only being mean because he missed his own father. Claire explained that the other boys followed his lead because sometimes people do cruel things in groups to show they belong. They put up a good front, but I felt their anger at my back pushing me up the stairs to my loft, out of its way.

"Don't you think it's time we moved to Berkeley or Amherst or somewhere like-minded people are raising children away from all these problems?" Claire demanded after she had settled me into my own bed, still feeling the sting of Theo's lie, heart breaking at the thought of me, holding the bag of clothes Drew's mother had brought down to her lobby.

"Great," snapped Theo. "Let's live in some hippie town full of tie-dyed T-shirts, vegetarians, and hairy women who can't raise their children in the real world. You could photograph people's auras and I could open a place called Tofu Take-Out, maybe adjust chakras in my spare time. Instead of saving for college, we could squirrel away two or three million dollars for the thirty or forty years of Freudian analysis Willy will need after a childhood like that."

"Stop making fun of me, Theo," warned Claire.

"I'm not making fun of you, I am simply trying to point out in terms you can understand that we will damage Willy irreparably by not showing him all the differences in life and allowing him to choose his own path."

"Well, he chose his own path, all right, didn't he?" Claire shot back. "Straight down to the lobby in his pajamas. Those kids showed him the door, Theo. I don't care what your prissy Miss Bitsie says, her son and his friends called our son names. They said something ugly like 'Your mothers are really dykes,' or maybe they just whispered it behind his back and Willy ran away as far as he could run in the middle of the night."

"If we could just go underground for a little while, Claire."

"Underground? Where is that, Theo? Is that where you get to be the mother and I get to be his aunt and Willy doesn't know who's who anymore?"

"What's the harm?" said Theo, asking herself as much as Claire. I wondered about that, too, thinking there wasn't much to recommend life above ground either.

Theo continued to see Bitsie and others like her. Some people came with husbands, some without. Some came with red dogs and houses in the Hamptons and lives full of charity work, others with full-time jobs and businesses of their own. But they all had one thing in common—boys my age, mean-spirited, spoiled, rich boys like Drew. In return for the pretense of lifelong friendship for me, Theo shared her prowess in the kitchen and her charm everywhere else. She played tennis with these women. She invited them to our apartment when Claire was off shooting (which she seemed to be more and more frequently), and she volunteered to take their children to the theater and to the park with us. She baked clown cupcakes for birthday parties, and devil's food with orange icing for Halloween.

I never let on that I preferred spending my time with Harry and Baxter, and Uncle Peter and with my new friend, Mr. Luis de Jesus Cosmopoulos, whom she did not know, whom nobody had ever met, except Uncle Bax, and even he hadn't realized he had.

One chilly afternoon in October, the phone rang and it was Bitsie. "Where is your mother?" she said.

"Which one?" I asked, stubbornly loyal to Claire.

"Well, Theo, of course, silly." I heard impatience and strain under the words.

Theo had a habit of smiling before she picked up the phone, the way people bounce a tennis ball a few times before serving. Bitsie had promised to phone when she got to the Vermont chalet with her new beau, as she coyly referred to the divorced father with whom she was currently sharing several homes and even more children, to confirm the arrangements for us to come up on Saturday morning.

"Theo, be a sport and don't come on Saturday night. It's going to be couples only and—well, you know what happens when a single woman shows up, all the women get edgy. Why don't you and Willy drive up for the day on Sunday and we'll have a nice lunch, maybe even have some snow."

"You know what's really funny?" Theo said when she realized I was standing in the kitchen doorway watching her. She was still smiling, even though there wasn't much reason to.

I shook my head.

"Claire isn't even here to say 'I told you so.' "

I didn't see much humor in this myself.

Like all children who live under the sentence of their parents' problems, I fought hard against the silence and growing distance by constantly nudging them closer to their shared history. I pointed to our wall and encouraged the languid reminiscing I remembered so well, which was always begun in the name of instructing me on my family history, but often as not ended up as their way of using the past to mend the present. But they no longer allowed themselves this luxury.

I pointed to the group photograph from Greece. "Tell me *Lesbians on Vacation,*" I begged, using the title of the movie Claire threatened to film about the kindness of a town that sent its entire male population to cheer up a planeload of widows, starting the story for them, easing them onto the common ground of that happy memory. I smiled at that first picture of Theo at the Fraser-Morris cheese counter and held their hands, but they would allow no blurring of the lines they had drawn.

WHEN SHE WAS HOME, Claire spent more time in her darkroom and in the Village with people who were "more progressive," people she claimed "understood the artistic nature," who believed in telling the truth about their sexuality and advocated flaunting it, if necessary, as a form of performance art and protest politics. "People," Claire informed Theo every chance she got, "who did not believe motherhood and lesbianism were at opposite ends of the planet."

Theo was usually asleep when Claire tiptoed into the apartment after one of her "evenings," as she called the frequent gatherings of intense and interesting women to which she was invited with increasing frequency and attended with one woman in particular, a hawkish person named Ruth who smoked incessantly and did not like me, even though she pretended otherwise.

Claire and I had been at Jessica and Baxter's; on the way home, just as we turned toward Sixth Avenue, Claire said, "What do you say, want to meet Mommy's friend Ruth?" I had wondered where she went at night when she left after dinner, but I was afraid to ask. I did want to meet her friend very much, but I simply shrugged my shoulders and we walked toward the river.

They talked for hours that afternoon, poring over photographs, reading aloud, eating oranges and drinking tea. They sat on a sticky leather sofa that creaked every time one of them shifted position or punctuated the conversation with a loud thump on the arms that sent the thick pottery mugs and plates clattering. I was left to my own devices in the book-strewn apartment, which smelled faintly of turpentine and a cat I could not find. Ruth peered at me from behind thick glasses that enlarged her eyes, but never once addressed me directly, instead asking Claire "if the child would like a soft drink or a cookie."

After one of those evenings—during which, I imagined, other women like Ruth gathered around the living room, their conversation multiplying the intensity I witnessed that day—Claire often headed straight for my loft, where she sat at the edge of my quilt, peering at me for a long time, her pale eyes glittering from the lateness of the hour, too much alcohol (which she never could hold), and something I would later recognize as coming as close to speaking her heart as she would dare.

One night, she padded upstairs, bent down, and whispered, "What shall I do, darling boy?" I felt the sadness and urgency in her voice, the warm breeze of it flutter past my ear, but I kept my eyes closed, feigning sleep, filling myself with the smell of tobacco and a dark, mossy fragrance that clung to her clothes and left her imprint on my pillow.

I don't know why I did this, why I didn't open my eyes and hug her that night. The fact that I didn't haunts me still, that she might have explained, told me something that would have changed everything, but I suspect I sensed she was communing with the idea of me and not the flesh-and-blood, stocky, red-haired reality. Maybe I was afraid to break the spell. Or maybe, if I woke up and spoke, I would not have been as lovable as I was in repose; I would have been easier to leave.

Theo used to say that taking pictures is a way of not participating, of staying out of the fray; it was preferable, she said, to dig right in and get your hands dirty, and even if life disappointed you, you could say you tried to affect its course. She said that was probably why she ended up a chef, because you could rearrange the elements, concoct something of your own invention, cut the bitterness with something sweet, add and subtract and know the second the experiment passed your lips whether you'd succeeded or not, and if you fell on your face, you always had the next meal as an opportunity to try again. She said this with no malice, no anger, and no accusation, as she had many times before, but with resignation and the deep sadness of knowing she was powerless to change what informs another's actions, even those of someone she loved.

It was the week before Christmas and Theo had just barely climbed out from under the exhausting pile of orders for pumpkin, mince, and sweet-potato pies and the mountains of cornbread stuffing customers begged her to make as late as the night before. This was the time of year Theo brought her work home, her concession to "making my numbers," which, she explained, meant doing a whole year's work in two weeks and being at home with us at the same time. Our red Parsons table groaned under the weight of the ingredients for other people's holiday dinners, brunches, cocktail parties, and office mixers. There were gift baskets in the making, platters of marzipan, pfeffernüsse, truffles, Christmas trees of spun sugar, and swarthy gingerbread men waiting for buttons, mustaches, and other distinguishing characteristics. When it was time for our own dinner, rather than move it all, we simply cleared a space for ourselves and ate around the gingerbread men as though they were friends of the family.

Most years, Theo did this work happily, humming carols and muttering silly stuff like "Never trust a cook who cannot lick his own fingers," while handing me a bowl of something wonderful—chocolate ganache, brownie batter, sticky cookie dough. Claire and I cheerfully proved we could be trusted as chef's assistants, licking something sweet from every available surface, inviting the pounds to add up to what Theo called her "seasonal seven" and to define the padding on my own large frame.

"Who said that?" she'd ask, humming into a bowl of something wonderful.

"Brillat-Savarin!" I'd answer without hesitation, my automatic response sounding suspiciously idiot savant–like in someone whose culinary horizons should not have extended beyond peanut butter and whose years barely added up to a decade.

There was none of that cozy closeness on this overheated night. Theo was bone tired and looked too thin, which was not only unusual at this time of year; it was not considered even remotely possible given her penchant for sampling her own work. Freezing rain needled our windows, and Theo worked with grim determination. In the harsh overhead glare of our kitchen, there were worried hollows in her cheeks, where last year at that time—before Mrs. Jacoby came into our lives—there had been only apples. The shadows carved bruised-looking half-moons under her eyes, setting off the sharp edge of a collarbone I could not remember ever having seen before. Standing out from each shoulder were knobby bumps that looked like the marks coat hangers leave in sweaters that should never be hung. But when I tapped them down, expecting them to give way to softly padded skin, they were hard and bony under my hand. She moved like someone begging for sleep.

I made a place for myself at our big red table and made a half-hearted pass at my homework. We were very much alike, Theo and I, in that we labored better in chaos than in the solitude Claire preferred and now demanded. Many years later, I found the manic buzz of a newsroom just the inspiration I needed for the noisy pursuit of journalism, but on this particular night there was no comfort in the clatter around me.

Theo worked silently and so did I. Afraid to interrupt her, and even more uncomfortable with the idea of being in another room with Claire, I plodded through the dull adventures of *Emilio y Los Detectives* for my beginning Spanish class, tripping over verb tenses to get to the sense of the simple tale, while the sleet clawed at our reflections on the icy pane.

Theo looked up but did not speak when Claire walked in, rubbing the darkroom out of her eyes.

"If anybody cares, it looks like I got some interesting stuff today," she announced to the refrigerator. Theo shook her head into the sink where she was rinsing out a muffin tin, but did not turn around.

I looked up and smiled at her. "I do," I said, as she sat down next to me.

"How's Emilio doing?" she asked. "Has he solved anything yet or are they saving it for when you have a bigger vocabulary?"

"It's kind of boring," I said, seizing on this tiny distraction as an opportunity to close the book.

"You know, they should put pictures in those books," Claire said to me as she looked at Theo's back, which stiffened slightly at the sound of this.

"That way, you could imagine what's happening before you actually learn the words," she continued.

"Or, you could decide what you want to happen and use the pictures to make your point," Theo interrupted coldly. Then, turning to me: "Got your favorite stuffing coming up, with a fresh cranberry sauce and roast chicken. Make a little dinner room on that table and I'm sure I could find some fudge brownies around here somewhere." She was working hard to smooth the sharp edge in her voice for me, and not quite succeeding.

"C'mon, Theo, give it a rest. We're all tired and overworked. Let's just have dinner," said Claire quietly.

Theo ignored this and arranged our plates over the stove, carrying each one to our chairs. When she sat down, she looked at Claire for a long time and said in a voice aching with sadness, "You know, I think taking pictures is a great way to avoid participating in life."

I stiffened, sensing something that would quickly accelerate into another one of their "discussions." These had already ruined most of our recent meals together—which were becoming much less frequent, Claire preferring to have me to herself during the day when Theo was at the store, leaving the evening to Theo and me and to her own plans, which did not include us.

Even though they never mentioned me directly, these discussions were always thinly veiled arguments. Each time I heard one of their opening salvos, I felt my food balling up in a knot at the bottom of my stomach, where it stayed, resistant to the forces of digestion for many hours. That night was no different. I prepared to turn up the volume on my thoughts to block out the sound of their disappointment in each other and mine in them.

Claire held her fork in the air for what seemed like five minutes and working her mouth, seemed to struggle against words that could not or would not make the final leap into the atmosphere of our kitchen.

"I'm not very hungry tonight," was all she said finally. She got up slowly, lifted her chair in to the table, taking care not to let it scrape, removed her plate, napkins, and cutlery, methodically transferred her dinner into the open containers from which Theo had just served it, gently closed the refrigerator, kissed me on the top of the head, put her hand on Theo's shoulder, and left the room. A few minutes later, we heard the sound of the shower, and some time after that, the front door closed softly behind her.

It would be many hours before we realized she was not coming back.

13

Theo and I didn't pay much attention to Claire's leaving that night. After a silent meal, punctuated by the buzzing of the timer, signaling several interruptions in which Theo jumped away from the table to execute a step that would not wait for us to finish our dinners, I returned to my homework, Theo to her baking, and each of us to our private thoughts about what was happening to our family. When Claire did not return late that night or the next day or the day after that, Theo fought her rising panic with calls to their friends.

"Don't worry, sweetheart, she'll be back. She has to sulk awhile," said Suzie, who was more concerned than she let on. "I'll call you the second I hear from her," she said, running a long nail down the pages of her own phone book, scanning the names of people who might have seen Claire.

"No, Jessica, I haven't called the police," said Theo to a very upset Jessica, who had just heard from Suzie. Theo was trying not to panic when she heard Baxter shouting that same instruction from somewhere at a distance from the phone. "Yes, I've tried the gallery . . . yes . . . and Thad . . . Peter and Molly aren't home. . . . Yes, I'll keep trying."

"We went to see somebody named Ruth who had a cat," I offered, realizing I didn't know any of Claire's other friends.

"I already called her, Willy. She says she hasn't seen Claire for a few days."

Theo took a long breath and dialed Mary Hirsh.

"We're having a rough patch, some problems," Theo began. "We had an argument the other night and I thought, well . . . I thought she might be with you, to cool off, think things over a bit."

As Theo struggled to find words that would not reveal the extent of her panic, but would say just enough to elicit the truth from Claire's mother, there was no response on the other end, no encouragement, none of the clucking and tsk-ing and other sympathetic sounds she'd heard from their friends as they listened to this fresh tale of disaster.

"If you know where she is, Mrs. Hirsh, please tell me. I'm beginning to get very worried," Theo pleaded, knowing she had exhausted herself, having said all she could without further encouragement from the other end. In the cold silence that followed Theo's plea, the evidence that my grandmother's "forgiveness" had been premature came down like a sentence.

"You know, Theo, we've discussed this situation with our son and we really must do the best thing for our grandson," Mary began.

"Well, I don't think you need to worry, Mrs. Hirsh. Claire and I can work this out ourselves," said Theo, shrugging off Mary's tone of voice and the chill it gave her, remembering that Doris always said this feeling was caused by someone walking over a grave. "I just need to know where Claire is right now," said Theo.

"I think it *is* necessary, dear," Mary continued, ignoring Theo's question. "We really can't allow this situation to continue—"

"*What* 'situation,' Mrs. Hirsh? What 'best thing for Willy'? What's Peter got to do with it?" The sudden pounding of the pulse in Theo's temple hurt, deadening the sound of her own words, pushing them into the buzzing blackness of the phone.

"May I remind you, Theo, that raising a young boy in a household like yours is unhealthy. I can't sit quietly by and allow my grandson to be pushed and pulled about in that sort of environment," said Mary coldly. "Your lifestyle is a form of child abuse and our attorney is appalled that Willy's grandfather and I have let this continue for as long as we have."

"Your attorney! Mrs. Hirsh, Willy may be your grandson, but Claire and I are his mothers and this is his home—"

"And may I also say, my dear," Mary interrupted, "that raising Willy in a household like yours is against the law; that any agency interested in the welfare of children would remove him immediately." Mary said this calmly, as though she were talking to a child or to a servant; as Theo hung up, she heard her say, "Did you really think we would allow this?"

Something in Mary's measured tone terrified Theo more than her words. It said that Mary had been waiting for a very long time. My mother thought about that night over nine years ago when I was born, when Mary had held Theo's hand and rolled her own tweed jacket into a ball to support Theo's aching, sodden head. Had she been planning this all along?

There's a photograph of my grandmother sitting stiffly on the ground in a pale pink linen suit which looked as though it might have been more at home at a garden party than at an impromptu picnic in Central Park. The spirit of that day is long gone—the sudden burst of enthusiasm for Jessica's romantic idea of transporting our Sunday dinner to the public lawn just beyond our windows, Claire laughing with her whole body as she skidded around the table packing our wicker hamper, plates and all, with the food Theo had just set out, Theo winding daisies into everyone's hair, including Uncle Peter's long blond wisps and my fiery mop, Uncle Baxter rummaging in the closet for Peter's old football, a bottle of wine in each pocket, Suzie slipping into an old pair of Claire's sneakers, Barnaby shaking his head at the silliness of "this new generation," Thad hoisting me up on his shoulders for the grand march into the park, Harry forgetting his sulk at Aunt Molly's refusal to let him eat the tops of the miniature cupcakes Theo had baked for Jennifer and Brooke's dolls, all of us singing our family version of Arlo Guthrie's song, "You can get anything that you want / At Theo's restaurant."

All of this is lost to the viewer now. All that remains is my grandmother sitting on a tattered Indian bedspread, her perfect crocodile pumps parked neatly on the ground next to her, heel lined up with heel as though they might be waiting for her on the scented floor of their closet, not on the scruffy lawn of Sheep Meadow. There is too much brightness around her eyes. At first glance, she seems to be working hard to appear oblivious to the imminent threat of grass stains on her expensive suit, but I now realize the people around her threaten her far more.

It is as though time has deliberately washed this photograph of all but its secret; I wonder what warnings live in other pictures, what signs I haven't yet seen.

I know my grandmother loved us very much, but even a child could see that she came alive whenever my mothers hit a difficult stretch. Even before Mrs. Jacoby and "the troubles," as my grandmother's Irish doorman called our bad times, the slightest display of temper or disagreement seemed to cheer her up. It would have been so much easier for her if Theo and Claire broke up.

Some say the heart already knows how everything is going to turn out, but the brain keeps it from telling anybody. I suppose I always knew my grandma Hirsh had never forgiven us, because I mentioned it to Mr. Cosmopoulos the first time we met.

I MET HIM just before Claire left for good. It was a few days after Thanksgiving, and I was walking back to school after lunch at The Latest Dish. Theo thought it best that I be given permission to do this, in order to avoid any further unpleasantness with Carl and the sizable following he had attracted in the wake of the "incident" the previous term, which had given him instant celebrity status as one who had been tainted by queers and lived to tell about it. I could not bear to see the proof that the most intense and important friendship in my young life had been forgotten in little more than a summer vacation, so I went to the store, where Theo wound a clean apron around her waist, sat at the round table she reserved for me near the door, nibbled at the edges of an onion bagel, and kept me company for as long as she could.

That frantic noon, we counted a record ten times that she had to jump up to wait on a customer before we decided I'd be late and she'd better wrap the rest of my meal to eat on the way back to school.

A heavy voice filled with gravel rolled up behind me and bounced off the back of my McCall blazer. "Hey mister, what's that you're eating?"

"Moussah-something," I answered, eyeing the man warily.

"Looks like moussaka to me," he said. "My mother used to make that when I was a kid in Crete. You Greek?"

"I dunno. Maybe," I said, holding my lunch close to me in case he made a move, the way Claire taught me to hold my tennis racquet on the way to the courts in the park.

"You gotta be somethin'."

I thought about the costume party my mothers had the year before I was born. I knew it had something to do with my birth, but I couldn't remember exactly what except that everyone talked about their family trees and what country their parents and grandparents had come from, so my mothers could pick my father, but I couldn't recall what they had said about ours. I knew Jewish and Protestant were religions; not where you're from.

"We're lesbians," I said finally, thrusting out my chin for the inevitable sneer.

"So you *are* Greek! I knew it!"

I was confused. People called my mothers many things, usually in a low whisper spoken from one side of the mouth in that deliberate way meant to leave you wondering whether you had actually heard or had only imagined what was said, but no one ever called them Greeks. I wasn't sure if I should hit him or run.

"Lesbos, mister. If you're a lesbian, you're from Lesbos. Coupla islands down from Crete, which means we're practically neighbors. Nice place. Clean. Not like here." As he spoke, he swept the pavement before him with a disgusted look and an imaginary broom. A rookie cop with a tender boy's neck that had not yet grown into the stiff blue collar of his patrolman's serge was absently writing tickets for the line of cars illegally parked along Third Avenue and ignoring the pleas of the owners, who dashed out of restaurants ahead of him, napkins still tucked into their well-pressed business suits, forks still in hand. He looked up from the tedium of his summons book over the bleat of his victims and narrowed his eyes at us. I didn't recognize it then—I had no reason to on the relatively vagrant-free streets of the mid-seventies—but it was a look that said, "Ain't you a long way from the Bowery?"

Just then, the man said something funny, something I didn't understand, which sounded like "teeny tie my shoe," but I was afraid to ask him what it meant. Maybe it was his name. Or maybe it was a nonsense word and he was crazy like Leon, who lived in one of the efficiency apartments over the store and frequently paced the sidewalk in front of Mom's window trying to decide what to buy before going in. Leon rubbed his head, rolled his tongue, and moved his eyes constantly, never looking directly at anyone, even Theo when she gave him extra cookies or a brownie.

He was odd, all right, and even from my taller-than-average fourth-grade perspective he looked at least seven feet tall, but I wasn't afraid of him. I couldn't tell you why. Something about his eyes. I just knew it. Leon always gave me the feeling he was capable of hurting someone and not remembering why. Even though Theo encouraged me to be polite, I always stayed behind the counter when Leon came in. He always looked dirty, too. But not this man. He just looked lived-in.

His hands were the biggest I'd ever seen. They hung at his sides like giant slabs of bacon, bright pink over the knuckles where the wind had chapped them and pale between the fingers where the weather could not penetrate, and they would have seemed dangerous if it were not for the fact that he kept them still as if he knew they could scare people if he used them too much.

Hair the color of octopus ink grew wild and as long as tentacles where the rubber band lost its grip on a thick ponytail and dark ropes coiled around his sharp cheekbones. They pointed to something high on the brow and in the proud aquiline plunge of his nose that hinted more at Diego Rivera than at Zorba the Greek.

Red suspenders held up a pair of faded jeans as soft and loose as a pair of Grandpa Barnaby's pajamas. I suppose what intrigued me at first was his interest in me and the fact that he called me mister, even though I was a kid.

He said it again. "Teeny tie my shoe."

"I guess they didn't teach you any Greek. I asked you your name, mister." The gold in his tooth glinted in the hard winter sun as he waited for my answer.

"Willy. Willy Bouvier-Hirsh," I said, still guarding the foam cup that held the rapidly congealing lunch Theo had spooned out of the long tin pan labeled moussaka.

"Mine's Mr. Luis de Jesus Cosmopoulos," he said with a crisp salute. "I know what you're thinking. Strange name. Everybody says so." He settled against a parked car the way a storyteller finds a comfortable position in an easy chair before leaning forward to cast his net with the words "once upon a time."

"My father met my mother the first and only time he ever left Crete," he started, folding his big hands over the pear-shaped stomach that pushed the suspenders to the breaking point. "He'd always wanted to see the Andes, saved up for years, and she was waiting for him right behind the front desk when he checked into his hotel in Lima. That's spelled like 'lima bean,' but pronounced '*Lee*mah.' " He barely paused for a breath before plunging back into his story. "Her name was Maria Teresa and she was the most beautiful girl he had ever seen. Part Castilian Spanish from some Conquistador way back and the rest pure Peruvian Inca." He was careful to pronounce the "th" sound in place of the "s" in "Castilian."

"Married her right on the spot. Well, a week later, anyway, after he talked her into it. By the time they got back to Crete, I was kickin' hard to get my start in the world and neither of my grandparents ever spoke to my father again. Can you imagine livin' in a fishing village no bigger than spit and never talking to your own flesh and blood when they passed you on the street? My grandmother wore black just like my father was dead. You know the word 'stoic'?"

I shook my head no.

"Well, that's the Greek way, boy. You could threaten to jump out of a twenty-story window and they just look at you. They named me Luis for my *abuelo.* Spanish for 'grandpop.' "

He wrote the word *"abuelo"* in the dust on the car's fender and next to it he wrote *"niño,"* with something he called a tilde over the second "n." He said, *"Neenyo,* that's what I was when all this happened, a boy, just like you," and suddenly his eyes went blank, the muscles in his face slackened, and he stared at me for a minute, seeing nothing.

"Mr. Cosmopoulos?" I was a little frightened, but I moved closer. "Are you okay?"

"Nah, I get a little lost sometimes," he said, pulling on his ponytail as though pulling himself back to his place in the story. His eyes brightened again, as if someone had switched on a lamp only he could see, and he continued.

"They named me Luis for my maternal grandfather, that means my mother's father, and Hay Seuss, that's how you say 'Jesus' in Spanish, for the savior who saved my father from marrying some moon-faced hick Cretan girl my grandparents would have picked out for him, and I can tell you they had no taste in women. Yessir, Mr. Bouvier-Hirsh. They named him for the good Lord who had the decency to drop him right on top of those Andes mountains where his bride and my mother, God rest her soul, was waiting for him to show up. Ain't that something? What about you?"

He talked as though he were running a race. I was tired just listening.

"That's my mother's store" was all I could muster, pointing to the red neon lips said to have once belonged to the owner of a famous speakeasy. Uncle Bax had found them in an estate sale and Theo hung them in the tiny shop window over the gleaming brass rod and the white lace French bakery curtains, just under the name, which was written in a graceful arc on the tiny shop's window.

I could make out the outlines of Theo's arms disappearing into the cases, then handing a square white box over the counter to someone on the other side. Later, when I understood such things, I could describe what I felt at that moment as the first stab of separation, the understanding that I was experiencing something wholly my own while my mother went about her business, oblivious to me standing just outside. I can't say this was altogether pleasant, and yet I felt an odd exhilaration.

"Some lucky one you are, mister!" He pursed his lips and whistled appreciatively. His eyes rolled in an exaggerated way I saw once in Claire's favorite Marx Brothers movie, *Duck Soup.* They shone like black olives in oil.

"I love her cannelloni with mozzarella, tomatoes and basil sauce. I take some home to Shorty every now and then. I wrap it in tin foil real good and it tastes like it just came out of the oven." He brought a huge paw to his lips and kissed his fingers when he said that and looked down at me.

"Now, Shorty would tell you he prefers your mother's puttanesca sauce. He says it's got just the right amount of heat and an authentic sense of immediacy. And I don't have to tell you why I'm an enchilada and moussaka man, what with my ethnic background and all, but those cannelloni . . . maybe there's a little Italian in me after all!" I guessed Mr. Cosmopoulos ate the way he spoke, with gusto and the singular enjoyment of a gourmet.

"When food is that good, you'd be surprised how far word of

mouth travels!" This last remark struck him as very funny. His booming laugh seemed to come up from the toes of his thick brown wingtips, which had soles like running boards. They were the shoes that fathers wore when dropping off my schoolmates in the morning on their way to the office, and they didn't seem right on Mr. Cosmopoulos, but he wore them with a certain eccentric panache, an incongruity Aunt Jessica would have described as "je ne sais quoi." "A regular underground sensation!" he snorted, these last words rocking him back into his private joke. "You're one lucky kid, with a mother who can cook like that. So Theo Bouvier is your mother."

"I've got two."

"Does the other one cook?"

"No. Claire takes pictures."

"What kind of pictures? Wedding and graduation pictures?"

"Nope," I said, trying hard to think of a way to describe Claire's photographs.

"They gave her a Guggenheim" was what I finally came up with.

"No kidding," he said, looking impressed.

"No kidding," I said proudly. "She takes pictures of strangers when they're not looking and people leave money with our doorman until they can take them home, but sometimes they buy them in a gallery after they're criticized and Aunt Suzie puts marks on them."

"Whaddaya say about that! Sounds real specialized. That's the ticket today. Everybody's a specialist. Not too much room for us generalists anymore." He seemed pleased that I had confirmed something he felt deeply, and he wore an exaggerated look of satisfaction tinged with resignation.

"So where you from?" he asked, changing the subject abruptly.

"Central Park West, but I go to school over on Seventy-fourth and Madison and my grandmother Hirsh lives on Seventy-second and Fifth and well, there's Mom's store. I guess we're from New York."

"I'd say you were. So what do your grandma and grandpop think of this two mothers business?"

"Grandma Doris and Grandpa Roy always say, 'As long as you're happy, that's what counts,'" and my grandpa Barnaby doesn't say much. But I don't think my grandmother likes it, even though she pretends she does."

I didn't tell him that my moms weren't as happy as they used to be and that I believed Grandma Hirsh wanted them to get a divorce, because saying that to someone, even a stranger, would have made it true. I was not yet able to acknowledge the fear that gnawed at me.

I didn't tell him that when we went to Grandma's apartment for Thanksgiving, even though Theo didn't want to go and everybody was on edge, I overheard her saying that I was Claire's boy and that Theo was her daughter's "friend."

"Sounds like you got yourself a grandma like mine, one of the Furies with a black dress and a personality to match, huh, mister?" He wagged his head at this and peered down at me with eyes that seemed to grow more luminous and unearthly, as though he had summoned a second sight that could see through me and all the way down to my secrets.

"Grandma Hirsh says black is too somber, and is appropriate only for funerals," I said, summoning a picture of my impeccable grandmother in her matronly pumps, pearls, and pale woolen suits with linings that rustled silk against silk, and the faint smell of lilies of the valley lingering wherever she sat.

"Aunt Jessica says she's a tweed-and-Chanel-Number-5 person."

"Who's Aunt Jessica?" he asked absently, looking at the policeman who was walking around a battered Chevy with an expired inspection sticker.

"She's not really my aunt, she's Claire's best friend. She tells women how to dress in her fashion magazine, and Mom says she's a glorified clothes hanger, but I think she's real neat."

"So your grandmother's a tweed gal, hey?" ignoring my answer to his last question, his gaze still moving off over my head.

I followed it, but could see only the wide avenue, people rushing along the sidewalk, heads down, eyes hard against the onslaught of horns, sirens, jackhammers, and any hint of trouble in the faces of strangers.

"You know, sometimes I think it's easier when you can see what you're up against, don't ya think?" Mr. Cosmopoulos said, now looking even more directly at me as though he had been less than attentive before.

I wasn't quite sure why I agreed, but I nodded at this and we stood on the sidewalk like two old friends who understood each other perfectly.

EACH TIME WE MET, I learned something else about my burly new friend Mr. Cosmopoulos. He worked odd jobs here and there. One day he told me all about the newspaper business and how trees were ground into pulp for only one day's use; he was about to make a killing in the new recycling industry.

He lived in what sounded like a cramped apartment in the twenties somewhere on Madison Avenue with a man named Shorty, who had a bad temper and couldn't keep a job long because, he said, "people didn't understand perfectionists anymore." Usually, I ran into him near the store; when I spotted his denim-blue and red bulk leaning up against a parked car, I ran in and got us both lunch, which sometimes he didn't eat, patting his stomach and taking care to keep the soot out of the wrapper. "Shorty's going to love this," he'd say. "I think I'll save it for him." After a while, I remembered to get enough for all three of us.

Once, when I asked Theo to ladle out far more chili than even a kid my size could eat, I told her I wanted extra for a friend, "just somebody I met," I said, looking down at the spotless French-blue tile on the floor. Theo smiled happily into the refrigerated showcase, leaning into the tray with the generosity of a mother delighted to know her son was finally becoming popular. I didn't really lie; I just let her think I'd made friends with someone from school. After that, it was easier to surprise Mr. Cosmopoulos with beef stroganoff and stuffed mushrooms, raspberry chicken, and lamb curry taped and wrapped tightly to take home to Shorty.

Some days, he was waiting for me near the hole in the fence near the McCall schoolyard. "Hey mister, what'd you learn today?" was his usual greeting. "Anything worth knowing?"

I'm not sure why I didn't tell anybody about Mr. Cosmopoulos. I meant to, but I never got around to it. I guess I wanted to keep him to myself a little longer, or maybe I just wanted something no one could fight over.

One cold Saturday afternoon, Uncle Bax and I were walking over to the antique store and spotted Mr. Cosmopoulos sitting on a bench in Sheridan Square.

"Well, well, if it isn't Mr. Bouvier-Hirsh," he bellowed, bowing and sweeping his huge arm to where his waist once might have been. "And who's this gentleman accompanying you on this fine day?"

I introduced Uncle Bax, who smiled politely but withheld his hand the way he did when a difficult customer took too much of his time and bought something trivial. I couldn't see his mouth under the handlebar mustache, which was just as well because I knew there was mistrust around the edges. Mr. Cosmopoulos sensed my discomfort immediately; he uncrossed his legs, looked at an invisible watch under one frayed shirt cuff, gathered himself up, and said, "Can't sit here all day. I've been transferred to the downtown office for a coupla days."

"For whom do you work, Mr. Cosmopoulos?" Uncle Baxter had started the polite probing that would pick my friend clean. I'd watched him do it at parties when Suzie brought someone he didn't approve of. He just kept asking questions until his victim made a fool of himself. Aunt Jessica called this being hoist with one's own petard; I had no idea what that meant, but I sensed it was the plan for Mr. C.

"For nobody, if I don't get there fast!" boomed Mr. Cosmopoulos over his shoulder. I turned to Uncle Baxter for only a second. No one had ever brushed him off so quickly, and I wanted to see his reaction. When I looked at the street again, my friend had already disappeared.

I waited for him for a long time the day after we found out Claire had left us and Theo cried all afternoon after talking to Grandma Hirsh.

I walked over to the store at lunchtime, even though Theo had not opened it that day, and I stood near the hole in the fence long after the last bus pulled up to the curb. I had to walk all the way home through the park, but Mr. Cosmopoulos did not pop out of any clump of trees as I had wished he would, nor did he materialize on any row of benches. If he had, I would not have known how to explain; I guess that's why he didn't show up again until I was able to say the word "divorced."

14

As word of Claire's disappearance snaked up and down the crooked aisles of fruity-smelling desks, ancient radiators clanging and hissing the news in the shorthand of that particular jungle, hostility toward me began to cool. The irony of my situation was that I was now getting along better at school. While there was no sudden flurry of invitations, no overture of outright friendship (and I believe Carl Jacoby did all he could to make sure there was no such thing), wary looks replaced outright scorn, and curiosity won out as the other boys found it impossible to resist my new status as a divorced kid, especially one who was rendered so moments before Christmas, when all but the most dysfunctional parents gift-wrapped the expensive face of family harmony. Most of them could relate to a missing parent, so I had become normal in their eyes; they offered advice on shared custody, divorced dating, stepsisters and stepbrothers, and the usefulness of mastering the art of pitting one parent against the other.

One ferret-like boy with old family money, called Rabbit because his mean eyes were always pink around the edges, shared the secret of how he started a bidding war for his affection.

"I told Mother that Father and his new girlfriend were taking me to Aspen for school recess, and I timed it just before the Thanksgiving holiday to give her enough time to take me somewhere better," he bragged, loudly enough for the whole class to hear.

"Where'd you go?" I asked.

"Barbados," he said with a smirk. "When we got back, I told her how much Father and Glynis—that's his dumb girlfriend's name—were looking forward to taking me to Aspen and teaching me to ski, just the three of us, like a real family, and guess what she did?"

"What?" I wasn't very good at this.

"She waited until he bought the tickets, then she beat him to the punch. Mother and I and some guy named Eduardo flew to Aspen for Christmas and she hired a ski instructor for me while they got dressed up and played kissy-face every night." At this, everyone rolled their eyes.

"Then he had to figure out something even better for spring break, so we're going to a dude ranch where I get my own personal horse. Now she's trying to figure out where to take me for the summer. Maybe we'll rent a farmhouse in the South of France so I can practice my French with her new boyfriend, Jean-Claude." A chorus of groans and "Jahhhn-Clawde"s swelled behind him.

"You're really lucky," I said, a little confused at his apparent lack of enthusiasm. "I wish I could spend that much time with Claire or Theo." I thought of how much time Theo spent at the store and Claire in her darkroom or away on shoots, and I was more than a little jealous.

"Yeah," he answered flatly. "It's okay."

I wanted to meet these people who took Rabbit on such wonderful trips, but I never did. Some mornings, an impeccably restored silver Bentley and an elderly chauffeur named Charles deposited Rabbit on the sidewalk without a word of encouragement or farewell. On other days, a Lincoln Town Car driven by someone called Tony squealed to a stop and dropped him off with seconds to spare before the first bell, leaving the acrid smell of burning rubber in the quiet street.

I didn't care if being divorced meant I could go to Aspen and on all those vacations and in fact, I didn't really know what Aspen was, even though I pretended I did. I just wanted Claire to come home and things to be the way they used to, but I didn't mention this to Rabbit or to the other kids in class. Having forgotten they didn't like me, they were having too much fun teaching me how to be one of them.

When I told Mr. Cosmopoulos that Claire didn't love us anymore and had left us, he said, "You know, mister, sometimes people are so afraid of what other people are going to do—of getting hurt—that they just strike the first blow just to get it over with before it happens to them. Doesn't hurt so much that way." I wasn't completely sure what he had meant by this, but I had a good idea. After I gave Carl a nosebleed, people looked at me differently and said I had a bad temper. I just knew where things were going, that's all, and I preferred the feeling of throwing the first punch to being laughed at. This strategy didn't get me any more friends (and, when I was a man too proud to risk his heart, I paid dearly for it), but people thought twice about picking on me.

We had stopped going out to the farm; whenever Uncle Peter called, Theo spoke to him in a flat voice studiously stripped of affect. Sometimes she hung up abruptly, her green eyes cold, the twin blotches of color that signaled trouble rising high over a dusting of freckles that fooled people into thinking she wasn't as dangerous as she could be. Other times she slipped the phone back into its cradle without a sound, before Peter was finished talking.

I really missed Harry, who had become my best long-distance friend; perhaps by virtue of that distance I believed he would not judge me as harshly as those who suffered my presence every day. We called each other when our parents weren't around and tried to keep the thread of this connection from unraveling, but it wasn't the same. Something between us always stilted these furtive conversations, infusing them with an overblown sense of loyalty to our parents—who, had they known of our attempts to keep our youthful bond unsevered, would certainly never have demanded otherwise. This, and the painfully short attention span of young boys, whose lives can change entirely within a few short weeks, conspired to lengthen the distance between the farm and the apartment, and add stiffness to the secret phone calls that were meant to continue our friendship. We drifted.

Afraid of my grandmother's threats of legal action, Theo no longer felt comfortable using the garage in the Hirshs' building, so there were no more late-night cab rides through the slumbering park. She began to park our car in the side streets around Central Park West; when Andy's voice boomed over the intercom, warning, "Better hurry Miss Bouvier, they're writing tickets down here!" Theo ran down the hall in her Chinese peasant slippers, nightgown billowing out from under the swirling chocolate wool of her warmest coat, and moved our VW Bug to safer ground.

We jumped when the phone rang, every artery pumping with hope, every muscle tense with anticipation, and then slumped when it was Suzie or Baxter or Jessica or Thad or Grandma Doris or Roy or just someone asking if we'd like to contribute to the American Cancer Society or the ASPCA. We scanned mail addressed to Claire, looking for clues. One night, Theo accused Suzie of knowing where Claire was, and slammed down the phone hard, but Suzie called back and explained that Claire had sent some film for her safekeeping, but no clues to her whereabouts; they talked softly until Theo believed her again. I heard her say, "I'm sorry, Suze. I just miss her is all."

During this time I developed the jump in my right eye that has appeared all my life to tell me I am under a great deal of stress just in case I am not completely aware of it; but in those days I did not know what stress was, only that it wasn't normal to feel something queasy in the bottom of your stomach from the minute you got out of bed in the morning until you closed your eyes at night.

To dispel the loneliness, I found it comforting to spend as much time as I could with Mr. Cosmopoulos, who knew how I felt even though I hadn't told him. I looked for him in what had become our special place, just around the corner from The Latest Dish, a few feet into a quiet side street where we could sit undisturbed on the stoop of a hulking brownstone, but not so far into it that the view of the avenue and its busy sidewalks was obstructed.

"You never know who's going to sneak up on you," said Mr. C. searching the windy corner beyond. There we shared the lunch Theo provided and I was always cheered at the sight of his red suspenders and the lightbulb that went on in his eyes when he saw me. I took care to watch out for him in the Village, too, and not to run into him on my Saturdays with Uncle Baxter, who asked me how I knew "a weirdo like that" and whose dislike was, I suspect, mutual.

When I mentioned Claire and Theo and the fact that Grandma Hirsh didn't like Theo anymore, Mr. C. answered with stories about his own parents and Greece and about a magic bean the doctors took out of his head that left him temporarily out of work and a little confused.

"Gave me second sight," he said, tapping the left side of his head, "but one day it went soft, just like a bad lentil."

I especially liked the stories about his own son, who was grown up and living somewhere in New Jersey, and I never tired of hearing that he was just like me when he was a boy. I begged Mr. C. to repeat those tales and I imagined what it must have been like to grow up with him. Whenever I asked if I could meet his son, Mr. Cosmopoulos drifted away from me as though he could see something I couldn't and said, "That boy's busier than a one-armed paper-hanger. He's doing okay. Got a pretty little wife, big job down on Wall Street, and a boy just like you." When I asked if he could meet us one day for lunch, Mr. C. pretended he didn't hear me, but that didn't stop me from asking.

"It's amazing what I see in the recycling business," he announced apropos of nothing, a strange light in his eyes, the day I pressed him too hard about his son. "I'm telling you, mister, the stuff people throw away. Not even broken. No, sir, nobody wants to fix anything anymore. Too much work. Easier to get something new."

Mr. C. always spoke to something beyond my vision: a bus that got stuck in the snow trying to make the turn onto Second Avenue, a purse-snatching that happened so fast he was the only witness, two blind people kissing good-bye, their guide dogs sitting patiently at their feet, speaking so softly only Mr. C. could hear them saying "See you later." That day, a woman had fallen on the slippery pavement; several people rushed by before someone stopped and offered a hand.

I learned to watch for these things on the street, too, and waited for Mr. C. to remember he was talking to me and swoop back in a gust of laughter and instruction. "Most people don't even see life happening right in front of them. Don't just look, mister, learn how to *see!*"

I often thought he looked elsewhere when he talked because he was afraid I'd see too much. Claire did this, too, staring into the faces of her photographs as she talked to me in the dim light of her darkroom, only the occasional pressure of her hand on my shoulder said she loved me more than her voice ever could.

I learned Mr. C.'s wife didn't love him anymore after he came home from the hospital because he couldn't remember her name. After the bandages came off, new hair grew over the stitches he described as "Frankenstein's zipper," and he was well enough to be on his own, she moved away and took their son with her and didn't tell him where. There was some trouble getting his old job back because even though he tried very hard to remember what it was he did there, he couldn't and the judge said if he didn't want to support his son, he couldn't see him either. I learned he named his son Angel because when he was born he looked exactly like one of Raphael's cherubim, but when Angel grew up, he changed it to Gabriel, preferring the abbreviated "Gabe" for its solid American ring. Mr. Cosmopoulos's round face dimmed when he told me this, but brightened again at the thought that at least his son had chosen an angel's name, and a very important angel's at that, for his alias.

"Then she got married again and I laid low for a while," he announced one bright snowy afternoon, "and one thing led to another. I figured I'd let the boy get to know his step-pop without worryin' about what I think."

I waited for him to get back from "his travels," as he called them. I did not always completely understand them but sensed they held something for me if I listened hard enough. That day I wondered if Claire would get married again, too. I got used to Mr. C.'s eyes suddenly going blank and the fact that he sometimes stopped short in the middle of something important. Sooner or later, he'd pull on his ponytail and say, "The porch light's on. Anybody home?"

"Maybe that's what Claire is doing," he said out of the blue that bitter afternoon in late January.

"What?" I asked, still lost in his travels, not realizing he had come back to the present.

"Laying low, of course."

That was the same day he said he'd take me home to meet Shorty.

I FORGAVE Claire for leaving long before I understood why. I saw her as a modern-day Joan of Arc, above the law, larger than life, yet exquisitely sensitive, using her camera, our lives, and even the fact of our lesbianism—for years I believed in the power of that word to define me as well as my mothers—not as something private, but as a form of performance art. Like many children of artists, I suppose I felt protective of her, more like the parent than the child. I really thought, as she did, that the world had a right to know about us and we had a responsibility to tell the truth, even if it meant being ostracized, which at the ripe old age of nine, I pronounced "Osterized."

I secretly believed that if Theo had loved Claire as much as I did, if she had taken her more seriously, hadn't fought with her so much, she would have stayed. I knew that if I had been better—not held that séance, not bloodied Carl's nose; pretended I was happier—she would not have left, and I would not have had to consider the drastic steps I was ultimately forced to take. I could not have said this at the time, but I believed Claire was a gift we had insufficiently appreciated and thus had driven her away.

After she left, Theo said to Suzie, who had come to the apartment for some photographs Claire had printed but forgotten to deliver in her haste to get away from us, "How can I compete with such heady affirmation of her way of seeing the world? If I'm lucky, my work is appreciated in small bodily rumbles and a request for seconds. Hers is praised on the public altar, serves as muse to Hollywood royalty, earns enough money to keep us in Beluga and weekends in Paris for the rest of our lives, and wins a Guggenheim into the bargain. I'd have made my neuroses art, too, if it paid off like that!"

Suzie held Theo's hand in her own, rings glittering in the brittle winter sun of our living room and said, "Don't you know she would trade places with you in a minute? You've made something she can't. This is about trust, Theo. This is about allowing her to be the mother, too."

"You know where she is, don't you, Suze?" said Theo, drawing her hand away.

"I wish I did," said Aunt Suzie, seeing the hurt in her face.

One afternoon when Theo was picking me up on Twelfth Street, Jessica said, "Darling, you know I love Claire dearly, but such a grandiose view of one's purpose can only lead to extreme disappointment. I've always felt she was biting off a bit more than she could chew. It's so much better to understand one's own devils before rushing off to record someone else's, don't you think?"

"You're just mad at her because she won't take pictures of ladies in fur coats and dumb clothes for your stupid magazine!" I bellowed, running down the stairs and slamming the front door before anyone, especially the twins, saw my bottom lip quiver with a baby's need to cry.

"She'll be back before you know it," said a shoeless and shivering

Uncle Baxter, who opened the big front door and sat down on the cold stoop next to me, pretending his strong hug, in which I allowed my anger to find its tears, was just to keep himself warm.

Uncle Peter called every day until Theo finally agreed to drive the hundred miles to his kitchen table for a talk. I listened to him tell her about my grandparents and how they had shut Claire out after Roland's death, how they rejoiced when Peter was born, and how they lost interest when Peter did not measure up.

"She didn't have a chance, Theo," Peter explained. "It's not that she doesn't love you—she does; she just expects to be hurt. Every second of her suffocating childhood reinforced that, every time she was compared to Roland and found lacking. I think what she does is get out before she gets thrown out."

"All I wanted was the best for Willy. She's got to understand that," said Theo, letting her guard down a little.

"She's got to, but she doesn't. She thinks that by rejecting the idea of being so open about your relationship, you're rejecting her. In a way, she's your child, too, and you're choosing the boy over her all over again."

"So what am I supposed to do, find her a good therapist, tell her all is forgiven, and let her whine about her childhood for ten or twelve years while our son grows up fighting everybody who doesn't like his parents?"

"Isn't that what kids do anyway?" asked Peter.

"Whose side are you on, Peter?"

"There are no sides, Theo."

"Yes, there are. There always are," said Theo, reaching for the car keys.

On the way home Theo explained. "Your uncle Peter says she's afraid we won't love her anymore, so she's pretending not to love us anymore, but she really does."

Uncle Thad spent an hour every Wednesday at three o'clock with a hippie turned psychotherapist, who wore long flowered silk dresses and brown orthopedic shoes. She encouraged him to cry, writhe, and relive his birth trauma in order to unlock his primal pain on the floor of her loft in the Flower District, urging him to set upon a battered vinyl pillow with a baseball bat and imagine he was beating his father. He was, in the jargon of the decade, "into his anger," and had his own version of why Claire had left.

"When Alan died, I thought my life was over, too, but I realized the grief I was feeling wasn't new. It was abandonment, the horrible ripping agony of separation, of being pushed out of the womb and knowing that I was able to move on. You know," Thad continued tearfully, "if we understand it, pain can become as familiar as an old friend warning us of danger. But if we don't look at it—try to understand where it comes from—and instead run away from it, as I suspect Claire is doing, it runs us, and life is just a boring repetition of our primal experience. Dr. Yvonne thinks you ought to come in for a session—and I must say, I think it would do you a world of good, working on yourself for five minutes instead of feeding all of New York from that expensive soup kitchen."

"You know what I think?" Theo had said, the exhaustion of so much advice clearly written on her forehead.

"Thinking is what gets us in trouble, darling," said Thad, rising to his subject again. "Feeling is what we need to do more of."

"I think you go for the flowers. I think on a hot day with the windows open and all those truckloads of freesias and freshly cut roses all over the street and Dr. Yvonne in one of her flowered numbers, that place must smell exactly like being with Alan," said Theo dully, but not without affection.

"And I came here to help *you.*" Thad smiled wistfully, hugging the friend who always gave him something even if she had nothing herself.

In desperation, Theo swallowed her pride and her fear and called the Hirsh household again, hoping Barnaby would answer the phone, but my grandmother was indifferent to her suffering and said coldly, "We all have to make choices, dear, and I think Claire has made hers."

Theo and I were the prisoners of our friends' opinions. This was what it must be like to be hospital patients, forced to lie in bed while people showed up unannounced, sat at the bed's foot, plumping covers, cranking us up, asking horribly personal questions until finally they got the idea they ought to leave.

Everyone had a version of why Claire left. No one had heard from her, but they all said she loved us and would come home when she was ready. I listened politely, but it had been over a month and Claire was beginning to feel as dead as Alan when the coffin lid came down with the heartbreaking sound of a falling piano, leaving the silence buzzing with questions.

I turned to Mr. Kimsky. And from his special vantage point as my mother's favorite photograph, he taught me my earliest lesson in the power of imagination.

Throughout my childhood, he presided over breakfast, lunch, and dinner, wearing a brown-and-yellow plaid shirt buttoned straight up to a long, old-fashioned collar that squeezed the skin of his talcumed neck into a turkey wattle. One wiry hair, having somehow escaped his razor, sprang from his Adam's apple and reached for the lapel of his only suit, a shiny double-breasted affair worn with the cocky dash of a man who knows he's too short. On the surface, it was a simple photograph of someone who got dressed up to play chess on the boardwalk, his dark eyes hooded in concentration and noonday glare, owlish glasses riding on the tip of a large and intelligent beak, his opponent an unseen shadow across from him, lost in the edges of the photograph.

If I lost a shoe or a button, I'd look up and ask him where it was and see it lying in the cobwebby darkness on my closet floor. I invented a history for him. He was my long-lost grandfather, my own father's father, who was himself a victim of amnesia and couldn't remember his own name, much less the fact that he had a son on the West Side; he was hit by a bus just as he was about to leave his grimy walkup in Coney Island and move in with us. He was my uncle Roland, or, on other days, my father, who had slipped into the body of an old man, come to hang on our wall and watch over me.

The implausibility of these biographies grew in proportion to my own need to escape the facts of mine. I believed that when the right moment arrived, Mr. Kimsky would tell me where Claire was.

While I found the picture of Mr. Kimsky a comforting presence, the shadow across the checkerboard terrified me. I hated its dark hold over my friend, the way it hovered over him like an oily stain, and I imagined that if I crept into the dining room in the middle of the night and suddenly turned on the lights, the unseen opponent would be sitting there, ugly, evil, grinning at me from his side of the picture, mocking me for cowering behind the kitchen door in my flannel pajamas.

Claire once said even though it is frozen in the past, a photograph can foreshadow the future and I think that's why I was so afraid of Mr. Kimsky's invisible challenger. He was the future I was up against and couldn't see but only imagine—and that's always worse.

At the time I could not have understood what was happening—besides the loss of Claire—but I sensed, as children always do, that it was serious. No one warned me of the rumblings from the apartment across the park, the lies that were being told about Theo nor of the swift and imminent change about to occur, but the minute I saw the nervous young woman from Social Services on the edge of Claire's prized Thonet hall bench, I knew she was there to take me away.

She wasn't sitting exactly, for that would have implied some commitment to comfort, some softening of the spine to the contours of her present circumstances. No, I remember a dull brown woman who seemed to be crouching and sitting, as impossible as this may sound. It struck me that she seemed to be both predator and prey as she waited politely for Theo and me, her hands folded quietly over the sheaf of official-looking papers in her lap while the expanse of skirt underneath, a suspiciously shiny, indeterminate fabric was involved in a struggle all its own, each stitch along its seam set in relief, stretched to its limit and threatening to give way against the pressure of thick legs that did not often hurry.

As though to delude the observer into thinking she was not interested in us or in our home, but merely in the execution of her job, her body remained deathly still while her eyes, the color of weak tea, slid around the room missing nothing, taking everything in. They scanned our pictures, rested for a moment on Claire on the cover of *Aperture,* Theo in *New York*'s "Best Bets," me as a fat baby with Thad and a drawn-looking Alan in his wheelchair (he had gamely covered the breathing-tube hole in his neck with a Fred Flinstone bandana from my collection) mugging for the camera, pretending not to see the shadow on the wall.

She squinted suspiciously at the picture of me with Claire, her arms draped around the shoulder of a strong, silent, and extraordinarily lifelike soft sculpture of a cowboy on a bench in front of a trading post in Arizona, the perfect American family if you didn't look too closely, and she lingered on the letter Jessica had sent when Claire gathered enough courage to tell her best friend she was a lesbian, but didn't seem to find it as funny as everyone else in our family did. Nor did she smile when her eyes rested on the one I loved the best: Claire and Theo, both in white, exchanging their vows for Uncle Father James Roy and all our friends and family, except Grandma Hirsh, who really didn't want to come, and Aunt Molly, who couldn't, with me right there between them in a white kimono and cap, blowing bubbles in my carriage, playing with the rings they were never to take off, a fat Cupid with a face a little too strained for the occasion, the only clue I was working on a little surprise that would add a certain pungency to the proceedings, a present of my own for the newlyweds in the depths of my own gift wrapping.

I had no idea there had been a hearing Theo lost, or that she had known this day was coming. How could she have warned me without telling me the kinds of things my grandmother accused her of? Instead, she prayed for a miracle that never came, she prayed for Claire. How could I tell her Claire had called earlier in the week just to talk to me?

Department of Social Services. Child Welfare Division. The seal of the City of New York. I saw the stamp, surrounded by a circle of raised bumps that looked like pimples on the top page in the pile of documents on her lap as her gaze slid, oily and dark, over our furniture, the collection of mismatched silver candlesticks on the big coffee table, the open box of chocolates someone had sent us to say thank you for dinner, letters to Claire Theo had steamed open and neatly stacked for the return we both wished for but never out loud, the tumble of books and the bag of groceries, which wore the slowly darkening stain of something melting inside, dropped on the hall table and now forgotten in the suddenness of that afternoon, assessing, measuring, making invisible black marks against us. An overstuffed and battered briefcase—no doubt bulging with evidence against other unsuspecting families—was parked at her feet like a cab with its meter running. She looked everywhere but into my mother's eyes.

The memory of that particular day is more physical than anything else. I remember it as a tearing sensation, a feeling so real, I believed it capable of leaving bruises on my skin. I actually looked for them the next day. I now understood why the expression "broken heart" is so apt. Something did indeed break that day; perhaps it was my heart, perhaps not. I suspect it was the premature snapping of trust, those more romantic than I might call this moment the end of innocence, but for me it was the first, shattering evidence of the existence of cruelty in people who claim to love you.

Many years later, Annie would tap quietly and insistently on the door that closed that February afternoon so long ago and I wonder sometimes if, in the beginning, before I loved her, I didn't open it because of my awe at the fact that she simply would not go away.

The afternoon Social Services came, I did what anyone would do under the circumstances. I slowed down the action. In the way that cars drift into each other and seem to kiss before slowly crumpling, glass floating over the scene like dangerous hail, in the silence before the sirens scream and victims hear the sound of their own terror, Theo moved as in a dream, gathering my things, stopping to refold a pajama leg, tucking an extra sweater into my duffel bag, dragging the entire length of the back of her arm across her eyes, as though to wipe away the sight of her loss. Her eyes were huge with fury and shock, made even more hollow and frightening by the long streaks of mascara disappearing into her ears.

Theo drew me close; despite the sting of fear and perspiration under the familiar scent of vanilla, oranges, and carnations rising out of the shirt, which clung to her cold, sticky back, I hung on to her. We moved from room to room as though we were one person. When she finally spoke, she swayed a bit and I was afraid she'd fall.

"Miss Rodriguez is going to take you to your grandma's for a while, sweetheart," Theo said in a thick voice I had never heard before, even the night Claire left so abruptly before eating her dinner.

"Why?" I demanded.

"Grandma doesn't think I can take care of you by myself."

"Why won't Claire come back and tell her you can?" I could hear myself shouting in a squeaky high-pitched voice that didn't sound like mine either.

"I don't know, baby."

"Why do I have to go?" I persisted.

"You have to go because Grandma went to court and asked the judge for a letter that says you have to and if we ignore it, they'll arrest me."

"For what?" I bellowed. What could she have done for them to take me away?

"It won't be for long. I promise," she said, holding my head in her hands, staring at me with a crazy, swollen face that scared me a little with its fierce determination to will what she was saying to be true. "We'll find Claire and we'll all be back together before you can say, 'Claire, Theo, and wee Willy, three for all and all for three.' "

I think we both wanted to believe that if Claire had been here, she would not have let this happen, she would not have let her mother do this terrible thing, but this thought remained unspoken as if to voice it would subject it to scrutiny it might not be able to stand up to. As Theo recited our family rhyme, tears rolling down her face into her collar, she drew the cord on my duffel and snapped it as though it were someone's neck.

"Grandma loves you," she said finally. "In her own way, she really does."

"Leave us alone! Leave us alone!"

I ran into the foyer shouting, sliding on the highly polished floor, punching at the air until my fists found the woman from Social Services sitting on our bench.

"Get off Claire's bench! Go away!" I screamed at the woman who had made my mother cry.

"Hey! Hey! No need for that, son," said a voice that did not seem to belong to the object of my anger.

I hadn't seen the policeman who had been standing just outside our door the whole time in case of trouble, a ruddy-faced Irishman with a cruel smile. He caught me mid-punch, lifting me up by my elbows and away from the frightened woman, who was nervously paddling backward toward our open front door.

"Usually, it's the parents getting violent in these cases, but this one's a real fighter," he said, winking at the social worker, with a mocking, sadistic laugh that told me he enjoyed what he was doing. The woman ignored him, gathered up her coat and briefcase, and headed for the elevator, past our neighbors who were standing silently in the hall, their faces a mixture of curiosity, genuine concern, and something else I couldn't exactly describe—only that the sight of it made me turn my eyes downward to the small mosaic tiles outside our door.

Theo was at my side in an instant. "Put my son down this minute, or I'll have you arrested, you goddamn pig."

"Don't be damning me, miss. It'll be you who'll be damned in hell for the mockery you've made of this poor lad," he threatened, deliberately raising his voice for the people in the hallway.

He towered over Theo, the leather of his holster creaking with a well-oiled and ominous sound, his fingers closing around a vicious-looking club hanging from a clip on his thick black belt, but the moment passed and just as suddenly as the sound of this afternoon had disappeared, as though an unseen hand had turned down the volume, it was back, deafening and full of the fear pounding in my ears. It was the first time I can remember wanting to kill someone. I could taste his blood in my mouth and it was mixed with the bitter taste of knowing I was only a boy, powerless to protect my mother.

Theo's face crumpled as she raced after us, parting the elevator doors like Atlas holding up the world, handing me the antibiotic the doctor had ordered for my recurrent ear infection. She kissed me one more time before they pushed her hands away and all I could see was her disappearing face in the diamond pane of glass on the wood-paneled safety door, saying something I couldn't hear and to which the mean-faced cop answered, "Tell it to the judge." The car began its descent to the lobby and to Andy, who was waiting with a crisp salute and a breezy "Don't you worry, Mr. Willy, your mom will get you back home with us before dinner."

I don't think it was my imagination that once I was safely through, Andy deliberately allowed our heavy leaded-glass front door to close within inches of the policeman's face.

The sunlight was blinding; it hurt my eyes to take in the brightness around the police car waiting at the curb. The woman was talking to me, trying her best to sound soothing, but I squeezed myself into the corner of the backseat, as far away from her as I could where the upholstery was cracked and full of lint from too many dirty and unwilling passengers. As we rode through the park, the driver, a younger officer with a weasel's face and badly pock-marked skin, slid open the grill between himself and the backseat and asked me if I wanted him to put on the lights and the siren.

"Play with them yourself," I said, twisting around to see if the cab I saw Theo wildly hailing just as we were pulling away from the curb was still behind us.

"Guess they don't teach you manners where you live." He muttered something under his breath as he swiveled in the driver's seat, giving the bumpy curves through Central Park his full attention. It sounded like "damn dykes" to ears accustomed to straining to hear what isn't meant to be heard.

If I had been paying attention, I would have seen this coming. I would have heard the whispers that stopped when I walked into the room, I would have understood the concern that tightened Uncle Baxter's jaw the day he took me to the shop so Theo and Aunt Jessica could talk, and if I had turned around quickly as we left the Baxters' house that day I would have seen an uncharacteristically muffled Jess standing at the window somberly watching us turn the corner. Even the twins, who always treated me with the superiority of older girls who have no time for the filthy habits of boys, had seemed oversolicitous and polite, speaking no French in my presence or behind my back as they usually did so as to exclude and drive me crazy at the same time. If I had thought about it, I would have realized Grandma and Grandpa Hirsh hadn't visited once since Claire disappeared.

THEO SAT in the Hirshes' lobby all night after they took me away. Every hour, the buzzer sounded upstairs and Buddy said in the most proper Irish-doorman voice he could muster: "Miz Hirsh, Miz Bouvier is here to see the grandlad."

In the vast empty echo of the marble, I could hear Theo coaching him: "*Son,* Buddy. I'm here to see my *son.*" Each time Buddy went through the motions that could have cost him his job, I saw Barnaby's jaw stiffen at the jolt of the buzzer and felt my grandmother's disregard for my mother's presence a few floors below.

Grandma found my pajamas in my hastily packed bag, clucking disapprovingly at their wrinkled condition. Grandpa Barnaby said, "I know you don't think so, but your grandma loves you." They put me to bed in the room that had once belonged to my uncle Roland, which smelled of camphor and plastic and they stood in the doorway like ghosts until I pretended to fall asleep. Around midnight, after making what Grandpa Barnaby called a scene in the staid hush of their building, Theo finally went home.

I did not know it then, but she left only after the police were called and informed her that if she did not go quietly, she would have to spend the rest of the night in jail. When I woke up and stumbled out of the unfamiliar bed and onto the thick carpet that cushioned my cries of alarm, Grandma told me that Theo had given up and realized it was better for me to be with people who could raise me properly; but the next day, when Barnaby insisted that I should be allowed to talk to her, Theo said that was a lie.

"I love you, honey," she said, with as much pain in her voice as I suddenly felt at the sound of hers. "I would never let Grandma take you away from me; not as long as I live. And I don't think Claire would want that, either." I know she was trying hard not to alarm me with her rage, but the panic was there.

"I want to come home," I wailed.

I slammed the receiver into its cradle on the highly polished phone table—which, up to that moment, had probably never experienced more than the refined snap of the Mark Cross crocodile phone book that lay on its gleaming surface. Grandma Hirsh heard the dangerous creaking of its legs in the next room, where she was quietly listening to my conversation.

"I hate you!" I cried, almost knocking my elegant and now despised grandmother off her well-shod feet. I barreled down the corridor, past Grandpa Barnaby coming out of his study with his half-glasses on the tip of his nose, and I slammed Roland's door, which I prayed was only temporarily mine and which I imagined welcomed the seething of another young boy.

On the musty blanket that had held my uncle's secrets for over thirty years, I gave some preliminary thought to an idea I could not articulate at the time, but that my mother alluded to in defending her decision to decamp the night before, something that would sustain me often in the course of my lifetime: the idea of losing a few battles in order to win a war.

15

My grandmother's apartment smelled of money that did not call attention to itself directly, but was applied in thin, tasteful layers until it shone in the apricot glaze on its drawing room walls and in the even more bottomless veneer of cerise in the dining room. It whispered its presence in the yards of cream silk damask that cascaded from tall, sunny windows (framing the impressionistic and unobstructed view of the sailboat pond, the reservoir, the Met's hulking Victorian conservatory and all the hollows and secret places in the park only the right floor on Fifth Avenue can afford) and fell into a large, extravagant puddle on the Aubusson below.

Money had built up an invisible barrier, like the thick restorer's wax that was carefully applied and expertly rubbed into the gleaming chests, semaniers, Chippendale chairs, a Philadelphia sideboard once used by William Penn, and her pride and joy, an eighteenth-century escritoire. My grandmother collected these at the annual show at the Armory and on trips to London and Paris with Barnaby and in the big auction houses on Madison Avenue, nodding discreetly but never showing excitement at the idea of acquiring the beauty before her.

Within the pervasive atmosphere of vanilla and lemons and cloves, those tiny green-striped candles that smelled of pine needles, cedar closets, and mink coats, I picked up something else, something faintly medicinal and vaguely ominous, like the sharp smell that lies undisturbed at the dark bottom of a pile of rotting leaves.

Even in good times, my grandmother's apartment was not the place to entertain a small boy. Sunday visits were always closely supervised; though Grandma always said my sticky fingers and curious feet didn't matter, we all knew they did. Something she did with her mouth, forcing it into the shape of a smile (one that never appeared when she was really amused), told me I had stretched her patience by hovering close enough to one of her priceless antiques to be considered a menace.

Meals were agonizingly long for me, full of arcane cutlery we didn't bother with at home, served by my grandparents' housekeeper and cook, Lucy, a reedy black woman who lived in the only room in which I didn't feel unwelcome. When Claire was small, Lucy left her family in Jamaica and came to live with Grandma. She fussed over me as though I were the King of England, or the son it was rumored she had left behind when she fled her father's Catholic wrath, and Claire assured me she did no less for me than for my predecessor, the young Roland who had been able to mend her shattered heart with a grinning sense of mischief and real affection for this woman. What Lucy's age was, no one knew, but it sometimes caused her rheumy eyes to blur the faces of the boys she had tended.

"Don't you fight with dat trout, precious. Lucy got sometin' in the kitchen fah yah!" said Lucy slipping easily back into the familiar pattern of the thinly disguised competition she and her employer had waged for the Hirsh children's affection for nearly forty years. "Yah mah don't remembah what leetle ones like," she said in an exaggerated stage whisper, shaking her head mournfully, making the most of the fact that everyone knew she was hard of hearing, forgetting for the moment which Hirsh boy I was.

I could listen to her lilting voice for hours. I knew no one who spoke quite like that except for Bob Marley, whose music made Claire happy enough to dance around the living room in her socks. But that night, alone at that long table with no one to gently tickle my slippered sole with a friendly foot in promise of a good giggle later, I did not enjoy Lucy's attempts on my behalf.

Grandma never responded to Lucy's criticisms directly.

"William dear," she said, ignoring my grim determination to starve in the enemy camp, nodding at me with a faintly aggrieved smile on her pursed lips, "give that trout a little try for Grandma. We wouldn't want you to grow up afraid of new things, would we?"

The fish that I had been taught to eat with a surgeon's skill and a chef's instinct for bones lay untouched, its dangerous spine intact. The pale, lukewarm lump reminded me of a happier evening at my grandparents' table when there was more appetite for adventure.

"Trout! That was whitefish in my book," Theo had said the second we were in the cab and safely out of Buddy's earshot, which was our signal to explode like errant children who have been nibbling their lips to keep from laughing in front of the teacher and find they are suddenly free.

"Only your mother could ask a good cook to take a perfectly nice fish and push it to the point of relative anonymity. Didn't you love the way she called the brisket *boeuf en daube?*" Then, flush from a glass or two from Grandpa's wine closet, Theo warmed to one of her favorite culinary theories, "cooking by obfuscation."

"She doesn't even know she's doing it," Theo lectured, trying to sound serious as she slid on the slippery taxi seat. "It's subconscience—"

"Subconscious," said Claire, trying not to make fun of her, enjoying her silliness.

"That's right," agreed Theo, grinning crazily. "Those proper Irish roots of hers have buried Barnaby and his nice Jewish food right up to the fish forks!"

"You've got to admit that was the best imitation of brisket by a *boeuf en daube* you have ever tasted." Claire laughed. "You know, Roland and I found out there was a Kingston in Queens, and we secretly believed Lucy never came from Jamaica the island, but from Jamaica in the borough, where she was kidnapped by a Jewish family and taught to cook kosher."

"Peter said she was kidnapped as a child and raised by retirees in Miami Beach, where she was forced to forget how to make fungi and conch curry and cook brisket instead," said Theo. "Imagine your grandmother serving fungi and jerk chicken." Theo wrinkled her nose and stretched her mouth into the "yuk" face we always made at foods that sounded awful, but tasted good. I couldn't imagine what fungi was, but I knew I didn't want any.

"What did he know? He was the youngest. At least my mother serves brisket," said Claire, still lost in the memory of how convinced she and Roland were of Lucy's shady past, how determined they were to unmask her secrets, always plotting to trip her up, quizzing her on Caribbean history, never once realizing that her total abdication of any life of her own was clue enough something terrible had been left behind.

"That's more than we can say for her neighbors, like the heiress upstairs who serves peanut butter and jelly on the family Meissen. She will deign to roast a beef, or in her case cremate one, only if she's entertaining the Pope. Who, if you ask her in the middle of the night, she admits is much too Catholic for her Presbyterian taste. What a building! A real hotbed of culinary adventure!"

By the time we crossed the park, Grandma and Grandpa Hirsh were forgotten and Theo was fuzzily philosophizing, not making too much sense.

"Isn't it amazing, the lower down people are socioeconomically, the more highly flavored and interesting their food? I mean, if a person actually enjoys eating, who knows what evils await?"

Claire kissed her on the end of a quickly reddening nose. "You're going to have to stick to vanilla extract from now on, my darling chef-a-rama. You have zero tolerance for alcohol, zip," teased Claire, helping Theo out of the cab while I held the door, bowing from the waist. Theo listed left and right, bestowing extravagant, blustery hugs in between pronouncements, and we burst into our lobby giggling.

"And what have the Bouvier-Hirshes been up to tonight?" Andy greeted us with mock disapproval and an exaggerated sweep of the door.

"Grandma's," I said.

"Brisket?" he deadpanned, which started us going all over again.

All of that had suddenly changed. There was no one to laugh with on the way home because I couldn't go home, only to school and back in the company of Lucy, who performed this new duty with an uncharacteristic solemnity that smoldered with her disapproval.

"Don' know what she's doin', your grandmother, fooling wit' nature like dat." Lucy would shake her head, muttering all the way to McCall, her white uniform showing under the hem of her thin, shiny coat, her skinny, slightly bowed black legs (chalky gray in white stockings), unaccustomed to hurrying, paddling furiously as she warily approached Seventy-fourth Street.

Every morning, I imagined the Latest Dish van with its red-lip logo would screech to a stop. My mother, all in black, grease on her face and a grenade in her belt, would spirit me off in a split second, leaving Lucy wondering whether to give chase on her rickety legs or to cheer Theo's commando style.

"You got two mothers who love you and lawd, dat's more dan most," she said one blustery morning. Some days, she told me about Uncle Roland and how she walked him and Claire in the park in their navy-blue pram, how proud he was with his sister right beside him, how protective of her even as a baby. I often wondered if my situation in the Hirsh household had reopened something she had closed a long time ago—the shock of Roland's death, the mystery of her own lost boy—and I suspected that my presence had toppled something that had taken her many years to construct. Unlike the rest of us, Lucy always had her status as an employee to fall back on, to protect her from the craziness of those times, and some days I saw her face bunch up in anger and in disapproval and felt her retreat like a door gently, but emphatically, closing.

Afternoons, Grandpa went to his club, or to his study at the far end of the long corridor that formed the cavernous apartment's backbone. Although I often followed him into its crisp, leathery interior, he soon tired of talking with me. When I asked him about Roland or why I didn't see Uncle Peter anymore or why Grandma always called Theo "Claire's friend" and never used the word "lesbian" or "mother" or called them partners, even though that was the word they preferred, he said, "Your grandma would do anything for you" or "Your grandma is thinking about what's best for you," and raised his newspaper as a signal I came to understand as dismissal.

Once he said: "You know, your grandmother was never the same after Roland." But he never finished, leaving me to wonder what she was like before.

Even in good times, we never ate dinner at home at the same time, probably because of the demands the store placed on Theo and Claire's erratic work schedule. But at the Hirshs', clocks could be set by the prompt arrival of meals. It seemed just as we sat down to dinner every evening, the phone rang; it was always Theo, demanding to speak with me. Lucy brought the phone to the dining room table, where I was expected to talk to my mother as though no one was listening.

"I love you, Mama," I said as Grandma's fork hovered over her plate, unable to go on with its work until its owner, suspended in the act of eavesdropping, remembered its presence just a few inches from the goal.

"I love you, too, sweet baby, and I miss you so much. Honey, I know they're listening, but just say yes or no, okay?"

"Okay."

"Have you seen Mommy?"

"No."

"Has she called?"

"No." I squirmed in my chair, feeling trapped.

"Have you seen Uncle Peter?"

"Uh-uh."

Grandpa stared at his plate, trying to give me a little privacy.

"If he comes over, will you tell me what he and Grandma talk about?"

"Okay."

"Do you know I'm going to get you home as quickly as I can?"

"Yes."

"Will you ask Mommy to call me when you see her?"

"Yes."

"I love you, honey." I could hear the throaty sound of Theo struggling to keep the tears out of her voice.

"Me, too."

"Mary, excuse the boy, for God's sake," Grandpa pleaded with his wife.

"Families shouldn't keep secrets from one another," she replied, her expression fixed and unbending.

GRANDMA SPENT her mornings at her desk ordering from the florist around the corner on Madison Avenue, never responding to my suggestion that she call Thad, who had kept Alan's shop and his lover alive in the beautiful arrangements he delivered to all our friends.

"Grandma, let's ask Uncle Thad to send flowers to your friends," I said, remembering how she praised the beauty of the flowers he and Alan brought to our Sunday afternoons.

"William dear, Peter is your uncle and poor Roland was your uncle, but Thad is *not* your uncle. He is a homosexual and he is not a member of your family. Do you understand?"

I didn't. I hated her.

Most days, the apartment sounded hollow, the small sound of Lucy's key in the lock amplifying its emptiness, the only response to my return from school. No Suzie, no Claire, no students looking up from their photographs to see their mentor transform herself from master teacher to mother fussing over the details of her son's day, no celebrity treatment at the store. Just an aging housekeeper trying her best to keep a boy amused. There was a bitter irony in the fact that my busy grandmother, who changed no plans on my behalf, honestly believed it was healthier for a servant to rear a child than his own mother, and would have been shocked to learn that motherhood requires something more than attendance at mealtimes and prayers.

Whenever I could, I waited for Lucy to lose herself in the small TV she kept on the kitchen counter, and then I gingerly slid the Hirsh telephone out of its cradle to call Theo at the store, each digit on the rotary dial a bomb going off in my ears, the ringing drawing her closer and closer, my panic rising until I heard her say, "The Latest Dish." But this was not enough to ease the unbearable silence of that apartment.

This was not the exquisite quiet of the darkroom, where I felt closest to Claire, or the afternoon lull that amplified the scrape of my chair on Theo's temporarily empty tile floor, one of her apple-banana muffins easing the wait for dinner, the day's drawing or composition hung on the shop's menu board for all to see.

Even when the tension and the separateness built up around my mothers, they had tried to rise above their problems for me. Often they succeeded, sharing themselves with me and not letting the growing distance between them intrude. There were moments I believed I was the only person in the world who could hold them together. Other times, as all children who try to be the glue in their parents' lives eventually realize, I knew I was the one who tore them apart. Now Claire was gone and no one knew where she was; not even Grandma, which Theo never believed no matter how hard I tried to convince her.

I had been at Grandma's for two weeks, but Theo was not allowed to see me until the judge made a final decision, which was not for another three weeks.

"Please, Lucy, please, just for a few minutes," I begged her to take me to see my mother. "Grandma won't find out."

"I can't, yah know dat."

But one day, when we were well past the school and the danger of one of the kids seeing me act like a baby, I sat down on the sidewalk and threw a tantrum, refusing to stop until Lucy agreed to take me to see my mother.

At last she relented, taking pity on me. "Only for a few minutes. If they find out I took you over dere, they'll fry me ahlive."

At the shop, she avoided Theo's grateful eyes, refusing her offer of food and stood guard at the door. She said she was looking out for my grandmother, but I knew she was really giving us some time alone. Theo felt my arms and legs and head for damage, while I insisted there was none, and she asked questions I didn't understand, questions I would realize later were intended to give her some clue as to my grandparents' next move.

She seemed delighted to hear that Judge Bailey, who had signed the paper in Miss Rodriquez's lap, was the same person who had dined with us at Grandma's earlier in the week, knowing this lapse of ethics could get the case thrown out and the judge himself thrown off the bench. When I asked if Claire knew what had happened to me and why she wouldn't just come over and tell her mother to let me come home, Theo's eyes narrowed. She was firm in the belief that Claire and Uncle Peter were behind this somehow.

When we said good-bye, a strangled sound came up from Theo's throat; this released the torrent of tears I too had been holding back, trying to be brave and failing miserably. Lucy didn't take me to the store again—not because she was afraid she'd get caught, but because "Lawd, it near tore my heart out to see you two say good-bye."

The school was instructed to make sure I stayed in for lunch because Grandma was worried Theo would kidnap me. Even though I assured my teacher only strangers could kidnap people, not their mothers, she didn't believe me, so I was forced to spend recess at school. I dined in the schoolyard on all but the most bitterly cold days, which required a march into the murky depths of the cafeteria I hated.

One afternoon, moments after the teacher stepped inside the heavy school door to warm up and the older boys who doubled as schoolyard monitors busied themselves shooting hoops, Mr. Cosmopoulos appeared, as though a frequency only he could hear announced my guards' departure. He cheered me up with stories about Shorty and their friends and neighbors downtown.

"Thelma had one of her parties and Shorty wouldn't go, so she walked right in and pulled him out of bed. Can you imagine the nerve of that?" whispered Mr. C. through the hole in the fence. "She said, 'What's the matter, isn't a formal invitation enough for you?' She's got his number, old Thelma!"

One gloomy day, he slipped me a portion of my mother's own moussaka through the cold metal of the fence and smiled as I ate, knowing without my telling him that this was as close to being home, to having the warmth of my mother inside of me, as I could get.

Before all this happened, I knew time moved, but I never actually saw it. Now time dragged—except for Mr. C.'s visits, which were always over before I was ready—and the sound of ticking and the slow scrape of clock hands moving on minute by minute is the sound I remember most from those days in my grandparents' apartment.

I had dreaded school and the sight of Carl, so smug and so popular in his orphaned state, disappearing into the cafeteria and up the echoing stairwells with boys we once whispered about and often disparaged, who were now his constant companions.

I hated the stinging humiliation of that, of knowing his growing popularity fed on my secrets. Before I moved to my grandparents', I couldn't wait for the final bell, but now I preferred the overheated rooms and the clang and rattle of the radiators, banging like Marley's ghost jumping off the page to wake an unsuspecting victim from the slumber of those long hours. I no longer despised the battered desk with its pencil shavings, notebooks, primers, and spitballs, its pungent baloney, mustard, and rotting-apple smell, and the anonymous taunts, furtively scrawled in turquoise ink plucked from the inside of my collar where they landed and hastily shoved under its dark lid. I perversely enjoyed my recent celebrity as the object of a custody battle, a dubious status that Rabbit had personally conferred on me, explaining to everyone in my class, including myself, that this was indeed what was going on. Anything was better than the slow, ticking silence of my grandmother's apartment.

In fact, I trace to those days my enjoyment of ironing, something for which Annie is forever grateful. I kept Lucy company for hours on end while she pressed my grandfather's shirts like a master plasterer, applying a new blast of starch only in the places that showed, leaving others soft on the skin, coming down on a cuff and staying there until it could hold its own against any weather condition and, with a graceful hand, lightly touching the iron to my grandmother's silk blouses and slips, linen sheets and pillowcases, neatly folding as she went, talking to me in words punctuated by the hiss of steam, surrounding us both with the reassuring order of a freshly laundered world, a place where any stain could be removed, any wrinkle smoothed away.

During those long hours waiting for my life to right itself, I wondered where my father was, what he thought about my grandmother stealing me from Theo, about the piece of paper that said she could and the judge who signed it. The judge had sat eating lamb chops with his bare hands as Lucy bore down on him with a clean napkin and all the scorn she could get away with. For the first time, the conviction that my father would appear and set everything right wobbled like the childish illusion it was.

16

If I looked hard, I could make out our tall studio windows in the line of Gothic spires, stone gargoyles, gabled roofs, and slate chimneys etched in a bleak winter morning along the western edge of the park. A smudge of weak sunlight glanced off its panes directly under the ornamental busts that glowed eerie and silver and kept the sleek art deco silhouette of our building from disappearing into an envelope of mist. When I was small and lost my bearings on the vast rolling green of the Sheep Meadow, I had only to look up and see the sleek carved heads and hooded eyes of home. Now, from my deep sill on the East Side, these guardians seemed poised to dive into the dull March sky and swim to me like two giant mermaids from the Jazz Age.

Theo seemed miles away, a faint glow in the swirling leaden soup, as I squeezed my eyes shut against the unfamiliar contents of Roland's room and tried to imagine my mother padding listlessly around the kitchen, the bright kimono no longer able to cheer, slipping off a shoulder, its magic sleeves forgotten in the ache of knowing I was just across the park and as lost to her as she was to me. I could see her starting the coffee, alone in the big apartment, missing Claire and missing me, sitting at the kitchen table staring into her cup with no heart for the day, feeling her loss in the explosion of a teaspoon in the cavernous empty sink.

I thought about home constantly, lying on my dead uncle's bedspread in the room that had been the scene of the dozens of naps I had succumbed to in happier years, where, facedown on the navy and white striped cotton duck cloth, I could hear Claire and Theo and Grandma and the muffled talk that never failed to cause my eyes to feel the weight of sleep. Now everything had been dusted, polished, aired, and wiped clean of any traces of its former occupant; it no longer comforted, but enclosed, like the circumstances that had trapped me beyond my understanding and my ability to affect them.

I looked for the toy soldiers I had admired during my earlier visits, for the neat stack of books (Jack London, *A Tale of Two Cities,* the Encyclopaedia Britannica), for the collection of wooden tennis racquets, and for the yellowed photograph, framed in silver, of Roland and Claire. Their faces, framed in matching wool and velvet, and the same blond curls, bobbed apple-cheeked above the sides of a pony cart drawn by the same sad-eyed creature on whose patient back I was sure I had bumped around the rutted track in the children's zoo. But everything was gone, replaced by the meager assortment of belongings Theo had packed for me the day I was taken away. I believed if I had been free to touch his things, I might have known what to do, but now there was no surface that held his thoughts. I wondered if he had run into Edgar and Marilyn Jacoby, still strapped in their seats on a smoldering wing, wild-eyed and dazed from their unscheduled plummet to earth.

My grandparents' apartment building, which had always been bright and safe and mine to enter and leave at will, had become a fortress. The welcoming *whoosh* of its elevator groaning under the weight of people heavy with packages, chill, and news of the outside, now creaked with warning and the heavy drag of chains. The richly polished hush of its hallways, once so full of mystery, rife with clues about the people living behind its doors; a whiff of something fragrant, a soft voice, a piano, a sigh, the secret click of locks, the slide of keys palmed in soft gloves, now gave off the dark smell of a prison out of which there was no easy exit. I think that was the hardest of all, seeing the cold edge of my grandmother's orders to block all possible escape routes in the watchful eyes of the staff, especially Buddy and Lucy, who could not conceal their sympathy for my plight.

"She just want her boy back is all, that poor dead child and she don't care who she hurts to get him," said Lucy more to the cloud of steam over her ironing board than to me.

"Theo is your real mother, and your grandma is tryin' to get you away from her before the court decides Claire's got no rights bein' a lesbeen and all. Nothin' to do with you, precious. The girls had demselves a big fight and broke up and your grandma's afraid Theo is gonna take you away, and she's gonna lose you just like she lost poor Roland. Understan, dahlin'?" Lucy leaned hard on one of Barnaby's cuffs as though pressing the truth of this into the cloth itself. I didn't understand. Claire was my real mother, too and I didn't see how making me live here would bring Uncle Roland back.

Even though he wasn't supposed to, Buddy always told me when my mom came to the lobby to ask him to phone the Hirsh apartment and announce her intention to see me. Under orders, Buddy invariably turned her away. "Your mama was here last night, lad. Sat here for two hours, she did, tryin' to get up to see you." The words slid from one side of his mouth, twisted in my direction while he kept the other side perfectly still, eyes front, on the door, all business, unblinking, as though only half of him were disobeying orders. "She misses you, you know. Don't you ever forget that." If anyone approached, he sang out his greeting extra loud: "Good morning, ma'am! And a fine day it is, sir!" as though to proclaim his innocence to anyone who might report our conversation to my grandmother.

Most nights, after listlessly pushing food around my plate, I left the table as soon as Barnaby nodded in my direction and said, "I'm sure you've got better things to do than to sit here with your old grandpa and grandma." Taking care not to scuff the legs, I slid off the stiff-backed Queen Anne chair that had become my place at the formal banquet table Lucy set for three. Sometimes Grandma followed me and sat on the edge of the bed while I brushed my teeth in Roland's bathroom.

"You know I love you, don't you?" she began, examining the corners of the bedspread as though secrets were contained in its cotton batting, but I let the force of the water drown her words and splash over the blue basin because I didn't know that at all.

"William dear, I know this is terribly difficult for you now, but some day, my darling, when you're older, I think you'll understand why I had to do it," she said, patting the edge of my blanket, inviting me to hop in.

"A long time ago I lost my own little boy, your uncle Roland, and even though I love your mommy Claire and Theo, too, in my own way, I want to make sure you grow up like other boys, go to a good school, enter a profession, or maybe go into business like your grandpa, and get married and have children of your own."

She did not look at me when she said this, but across the room, at a point beyond this moment. The thin skin on the backs of her hands sounded dry and old like crepe paper as she nervously drew one hand over the other, then let one flutter up to her pearls, which encircled a neck that rose, stiff and patrician, out of one of her dozens of pale cashmere twinsets. These never failed to remind me of the luminescent seashells, baked bone white, that lined the path to the tiny Bouvier trailer, where I imagined Doris and Roy planning to fly to New York to talk sense into this grandmother who claimed to love me.

"Theo says that when I get married, she'll bake the tallest and most beautiful wedding cake anybody ever saw. And Claire promised to take pictures that Aunt Jessica will put in her magazine," I said hopefully, managing a weak smile at the memory of the day I asked them who I would marry and how we laughed as I made sick faces at their suggestions—Jennifer, yuk, Brooke, double yuk, goggle-eyed Georgine Feinberg who cornered me in the laundry room and planted a slobbery kiss on my four-year-old cheek and cried when I rubbed it off with the tail of my shirt, blech—wondering if Grandma knew they too hoped I would find someone nice when I grew up. I wondered if I'd go to hell for wishing she would clutch at her heart and die that night, so I could slip past the ambulance driver and the medics and poor shocked Barnaby in the confusion. People in bathrobes would peek out of the doors on my grandparents' floor, shaking their heads at the little boy pretending to follow his grandmother's lifeless body out the door.

"If you love me, you'll let me go home," I said snapping the sheet out of her hands, full of the need to pound something, grateful for the pillow, remembering how upset everybody got when I could not stop pummeling Carl.

"I *do* love you, William dear, that's why I can't," she said sadly before she left the room, leaving behind a cloud of perfume that drifted down onto my bed and settled into the folds of my pajamas, heady and sweet; that, and the slippery sound of silk-lined clothes I would forever associate with deception. When these conversations became too difficult, I pretended another person was posing as my grandmother; one day, my grandfather would realize this, pull off her rubber mask, and have her arrested. But something in my grandfather's eyes told me he had long since given in to the strength of my grandmother's will and could be counted on merely to offer the illusion of threat, like the occasional low growl of an old dog who still dreams of blood but has no teeth for the fight.

"Why can't I go home, Grandpa?" I asked the man who had no say in this house—who'd wanted no part of it for so long that he'd forgotten what to say.

"You've got to bide your time with your grandma," he told me.

When I could no longer hear the soft creak of shoe leather on the deep Persian rug that rolled past my bedroom and carried my grandmother to hers, I tiptoed out of bed over to the pale window, where I sat for hours on Roland's sill, dreaming of escape while I watched a half-hearted moon float over the trees, which seemed to beckon me with bare arms as the wind moved them against the cold black semicircle of night. I imagined the trees were alive; if I ventured out, they would warn one another of my approach, then laugh at the futility of my effort as I plunged through the sleeping park, past the grinning, riderless horses in the carousel, the ghost skaters on the pond, who traced sharp circles in the black ice and the bundles of rags huddled in the deepest hollows and exhaling foul breath into dreams of soft beds from grimy blankets of sharp-smelling newsprint. The trees would become a low, unearthly cackle deep in the throat of the dark gusts that gave them voice, mocking my passage as I became hopelessly tangled in the sharp brambles that lay at their roots, grabbing for my bleeding ankles on the dark, heart-pounding journey home.

I think I would have tried to run for it anyway, in spite of my fear of the cold and the monsters lurking in the dark woods between Fifth Avenue and Central Park West, which now stretched before me like the shark-infested waters of Devil's Island. But I was not sure that Theo wouldn't drive me back herself. I did not want to see the side of her that knew her chances were better if she played by the rules and returned me to my grandmother's. I couldn't have stood that.

I wanted the Theo who deliberately provoked Mrs. Langelotti's anger, who baited her and shamed her for taking her disapproval out on me; I wanted the Theo who called and told Mrs. Jacoby *she* was the one not welcome in *our* home. I didn't want the Theo who lied that she had lost my father to something tragic, who stopped using the word "lesbian," until finally Claire left us forever.

I wanted to be important enough to break rules for, no matter the consequences, and I did not want to be left out the way I suspected Theo had cast Claire out of our lives. I suppose most boys dream of fathers who ride to their rescue on white stallions, but in the absence of such a man—and of Claire, who gamely tried to play the role—my fantasy put Theo squarely in the saddle (which was really the bucket seat of James Bond's deadly Aston Martin). I imagined her smashing down the richly paneled Hirsh door, gun blazing, demanding of my shocked and terrified grandparents that her son be returned to her immediately or else. She and I would disappear into the night, and would laugh at her audacity from the safety of our hideout in Baxter and Jessica's snug attic.

I wanted no part of the Theo who could be controlled by a law, even if the penalty for breaking it was a guaranteed prison term, and I didn't care that this was not convenient for the raising of a young boy. Maybe that's why, when I saw my opportunity, I headed in the opposite direction.

"I GOT AN AWFUL fiah in my head, precious," said Lucy. Her eyes glittered with the fight her body was waging against the new strain of flu circulating in New York that year, felling the hardiest of the hardy. The virus was so potentially lethal the Health Department had set up makeshift clinics where rich and poor eyed each other suspiciously from hard benches, while they endured the wait for free shots.

"I'll tell you why they call it the swine flu," Lucy said, drawing the shawl collar of her robe over her puny chest to cushion a cough that was phlegmy and deep and full of warning, working its way up from her lungs, " 'cause it puts ya lower than a pig in a sty, dat's the truth."

She peered around my bedroom door and spoke in a thin, conspiratorial wheeze. "I trust ya'll get to school today without telling ya grandma old Lucy is too sick to take ya," and I was sure she would hear my heart clanging under my pajamas, but she shuffled back to the kitchen, moving like the living dead who wore their hair in dreadlocks and stalked the abandoned sugar plantations in her tales of Jamaica.

I remember warm flannel slippers on cold tile, a feverish Lucy absently scraping the pot for the last gummy spoonful of oatmeal. As I slid into my place at the large worktable, she set my steaming cereal bowl before me and lamely pushed a thick faience pitcher and sugar bowl in my direction; I believed she would now read my thoughts, but she just stared into the bottom of her mug of strong Caribbean coffee laced with something far more fortifying than cream. Lucy was lost in the rattle of her bones, seeing nothing but her misery.

As was the custom with women whose circumstances did not provide a compelling reason to rise early, my grandmother slept until those who were not so fortunate were safely off the street. She avoided the sullen commuters huddled in their coats, who rode in from Queens and the upper reaches of Manhattan and issued forth, up urine-splashed subway stairs and into the dazzle of Fifth Avenue just beyond. There they stood a little taller, strode a little more purposefully, hoping to blend in, knowing they never would no matter the cut of the cloth that kept the biting wind from its work.

It seemed so long ago that I dressed in the dark to ride the subway with Claire. I watched her, fingering the metal skin of the Leica as it lay quietly in the black shadow of her leather satchel waiting for the right moment to photograph the people who lived in exotic places like Corona and Bayside, Hunter's Point, Astoria and Beechurst and tunneled to work under the river, racing the sun to the day. Flashes of soot-streaked windows, the sound of an alarm, the bitter smell of coffee, a curse, a prayer, a tumble of life with the sleep still in it, rushing by in houses built long before the elevated tracks brought strangers to within inches of their thin curtains, close enough to smell last night's dishes still in the sink, to see the deadness around the eyes, not long enough to know why, as the train hurtled between stations, then plunged underground for the final sprint, full of hair tonic, cologne, and sour breath.

When we surfaced hours later, we were stiff from standing most of the way, sore from bracing against the sudden stops and hairpin turns that could roll those who dangled from the overhead straps into another without warning. Propelled upward in the crush, we often found ourselves face to face with Buddy, who, from seven-thirty to nine every morning, including the extra quarter-hour that held potential for stragglers, stood guard over my lightly snoring grandparents, asleep twelve stories above the crowded pavement, with the fierceness and the single-minded sense of duty of a Doberman. Some mornings, Claire sipped coffee with Mary until, as my grandmother liked to say, "the streets were respectable again."

Buddy and José, a shy, smiling man from Bogotá who came on at midnight and was hoping to assume Buddy's exalted position when the senior doorman retired, were the only people with a key to the building's massive front door; not even my grandmother or the cardinal's ancient sister, who lived in an endless series of vast and musty rooms next door, had one. When residents or guests arrived, Buddy simply let them in; if he wasn't on the door, it was correctly assumed to be locked, so the visitor waited for his hasty return. Only the uninitiated would disturb the elegant hush and press the bell discreetly built into the building's ornately carved entrance; everyone else knew Buddy's absence meant that a delivery person was being escorted up the back elevator to one of the service doors behind each apartment, where one of the building's housekeepers would greet him cordially and accept the parcel with no idle chat or undue delay.

In better days, Barnaby had bragged to Uncle Baxter that this minor inconvenience resulted in zero burglaries the year it was instituted and that at the quarterly co-op board meeting all objections had been voted down, including those of his own wife, who was appalled at the idea of having to wait on a public street like a common person, even if that street was Fifth Avenue.

After breakfast, I dressed quietly, filled my duffel with extra pajamas, underwear, and a well-thumbed photograph of Claire and Theo and me. This was creased from my jamming it into the bag with the cotton shirts Theo had folded with great care, defiantly slowing down the events of the afternoon of my arrest—which, contrary to patient explanations of the difference between temporary child custody and police custody, I believed for years was the case. I was careful to leave a pair of socks draped over the edge of an open drawer and my comb on the broad rim of the sink along with an uncapped tube of toothpaste. My grammar lay open on the small desk at the foot of Uncle Roland's bed. This, I hoped, would give me until at least four o'clock that afternoon before suspicion turned to alarm and the police issued a new warrant for my capture.

I was careful to take the photograph, not just because I wanted it with me, though I did, but because all Grandma had was a picture of an eighteen-month-old baby, all cheeks, red cowlicks, and bracelets of fat, peering out from a heavy, velvet-backed silver frame. I foolishly believed it would be more difficult for them to draw a Wanted poster without a recent photo of the escapee.

The bag was heavier than I remembered, but I swallowed the sound of my own effort as I padded down the long hall past my grandparents' separate bedrooms, past the Manet suspended in its place of honor over the English sideboard on the butter-yellow wall of the dining room.

"William dear, aren't you forgetting something?" The rope of my grandmother's voice uncoiled at my back, hit its mark, and pulled tight.

"Late for school," I muttered, hoping she wouldn't smell the fear crouching in my chest.

"Grandma's good-bye kiss," she reminded me, the sound of her dressing gown rearranging itself, the sweet stale morning smell of her pouring over me as she smiled and lowered a cheek for my dutiful peck. I put the duffel down and met the swaying pouch of her face halfway, planting what I hoped was a kiss as half-hearted as the ones yesterday and the day before that, hoping I would not give myself away by trying too hard.

"Where's Lucy, darling?" she asked, looking over my head in the direction of our housekeeper's room, while I prayed Lucy wouldn't suddenly explode this lie with the terrible racking cough I had heard earlier.

"In the hall. She's waiting. Bye, Grandma."

"This afternoon, we'll take a taxi down to Mark Cross and buy you a proper school bag, how's that?" she said, eyeing my lumpy luggage.

"This is okay," I said, barely breathing. I tried not to wobble under its weight or that of the older, more calculating version of Claire's gray eyes.

First there was the long gangplank of polished parquetry on either side of the Tabriz runner, a line of cedar closets holding Grandpa's

British warmer and Grandma's mink coat, the Empire table, masses of tulips lolling on broken necks, chosen for the tenderness of their apricot tint and spilling over the side of a Baccarat bowl, a silver shell holding a small key, a flyer from Bergdorf's announcing a fur sale and a petal dusted with pollen on a small rug upon which simple desert people once prayed.

Six more steps. Five. The smooth click of the lock. Three. A door closing on well-tended hinges, the sound of my grandmother's velvet slippers walking away from her last chance to keep me from my mothers.

The elevator door opened quietly on the empty lobby. An open can of Brasso and a soft cloth left discreetly behind the bench, and a panting Mr. Cowperthwaite from the floor below my grandparents, in baggy sweats with his soft-eyed beagle waiting patiently in the lee of the snapping canopy told me all I needed to know. I could feel my heart pounding in my mouth as I walked as quickly and as nonchalantly as I could toward the bright light pouring into the gloom. I was convinced Buddy would descend any second and stop me.

"Glad you came along, son," beet-faced Mr. Cowperthwaite said as he and his frozen dog slipped in out of the chill. "It's cold out there. I hope you're bundled up."

"Yes, sir," I said to my left shoulder as I braced for the gust that blew me around the corner toward Madison Avenue and downtown.

17

Grandma Doris was making cactus tea in an ancient pitted kettle that blew its whistle with the urgency of a much younger utensil. Everything in the Bouvier household seemed afflicted with this leaping energy; people and objects moved as though stung, except Roy, who presided over the poltergeist from his green leatherette BarcaLounger in the salon, as Doris called the living room. It was no wider than a hallway, but back in the twenties she had read about Gertrude Stein and Alice B. Toklas and other patrons of the arts who had opened their Paris apartments and country houses to disheveled, poor, often drunk but always brilliant bands of painters, writers, sculptors, musicians and that these spontaneous gatherings were called salons.

In Broken Arrow, Doris Bouvier was known as an arts patron of sorts, and even more as a refuge and mother confessor to rebels, runaways, clairvoyants, religious fanatics, and all manner of oddballs who were not exactly well received or even remotely understood in this conservative and solidly Protestant town on the edge of the plain that had been built by fiercely independent people who risked everything in the great land rush. Their descendants never took another chance, even if it meant ordering the same thing for lunch every day of their lives.

"I can't understand how you can put everything you own in the back of a gut-jolting prairie schooner, have your babies in the open, freezing cold back of the wagon while the wind or worse howls for your scalp, risk dysentery, dementia, and sudden death from every direction, then give rise to generations of people who are afraid of herbal tea and a little chanting, as though even mentioning these things were tantamount to becoming a member of the Communist party or some Satanic cult. Makes no sense to me, no sirree. I think these people lost more than their spokes on the way out here." Doris clucked, shaking her head at the narrow opinions of her neighbors.

The old Bee-Line, with its silver bullet lines, neat rows of rivets marching along its seams, its front door hatch hung with a spirit pouch, and the collapsible clothesline out back flapping with Roy's three-to-a-pack plaid shirts, stood in shining tribute to Doris Bouvier's sense of the eclectic. A tidy herb garden eked out of the hardscrabble in front contained rosemary, thyme, sweet basil, and chives, as well as strange medicinal things like mugwort, comfey root, and belladonna. Doris mixed people with the same flair and you never knew who you might find at her red and white Formica kitchen table. Once, when I was too small to understand but big enough to be curious, Claire and Theo dropped in on Doris and Roy unannounced and sent an entire family of Salvadoran refugees scrambling to the top bunk in the spare room.

As the kettle hissed and rattled on the tiny burner, Doris banged cupboard doors, stretching fleshy arms into dark corners, running fingers over the edges of crockery for chips, passing up the "Make Love, Not War" mug and settling on the baby-blue "I Love Grandma" mug we had sent one Mother's Day, and another decorated with daisies and peace signs that announced her determination to suffer "No Nukes." More rattling. Cutlery. Plates. A plastic bear filled with organic elder blossom honey. Tiger's milk. Boxes of saltines and cookies encased in plastic and twist-tied to bar the insects that crawled in out of the Oklahoma dirt.

"Damn ants," Doris said to the flat ground, which rolled away from the porthole over her sink in shimmering waves toward a horizon straight and sharp enough to shave a man's face clean. As she poked in and out of cupboards, she fashioned a stiff cardboard gangplank out of the back of a cookie box. Then she hit the front door with one practiced and well-padded hip, gently placing the dazed ant on the front step. "Too cold for him out there. He'll be back," Doris muttered, as the door slapped shut. She cracked two ginseng capsules into the green liquid and finally came to rest at the table, parking her heaving bulk alongside a plate piled high with Mallomars.

"Does she know you're here?" Doris asked. She peered out from under a mop of frizzy straw-colored hair so white at the roots, she could have been wearing a tennis headband. Eyes the color of pine needles fixed on her guest.

Claire shook her head dumbly without looking up from her tea. She hadn't planned to come and now she didn't know what to say to these good people; they lived too far away from their daughter to see the small changes that added up to the stranger who had once been Theo. It seemed like a good idea to look for answers here, to search the faces of Theo's parents for clues, to ask these people who said they loved her and adored their grandson for help, but now the trailer felt hot and claustrophobic and Doris and Roy seemed smaller and a little seedier than they had on Claire's last visit, when things were different, when she didn't see them quite so clearly, having observed them only through the filter of her feelings for their daughter.

"Theo has changed," Claire began, sensing the need to start somewhere outside herself.

"Everyone does, sooner or later, darlin'," Doris countered. She waited for the rest of the story, which never had much to do with how it began, and she wondered if Claire really was in cahoots with Mary Hirsh, as Theo had said she was beginning to suspect.

"I can't believe Claire would do this. How could she? No matter what happened between us. He's our son. *My* son." A small gasp, amplified by the phone cable. Doris remembered the tumble of words, tears, and silences that said more about it than her daughter ever could.

"Theo was brave and daring and reckless and I loved her for that," Claire said quietly into her tea, starting fresh as Doris knew she would. "She saw life differently; it wasn't just about sex." Claire colored a bit, remembering where she was. "Something happened and the Theo I knew started to disappear, a little bit at a time, as though she was becoming someone else, someone I didn't know."

Doris felt the truth awaken and begin to flow around her. "What happened, honey?"

"I guess it's what didn't happen, really. She never lied about us, you know, about our relationship. Even when my mom refused to acknowledge her existence, she never stopped encouraging me to just keep saying the truth until it became easier to hear, as natural as my name. She used to send food to soften my parents up and when I was really down about it, she'd tell me it could be worse and say, 'Her daughter may be a lesbian, but at least she's eating right,' and I'd laugh in spite of myself." Claire wore the look of someone who believes all happiness is behind her. Her memories had not yet been reduced to nostalgia; the hurt was too new for that. "I don't know, Doris, I just don't know."

"Yes, you do, we all know everything there is to know, we just have a hard time seeing it is all," said Doris, willing herself the time to wait for Claire to get around to it.

"At first, when Willy was born, we told everyone we trusted we were his parents and damn anybody who thought less of us and I felt more part of things, part of a family, than I ever have, half mother, half father, happy. Then Willy started school, and we both knew it wasn't going to be easy, but I didn't think Theo would turn on me and side with people who punished our son just because lesbians made them uncomfortable."

"Are you sure she was siding with them?"

"What do you call it? She said Carl's grandmother was right. She deliberately went out of her way to make new friends with all those Upper East Side phonies from Miss Porter's and the Junior League who wouldn't know a lesbian if they fell over one. Then she let them think she had a dead husband somewhere, so their kids who all just so happened to be exactly Willy's age would play with him and he could have normal friends," said Claire, still reeling from the shock of overhearing Theo's conversation with Bitsie Clark.

"Do you think she meant that Mrs. Jacoby was right, or that Mrs. Jacoby was an example of the reactions Willy would face if you two didn't try to keep things secret?" Doris had her own thoughts about not correcting other people's perceptions of you, letting them think whatever was easier for everybody concerned.

"Do you know, one of them actually asked me if Theo would mind if she invited an interesting man to accidentally drop by while she and Willy were visiting for the weekend? What was I? Her roommate? What was I supposed to say? 'Sure, Missy, or Muffy, or whatever the hell her name was, fix her up with her next husband, I don't mind. I'm just her brokenhearted lover'?"

Doris could see the sting of humiliation, more than anger, mottling Claire's pale skin, riding high on her brow.

"You know," Doris interrupted her, "I've always been a wanderer, never stuck with anything, stayed with anyone, loved something long enough to claim it. I borrowed people, wore them for awhile, then returned them like overdue library books, a little ashamed of myself, but not enough to stop doing it. I guess I never wanted to wait around for things to be different from the way they started, or for them to be over." Claire saw Doris begin to drift away from the troubles on her kitchen table and she relaxed into this new course.

"Until Roy?"

"Nope. Until Theo," Doris answered, holding Claire in a deep gaze. "I could have left Roy anytime, and he knew it, told me it was what held him, the idea that I could up and disappear any time. Kept him on his toes, he said. Even as the babies came, I never felt my roots sink in; I figured one day I'd take off and write them postcards from the next place and Roy would raise them with the romantic version of their mother. But all that changed with Theo."

"Why Theo and not the others?"

"Because from the minute she was born, she was just like me, and I saw in her what I could never see in myself, a person who wants to belong, to be like other people who are satisfied with the life they're dealt and don't haunt themselves with what's around the next bend. I was fascinated by her and the fact that the part of me I was afraid of most had to be born in another person before I could love it."

"But she's not like other people, she's different," Claire insisted.

"I encouraged Theo to break the rules because I knew how easily she could be hurt by them. Down deep, she's a sweet girl whose crazy mama taught her being a little different is a great place to hide."

"Are you saying, deep down she's not really a lesbian?"

"No, sweetheart, I'm just sayin', deep down maybe she didn't mean it the way you took it. Maybe she was just being a mother, the mother she taught me to be," said Doris, thinking about men and women, husbands and wives, mothers and daughters, *her* daughter with someone else's, and the shock of it happening in her own family, an idea that she'd taken a long time getting used to, still had trouble with, that she never let on about except to Roy. Theo's mother thought about the silent bargain of any alliance built on the delicate and scarred ground of feelings, and for the first time felt her years.

"She didn't even want Willy! I was the one who wanted a baby! I wanted a baby more than anything and it almost made me crazy. It almost ruined my career, all those sappy pictures of fetal development and fat Madonnas and everybody reproducing but me. But I didn't have any damn estrogen left and I begged her to have our beautiful boy and then, bit by bit, she started acting as though it were her idea and just threw me away like some dyke who embarrassed her in front of her friends. Is *that* being a mother, Doris—is it?" Claire's voice rose and alarmed Roy, who was napping on the recliner.

"You know, most people don't really change at all, they just become what they really are and it takes the other person by surprise. Kind of like buying a house, then finding out the roof leaks. If you love the house, you'll stay and fix it." Doris allowed these words to drift down over Claire, wondering if they would eventually sink in.

"How are my gals doin'?" Roy called out from the BarcaLounger, aiming his voice at the kitchen door.

"Just fine, Roy sweetheart. You want some Mallomars in there?" Doris shouted back.

Roy ambled into the narrow kitchen, palmed a handful of cookies, and touched his wife's shoulder with the tenderness of a bridegroom, smiling a broad smile at his wife and at the young woman he, too, had not come easily to thinking of as his daughter-in-law.

Claire and Doris watched him edge around the kitchen furniture like a cat measuring space with his whiskers. Claire pulled the cake off the back of her cookie with her fingers and took baby bites of gooey marshmallow.

"How's our boy Roy?" she said, forcing a smile.

"I'd be better if I knew where my grandson was," he said, knowing Doris would be cross with him for getting to it so bluntly. Doris liked to draw people out, but Roy couldn't stand not knowing where I was.

"What do you mean, where is your grandson? He's at home with Theo where he always is," said Claire, panic growing inside her as she watched their reaction, faces hardening into a mixture of confusion and disbelief.

"When did you last speak to Theo or Willy?" Roy asked, hunkering down for the duration. Doris shot him a cross look that said, "Now you've done it, nobody tells the truth when they're cross-examined."

"One afternoon a few weeks ago—I knew Theo would be at the store—I talked to Willy." Claire spoke haltingly, remembering the sound of my voice asking her why she left, when she'd come home, telling her I was sorry for making her leave, promising to be better.

"It's not your fault," she had said. "It's a problem your mama and I are having. I didn't leave *you,* Willy Wonka. I love you. I'll always love you even if Mama and I live in different houses."

"Am I divorced?" I had asked and Claire now regretted that she had answered truthfully, "I don't know honey. Maybe."

Now she faced Doris and Roy. "I've called the apartment several times since, but Theo always answers the phone and I hang up because I don't know what to say that will change anything. I called from the road just before I got here, but no one was home."

Claire didn't say "the road" was an apartment belonging to a pretty young woman named Dakota whom she had halfheartedly picked up at one of the many truck stops she was shooting along the way, believing her own ruse, looking for the truth about the lives of strangers so she could tell herself lies about her own—*I haven't really left. I'm on the road. I'm working on a show*—she reminded herself as the miles and weeks ticked away.

"Lotta tattoos around here," she had said when she sat down at Dakota's counter and noticed bright red hair skinned back under an old Orioles cap. "Beats Miss Grundy hairnets," Dakota had said when Claire focused her camera on the tip of the peak and the face under it: cat's eyes penciled out to her temples, downy young skin in the spots the Pan-Cake had missed. This face had seen more than one brush with the bad side of people.

What is it about women behind counters? Claire had thought.

They drank coffee and talked about the men scattered around them. Claire told Dakota they reminded her of crumpled cigarettes, bleary and stale, stinking up the place from haulin' ass, drinking too much coffee, downing too many reds, and living with the constant fear of eighteen wheels skidding off an icy road with ten tons behind them, making an instant coffee table out of the cab.

When Claire asked her if she ever got tired of CB talk, slinging hash, having her butt pinched, and hearing propositions made by her grizzled customers, never seeing normal people out for a drive, Dakota leaned over the counter, smiled deliciously, lightly touched Claire's fingers on the Leica and said, "I'm okay around here. It's around my type that I get in trouble."

Later, in Dakota's tiny ground-floor apartment in what had been the Blue Bird Motel, they drank a rough wine that needed food neither was willing to make.

"Whew!" Claire wondered whether she had gasped at the fiery vintage burning her throat or at the fierceness of her own intent. "What is this stuff?"

"Road Kill Red," Dakota answered, smiling sweetly, raising her jelly glass.

It wasn't the first time Claire had discovered the brief but powerful anesthesia of someone who wore off as soon as the sharp edge of loss returned, each time a little sooner as though she was building up a tolerance with each dosage. When Claire saw Theo's face in the one Dakota wore to bed, pale and dusted with freckles in the merciless morning light, it was time to move on. That was this morning, before she decided to make a run for Broken Arrow.

"Your mother got a damn court order, claiming abuse, probably from one of her fancy judge friends, and took him away from Theo. And now he's gone, Claire. We think you might know where he is," said Roy bluntly.

"My son is missing and you think I *kidnapped* him?"

"Roy doesn't mean to accuse, Claire. We just want to know why your mother has taken Willy away from Theo and where he is now," interrupted Doris, who was working hard to keep the anger out of her voice. "We're very worried."

"Do you know where he is?" continued Roy, ignoring his wife.

"No, I don't, and you're going to have to believe that!" Claire said, hurling her cookie back onto the plate and slamming her shin so hard in her haste to get up from that table and away from her accusers, the pain made her dizzy.

"I guess we don't have much choice," Roy said in a voice that did not need to shout its threat.

After she left, Doris didn't see much reason to criticize. As she watched Claire squeal off in a rented black Camaro, which left a streak of rubber on the blacktop in front of the trailer, she thought: *When Roy gets that riled, there's no turning him back. May as well stand with him and fight his way.* Before she turned her back on the window, she composed herself and wrote the license-plate number on the blackboard over the dryer rack.

There was a cough and the faint whistle of air in a windpipe before she heard the familiar "Hirsh Residence."

At any other time, Claire would have spent at least five minutes politely inquiring after Lucy's health, she would have asked what she was taking and why she was not in bed. But today she simply said, "Lucy, please ask my mother to come to the phone."

If it had been any other time, Lucy would have reprimanded the girl she loved like her own for being so rude, so dismissive, but she said, as formally as the flu would allow, "I'll get huh, Miz Claire."

"What the hell have you done with Willy?" Claire shouted over the roar of traffic on the exit ramp over her head. She had driven for a while, too fast, as far as she could get from that stupid capsule Roy and Doris called home, then pulled over at a foul-smelling phone booth in the middle of East Shit, Nowhere.

"Where are you dear? We've all been worried sick about you." Claire remembered how infuriatingly genteel her mother became when cornered. She sounded as though she might be making plans for lunch.

"You got a court order and took Willy away from his home. You said you suspected abuse. Abuse! I can't believe it. How could you do such a thing?

"I did it for you, darling, of course."

A whirring sound rose up out of the wire, followed by the sound of a blow-out on the adjacent highway, and for a crazy second she wondered if luck had run out for one of Dakota's truckers.

"You did it for me? I didn't ask you to do such a horrible thing!" Claire shouted down the buzzing and clicking on the line.

"Where are you?" Mary asked again. "This connection is dreadful." The imploring voice was receding.

"I'm on my way home. And you had better have an explanation!" Claire shouted into the dying phone. She had no idea whether her mother heard her. She remembered, with the clarity of yesterday, the young bully in the butcher shop who threw straw in her face when she was four years old. She remembered how it clung to her hair and to her coat, how her child's voice had said "I'm going to hit you" as she shook her small fist at him, and how he mocked her empty threat. Now she stood in the middle of the Oklahoma flats, thinking *I'm almost halfway through my forties. I've just lost my lover and my son and I'm absolutely nowhere in my life.* Claire remembered how she wanted to bloody that fat kid's nose so badly, pummel him into the floor until he spat sawdust, but was powerless to lower her arm, which had frozen in mid-threat. She felt the humiliation of that moment all over again until she realized that the buzzing in her ears was not remembered shame, but the sound of the dial tone pushing her out of the booth, back into her life. And mine.

18

Mr. Cosmopoulos had said, "If you want to know how things stand between your folks, look at that picture you're carrying around in your duffel. It's all there, mister. The mouths are smiling, but the eyes are hard. Look at the distance between them. Are they touching? Or holding themselves apart? People break up long before they know it themselves. Take a real good look. Yep. You'll see it, mister."

I pretended not to hear him and I think he knew it, but I did see what he meant—in the offered hand gone empty, in the space between their bodies—and I felt my own spine stiffen, resisting its natural inclination to melt into another's. I thought of our wall of photographs at home and wondered why I'd never noticed how death, masquerading as the long afternoon light, had cast Uncle Alan's face in shadow. Something in Uncle Baxter's sidelong look at Aunt Jess just before the click, her eyes gone flat and black, like a darkened stage where the players are hiding in plain sight, flashed a warning. Divorce, illness, something worse? His face said he didn't know either.

The Thanksgiving before last. Uncle Peter's house in South Neck. The turkey carcass, a row of half-eaten pies, apple-sausage stuffing, cider, corn bread, buttered beans, Brussels sprouts, and something I wouldn't eat, succotash, congealing in Pyrex dishes, mashed potatoes redolent of sage, spoon lakes drained of gravy, sweet potatoes with marshmallows for the children's table. Molly and Theo and Claire wrapping platters, licking the last bits off their fingers, patting their stomachs, sponging counters, talking food, work, the whispering of women. Harry and I racing up the back stairs to stare at Charlotte's boyfriend, an awkward South Neck senior pulling at his collar and badly knotted tie, giving the impression of being strangled by his clothes as he nervously waited for my cousin. The noisy and important business of boys. The sofa I believed was made from a real camel's back; soft chairs draped in old shawls; Molly's needlepoint pillows; Peter on the fireplace bench, absently stirring the logs; Barnaby and Grandma Hirsh in opposing corners of the room; the room itself wrapped in its own thoughts, punctuated by the soft ticking of the silver mantel clock, the fat crackle of applewood, a gust of laughter from the kitchen. The sudden tumble, coatless, to the porch, Grandma protesting the cold, Claire's camera on the tripod, timer ticking, giggles. "All together, one, two, three, hurry now, smile. C'mon, c'mon, c'mon. Click."

And there, frozen on the wall, just as Mr. Cosmopoulos had said, was everything I needed to know: a small angry girl hiding in the set of Claire's jaw, the wide-open longing in Theo's; their hands rest on my shoulders, but they are careful not to touch each other. An old man searching his youngest son's face, measuring him against the memory of another. Uncle Peter, sensing this, is caught turning away and offering his hand to Molly, who stands apart from the group, feet planted on the top step, arms clamped firmly around Harry in a pose as clear as a sign that says "Keep Off," fingers wiggling in empty space, reaching for Charlotte, who is already reaching for her own life in the arms of a boy whose name she will soon forget. And the tightness around my grandmother's mouth tells us all we ever needed to know of her intentions.

Something Mr. C. said about people always watching for something that doesn't come, which keeps them from seeing what does, made me think of the afternoon we hung Mr. Kimsky over our red dining room table. I had no idea this would be the last time things felt normal, or the last photograph of us together, Theo and Claire, Suzie, Uncle Baxter, and me, smiling dumbly at the ticking timer and the tripod from which Claire had hung a sign that read "Fromage." I had no idea how important it was until the morning I left and found myself wishing I had remembered to squeeze it into my bag with the one I had already packed. Of all the stories I told Mr. Cosmopoulos, the story of that day seems to hold the most clues. I was learning the lesson of secrets revealed not only in photographs, but in the details of a story chosen for the retelling.

Aunt Suzie had kept in touch with everyone who signed the gallery guest books or even casually considered the possibility of buying a print, and dutifully mailed announcements of new shows. She was especially solicitous of important collectors and people she thought might be, like the director of Amnesty International, who had, through an oily and rather menacing-looking representative, purchased the one Claire called "The Vigil," a quiet and powerful image of a woman in a frayed blue coat, red scarf knotted tightly under her chin, squinting out to sea. But after the first post-show rush of courting the artist, interest dropped off and Mr. Kimsky never sold.

Uncle Baxter had had Mr. Kimsky framed for Claire. As he carefully untied the twine and brown paper that had protected the special nonglare glass from injury during the cab ride uptown that day, he wondered aloud if people who bought Mr. Kimsky's friends and neighbors were art collectors or actually Holocaust victims themselves.

"To think," he said as he neatly folded the paper he still saved, a habit left over from his youthful introduction to rationing, "these poor devils were being gassed, while my schoolmates and I looked at the whole war as a school holiday. All we worried about was London's supply of Malteasers dwindling down to the danger point."

Aunt Suzie perched on one end of the dining room table, bracelets clattering on its hard lacquered surface, holding forth on what sounded to me like gibberish then and, in retrospect, may well have been—the tragicomic symbolism of Coney Island itself lurking beneath its rusting rides, its decrepit boardwalk, and its seedy clown face. All the while she eyed the front door for a signal to put out the cigarette that punctuated her remarks with acrid commas and exclamation points.

"Jessica swears this one didn't do as well as the others because it's so stark, no kitschy salt and pepper shakers like the ones on Mrs. Klein's windowsill, no painted ties or cat's-eye sunglasses studded with rhinestones. She thinks Mr. Kimsky is too serious, not collectible enough," said Suzie.

"Why does your wife have to reduce art to fashion?" Claire asked Baxter with no animosity.

"It's her job," said Baxter, measuring the wall against the frame with a practiced eye. "Besides, she's very cute."

I watched them mark the wall, stand back, and envision the white space shimmering at the edges of Mr. Kimsky's brown-and-yellow plaid shirt, the hooded eyes, the beakish nose, the sun burning out the chessmen, leaving only the shadow of his unseen opponent.

St. Kimsky of the dinner table.

Claire stood on a chair and pounded a nail.

"Do you all know why this is my favorite?" she asked, not waiting for the good-natured groaning of friends accustomed to the unsolicited opinions of the artist. I listened to their talk; I was like a sponge that would someday be asked to squeeze out an opinion.

"It's my favorite because it makes you work. It doesn't lead the witness. It's full of clues. Look there, see that tiny hair insinuating itself into the picture, like a cockroach that won't die?"

I looked closely at the lone hair that had escaped Mr. Kimsky's razor. It was barely visible, yet tenacious in its quest for his collar and the lapel just beyond its reach.

As Baxter handed Claire the picture and she found her balance on the chair, gingerly sliding the wire onto the nail she had just hammered, I thought of a commercial I had just seen: "No more guesswork, no more holes in the wallpaper, unsightly marks on the paint job. Now anybody can decorate like a professional with EZ Hang, the invisible nail."

"Honey, what's so funny?" she asked over Baxter's head.

"Nothing, Mom."

"Pay attention. This will be important some day."

"Okay."

"The thing about roaches," Claire continued from her precarious position on the chair, "is no matter what people do to them, they won't die."

"Mine leave little suicide notes, but they never do it," said Suzie, shrugging off the losing battle her own building waged against these prehistoric pests.

"Willy, did you know they can live on nail clippings and squeeze themselves through electrical sockets to get out of a place that's been sprayed or freshly painted?" Claire continued.

"Nope," I said, squirming at the memory of the time a huge

water bug fell right out of a crack in the bathroom wall into my tub. Theo had said, "If he can afford the rent, he can stay."

"That's just like the human spirit," Claire said, "impossible to kill."

I nodded, still thinking of the vile greenish-black creature paddling furiously toward my soapy toes, Theo scooping the water behind it with an empty jam jar, beating a hasty retreat to the incinerator.

"And the shadow of the other player—well, darling, isn't that how we all get through life? We play the game with a shadow, against what we think might be life's next move. And look at Mr. Kimsky's eyes. We can't see them." Claire pointed.

"They say it's impossible to look an animal in the eye and kill it," said Baxter, nodding his agreement up to Claire.

"Leading the witness? Life's next move? The human spirit as cockroach? Claire, this is your nine-year-old son, Willy, not the art critic for the *Times!*"

Suddenly Theo was there, looking at us with that aren't-we-all-getting-just-a-tad-pretentious-here expression on her face, laughing at us in that way she had of pretending she was being funny while saying something mean, so you couldn't really get mad at her without being accused of starting a fight. We had no idea how long she had been standing there watching the installation (which Suzie had earlier explained was the proper term for hanging a work of art).

"Maybe Mr. Kimsky is still with us because he didn't remind anyone of their uncle George, or there was no more room for another picture over the TV and the snack trays," Theo said, reaching for the coat she had draped over the back of a chair, bending to pick up the shopping bag she had set down on the dining room floor while she observed the proceedings.

"Wouldn't everyone love a nice hot cup of tea and, for a certain person, some hot cocoa?" She asked as the swinging kitchen door slapped her into the kitchen. Claire said nothing. Baxter and Suzie looked like children who had been caught at some mischief.

Before anyone could recover, Theo's disembodied voice coiled around its victim and squeezed. "Suze, air conditioners and water heaters are installed. Pictures are hung. And I know you were smoking."

By the time Theo returned, the tension had dissolved into the civilities of tea. A fragrant pot of Darjeeling was brewed, hot cocoa poured, a plate of blondies passed. Baxter told stories of Brooke and Jennifer on location with their distracted mother, and Suzie pretended no one knew she was smoking behind the bathroom door.

Claire said no more about the picture, but I felt something pass between us, something I would save for later when I looked for reasons why things had turned out the way they did. It was a feeling I would someday examine as closely as the photograph of us with the newly installed and dour Mr. Kimsky hanging over our heads like a long-lost relative.

After Baxter and Suzie left, Claire said to the line of hangers in the open closet in front of her: "Damn it, Theo, you come in and you don't even have your coat off and you're at me already."

"You don't even listen to other ideas, Claire. You use that camera of yours to club people with your point of view, and God help anyone who disagrees with that withering, what-do-you-know-about-art-anyway look of yours."

"Oh, yeah, what about you?" Claire wheeled around and snapped, "If a cement block sat on the table long enough, it would never occur to you to ask how it got there or what it might be trying to tell you, you'd just feed it. Maybe some things are not about eating, Theo, ever think of that? Maybe my art is about feeling connected."

"Connected to what?" Theo shouted at Claire's back just before the front door slammed. "The idea that no matter how intractable and selfish your position, there's a photograph to support it?"

I padded into the kitchen that night where Theo was sitting in a pool of light, blindly turning the pages of a cookbook.

"I love you both and I don't want you to fight anymore."

"I know you don't, honey. I love her, too, and I don't want us to fight, either. We're very different, your mother and I, and we can't help it sometimes."

"You're both lesbians," I offered, looking for some common ground.

She slipped an arm around my shoulder, drew me close, smiled in spite of herself, and sighed into my hair, "If only it were that easy.

"Do you know why I cook, baby boy?"

"No."

"Because sometimes it's hard for me to say 'I love you.' "

"You say 'I love you' to me."

"You're easy."

In spite of the shock of green between dark lashes, the flashing red siren of hair, the freckles that left a trail of gingersnap crumbs across her nose, she seemed so pale, so tired and defeated. She sat, face sagging, shoulders down, feet apart and flat, slipperless, on the black-and-white tiles like someone who had taken a drug to quiet the nerves and killed the spirit instead.

Another picture to carry into the numbing cold of the day I left my grandmother's apartment.

I WALKED for a long time, and I had begun to shiver from the bitter wind that pressed my chin into my collarbone, from the tension of expecting to be caught any minute and from the slow realization that Mr. Cosmopoulos might not come as he had promised yesterday when I told him that Lucy was so sick, she had barely made it to school.

"Well, mister, looks like tomorrow's the day," he had said. "If you don't make it, I'll give you a rain check."

After I had safely turned the corner off Fifth Avenue, which seemed like miles away, but was only about a hundred yards, I walked east and crossed to the southeast corner of Madison, careful to avoid the greengrocer who always tossed me an apple and said, "How's my girl?" to Lucy when we walked by. I turned right, watching for classmates and neighbors who might stop me and ask why I was going in the wrong direction on a school day.

I headed south, afraid to look back, trying to act as normal as I could, walking quickly without breaking into a run, imagining baying hounds on my scent and a red-faced policeman at my back. I did not draw an even breath until there were at least six blocks between Grandma's building and me. As I escaped down the humped spine of Madison Avenue, art galleries gave way to small apartment buildings and expensive boutiques and coffee shops where models huddled over black coffee and grapefruit sections in beautiful starvation.

Somewhere in the sixties, I slowed down and began to pay attention to my surroundings.

Drivers lounged against long black cars, their caps tossed on front seats, smoking cigarettes and stamping the chill out of their thin black shoes as they waited for their regulars to down the last piece of toast, pull on their coats, and promise to return at a decent hour to the brownstones and maisonettes in the quiet side streets just off the avenue. Hotel doormen whistled for taxis, while French, Italian, Japanese, Swahili filled the cold morning, the guttural sounds of German, snippets of an argument drifted over snapping awnings.

Farther down, the human swarm grew, the blare of traffic with it; cabs, buses, hired cars and the occasional tourist who had not seen this coming, horns, brakes, speeding bicycles, all converging in a great seething wave of noise a few steps away from the Plaza. Every bus and subway stop fed long columns of workers into the General Motors Building, the IBM tower, giant hives with names like Helmsley Spear and Graybar. Miniature tornadoes lifted my hair and reddened my face as I watched huge revolving doors usher people inside and swallow them whole. I followed one group into a crowded lobby only to watch them turn, one by one, to stare at me, before the elevator door closed and took them away. I fled the building and caught the sharp edge of an increasingly nasty day.

I passed Schrafft's, where Theo took me for hot chocolate in thick pottery cups with vanilla sandwich cookies on the saucer, and my stomach rumbled thinking of the dark sweet taste under the warm creamy head. I passed the gloomy Archdiocese building, black as a nun's habit. Grandpa Barnaby said the old Cardinal lived there and used the money in the poor box to buy caviar.

As I walked in the tall shadows of Madison Avenue, I glimpsed the wide luxury of Fifth every now and then, as though through a giant deck of flash cards, the grand department stores inhabited by gracious older women with tinted hair who knew my grandmother by name and wrote her tastes in their red leather books. A pair of old lions guarded the Public Library at Forty-second Street. Down farther, I began to see hunted-looking, long-haired men carrying the large black cases I later learned contained ideas for the television commercials we enjoyed and made fun of during happier days, but none of them noticed me in their headlong plunge toward meetings with clients, dark screening rooms and editorial suites and the taxis waiting for them three deep on the busy curb. They all seemed too serious to be people who could invent talking spicy meatballs, hot dogs rendered filler-free by someone who sounded like God, and a man who looked like his chickens.

I descended the small hill down to Altman's, and when I spotted the knot of shoppers waiting for the doors to open, I realized it was almost ten; I had been walking for over an hour. When the guard unlocked the big glass door, I let the crowd carry me into the overheated building. To avoid the suspicious store detectives I imagined lurking behind every mannequin with a police sketch of me in hand, I trailed discreetly behind a large, lonely-looking red-haired woman who could have been my mother or an aunt. Together we marched through Handbags and Gloves, and by the time she got to Scarves, I was steps away from the main door on Fifth, nice and warm from the shortcut Claire taught me one rainy Saturday when we looked for an anniversary present for Jessica and Baxter.

I didn't see the bike. I just felt a rush of wind as it came so close to hitting me that it ripped the handle right off my duffel bag. A man in a topcoat and what I might have identified as a bowler hat, if I had known at the time what such a hat looked like, helped me to the sidewalk as I tried very hard not to cry.

He dusted the front of my jacket, looking for broken bones. "Are you okay? Do you want me to call somebody, a doctor maybe?" He held my sleeve and searched the street, then brightened as he spotted a blue uniform walking toward us. "Here comes a cop; you want me to call him, maybe you want to report a hit-and-run?"

"No thanks. I'm going to see my father. He works in that building over there."

"Okay. You sure?"

I pointed to the Empire State Building. I know he was watching me as I walked in.

I WAS EATING a hot dog at Nedick's on the corner of Thirty-fourth and Sixth when he finally came. I had waited as long as I could on the corner of Fifth and Thirty-fourth; Mr. Cosmopoulos had whispered through the school fence that he'd meet meet me there at twelve o'clock sharp and take me the rest of the way to his place. But by three, the wind had bitten through my coat and I knew I had to keep moving. I had been to Macy's many times and remembered Mr. C.'s face had brightened when I mentioned this to him. I thought he might be there, so I let the crowds sweep me along Thirty-fourth Street where I wasn't noticed as much and lost myself in the huge store's maze of buildings. I badly needed to use a bathroom, so I felt much better after finding the "Lounge" with its high ceilings, marble floors, and rows of creaky wooden stalls at the bottom of the oldest and slowest escalator I had ever seen. I imagined it, too, shivered as its passengers put their cold feet on its creaky wooden back.

Back outside, on that peculiar corner in front of The World's Largest Department Store, built around the tiny business that would not budge for all the tea in China, hoping to be offered just that and was finally forgotten by the giant but remembered forever by New York for its pluck, the seethe of Herald Square was strangely silent, muffled. It had begun to snow. Big wet flakes flew over lowered heads, raised collars, shoulders hunched into the task of getting home early. I thought of cockroaches in the wall. *If everyone came out of their apartment at the same time, would there be room in the streets for cars?* Umbrellas had sprouted up everywhere, black, yellow, plaid, sprays of flowers, peek-a-boo vinyl, cheap vendor models that snapped in the wind as soon as you paid your money, and expensive English ones with monograms on their gilded collars, mushrooms on a field of vanilla frosting, this new dusting blotting out the blackened crust of winter's previous attempt to promise sleigh rides, snowmen, a day off from the adult equivalent of school. No Mr. Cosmopoulos.

I felt a cold flake land on my warm cheek and melt into a tear, then another and another, coming faster now, soaking my hair. I slipped a cold hand inside my jacket, felt way down to the bottom of my school khakis and counted my lunch money. Two dollars. I hadn't planned on snow or Mr. C. coming so late. Was he coming at all? Had he forgotten? If it snows, do you still get a rain check?

I had already eaten the muffins I had packed for Shorty, nibbled from my coat pockets as I walked along the street. Grandma told me never to eat in public, but I couldn't help it. My stomach growled at the thought of Lucy fixing one of her snacks, usually a meal in itself, to tide me over until dinner, and even the thought of something brown and mushy from the McCall cafeteria was appealing at that moment, but I knew no one was thinking about food back at Grandma's. By that time, they had known for hours that I was gone. I felt a twinge of guilt as I thought of Lucy, shaken from her sickbed, told it was all her fault, packing her bags in shame, fired. I decided I couldn't ever go back. I'd join a gang of street urchins and live on the streets by my wits as I had seen on the six o'clock news.

The hot dog was still sizzling when the man in the white hat put it into a thick roll. I nodded yes when he pointed to the onions and again at the relish. He just smiled when he got around to the chili and the cheese. He filled up a large paper cup with pulpy orange juice and watched me try to find a place for the mustard.

"Where you been, mister?" The familiar red suspenders were peeking out from a stained parka, black ponytail curling under what looked like an old sock stiff with frost. The counterman eyed him suspiciously, ready to intervene and turned away when I jumped from my stool and hugged the gentle giant.

"Been looking for you hours and you're sitting here, eating hot dogs. What happened?" He frowned at the lump at my feet.

"Bike hit me."

"Lucky you had that bag."

"I guess."

"Glad you could make it," he said as he pulled his huge gloves over my trembling hands, his stocking cap way down to my melting eyebrows. We walked along in silence and I watched my friend concentrate on the swirling white ahead of us. "So clean, snow. When God can't stand looking at how dirty we make things, he just sends down a coat of this stuff. Makes everything nice and quiet. Gives him a rest. Doesn't have to hear everybody bitching and moaning, if you'll excuse my French."

I hadn't heard him say anything in French, but I didn't mention it. I was just so glad he hadn't let me down, he could have said anything. We walked for a while in the wet silence, the unknown ahead, the noise of workday New York at our backs.

When I asked him why he was opening the manhole cover on

Twenty-ninth Street, he said, "Didn't ever say I lived *on* Madison Avenue, did I?"

My fingers cramped on the cold metal bars but Mr. Cosmopolous was just underneath me, accustomed to holding on with one hand, guiding my foot with the other. His voice spiraled up through the darkness. "Hold on, mister, these steps are slippery and doctors don't make house calls down here."

When we stepped into the dark tunnel, my legs and arms were still wobbly from the climb. We walked for what seemed like hours, but was only a few minutes, and as my eyes became accustomed to the pitch-black, I saw that we were moving toward a feeble light strung up on makeshift wires. In the broad apron of what might have been a subway tunnel were two tattered chairs, a large shelf of books, maps, magazines, and newspapers, a mirror, some toiletries, toothpaste, brushes, some shaving things, a cupboard neatly stocked with cans of soup, beans, hash, chili, and some clean Latest Dish containers. And there were three cots, one freshly made up with a new blanket and a pillow still in plastic.

"Home, sweet home!" my friend announced as he swept his arm across the entrance to what looked like a campsite. *"Entrez!"*

A small, dark man with the dense build of a boxer and a pronounced limp walked toward me and as he drew closer, I saw that he was wearing a plaid shirt and round wire-framed glasses that had been mended with a little tape balanced on the end of a rather large nose. He did not smile, nor did he frown.

"Meet Shorty!" Mr. Cosmopoulos bellowed.

"What took you so long?" the tiny man complained.

"Mr. Kimsky?" I whispered, too softly for anyone to hear.

19

Shorty's uncanny resemblance to Mr. Kimsky, along with the motley band of souls who inhabited the dark corners of the tunnel and formed a neighborhood of sorts along the abandoned track, reinforced my belief in a parallel universe. (Of course, those words came much later when I grew up and realized that in order to be taken seriously, it was necessary to give one's theories serious-sounding names, names like "big bang," "the Creation," "global warming.") I put my nine-year-old's faith in the elegant, if not scientific, idea that carbon copies of ourselves lived somewhere, millions of light-years away, on a green planet just like Earth with cities like New York and Chicago and Broken Arrow, Oklahoma, and Greenwich Village and South Neck. But *that* planet was way ahead of us: I was a senior in high school up there, S.A.T.'s behind me, an acceptance letter from Harvard in my pocket to show to all my friends; Grandma had given up and let me go home; Alan, Roland, and the Jacobys had not perished after all, but were merely victims of amnesia; Claire and Theo were together and happy again, and it was discovered that children with two mothers had, on average, higher I.Q. scores, better relationships, and a higher level of creativity than kids who had one of each kind of parent. I suppose this was where I got whatever small shred of courage I possessed, believing in a world where my present was already history, where what was happening to me was no big deal, was old news about somewhere else.

I imagined a handful of intuitive people like myself who sensed the existence of my world, too, in dreams, ESP, flashes of recognition, in the oddly familiar faces of strangers, and in those bursts of clarity when a course of action is lit up like Rockefeller Center at Christmas. I imagined my father, broad-shouldered, proud in the hard November sun, his breath curling over the crowd, watching a football game in which an older, handsome version of me is the brawny fullback running a touchdown to wild cheering, to the waving red flag of my father's hair in the row reserved for parents. I am unstoppable in the last minutes of the game, single-handedly turning the Crimson back from certain defeat at the hands of the evil Elis. I imagine telling my own children a story about a boy who ran away to join the underground people while my pretty wife and their grandfather, his once fiery crop now burnished to copper threaded with silver, framing the pale skin over his temples, look on and chide me for frightening the children so close to bedtime. I imagined many things, but never that my parallel world had been under the sidewalk the whole time.

If I am here, is the other me taking my place above ground? Is he sitting at Grandma's table right now, politely waiting for Barnaby to excuse him, getting ready for bed in Roland's room, putting on the pajamas I left under the pillow, wondering what will happen if Theo doesn't win in court? Does anybody know I'm here?

Mr. Cosmopoulos had gone "upstairs," as he called the rutted sidewalk above us, and I was sitting across from Shorty, who was carefully tapping cocoa into a chipped enamel saucepan balanced on an electric coil. A black extension cord snaked up from this contraption and was clipped to a thick cable that ran along the grimy rock roof of their makeshift home before it disappeared into the gloom farther down the line.

"Not like your mother's, but it'll have to do," he said, using his shirttail to wipe a bent Horn & Hardart spoon, delicately peeling back the surface of the bubbling liquid for scalded curls of milk skin. "Milk's easier to get than water down here, you know."

"Is my picture in the paper yet?" I asked Shorty.

"Didn't want Luis to bring you here, you know. We got enough trouble without a kidnapping on our heads."

"You didn't kidnap me. I ran away."

"Tell that to the cops," he snorted. He limped over to me with a steaming mug. His face was not friendly, but his gesture was, and I was not as confused by this as I once might have been. My grandmother looked friendly enough, but was not. Until just then, I hadn't thought about how it might look to other people, my running away to visit Mr. Cosmopoulos and to meet his friend Shorty, maybe stay with them for a while until I figured out what to do, and I worried about the trouble I caused. We sipped the cocoa, which was silky, dark, and rich and, surprisingly, as good as Theo's.

I sneaked looks at Shorty as we drank in silence.

"Do you play chess?" I asked.

"Do you?"

"Grandpa Barnaby was going to teach me, but I left before he got around to it."

"I might."

In the glare of the bare bulb that hung over the section Shorty called the parlor, I saw tiny nicks in Shorty's face, as if someone had been chipping away at him.

He saw me look away and brushed a hand over his cheek.

"I fall down."

"Oh," I said, sorry I'd hurt his feelings.

A woman's voice, raspy and thick with cigarettes, rose behind me. "Don't let him scare you, Red. His bark is much worse than his bite. Fact is, he's got no bite. Teeth are rotten. Aren't they, Mr. Shortypants?"

As she moved into the circle of light and peered into my cup, I could see she wore grimy brown corduroy trousers and a pair of black high-topped sneakers. An old sweater that had been darned with bright thread and masking tape clung to her with its last button, and a faded blue terrycloth-towel was safety-pinned around her head as a turban. From it a fringe of dirty blond hair stuck out. She dangled a battered purse in the crook of her left arm, palm up, forefinger leading, just the way my grandmother and her friends carried theirs when they went out to lunch.

"What's that?" she asked, and answered herself before I could. "Cocoa? Ha! I knew it! He doesn't know how to properly entertain a guest. Been down here too long." She arched one scraggly eyebrow right up to the frayed edge of her turban, ran a finger over the cardboard box that served as our table, and sniffed. "Where are your manners, sir? Not even a tablecloth!"

She made a clucking sound and murmured something about expecting a package and bent down for a closer look at me, lingering on a point above my eyes. As she moved toward me, she sounded like loose clothes in a suitcase.

"I will call you Monsieur Rouge," she pronounced, stepping back to peer at me with an odd combination of approval and mistrust. "Everyone calls me Mrs. DeVries, and so you must, too. You'll come over to my pied-à-terre when you're settled in and we'll have a proper visit. I'll serve hors d'oeuvre, make a nice roast, some mashed potatoes and homemade apple pie, and you'll tell me how my boy is doing in school. You will call first, though, won't you? I must check my schedule and straighten up a bit, Cornelia hasn't come in a while. I'll let myself out, Shorty dear, don't get up."

We watched her pick her way back into the dark and toward a feeble light farther down the broken track. "That's Thelma, she lives down the street," said Shorty, tapping his temple. "Her elevator hasn't gone all the way to the top for years, if you know what I mean."

I didn't know what he meant, but even though she didn't look like any of the women I knew and she smelled strong, like Claire after she'd been running hard, I thought Mrs. DeVries was a lot friendlier than Shorty and I looked forward to going to her house for dinner.

Mr. C. returned from upstairs with Chinese takeout and soon the milk crate was covered with cartons of sticky white rice, crispy noodles, sweet and sour chicken, and ginger beef and pork in black bean sauce. Shorty dug around in a shoebox for chopsticks and little packets of soy sauce, hot mustard, and sweet plum sauce; I stared at my Horn & Hardart plate, waiting for a fork, too embarrassed to say I didn't know how to use the long wooden sticks my hosts had provided.

After dinner, we sat and talked awhile. As I followed Shorty and Mr. Cosmopoulos from the orange crate to the tattered chairs a few steps away, I thought of how Claire always stayed behind in the kitchen to start the dishes—"You cook, I clean up," she always said—and Theo led their friends into our living room where coffee and chocolates waited on the low square table that was surrounded by cushions.

While Mr. C. excused himself to tidy up and disappeared into a room I hadn't noticed before, Shorty told me about the plate.

"Got a plate in his head, you know," Shorty began and I wondered how a dish could get inside a person's skull.

"Happened before I met him. Had a family, then one day, he just wandered off, couldn't remember who he was. Amnesia."

I thought, wouldn't it be great if Uncle Roland and Alan had that, too; that they weren't really dead.

"When they found him," Shorty continued, "he was in bad shape. Crazy. They took out a tumor the size of an orange, stitched him up with cat gut and Krazy Glue, and covered the hole with a metal plate. Down at St. Vincent's. Says he can tell when it's gonna snow, even down here."

I wondered if Mr. C. really did forget to meet me, if his plate told him to come get me out of the snow.

"Did his memory come back?" I asked.

"Most of it, but he forgets a lot. Goes blank. Forgot to tell me you were coming."

"Did they find him?"

"Who?"

"His family," I said.

"Nope. He didn't want to be found and they didn't try real hard. Writes to his son, though. In Jersey somewhere. Pretends he's a traveling salesman. Kid thinks he lives in a fancy apartment on Madison Avenue. Doorman, another Greek, took a liking to Luis and saves the letters for him, nobody's the wiser. Says he'll go see him when we move into a better place."

"How long have you lived here?"

"Since '59."

Shorty rolled his eyes and tilted his head in the direction of Mr. Cosmopoulos's heavy step. "I hear you're Greek, too," he said, quickly changing the subject.

"Not exactly," I answered.

When Mr. Cosmopoulos sat down, Shorty got up and moved toward the commode they had hidden behind an artificial palm tree someone had left on the sidewalk upstairs. A battered twelve-string guitar stood in a corner; without looking at it, he absently ran his hand over it the way parents touch their children in passing. A few notes scaled the grimy wall and fell.

"Shorty telling you about my plate?"

He curled his hand into a fist and knocked his left temple. "It's right here. Go ahead, hit it."

I politely shook my head no as he kept on knocking. "It's as hard as a rock."

When Shorty was out of earshot, Mr. Cosmopoulos told me Shorty had been in the Korean War and had gotten shell-shocked, which meant he still saw pictures of the war in his head and no matter what he did, he couldn't make them go away.

"Got his leg blown off, trying to save one of his buddies," Mr. Cosmopoulos said, shaking his head. "They pinned a medal on him, put him in the Veterans Hospital on Welfare Island, then forgot about him. One day, he packed a single shoe and the wooden leg they gave him and left."

Mr. C. drifted away as he spoke and I waited for him to come back, as he always did.

"He was in the bed next to mine in St. Vincent's free ward. That's for charity cases, you know, and if you don't make it there, they put you right in Potter's Field and nobody comes to cry at your funeral except a couple of guys who have to dig the hole in that godforsaken place.

"We were both in pretty bad shape. He had a bad case of the DTs; you know what that is?"

I shook my head.

"That's delirium tremens, mister, means the booze got you and won't let go, makes you shiver and sweat and think you've got bugs crawling all over you. You think you're gonna die, and some do."

I gave my head an involuntary scratch, and a chill ran through me at the thought of roaches on my skin.

"Well, I wasn't any good to anybody either, talking nonsense, big bandage wrapped around my head like the mummy's tomb. What a pair we were, the blind leading the blind, but we got along all right, and afterwards we helped each other out. Stayed in a coupla roomin' houses down on the Bowery, give ya the creeps. Heard about some people goin' underground and decided to give it a try. Been together ever since. The world forgot him and I forgot the world! Whaddaya think about that? Two peas in a pod!"

Mr. Cosmopoulos laughed at his joke. I thought of how telling secrets on someone you love is a form of getting new people to like them, protecting them, so they don't have to explain things themselves. I remembered how Theo used to say, "She really wants to see you, it's just that she's working on a show," when Claire got up and wandered out of the room when we had company.

"If he likes you, he'll show you his Purple Heart," Mr. C. confided.

I didn't discover the damage the bike and the snow had done to my duffel until it was time to settle in for the night. One by one, I pulled out soggy pajamas, stiff jeans, sodden underwear, a shredded book, an extra sweater stained by the tube of toothpaste, which had ruptured on impact with the bike and left sticky stripes of white and green all over everything.

"Don't worry," Mr. Cosmopoulos said. "Tomorrow we'll take 'em to a place I know that'll wash 'em for you, good as new. And Shorty'll iron them up. Shorty's a real spit-and-polish, knife-edge-creases man, aren't you, Shorty?" he called over his shoulder to the lump in the next cot, but Shorty had gone to bed without saying good night.

"If I have to," came the muffled response.

"He doesn't like me, does he?" I whispered.

"Sure he does. What makes you think that, mister?" Mr. Cosmopoulos asked, as he felt inside my bag for more breakage, lifting out the toothpaste tube slit side up to avoid wasting any more of the precious goo.

I shook my head.

"Shorty's idea to invite you down here, give you a little break from your troubles while you figure out what to do."

"He said it was your idea and that people might think you kidnapped me."

"Nah. That's his way of not letting you see how soft he is."

"Are you and Shorty married like my moms?"

"I guess you could say that. Been together long enough to qualify. We don't have any fancy name for it, though, we just watch out for each other, make sure we got enough to eat, don't get sick or too lonely. Somebody to talk to, fight with. Nothin' sadder than not having anybody to pick a fight with."

"My picture!" I suddenly remembered I hadn't looked at it for a while.

"What picture?" he asked, looking at me over the piles he was making—stuff to fix, stuff to wash, stuff that's okay.

"Us. My moms and me. I put it right there." Little spirals of panic now curling up from my knees.

"Where?" He turned what was left of the front pocket of my bag inside out.

"Not there now," he said.

Loss. The sudden, aching loss of that picture hit hard and unleashed something I had been holding back all day, maybe a lot longer than that. Everything came flooding back. Poor Lucy. Grandma. Buddy. Mr. Cowperthwaite and his dog. The unbearable tension of maybe being caught at any second, terrified, yet willing my feet to move to the door, shivering in the wind, long blocks, the hard faces of strangers hurrying past, the bike, its rider aiming at me, never looking back, the snow freezing my eyelashes and the sudden gut-pounding fear that Mr. C. wouldn't come and I would starve or be killed by bands of muggers who slept on the streets and preyed on little kids like me.

I was shivering uncontrollably—not from cold, from something else. The long walk, the dark descent to this place, a sudden slip, skin curling away from my knee, bubbles of blood rising to the surface in time to the panic reaching for my throat, scratching rat feet scurrying away from the loose rock, Mrs. DeVries, Shorty. Claire gone, Theo gone. And now, all I had to remember us together was gone too.

Mr. Cosmopoulos saw my shoulders moving and rubbed a huge hand up and down my back to dislodge the tears that were stuck inside my head.

"Let's fix up this bed. You've had a big day, mister," he said gently.

He opened the plastic cover on the new pillow, careful to keep it intact, folded it with delicacy surprising for someone so large, and wrapped a soft flannel shirt around it for a case, tying the sleeves so it wouldn't slip while I was sleeping. He opened the blanket next, again taking care with the wrapper, and I saw the big white streak in one corner. "That's nothing," he said, following my gaze, "just a bad dye lot. It's amazing all the perfectly good stuff that gets rejected. It'll keep you just as warm as one that's got all its color." There were no sheets, just more shirts sewn together, which he fussed over, smoothing and re-smoothing just like my mothers.

"You don't remember people because you carry their pictures," he said finally, after I had climbed into my one dry pair of pajamas and got in on the side he had turned down, "and you don't forget them because you don't have any."

He padded away and I lay there listening to the distant rumbling of traffic overhead, something dripping somewhere, and the soft chords of "Malagueña" from the other side of the dark.

I fought sleep for a long time, trying to keep the lost photograph in my memory, squeezing the images into the space behind my eyes. A sunburned Theo wrapped in a pareo and Claire in shorts smiling on a dock, both listing a bit from their day on Uncle Peter's boat. I am closer to the ground than they, and have already found my land legs, a small anchor in a tennis hat between them, hands extended as if to keep them from drifting away.

When the music faded and was replaced by the big man's soft snoring, the silly sidewalk rhyme that had been playing over and over in the back of my head became louder and louder, the last thing I remember before exhaustion finally washed over me.

Don't step on the cracks!
You'll break your mothers' backs.
Make three wishes,
And break the devil's dishes.

20

In the following days my routine was that of people who live one day at a time, with one primary focus: food. What was simply taken out of the refrigerator, oven, freezer, delivered from the pizza parlor on the corner, snipped from Theo's herb garden on our wide kitchen sill, stirred and prayed over by the superstitious Lucy, or blindly grabbed from the snack jar on the counter was an entire day's work for my friends underground.

There was no other work: no store to open, no photographs to take, no business to run, nothing beyond the basic three squares and little extras to be secured daily. Every meal was the direct result of enormous effort and creativity on Mr. Cosmopoulos's part, and of Shorty's talent for merging disparate ingredients into something at least palatable, and more often than not very good. A network of contacts "upstairs" abetted their efforts. Dimitri, a friendly ex-Marine who washed dishes at Fong's Szechuan Garden, had been responsible for my feast that first night, and a newspaper dealer named Jimmy the Scoop, who, according to Mr. Cosmopoulos, was known to enjoy the bottle every now and again, donated his unsold papers to our cause and never failed to tuck a chocolate bar, a bag of peanuts, or a two-pack of devil's-food cupcakes between the torn ink-stained bundles. Even my clean clothes were courtesy of Leroy at the coin-op who donated slugs when the owner wasn't looking.

A backbreaking day spent collecting old newspapers and scouring the sidewalks for small change netted some meat for a dish Shorty called Hamburger Hill, a mound of mostly beans and rice faintly seasoned with traces of something mysterious and hot. The pint of milk, the dented can of orange juice reconstituted with a soda bottle full of the fire hydrant's best, the loaf of stiff rye bread, and the eggs I enjoyed two at a time at breakfast, their yolks unbroken and glistening on my chipped plate, cost Mr. C. a whole afternoon of delivering sale leaflets for the man in the red-striped jacket who managed the D'Agostino's on the corner. Shorty rarely ventured out except for a checkup at the veterans' hospital clinic or to the occasional "meeting," the announcement of which usually came on the heels of a foul mood even Mr. C. couldn't shake him out of, a few straight nights of tossing and turning and often after a bad bout of "ghost pain," which was the strange sensation Shorty still felt in the general vicinity of where his leg should have been. He returned from meetings a little softer around the eyes. He said he didn't like to climb up and down stairs and preferred their dark nest, despite the constant rattle of wheels over his head, the idiosyncrasies of neighbors like Thelma DeVries and the shadowy Raul who spoke to no one but his cat, a punchy looking one-eared stray tabby named Valentino who seemed to share the same opinion of humans held by his owner, and the dangers of flooding from the water mains that crisscrossed the walls. He left it to the gregarious Mr. C. to venture out for supplies. My friend never bought a cup of coffee without scooping up all the sugar, salt, pepper, mustard, ketchup, and those plastic tubs of jelly his big hands could hold, taking every opportunity to see to it that the larder remained amply stocked.

I understood that it was my job to play along and accept these gifts without protesting the hardships faced on my behalf. I never questioned Mr. Cosmopoulos, who was far too proud and extravagant in every gesture, to admit the perils he faced in securing my comfort, nor did I ever confront Shorty, whose own grumpy, begrudging style of giving was all the sweeter for all the discomfort it seemed to generate in him. I was the guest, and as such I was bound by the same rules that my mothers applied when a particularly irksome task was undertaken in the name of the invited. So I steadfastly ignored the reality of their situation, enjoyed the adventure, accepted their hospitality, and pulled it off with an ease only children can bring to such an endeavor.

I had been there a week and we were doing our laundry in Leroy's coin-op several blocks south of the "front porch"—which is what we slyly called the old manhole cover over our tunnel, sharing a chocolate bar Jimmy had slid across his newsstand to me, counting the squares and neatly dividing it along the lines. We sat on plastic chairs watching Shorty's plaid shirt and my flannel pajamas and Mr. C.'s baggy jeans, arms and legs and buttons clacking against the sides, stand up for a second, then collapse and tumble around in the big porthole of the dryer that smelled of lint and other people's clothes. Then carefully folding our things, pressing them with our hands, holding each garment up against our faces for a sweet whiff of the previous customer's fabric softener, we packed it all into my duffel and a couple of worn shopping bags. I decided to ask Mr. C. if he and Shorty were bums like the men we had seen sleeping on the glass-littered sidewalk when we walked down to the Bowery and looked up at the dark windows of the hotel where they once had lived.

Mr. Cosmopoulos thought for a second, tugged on his ponytail a couple of times as though he were jump-starting a car, and said, "Let's see, are we bums? Well, mister, we've got a roof over our heads—such as it is, a little inconvenient and out of the way—and we earn every bit of food we eat and trade honest work for extras. Nobody sleeping on a bench in our neighborhood and no winos. No crazies either, except Thelma, but she's harmless. And no drugs, anybody tried that in our tunnel, out they go.

"No," he said with a thumping finality, "Shorty and I are just down on our luck. In between things, you might say." And then quietly, with a wistful expression that ran counter to his words, "No, not bums. Maybe independents is more like it."

A few steps from the laundry, we noticed a pile of greasy blankets and newspapers huddled in the doorway of an abandoned tenement. As we got closer we saw it was really a man, hunkered down against the sooty wind. His hair was long and matted, and under it was a face full of deep creases where dirt had hardened and fanned out in streaks that resembled war paint. His skin was as deeply tanned as Aunt Suzie's when she returned from her winter vacation, but his eyes were bloodshot and crusted. A mixture of urine and sweat and excrement rising up from him forced me to breathe through my mouth.

Mr. Cosmopoulos opened the shopping bag we were swinging between us, took out a freshly washed blanket, and bent over the man and placed it around his thin shoulders, gently prying away the filthy one he had wrapped around him. "Here you go, still warm from the dryer," Mr. C. said. "We'll get yours washed up nice and new. Be back with it next week," said Mr. Cosmopoulos, as the man touched an invisible cap in salute. Then, as though he had not planned to do so but had changed his mind at the last minute, Mr. C. leaned down into the awful stench, and handed the man the coffee we had just bought from the machine in the laundromat. I heard him whisper, "God bless you, brother."

We walked along for a while, each of us lost in something too private for words, I in thoughts of my warring family and of that man who could be me when I grew up, never getting home again. I didn't realize that I was seeing the first of many lost and tormented souls who would be victims of society's best intentions, forced to leave the comfort of a warm hospital bed, medication, and regular meals for something more humane, for a freedom that never materialized. I could not have known that this was a chilling omen of a skid row that would soon overstep its bounds, but in the way he shook his head, slowly and with great sorrow, I suspect my friend knew more about it than he would say.

Our shoes made a slurping sound on the slushy sidewalk and we walked a little faster as the temperature plunged and the ground underneath became hard and slick. Mr. Cosmopoulos tilted his head at an unfriendly sky full of snow and said, "That's what a bum is, mister."

AS PROMISED, we paid a social call on Mrs. Thelma DeVries.

Shorty had walked down the track ahead of time and asked her if it was okay to come for dinner the next evening. After consulting her "schedule," which was really a grimy three-year-old calendar open to May and a picture of Mount Vesuvius, stamped "Bellevue Dermatology Associates," she thought for a while, frowned at the blank pages, and said, "Well, we must do it tomorrow because as you can see, the rest of the week is simply out of the question. Yes. Let's."

When Shorty came back, he said, "She'll fit us in," and rolled his eyes.

"Ah, Luis, Shorty, and my dear Monsieur Rouge, how good of

you to come. Welcome to my chez moi," said Mrs. DeVries, ushering us over the threshold of the niche she called home, thanking Mr. Cosmopoulos for his thoughtfulness when he offered the jar of briny black olives Shorty had remembered at the last minute. "We gotta take something," he had said.

Her front door really *was* a door—battered but once beautiful oak, with delicate stained-glass panels and a crystal knob. "My treasure," she said when we entered. "It was winking out at me from a pile of junk in front of an antique shop. A rose among the thorns, like me."

Somehow she had gotten it to stand upright long enough to attach its richly carved molding to two old bed frames fanning out from either side, upended and draped with old sheets and a piano shawl to give the impression of entering a real room and to shield her from "the prying eyes of passersby," as she put it. She was still wearing her turban, but this time she was dressed in something that resembled a man's bathrobe tied with a piece of velvet ribbon.

"You must try one of these canapés," she said to me, offering an empty paper plate with a grand flourish. "They're frightfully good."

"Just play along," Mr. Cosmopoulos whispered.

"Thank you," I said politely, and pretended to take one, thumb and forefinger together, pinky extended, the way my grandmother's friends did it.

When Mrs. DeVries offered another, I said, "Oh no, please, you must take the last one," just like Aunt Jessica when she really didn't like something.

"Such manners you have, my dear. Just like my darling Jack," she gushed, beaming at me through a shock of limp hair that had fallen out of her turban, unable to see Shorty sneering behind her back.

She served one course after another of empty plates and glasses: mashed potatoes, *haricots verts,* rack of lamb with mint jelly, apple cobbler with a touch of burgundy, and a nice, mellow port with some double Gloucester for afterwards, which she was careful not to offer to Shorty. After a reasonable amount of time, during which we made appreciative noises and commented on her extraordinary culinary skills, we thanked Mrs. DeVries for a lovely dinner and bade her good night. Even though Mr. C. said it was kinder to pretend along with her, I felt sorry for her all the same.

"Who is Jack?" I asked when we were safely into our own section of tunnel.

Mr. Cosmopoulos, unwrapping the jaunty scarf he had wound around his neck for the occasion, said, "That's her son. She was married once a long time ago. When they found her wandering around the streets telling people she was Anastasia, the daughter of the last czar of Russia, her husband took the kid away from her. Never found him again when she got out of the hospital. He's probably older than me by now.

"Her family's got some money, old money I think, and they tried to get her to come home, but she wouldn't. They send her packages every now and then. They tip the parcel post guy real big to come down here and deliver them personally."

"Still crazy, if you ask me, wearing a dish towel on her head and serving imaginary food. Better off without her, wherever he is," sniffed Shorty, limping around looking for something to tide us over until morning. "I don't know why we didn't just stay home and eat our own olives," he said grumpily.

I thought about Theo, wearing a towel and a man's bathrobe and looking all over New York for me, and I wondered if she would serve imaginary tea while Claire pretended to develop pictures that were not there.

Mr. Cosmopoulos was upstairs "recycling" and I was helping Shorty straighten up when he asked, "You know why they call me Shorty?"

"Because you have a short temper?"

"Thelma tell you that?" he snapped.

I shook my head in a way that looked like a yes, but really wasn't a lie, because I was afraid he'd get mad if I said it was Mr. Cosmopoulos. He ignored me and kept on talking.

"I was a short-order cook for a while," he said. "Greek joint. Hotter than Hades in them kitchens. Would have still been there, if they didn't hire that draft dodger, spouting junk about us minding our own business and leaving the Vietnamese alone to solve their own problems. Would have stayed on if he hadn't got on my nerves and made me go after him."

"With a bread knife" is all Mr. C. said when I asked him about it later.

Shorty's face darkened at this memory, and he rubbed his leg as if to remind himself that he had been right to go after the kid.

"Gimme a side of down!" he shouted suddenly. "Know what that is? That's short order talk for toast, kid. Adam and Eve on a raft, that's two eggs on toast. What's 'over easy'?"

I didn't know.

"C'mon, that's easy. Fried egg flipped over just for a second until the yolk gets cooked," said Shorty. "Hard to do without breaking it. I'll bet your mother can flip eggs with her eyes closed. Boy, can she cook! I'll bet she's a real dish, too, no pun intended. Nobody makes a chicken fricassee like hers. A real underground sensation, hey kid?" As he closed his eyes and smiled at his joke, I wondered why it sounded so familiar. Where had I heard this before?

"I could do with some of that right now, couldn't you?"

At that moment, I could do with a lot more than Theo's cooking. A wave of loneliness swept over me. At least at Grandma's, I got to *talk* to my mother.

I watched Shorty scramble some eggs in a cracked dish balanced on a hot plate. He limped around the dark corner that served as his galley and muttered into his task, face clouding over with the anger that raced through him, that could turn him mean at any moment. I gathered my nerve.

"Shorty."

"Yeah?"

"Have you ever lived in Coney Island?

"Yeah." He brightened. "Learned to cook there. Hot dogs. A place called Nathan's. It's pretty famous, you know."

"I know," I said as calmly as I could.

THE DREAM had changed. It was very different from the one that rose up from the "Peanuts" sheets at home, or from Uncle Roland's nautical blue bedspread, or the mismatched flowers and stripes Aunt Molly stretched to the corners of my fold-away cot at the farm. This dream came up from the pavement, snaked through the steam vents, and hissed me awake in my cave under the sidewalk. It slithered through the arms of my shirt pillow and wrapped itself around me like an old friend.

Like my Cherokee great-great-great-grandfather on Grandma Doris's side, who could shape-shift into any living creature and back into human form just by thinking it, my father-spirit assumed many forms and followed me into the dream. He was a bundle of rags on the sidewalk, hair bleached white from the sun, eyes peeled back from the effort of searching for me, always searching for me. The face that rose to take the coffee I offered was a mirror held up to mine; then it was gone, lost again in deep ruts of dirt and despair.

He was a crazy old woman who pressed her face close to mine and rubbed a callused thumb into my brow, anointing it with holy oil. "I now pronounce you Sir William of Rouge. You may rise, Sir Knight."

He was a stranger in a bowler hat who came out of the crowd and offered a steadying hand. "Have you run away to lose your life or to find it?" he asked as the bicycle tore away. The man on it looked back to see how close he had come, smiling at my quick reflexes under his black helmet.

Thunder growled in the distance, growing louder and louder, moving toward me, until finally a towering flume of water burst through the tunnel. Just as it was about to wash us away like roaches in the wall, Shorty stirred, leaped to my rescue on two good legs, and carried me to safety as Mr. Cosmopoulos flew overhead on wings of red suspenders.

In this dream, the man I saw through Uncle Peter's fence played chess with a photograph in a plaid shirt and turned himself into a shadow until the blond woman and her camera were safely out of the picture.

I COULD NOT KNOW then that it had taken everyone a few days to realize I was really gone, not spirited away by someone in the family. Later, I was told that Theo had accused Uncle Peter of being in cahoots with my grandmother and getting me, via some kind of underground railroad, to wherever Claire was.

Grandma Hirsh accused Theo of kidnapping me, then sending me to Broken Arrow to stay with Doris and Roy because Oklahoma did not have a reciprocal agreement with New York State.

Lucy believed that I had been killed and that if she hadn't gotten the flu, I would still be alive, an opinion no one in the family wanted to hear. And when Claire showed up one night, tearstained, repentant, and worried sick about me, it took a lot of talking and begging before Theo would believe she really hadn't any part of it and let her sleep in my loft. Deep down, Theo still wasn't convinced, but she desperately wanted Claire to prove she could be trusted again.

After a few days of this, Barnaby broke his characteristic silence, cast a disgusted look at his wife and daughter, who had been threatening each other with lawsuits and disinheritance, and said: "Maybe Willy just ran away. Maybe he ran away because you're all so busy pretending that what you want is for his own good, nobody bothered to ask him what *he* wants."

Taking no chances, Theo had filed a missing-persons report, with both the 19th and 20th Precincts, and when Claire came home, they took turns riding around the streets in police cruisers, a photo of me taped to the visor. Desperate and frightened, Claire chain-smoked as she conducted her own search from behind the wheel of our yellow VW, praying my body wouldn't be found in the slimy grass across the river in New Jersey and promising herself that if I were found alive, she would be the mother I needed and try to work it out with Theo. But all the while she secretly suspected everyone: Uncle Thad, Uncle Baxter, Aunt Jessica, and Aunt Suzie were getting tired of phone calls in the middle of the night and surprise visits aimed at rousing a sleeping boy from his hiding place in their homes.

I had no way of knowing then that the drastic action I had taken gave me an enormous advantage over all of them. But I sensed in some telepathic way that my decision to leave them rather than suffer choices made on my behalf opened the window of opportunity a crack, just wide enough to blow into my childish heart courage and the belief that I could really change things.

In the insight that sometimes comes with distance, I understood completely that the simple act of saying no gave me tremendous power over my own fate. I knew I had to use it before I went back to being a child in their eyes and they went back to being grown-ups who knew what was best for me.

Mr. Cosmopoulos came home that night with a large shopping bag. Inside were several containers from The Latest Dish, sour-cream corn bread with flecks of Monterey jack and jalapeños, four-alarm chili with black beans, and a crusty loaf of sourdough.

"She looks tired, mister, like she's missing you," said Mr. Cosmopoulos as he handed the bag to Shorty. "Didn't have her usual smile; she's real worried about you." I did not ask how he managed to get these things from my mother's store, but I was grateful to him for news of her, even news of the pain I had caused. I closed my eyes and felt the hot chili in my mouth. I swallowed slowly, pictured my mother's hands stirring the big copper restaurant pot, using the scissors she wore on a ribbon to snip slender green shoots directly into the stew, seasoning the mixture with spices I could not name but identified as clearly as her signature on my report card. I imagined her tears accidentally spilling over into the bubbling liquid, and I felt her need in every mouthful.

The picture had been taken when I was eight, before my body had begun to find its lines, before shapeless moons of baby fat melted to reveal cheekbones, carved a brow, and gave my silver-gray eyes their present seriousness, before the series of rings above the pullover I wore that day yawned and stretched and grew into a neck showing the first sign of an Adam's apple. When I saw that slightly younger version of myself, I realized that people do not record their unhappiness in the same way they photograph and frame their contentment; they do not reach for the camera when there is nothing to smile about.

I did not recognize myself at first when Mr. Cosmopoulos handed me the newspaper, from which an inky smudged image of another me smiled dumbly back and I realized this was the most recent picture they had.

Nobody had to say it was time for me to go home.

21

I rehearsed the voice I would use to convince my grandmother to call off the police, who I imagined were now shining flashlights and badges into alleys slick with fish heads and blood, abandoned warehouses, tenements, shooting galleries, lovers' lanes, the soiled nests of predators known for their particular interest in children, the forsaken trailers that had long spilled their contents and lay on their rusting ribs under the dangerous lacework of the West Side Highway, places forgotten by all but those who needed them for deeds not tolerated in the light of day.

I practiced the tone that would call off the grim-faced people in the newspaper picture who surely were dragging the Central Park lake for a pale bloated boy dangling under a small, undulating slick of red hair, people who would not be amused to find the freckled body alive and in its mothers' apartment.

I practiced a determined pitch, so when the time came to tell them that I would never go willingly, would run away again and again until my grandmother told the courts to leave us alone, my voice would not waver or crack in the presence of that same grinning sadist. I was sure they would send him again, the one who took me away from Theo, and this time he'd enjoy his official cruelty even more.

I looked for courage in small victories, remembering last term when Theo made me try out for the third-grade version of *Fantasia.* All I got to play was a wild mushroom in a singing forest of vegetables, but I had quickly forgotten my embarrassment at having to wear the stupid brown costume designed by the only mother who actually knew the difference between a wild morel and the pale buttons that passed for mushrooms in most of my classmates' kitchens, how ridiculous I felt wearing Claire's tights (which had to be rolled into a fat tire around my waist), all forgotten in a wonderful and unexpected moment under the shaky spotlight of McCall's pimply-faced lighting director.

Carl Jacoby, the production's little orphan star, still a little puffy from where I had just recently slugged him, strode onstage to sing a solo and, struck dumb by the footlights, forgot every one of his lines. He stood in mute disgrace as our classmates snickered, snorted, then howled and I, confident in the fact that my identity was disguised, laughed so loud the whole audience could hear, becoming the only happy vegetable in a field of stiff human produce and the mysterious new star of the show. Kids laughed and hooted and whistled and parents clucked in mock disapproval at the boy they mistook for one of their own and I got the best applause of the night. I remembered what I could do when I believed I was someone else.

In my hunger to *be* someone else, stronger, older, smarter, more convincing, to be anybody but a boy whose fate rested so wholly on the opinions of others, I began to see why I was so drawn to my aunt Jessica. She, too, found her courage in costume, in the berets, fedoras, feather boas, and long slides of silk that were always scattered around her. She was looking for the mushroom costume that would set her free. And now I was looking for the words she found instead, persuasive, bold, irresistible, sweet in the mouth for a second and gone.

From the distance of flight, I saw the lesson she had been teaching me all my life and I understood why she and my mother were best friends, why one rewrote the words, the other rearranged the pictures. "If you can imagine it, you can have it. If you can see it, it is yours."

In my last hours with Shorty and Mr. Cosmopoulos, I pictured what I so desperately wanted. It was clear and shining and so real, I believed in it entirely. I saw my mothers together again and happy.

When my friends gently explained that this might not be what my mothers wanted, that they might be happier apart, I resolved to convince my grandmother and the judge that I should live with Theo and visit Claire or live with Claire and visit Theo; I didn't want to be difficult. I just wanted to be normal or at least like other divorced kids who lived with one parent and got to spend weekends and holidays with the other.

I saw myself riding a bicycle to a new school where there was no Carl Jacoby, no nannies, no limousines, no uniforms, and no kids who saw me as a curiosity. I imagined a perfect life with my mothers, together again, loving each other and me as they once did, summers with Harry at the farm, trips to exotic places with my uncle Bax and Aunt Jess, visits with Shorty and Mr. C. whenever I pleased.

Mr. Cosmopoulos had said that some things can't ever happen the same way again and some never happen at all, and asking for them can ruin what's left. I closed my eyes, moved my lips, and saw myself living this life with all the power I could muster, ignoring the fear that slept in a dark coil at the bottom of the picture, again feigning sleep, knowing Shorty would not want me to see him sitting at the edge of my mattress, smoothing the blanket around me, just like Claire.

THE PLAN WAS for Mr. Cosmopoulos to walk me home. "No need to meet up with the wrong people," he had said. We had talked about my going straight to the store, to Theo, but decided that was too dangerous. The police might be watching her, and then they'd return me to Grandma's before I got a chance to talk to her; also, they might see Mr. Cosmopoulos with me and arrest him for kidnapping. We discussed calling first, but abandoned that idea, too. Mr. Cosmopoulos said there is an advantage in surprise.

It was Thursday, the week before the newspaper said a custody hearing would take place, deciding whether or not two lesbians would be allowed to care for a minor child, despite an old New York State "statue," I thought I heard Mr. Cosmopoulos say, and another word he mumbled that characterized their sexual activities as criminal.

The paper went on to say, "Mrs. Mary Hirsh, the child's socialite grandmother, believes her grandson was removed from her apartment by a group of women who drugged the housekeeper, Lucille Thomas, who usually escorted the boy to the exclusive McCall

School. These women, Mrs. Hirsh believes, hypnotized the boy into lacing the housekeeper's coffee with an undisclosed and powerful substance."

Mr. C. continued reading, frowning into the page, "Miss Thomas is quoted as saying, 'Willy wasn't himself that morning and could have been "under the influence." ' Danforth Cowperthwaite III, a resident of the posh Fifth Avenue co-op, stated he had just returned to the building's main entrance after his morning run as young William was exiting the lobby, Mr. Cowperthwaite reports that he became suspicious when the child did not return his greeting and seemed to be struggling with an overly heavy school bag. When questioned, Mr. Cowperthwaite stated the boy had previously been extremely well behaved. He conceded that drugs could have been responsible for William's unusual behavior on the morning in question.

"Theo Bouvier, founder of The Latest Dish, the popular East Side eatery and catering service, is the child's natural mother. Claire Hirsh, the prominent photographer daughter of Mary and Barnaby Hirsh, who also calls herself the boy's mother, had been missing for several months and is believed to be withholding information regarding the boy's whereabouts.

"A gang of lesbian child hypnotists!" Mr. Cosmopoulos howled, snapping the paper viciously and letting it fall in a rustling pile at his feet. "People will make up anything to keep themselves from seeing what's right in front of them, won't they?"

Shorty had repaired my duffel bag with masking tape and some pins donated by Mrs. DeVries, and Mr. Cosmopoulos had carefully folded my clothes in a neat stack, including a shirt of his, the one that had been wrapped around my pillow. "Make you think of us down here," he said, when I noticed he had unfolded the arms and tenderly placed it on top.

I walked to Thelma's alone; the tracks were now familiar under my feet, and the dark tunnel no longer held any fear of the unknown. The constant rumble of traffic overhead, the occasional thunk of a tire on metal, the scurrying of the other residents, more terrified of me than I of them, the faint *plop, plop* of water echoing in the damp walls—all this was now as commonplace as the steady wail of sirens tearing through the park and into my loft window, or the smooth hum of the elevator, or the thumping bass of the stereo in the apartment above ours. And in an odd way this new world was more comforting—so protected, so still, forgotten by the world above and yet, in many ways, far ahead of it.

"You must stay longer next time," Thelma said as she swept me up in an embrace and planted a kiss on both sides of my face. "I'll have a cocktail party and invite *everyone!*"

"Good-bye, Mrs. DeVries," I said, remembering what Theo taught me to say when someone invited me to their house. "Thank you for everything."

"Do write with news of Jack," she said.

"I will."

When it was time to leave, Shorty limped over and fussed with my coat collar, pulling it up to my ears.

"Gonna snow up there," he said, giving me a nod that felt like a salute. That was all it took to slip the loose knot of my resolve not to cry. I looked at a point above Shorty's head. It had only been two weeks, but I felt safe with the little man, knew where I stood with him, even if that was directly in the path of his stormy temper.

"Get outta here," he said, and turned away.

We climbed "upstairs" for the last time. Mr. C. said it was a shame I was leaving now that I could take them two at a time. "You're a regular mountain goat, mister," he blustered as he lifted the heavy metal plate that served as our front door.

Jimmy waved to us from his newsstand. "Hey kid, you must have done something pretty special to deserve that," he called through yellowed gap teeth, a crooked grin under the bulbous clown nose of a drinker.

"Deserve what?" I called out.

"That."

We turned the corner and walked into our reflections in the barred window of what used to be a furniture store, the wind banging a tattered "For Sale or Lease" sign against its padlocked plate-glass door. I saw a big man with wild black hair, and a boy, hands jammed in his pockets, shoulders reaching for his ears in the biting cold. The boy was taller than I remembered, or maybe just thinner, and there was a new seriousness in a face that seemed a little less pale, not as milky, framed in copper and dominated by dark pools of liquid mercury, icy, determined. He seemed to carry the duffel, mended and packed to within an inch of its seams, with a new ease. Something gold shone from the front of his coat and he came closer to the grimy glass.

Shorty's Purple Heart.

"I told you he liked you," said the taller reflection.

IT WAS bone-rattling cold, a pewter sky full of snow and sudden wheeling gusts. Mr. Cosmopoulos and I traveled uptown via his secret underground route, which I now understood as the reason he was able to move around the city so fast. We did this to stay warm and to avoid policemen, knowing the cabs that drifted slowly against the curbs were often driven by detectives in plainclothes.

I made Mr. C. promise to visit, no matter where I ended up, no matter what happened, just like before. He said he would, but we both knew it might be impossible, for a while, anyway.

Mr. Cosmopoulos went ahead and I watched him disappear up the steep subway stairs, first the wild black ponytail bobbing between the backs of his sizable ears, then the secondhand overcoat, a once-elegant chesterfield with a velvet collar and sleeves that exposed his huge hands and his wrists. The coat was now moth-eaten and pulled tightly over his bulk. Next came faded denim legs waving out from a ragged hem, and finally, just wing tips, all business and incongruous on an unmade bed like him.

We had been walking alongside the subway tracks in an abandoned tunnel used only by repairmen when we saw light flickering eerily against the white tile of the station in the distance, heard the rumble of an oncoming train, and felt the receding safety of darkness at our backs. It was only a few short blocks to Central Park West from the subway entrance on Columbus. We agreed that Mr. Cosmopoulos would go up first, then let me know when it was safe to make the final dash to the door.

"You know, I'm going to Jersey after I drop you off," he said, just before we climbed up on the platform and blended in with the crowd pressing toward the approaching train.

I nodded dumbly. I didn't want him to see how much it hurt to know he was planning his time without me, that he had already moved on, that it was easier for him than it was for me.

"Gonna visit my boy."

Mr. Cosmopoulos was looking at me squarely now. No vacancy, no tugging on his ponytail to clear the fog that rolled in from his brain, collected around his metal plate, and kept him from seeing where he was going.

"Used to think he was better off without me. Figured if he thought I was too busy to see him, he'd stop looking. He wouldn't end up finding out his father is really a bum who lives hand to mouth in a tunnel with a shell-shocked wino."

"Shorty is not a wino!" I shouted, surprised at what I felt for the grumpy man with the wooden leg, remembering how he let me touch the stump one night and how it felt exactly like real skin that had been neatly folded over where there was extra. It wasn't as scary as I'd thought it would be. "He's on the wagon," I said, defending my cantankerous new friend with the words Shorty used himself to proclaim his sobriety during his infrequent visits to a small mission for men who told stories scarier than his.

I saw Mr. C. doing what Theo used to do, picking a fight with Claire so it would be easier to accept her leaving, and I wasn't going to let him off that easy.

"I wish you were my father," I said.

"Yeah, I know, mister," he said. "Maybe my boy will, too."

He wrapped me in a bear hug that forced all the air out of my lungs and before I could draw an even breath, I was on the street and he was gone. Just like in the old days, when I turned away for a second and the street was empty save the echo of his words shivering the icy trees.

I walked the last few blocks alone.

Andy saw me first. He abandoned his post, forgetting his composure under his stiff, plastic-covered doorman's cap, gold braid lifting away from his shoulders as he ran to see if I was real.

"Jesus, Mary, and Joseph," he repeated over and over. "Jesus, Mary, and Joseph!" And he thumped me against his thick greatcoat. "I thought you were—" He didn't finish. "Oh, look at you!" He scooped up my bag and swept me off the sidewalk, into the paneled gloom of our building. With one hand on my cold cheek and the other on the old intercom, he rang our apartment.

"It's a miracle, miss! It's Willy come back!"

I could barely make out her voice. A popping sound, like a shriek, then a higher, angry sound, suspicion, disbelief.

"Yes. Yes. He is. He's right here. He's really here!"

As Andy shouted into the old-fashioned receiver, he beamed down at me, smiling, thanking God all at the same time. "Just now! No, he's alone. Yes! Dropped out of the sky he did, like a regular angel!"

I heard the crack of static as our intercom hit the floor. I ducked out of Andy's grasp and bolted for the elevator.

It moved in slow motion, creaking its way up the cable. It groaned as it approached our floor, sighed again loudly before stopping, taking an eternity to line up with the other door, and as it inched open, I heard our apartment door flung wide, its security chain banging against the dead bolt. The slap of bare feet running. Bacon frying somewhere. My name bowled across the empty hallway. "Willy! Willy!"

"Oh my God," she cried. The elevator door was still opening when she reached in and grabbed my outstretched arm. "Willy, my baby, oh, thank God!" She was crying and I was crying, from relief, from the cold, from the shock of seeing her, not just longing for her.

Claire.

22

"Where did this come from?" she asked.

"I found it," I replied, deciding at that moment to evade the truth as much as I could without technically lying.

"Honey, it's extremely unusual for someone to lose a Purple Heart. People keep them forever. In fact, most people would rather starve to death than sell theirs."

In one of the moments of calm between recurring surges of excitement at seeing me, during which she held my face with both hands, patted me down for broken bones, and squeezed until I squeaked, muttering, smiling, crying, and laughing all at the same time, Claire had spotted the medal glinting out from under the collar of my jacket.

"Where did you find it?" She was smiling the kind of smile that is meant for someone else, a dreamy one that is mostly in the eyes and doesn't wait for the answer.

"Under the sidewalk."

I held my breath for the next question, the one that would expose me as a liar, that would force me to feel loyalty tug in two directions, the first duplicitous stab of guilt that would soften as I got older and learned to accommodate its place in my life, but it did not come. I was spared for the time being. Claire was somewhere else.

The apartment was smaller, different somehow. The long corridor of photographs, the French doors with their beveled panes revealing a slice of the comfortable room beyond, soft pillows scattered everywhere, the big sofa that swallowed people whole, the low, square table stacked with books, photographs, recipes, the pale sweep of floor where Claire and Theo kicked off their shoes in front of tall windows, danced to Chubby Checker while Suzie and Thad and Baxter and Jess and Uncle Peter and Molly clapped and candles burned down to smoky stubs. Black-and-white kitchen tile, our red Parsons table, my loft, once an aerie under a canopy of clouds, planets and stars, all diminished, ordinary, unfamiliar, and tinged with sepia, the color of the past.

As I looked around me, trying hard to reconnect, I wondered, *Am I really here? If I'm not, where is the boy who is?*

Nothing seemed real to me in the four o'clock light that darkened even as I watched, reddish gold streaked with umber, afternoon with night already mixed in, brushing small shadows under the legs of chairs, to creep across the rug, inch up to the carvings on the ceiling, darkening everything, even the thick curtain of hair I remembered as paler, the eyes less gray, more metallic. That light somehow heightened the odd, prickly feeling that I had arrived at a place that did not feel as familiar as it should, somewhere that was already in the past.

When Claire was satisfied it was really me turning up out of thin air at the front door, she shouted my arrival into the red phone in the kitchen, causing a tearful joy in the small restaurant kitchen across town.

"Yes! He's here! He's fine. No! Don't tell anyone yet. Let's just have him to ourselves. No. Not even him. *Especially* not him."

Claire slid me over to the half a lap she had made and gave me the receiver, from which Theo's happiness overflowed and shouted. "Oh, honey, is that really you?"

"It's me, Mama. Come home soon."

"I'll be right there. Put on your mom, again, okay?"

"I'm right here," Claire announced. While I was talking, she had laid her head against my hair, as though Theo's voice could travel through my ear to hers.

Theo said something I couldn't make out, as I tried to do the same against Claire's head. Up close, she looked pinched, as though sleep had not come easily, and the latticework of tiny lines on her face seemed to have multiplied, giving her skin the look of one of Grandma Hirsh's priceless porcelain vases, more crackled than I had remembered. As I listened, I saw a baby's face peering out from the newspaper clipping on our bulletin board. The headline said, "Boy Missing in Lesbian Custody Battle." Next to it was a scrap of paper with the name of a Detective Maloney and two phone numbers, scrawled in Theo's loopy hand. It seemed odd seeing a stranger's name up on our board, knowing he was probably still looking for me at that very moment.

A cardboard box with a mailing label from the McCall School was sitting on the counter, stuffed with cards and notes and clippings. I wondered who there would willingly write to me. I saw them in art class, biting the tops of their pencils, sullen, staring at the pristine expanse of kraft paper before them, thinking about how little they could get away with doing.

We waited for Theo to come home as though we couldn't begin without her. I got the feeling Claire was as dislocated as I. She absently ran her thumb around the Cupid's bow of the Purple Heart.

"You know, I tried to find one of these for your mom, for putting up with me, but I couldn't," Claire mused out loud. "Uncle Baxter even called all the dealers he knows who buy medals and military paraphernalia and they all said they'd keep an eye out for him, but not to count on one turning up, nobody ever lets these things go." I wondered if anybody ever found Shorty's leg after it got blown off, if the President had come to the hospital to pin the medal on his pajamas, why the heart was purple and not red for blood, what Theo had done to earn it, and why Shorty had given me his.

"We thought someone had kidnapped you," Claire said suddenly, then whispered hoarsely: "We thought you were dead."

Claire almost never cried, preferring to make jokes to cover up her feelings (not that she fooled any of us), so when she did cry it was pretty serious, and she fought it tooth and nail. Her hands began to tremble as I watched the red blotch move across her face, up her neck. Tears never arrived quietly with Claire, the way they did with Theo, glistening, brimming, filling her eyes until they could not be contained and spilled over in silence, "clearing up the fog," as she called it.

"A good cry is like a good soaking rain," Theo would announce, blowing her nose, never apologizing for the outpouring of feeling. "Afterwards everything is washed clean, and for a while, you can see for miles," she'd say, punctuating herself with a loud and final honk.

Not Claire. Tears had to be torn from Claire in a purple violent way and when they finally appeared in eyes that were swollen with misery and the fear of going too far, they signaled a struggle lost. Sadness trying to pawn itself off as anger. Because of her, I believed tears could run out and needed to be hoarded.

This was the war she eventually lost in a big, loud, sloppy way the afternoon I came home and discovered she had not been able to stay away either.

"I didn't know you were lost until I visited Grandma Doris and Grandpa Roy. They told me and I called your mama and she said your grandma Hirsh had taken you and I came home right away to help find you," sniffled Claire as she rubbed a fist in her eye and swallowed hard. "I thought you were right here with your mother the whole time. If I had known, I never would have stayed away."

I felt sorry for her, but I wanted her to say she had come home because she still loved Theo and wanted us to be a family again. I didn't want her back just for me, I wanted her back for us, and I wondered how long she would stay this time. But she didn't say these things.

"Grandma said she had me arrested because if I stayed with you and Mama, I'd never get married like normal men. She said I'd grow up queer."

"Oh, Willy Wonka, you weren't arrested. You have to do something bad to be arrested, like rob a bank or hurt somebody or break the law."

"Grandma and Grandpa said we broke the law," I insisted, remembering what I heard after I was excused from the dinner table and stood at the door listening to their conversation. "Judge Bailey thinks so, too."

"How do you know Judge Bailey?" Claire asked, suddenly alarmed.

"He came over to Grandma's apartment for dinner."

"Oh, God." She shot a disgusted look at the window as though Grandma could see it over the tops of the trees in the deepening silence of the park. "That will be your mistake, Mother dear."

Claire muttered something mean under her breath, a word I wasn't suppose to know, but did: *"Bitch.*

"You didn't break the law, baby. We did. Your mother and I. But it's not a good law and we didn't hurt anybody and we love you and of course, you'll grow up and fall in love with somebody wonderful and get married like your uncle Baxter and uncle Peter. But if you grow up like your uncle Thad, that's okay too. He wasn't bad for loving your uncle Alan. Just different from other people. Do you understand that?"

I didn't, but there was no need to say so just then. Keys fumbled in the lock, then the front door swung wide on its hinges, slammed shut and Theo was with us on the floor in a second, crying and hugging me and tumbling me over and tickling and swatting and saying how much I scared her, like the mother bear I saw at the zoo, licking and pawing, batting and petting her stray cub in her big mitts all at the same time. Claire watched us, smiling weakly through sticky lashes, limp hair, and a face full of spots.

When Claire told her that she had already broken one of my ribs looking for injuries, we all laughed; then the room got quiet and we held on to one another for a long time. When we finally let go and looked around, the lights in the park had come on and the shadows had crept past us, swallowing up the room; we had to switch on the lamps to make sure we were all still there.

For a little while, we were *Claire, Theo, and Wee Willy, One for All and All for Three* the way we were before all the trouble. I watched Theo open and close cabinet doors looking for ingredients for our dinner, grating cheese, chopping tomatoes, sautéing mushrooms, assembling omelettes, buttering toast, spooning jam out of thick glass jars. We all followed each other around as if to make up for lost time, as though if one of us left the room, we'd all disappear, and I couldn't help thinking of Mr. Cosmopoulos and Shorty, wondering what they were eating and whether they were entertaining a special visitor named Gabe. I thought of tipsy Jimmy the Scoop at the newsstand, Leroy at the coin-op, watching for trouble in every laundry bag, Dimitri's neatly wrapped cartons of steamed rice and kung-p'ao chicken on the steps out back of Fong's, and Raul's mean-looking mouser who never let me pet him, but always knew when Shorty was cooking. I thought of all the people who'd stopped by one by one to say hello, then to say good-bye.

I was too glad to be home to miss my new friends that night, but as Theo stirred and seasoned and moved from cupboard to stove with practiced ease, as Claire set out napkins and cutlery and laid all the colors of our bright Bonnier plates down on the red lacquered table with an awkwardness I had never seen before, as we scooped Rocky Road straight out of the half-gallon tub she put between us on the table, I couldn't help wondering if Thelma pretended to eat when she was alone, too, and not just when she had company.

After I climbed the stairs to my loft, I opened every drawer looking for the smell of my old life. I looked at my schoolbooks, tennis racquet, pencils, paints, the jumble of toys that lay abandoned among the dust bunnies on the closet floor and the tennis shoes that had lost their treads. There was that pair of shiny red Wellingtons I'd tried to lose, and the dusty G.I. Joe Uncle Baxter sneaked into my room one Christmas, ordering me not to tell anyone I had a war doll or they'd kill him. My old "Peanuts" sheets were neatly folded in the big chest under the top half of the tall window that swept up from the living room. My secret shoebox was undisturbed, and in it I still found a stone from Uncle's Peter's field, a shell from our trip to Aruba, a picture of a cowboy swiped from Claire's darkroom, the tooth I found dangling from my pocket the day I punched Carl in the face. Only after this ritual touching and examining of things that would reconnect me did I truly feel at home; only then did the faint parchment color that still clung to the edges of the furniture finally recede.

I SLEPT between them in the big bed that night, and where I once fit neatly, I was now all arms and legs and protruding sharp angles, an ungainly anchor they held onto for dear life.

No one else knew I was home. And for this short while, our lives stood perfectly still. Claire had not left. Grandma had not taken me. I had not run away. And Mr. Cosmopoulos and Shorty were part of a dream I remembered in fragments. Only Mr. Kimsky knew better, up there in his frame on the dining room wall, locked in a chess match with a mysterious shadow, and I imagined he winked at me, knowing I was the only one who knew he was a war hero; somebody who pretended he didn't like you when he really did, a man who had promised himself a hot dog at Nathan's when the game was over.

Theo got Grandma Doris and Grandpa Roy out of their bed in Broken Arrow to hear the good news and me out of mine to prove she wasn't just dreaming.

"We've got to tell Detective Maloney that Willy's home," Claire said.

"What's the harm having one more day to ourselves?" Theo asked.

"The harm is he's going to find out soon enough and it would be better if he didn't start out pissed off," Claire snapped. They called him. Next was Grandma Hirsh.

"No, you can't come over and see him," hissed Theo into the receiver. "I don't give a damn that you were worried. In fact, I hope you never see him again. You drove him away, you stupid old woman. You're lucky I'm letting you know he's alive."

"That's my mother you're talking to," said Claire quietly as Theo stared at the phone she had just slammed down.

"I don't care if she's the Queen of England. She's trying to take our son away from us. *Your* son away from *you.*" Theo snapped back to remind Claire whose side she was on, as though this was necessary.

"I didn't mean it that way, Theo. I just thought we should be civil. Maybe she'll drop the whole thing now that he's back," Claire said, trying to placate the anger that was roiling at the surface of Theo's relief.

"Oh, really, just like that? And where have you been all this time—the moon? I've been here, Claire. Out of my mind with worry, sick with fear, while you were God knows where." Theo said this with a blame that cut deeply because I saw Claire tremble.

"I know, Theo. And I'm sorry. We can only hope Grandma will let you stay here, right, Mr. William Bouvier-Hirsh?" Claire asked, turning to me.

"Yup," I answered without much conviction.

Jessica and Baxter arrived unexpectedly.

"Doris phoned us this morning. Sorry we didn't ring first. I closed the store. We just wanted to be here with you," Uncle Bax said almost shyly. Aunt Jessica, dressed in one of the black suits she always wore to work, and looking rather like a model in her own magazine, picked invisible lint off my sweater, made sympathetic clucking sounds, shook her silky head, and looked straight over me to Theo, shooting Claire a black look that said, "It's about time you got back."

The doorbell rang again. "We thought Suzie and Thaddy should know," explained Baxter.

I had forgotten how much Aunt Suzie glittered in the daytime. She swept me up into a blaze of sequins and kept me in a hammerlock until the need for one of her Nat Sherman's took over and she grinned at me from her position near the open window where Theo demanded she station herself.

"He didn't get killed on the street and I'm not going to let you murder him right in his own living room with those disgusting cigarettes," Theo said angrily, tossing Suzie a chipped saucer to use as an ashtray. "This is the one Claire uses when she thinks I'm asleep."

Uncle Thad soon followed, and when Theo asked him if he knew any really good lawyers (painful experience taught her the one who represented her in the hearing, the friend of a friend who said it would be a "piece a cake," was not), he flew into action. Thad sat at our table all day, drinking coffee and flipping through pages inked with people's names and phone numbers, stopping every now and then to call someone in something he called his support network. If one of us passed near him while he spoke in urgent whispers, encouraging the listener to "do everything possible," he shook his head as if to say, "It will be all right, don't worry, Thaddy is here." I got the feeling he was very much at home in the center of our trouble and maybe even enjoyed all the excitement a little. It had been a long time since he felt so needed.

Aunt Molly brought a pie and wore a troubled look. Uncle Peter said the traffic on the expressway was terrible all the way in; when he saw the disappointment in my eyes that Harry hadn't come, muttered something about my cousin really wanting to. "Maybe next time" he said as much a question to Theo as in answer to me. They too, joined the huddle, which grew with every announcement from Andy.

Theo picked her way through our crowded living room carrying bowls of chips and platters of chicken sandwiches, refilling empty glasses, replacing sticky napkins, but she did so without her usual gusto. The thin skin under fine lower lashes had a bluish cast, as if she had smudged shadow under her eyes instead of on the lids, and the freckles mixed into her creamy skin now seemed separate, floating on yellowish wax. Like Claire, she too, looked tired, but in a different way, a way that seemed deeper and more permanent, and would take more than a few nights' sleep to fix. She fed us in the uninterested way some people feed pets, opening a tin and stirring up the meat with a little water to make it go further. She might as well have left our bowls on the floor.

I was acutely aware of the fact that I was the focus of all this, but once our friends got over their excitement at seeing me alive, they seemed to forget I was there. The talk centered on the hearing and on the chances they had of winning, which were thought to be very slim, especially in light of all the publicity, which I came to learn had been considerable and damaging in my absence. Theo's business had fallen off dramatically, and a perverse fascination with Claire's sex life had eclipsed interest in her art, according to a very down-in-the-mouth Suzie.

Detective Maloney was the only person who questioned me directly regarding my whereabouts.

"I was under the street," I said.

"Exactly which street were you under, son?" he asked, waiting politely for a real answer, unlike the others, who didn't challenge me and who gave me the feeling they had chalked up my answers to an overwrought and childish imagination.

"I don't know," I said as he tapped on an open notebook that was already filled with other people's answers. "It was dark."

"Were you alone?" he asked.

"No," I answered politely.

More tapping. The detective was wearing his coat indoors, just like in the movies.

"Who were you with?" he continued, patient and friendly.

"My friends."

"Would you like to tell me their names?"

"If I don't tell you, will you arrest me?" I had seen enough episodes of *Columbo* to know that policemen ask you innocent questions, then trick you into a confession before you even know what is happening.

"No, son, I won't arrest you," he said, looking up from his notebook.

"No."

"No, what?" said Claire to me from across the room.

"No, sir," I said, "I wouldn't like to tell you their names."

Theo stopped talking to Uncle Peter and exchanged a puzzled look with Claire. "Why, honey?" she asked, moving toward me, puzzlement and concern moving her brows into worried commas.

Everyone waited for my answer as if they had just realized I was there. And then I said something I'd heard Aunt Jessica say once. "If I tell you, it won't be a secret anymore, will it?" But no one laughed the way they did when she said it. No one even smiled. And Theo ordered me upstairs to think about being fresh to Detective Maloney. My face burned with her betrayal. If she'd been half as loyal to Claire as I was to Shorty and Mr. C., none of this would have happened.

"I hate you! And I hate you! And I hate lesbians!" I was crying and banging my fist against the door, and I saw Theo's face crumple, I knew I was hurting her, but I kept on yelling. "You made Mom leave and you're going to make her leave again! I'm not telling on my friends because they'll get in trouble. And if they make me live with Grandma, I'm going to run away again!" Claire had rushed to me, but I pushed her away. "Why did you leave us?" I cried, releasing something that could no longer be contained.

"You've got a pretty good reason to be mad, kiddo," said Uncle Baxter. He had waited a few minutes, then followed me after I ran down the hall and up the stairs to my loft, leaving a gasp of adults behind me. By the time he got there, I felt better, lighter, like everyone who has ever let go and experienced the temporary exhilaration of knowing his burden has moved to another shoulder.

"If they weren't lesbians, they'd be something else you didn't like," said Uncle Baxter, moving into the center of my room. I wondered what could be worse than having two mothers nobody liked and who now didn't even like each other.

"My mother and father didn't get along, either. They told my brothers and sisters they stayed together for us, but they weren't fooling anybody. Instead of being honest with each other and doing what was right for themselves, even if that meant separating for a while to think things through, like your mothers are trying to do, they made all of us miserable. It's not your fault, sport."

"Uncle Bax . . ."

"Right here."

"Does Grandma hate us?"

"Nope. She really thinks she's doing what's right. And if you ask me, and nobody has, I think she's afraid that if your moms get divorced, Theo will take you away from Claire and from her. She doesn't know Theo like we do, right?"

Uncle Baxter hugged me as he said this. Just then I wanted to ask him the question I told myself I would never ask anybody, but I didn't. I would never ask that. I would never let anybody see how much they could hurt me with the answer. Instead, I told him a secret. As a test.

"When Mr. Cosmopoulos's father married someone his grandmother didn't like, she never spoke to him again even though they lived on the same island. She wore black and acted like he was dead. Mr. C. says she was a stoic, which he said is another word for stubborn."

"Mr. Cosmopoulos is your friend, isn't he, the man I met in Sheridan Square that day?"

I nodded.

"I thought so," he said. There was a pause. "I'll go tell them you're sorry, okay?"

"Okay," I said, not quite sure that I was.

What I was sure of, though, is that everyone takes you seriously when you draw a line in the sand that says, "Cross this and there will be consequences." I was beginning to see that anyone can do it, even a kid, as long as people get the idea you really mean it. I think they knew that if they made me live with Grandma, I would run away as many times as it took. They didn't push me after what I said to Detective Malone.

23

Theo had wanted a man to represent us. She said it would look better if a man stood up for a mother fighting to keep her child. Claire did not agree. She wanted an activist, someone who was passionately and personally committed to the plight of lesbian mothers everywhere, and who was a mother herself—and preferably a feminist, who wouldn't think twice about involving the American Civil Liberties Union, a firebrand who was willing to take us to the Supreme Court, if necessary.

Claire hovered at the edge of the command post Theo and Thad had set up at our dining room table to plan our defense. "Don't you mean *mothers* plural who are fighting to keep *their* child?" Claire said with a quick jab, hearing only the exclusion, not the fatigue wearing Theo down.

"Claire, darling, if a man speaks on our behalf it will be construed as acceptance. We will blatantly play on the judge's paternalistic instincts, which I'm sure he possesses in larger portion than most men, being a judge and all," said Theo, ignoring the shot, speaking to the issue between them, trying to be patient, not looking up from the list of attorneys Baxter had supplied.

"Louis Andrew. Bax says this guy is a killer," said Theo, pushing her finger into his name as thought the ink might seep into her pores and tell her the truth about his skill.

"We need a lawyer, not a hit man," Claire said stubbornly. "Ruth knows a woman who's represented some of the people from the Stonewall riots." "Claire," Theo interrupted, "this is not a publicity case for some lesbian Ralph Nader whose only claim to fame is representing a man's right to wear pantyhose. This is our son. We want to win."

"She's right, Claire." Thad looked up from his fat telephone book. "Much as I hate to agree, this is war. You need a nice heterosexual Connecticut lawyer with a wife and two kids, someone the judge knows for a fact is virile and middle-class. And who, of course, is as well connected as they come. With all due respect, darling, you really don't need some storefront bleeding heart, the likes of whom said 'piece of cake' last time, as I recall."

"Who asked you, Thad?" said Claire, before she skulked away.

CLAIRE SAID Theo was selfish and insensitive to the fact that this was a precedent-setting case that could conceivably produce an entirely new definition of family. Theo accused Claire of wanting to politicize our problems, of making something very private into a public circus.

Theo fled to her stove, producing meals with the determination of a line worker. Her anger assumed the sound of wood and metal clicking into well-worn grooves, the steady breeze of the kitchen door, footsteps, one, two, three, four, five, a solid thunk following close behind as the opponents sought fresh arguments in separate rooms.

Claire retreated to her darkroom, where new images gathered during her recent journey took shape: grizzled bikers and the hard-bitten women who rode with them; outlaws in black leather and studs, which did nothing to hide a look in the eye that said, "I'm not really so tough, I can still be hurt"; truckers sporting Road Runner tattoos and nicotine-yellow teeth, posing in front of their rigs, dwarfed by mud flaps and wheels big as a man, massive grills the color of candy apples, sporting names like "Rosie" and "Lurleen" traced in swirls and curlicues of gold leaf, written in the aching loneliness behind the foul-mouthed and incessant bravado of the CB, pictures of men who washed and shaved in public restrooms and talked of highways with the reverence of lovers, lowering their voices to a whisper in the presence of outsiders.

"I dunno," Claire had said when I asked her how come they let her in the men's room for the one I like best. She called it "The Trucker's Toilette"; two men, two pairs of eyes, two white Jockey T-shirts, looking back from two mirrors, each one reflecting a face full of soap, chins stretched tight, lower lips reaching for lantern jaws as two stainless steel razors, held as delicately as teacups, scraped the highway off their sunburned necks, a transistor radio on the shelf between them. These images told us more about where Claire had been than she wanted to say. One in particular, of a waitress in a tight uniform winking across the counter of a diner, held a terrible power to disturb. When Theo saw it, a tiny muscle in her cheek began to quiver and she stared at Claire so hard, Claire had to turn away.

As it turned out, we hired Alice Coombs, who had represented Uncle Thad against the insurance company that had dropped Uncle Alan when he got sick. We hired her not because Theo had conceded to Claire, but because no one else would take our case.

"Honey, you can't get better than this—whip smart, top ten at Columbia Law. She took on Alan's landlord once, and the guy didn't know what hit him," Uncle Thad had said, fingering the page in his red leather address book, where Alice's name and number were neatly printed above "Croissants" and below "Cleaners." "I don't know whether it's because of a defective gene, boring parents, or a childhood spent at math camp, but she has absolutely no sense of humor. Not that we need Bette Midler at a time like this."

Alice stared down a punch line the way most people look at bad food. The day she came over to take statements from Baxter and Jessica, Thad, Suzie, and Peter, Claire slid her arm around Theo's waist as she introduced Alice to the shuffling group.

"From now on, it would be a good idea to avoid any public displays of affection," the dour lawyer had said, ignoring the offered hands, "especially where the other side might see you."

"I guess that rules out French-kissing in front of the judge," Claire said.

"Claire, for God's sake, this is no time to be funny," said Theo, trying her best to be severe and failing, grateful for a reason to smile. But Alice's face simply emptied as she waited for the nervous laughter to die down, giving no sign that she understood, as we all did, that my mothers were very nervous.

Theo led Alice into the living room, where she would talk with each person privately. The lawyer seemed dull and brown against the soft colors of our lives and the vivid parade of our friends.

The French doors became the curtain that rang down each act in the pantomime playing out behind its faceted glass, a sudden gesture, a sharp reply, raised voices, not a sound beyond its glittering perimeter as we strained to hear. Suzie went first. Alice never looked look up, did not respond to Suzie's frequent volleys of nervous patter, and glared when Suzie reached into her purse for one of her Nat Shermans.

"I always smoke when I'm cross-examined," Suzie said from the interior of her enormous bag, announcing the hunt for her lighter with the clatter of bracelets against leather.

"I'd prefer it if you didn't," said the unsmiling Miss Coombs, warning Suzie of private detectives, tape recorders, phone taps, and other dirty tricks from any number of professionals hired by my grandmother to report any "unsavory activities a small boy might be exposed to," pelting her with questions about her marriages, her business dealings with Claire, her relationship with me, her frequent and short-lived relationships, her own sexual preferences. Alice asked these things flatly, with no judgment, no accusation, with no affect at all really, nor any regard for their effect on the other person.

"It would be very good for Claire and Theo to have a character witness whose own character cannot be impugned," said Alice, frowning into her notes.

"Well, I'm a character, all right," laughed Suzie, looking for a reprieve in the lawyer's unblinking eyes. Suzie was visibly shaken after her exhaustive interview, happy to be out of the box.

When Aunt Jessica came out, she tossed her hair and sighed in that way she had of dismissing people who did not interest her and said, "She's a hopeless frump."

Claire rolled her eyes.

"Yes, I know, Claire: What has fashion got to do with this serious problem? Please don't take this the wrong way, but she dresses like one of those awful dykes and if she looks like that in court, we haven't a prayer. Appearances count, whether we admit it or not," said Jess, encouraged by the reluctant agreement she saw in Claire's tense nod.

Uncle Baxter put it another way: "She's just very smart and very dull and has absolutely no charm. Okay, no social skills at all," he added, seeing them elbow each other for the opportunity to be first to pounce on this understatement.

Thad looked stung when he reappeared in the dining room. Alice had bluntly asked him not to come to court. "It would be better, given your obvious homosexuality, which would exacerbate the situation," she had said, never looking up to see where the punch had landed.

"Maybe she didn't like me asking her who did her hair," he said, tossing his own perfectly shaped cut, trying to pretend it didn't hurt. "Putting on the drag," as Theo called what Thad seemed to be doing more of in Alan's absence.

I didn't like Alice, not for the kinds of reasons you can explain with words, but for the kind you know without them.

I watched her when Theo told her the story of the afternoon the court had sent Miss Rodriguez to the apartment to take me to Grandma's and the cop was so horrible, humiliating her, threatening her. Alice never once said, "Oh, that must have been terrible," even when Theo got to the part that always made her cry, about how he reached for his gun and raised his voice at her in the hall in front of our neighbors, who hadn't really been the same to her since, about how scared she was that she would never see me again.

Alice just kept on writing, and looked up every now and then, saying, "I see . . . Yes . . . What happened then? . . . Go on," then scribbled some more, chewing on the inside of her lip, nodding to herself, filling up a pale blue tablet and then another with words and punctuation marks only she could understand.

Afterward, she read back what happened and none of what she wrote seemed to have anything to do with us anymore; her words were stiff and formal—words like "rules," "writs," and "versus" this and "versus" that—and there were no pauses in which to look away from the page and draw meaning from the pictures they formed. Anytime a voice wavered slightly, an eye shined suspiciously, or a coffee cup betrayed a trembling hand, Alice fixed her gaze on her ever-present legal pad, twisting the top of her black-and-gold pen until it was over. I got the feeling that she knew if she ever started crying, she'd be no use to anybody.

The problem was that Alice didn't understand anything that wasn't a fact; she liked to talk about things people did, not what they felt. I told Alice that nobody said a word when Jeffrey Tannenbaum's mother didn't tell his father and his new wife she had left him home alone with the maid for a month when she went to Switzerland to have an operation on her face, and nobody cared when Henry Paste's dad let him stay all by himself at the Pierre and order anything he wanted from room service in return for not telling his mother that two girls named Cindy and Irene were living in his apartment when she sent Henry over for the weekend.

Alice listened politely to my mothers and to our friends and to Grandma Doris and Grandpa Roy (who had arrived in a flurry of hugs and kisses and their battered blue Samsonite packed to overflowing with odd bits of luck, a prayer arrow, a medicine pouch, a foul-smelling amulet, and a Catholic mass card) but I could tell she thought they were all nuts. She narrowed her eyes at Uncle Peter when he insisted the trouble was Claire's childhood and not feeling loved as much as their dead brother and when he explained that he never knew of his mother's intention to petition the court for custody until it happened.

I told her how Theo was so upset at what Carl's grandmother did that she cut her hand and had to go to the emergency room for stitches. I told her how Claire drove all night and slept on plastic chairs in the airport when she found out I was gone. Theo had closed the store so they could help Detective Maloney search for me. Grandpa Barnaby had stopped talking to Grandma while I was there because he couldn't stand what she was doing to our family. Aunt Jessica sent Roy and Doris airline tickets, so they could come to New York to fight for their grandson and "tell that woman off." But Alice said these things were irrelevant. I didn't understand how you could show how much we wanted to stay together without telling these things to the judge, but Alice wasn't the slightest bit interested in my opinion. Whenever I tried to tell her how things really were, she tapped her pen and waited for someone to explain to me that lawyers don't discuss cases with children.

The other problem was that Alice never smiled. She just drew her lips tightly against her teeth, the way some people did when they met us for the first time and pretended to like us.

* * *

CLAIRE KEPT our record albums under the stairs, near the darkroom. One in particular, which she loved to listen to while she was developing, said "chamber music" on the cover—which, I suppose, is why I thought judges' chambers were a series of special secret rooms where important cases were discussed while someone played the cello. But it turned out chambers weren't anything special at all, or even plural for that matter. *They* were really just a singular stale-smelling office with a water-stained ceiling in a heavily trafficked corridor of the courthouse, with no music at all except the static of a police radio coming in from somewhere on the other side of a transom that cried out for Windex. *They* had just a row of cracked venetian blinds shielding the windows from undue interruption from the boisterous world of felons, detectives, jurors, and marshals loitering in the din outside.

On the way to this dirty peeling place called chambers, where I was told the judge would listen to the arguments each side would present in court before deciding where I had to live until I was "emancipated," we passed a fierce-looking, pockmarked bride in a pillbox hat and a tight, sequined dress; she seemed to be egged on by a handful of sullen relatives who did not look pleased with her choice. The swarthy young groom wore a lavender tuxedo and a downy mustache, which made me laugh because it was softer and more feminine than the one that darkened his fiancée's upper lip. They were looking for City Hall.

Even though I knew it wasn't polite to stare, I could not pull my eyes away from a man sitting on one of the scarred benches in the ammonia-choked hallway, whose grizzled hair and woolen cap blurred the beginnings of a scar that rode his cheek from earlobe to nostril, carved an angry furrow across a mountainous forehead, dropped down through muttonchop sideburns, appeared again at the edge of his bottom lip, then disappeared into the tangle of his beard. It was not a fresh scar—its slash was a timeworn mother-of-pearl against ruddy skin—but it warned of a danger that was far from over, a fuse that could be easily lit again.

If I looked like that, nobody would be telling me where to live, I thought as I heard the soft click of Claire's Leica behind me, the same familiar sound as when we passed the mustached wedding party. I knew the man on the bench, too, would be developed, catalogued, given a point of view, and memorialized as part of a larger work I imagined she might dub *Fighting City Hall.* And after that, the escaping steam of Theo's disapproval, a sharp tug on Claire's sleeve and a look that said, "How can you be thinking about that now?"

"If I didn't do this, you'd be carrying me at this point," Claire whispered. "Don't you know that?"

"I guess I do," said Theo quietly, squeezing Claire's free hand.

Claire returned the gesture with a sad smile, and held up Theo's delicate finger, which still wore the six gold bands and a small plaster from a mishap with a paring knife. "Look who's talking, the one who cooked all night with nobody coming to dinner."

When we entered the large room, it was bare except for a series of bookcases painted a bilious green, the poorly constructed shelves buckling under the weight of dozens of thick lawbooks emblazoned with gold-leaf spines. A dozen or so metal chairs had been arranged in haphazard rows fanning out on either side of a desk, with a crooked aisle in between.

The desk was a virtual paper skyline, piled high with several stacks of yellow manila folders, each one bearing bold black Magic Marker letters. One thick file had been separated from the rest, set out like new pajamas on a scarred plastic blotter in front of the judge's leather swivel chair. I could see by tilting my head that the letters spelled out *Hirsh v. Bouvier.* A plaque, barely visible under this burden of paperwork, bore the name Albert J. Shapiro, the *Honorable* Albert J. Shapiro; not Bailey, who had come to dinner. Claire, Theo, and Alice slumped at the sight of it. When he entered the room, this judge did not smile as Judge Bailey had at my grandmother's table. This one looked at us with a weary expression, the kind teachers wear when you're late for class.

Alice said Claire and Theo and I should take the seats to the left of the big desk. Grandma, accompanied by her lawyer and friend Chester Darlington, and that awful woman from Social Services, Miss Rodriguez, settled in the chairs to the right.

Grandma Doris was glaring at Grandma Hirsh, who was looking straight ahead pretending she didn't see. Grandpa Roy was holding

Theo's hand; Uncle Peter was holding Claire's; and Suzie, Jessica, and Baxter, who had been asked to be character witnesses, took turns leaning forward to tousle my hair, tickle my sides, and tell me everything was going to be okay, which I did not believe for a minute. Alice sat in the chair closest to the judge's desk, scribbling furiously. Detective Maloney was there, too, but he stood in the back, so I couldn't tell which side he was on. When I saw him leaning against the door, squinting suspiciously at everyone in the room, I was glad Mr. Cosmopoulos hadn't come after all, even though I'd hoped he would.

Jimmy had given us the newspaper that said, ". . . The matter will be decided at a hearing set for March 9," and Mr. C. had said, "You'd better be there, mister. You can't have people deciding things for you without speaking up for yourself." When I asked if he could come with me, Mr. C. went blank for a minute, then shook his massive head, setting the springs in his ponytail in motion, and said, "Some things you've just got to do on your own."

I knew he was right, but I was scared. So, just before we left the apartment to go to court, I ran back up to my room and pinned my Purple Heart to the inside of my sweater where only I could see it, just in case Shorty was right when he told me the medal had the power to transform ordinary people into heroes.

Judge Shapiro was talking. Something about this matter being best resolved quickly, avoiding even more damage to the family than had already been done in the newspapers.

"We have a small boy here," Judge Shapiro continued, "an impressionable nine-year-old—"

"I'm almost ten," I corrected him, surprised to hear my voice lifting away from me.

"Thank you, William," said the judge a little too quickly, in a tone that did nothing to soften the fact that he did not take kindly to interruptions, "and I would appreciate not having to remove him from this important proceeding, which I understand he asked to attend. So I warn all of you: Anyone who disrupts the proceedings in any way, uses language or pursues any line of questioning I consider harmful to this child, can expect to be reprimanded, and held in contempt of this court, despite the informal nature of this venue. I will not tolerate offensive behavior. Is that clear?"

Alice and Mr. Darlington tilted their heads in assent.

"Well then, shall we proceed?"

No one answered this question, and so Judge Shapiro continued talking, looking squarely at Alice, then at Mr. Darlington, then back to Alice again the way Mom watched Theo and me play tennis, over the same half glasses Grandpa Barnaby wore to read *The Wall Street Journal.* I wondered where the jury was.

"This is not a jury trial. This is a hearing, which means I will hear all arguments for and against keeping William in the custody of his mother, Miss Theodora Bouvier, and her companion, Miss Claire Hirsh, and arguments for and against making permanent the temporary custody granted by family court and the Child Welfare Department of the City of New York to his grandmother, Mrs. Mary Hirsh, for the reasons stated in the original court order obtained by said custodian and case worker Rodriguez of that department. I will hear all relevant arguments which will be recorded for the public record."

I looked around the room for places a jury could hide.

"Of paramount importance to me in rendering this decision is the welfare of this child and only the welfare of this child. I will award custody based on what I believe to be in his best interests. I have chosen to hear your arguments here in chambers in order to expedite the proceedings in open court, and in the hopes that we may reach a compromise, thus sparing the family the lascivious interest the public seems to have taken in the details of this case. If anyone has a problem with this, now is the time to say so. If not, we will proceed. I remind you all that despite this informality, we are in a court of law and my decision is legally binding to all parties. Anyone who fails to comply with my decision in this matter will be held in contempt and prosecuted in accordance with New York State law. Is that clear?"

More nods. My heart pounded so hard, I was sure everyone could hear, but no one made a sound as Judge Shapiro filled the room with words that neither waited for a response nor expected any, words that ran over their meanings as they were spoken, like the Pledge of Allegiance or the Lord's Prayer.

Judge Shapiro glanced toward the right side of the room. "Counsel?"

Mr. Darlington remained in his chair, but squared his shoulders and raised himself up from his waist in such a way that he gave the impression of standing. There was something too easy, too confident about this posture; it resembled that languid way gunslingers yawn in the face of a shoot out. I imagined him practicing it in his room, over and over again until it looked as unrehearsed as an actor delivering his lines.

He cleared his throat quietly, the way Grandpa Barnaby did when he was ready to make a toast. He kept his hands perfectly still, resting them on the balls of his fingers, and began. "I think it should be clearly stated from the start that New York State does not recognize the intimate relationship between individuals of the same sex, and in fact, considers it a crime—one not prosecuted with any vigor, but nevertheless a crime."

Mr. Darlington's voice was like all the voices I heard when Grandpa took me to his club; not unlike Grandpa's, it was reasonable, silky, cultured. If not for what he was saying, it would have sounded almost kind, like the voices of all the others who sat in tall leather chairs and wore suits that smelled faintly of talcum, and who spoke as warmly to friends as to enemies. It contained no clues about what its owner really felt. It fell on us like smooth stones.

"Whether we agree with this or not is irrelevant," he continued in a tone that never traveled very far from this affectation of neutrality. "I, for one, like to think consulting adults have a right to their privacy, even though I consider such behavior a sin against nature. My client, Mrs. Mary Hirsh, also considers herself a modern person, and has tried to be objective, even forgiving, in spite of the fact that her daughter's way of life has broken her heart."

Claire winced at this, and Alice glowered.

He waited a beat for the reaction to this to register, never moving his eyes to where we sat, and continued. "We are not here today to pass judgment on these two women, much as some of us here may think that appropriate."

Now he turned and looked directly at my mothers; when he formed the words "these two women," he did so with a slight purse of the lips that seemed to emphasize his distaste for them, even though he had known Claire from the time she was born.

"Your Honor, since the law does not recognize marriage between people of the same sex, there can be no discussion of custody for both women. The only issue here today is whether or not the natural mother, Theo Bouvier, and only Theo Bouvier, is considered fit to raise her son." He paused here to let this sink in. "My client submits that Miss Bouvier is not fit, and she does so with a heavy heart because the very basis of that charge rests squarely on the fact of her own daughter's lesbian relationship with Miss Bouvier, which has created an environment unfit for the raising of children and specifically of this child." He swept his arm in my direction. Theo pinned my hand to her lap to keep me from reacting.

"Your Honor, Mary Hirsh understands her actions will cause her daughter much pain, but in spite of that, she cannot sit idly by and watch this poor child go through life as a misfit, scorned by his schoolmates, to end up an outcast, perhaps even become sexually confused himself, just to protect her daughter's deviant life-style." Now Peter reached for Claire.

"Mary Hirsh has already raised her children," Mr. Darlington continued, smiling sweetly at my grandmother, "and at this time of her life, she should be enjoying her leisure years. Yet she is willing to take on the responsibility of child-rearing all over again out of her love for this boy who believes her to be his grandmother in every decent sense of the word. She asks that young William not be remanded to foster care as the law provides in situations such as this, but that the court make an exception and allow this woman of means to provide for this child she loves so dearly. We ask you to set this important precedent, Your Honor, and grant Mrs. Hirsh sole custody of this boy, so that she might undo the damage that may already have occurred in that"—and here he paused, searching for a word that would give everyone the impression he was sparing the room his first choice—"in that *unhealthy* home, to generously direct her considerable resources to provide a wholesome atmosphere in which William can develop, grow, be educated properly, and take his place in society." Mr. Darlington paused again. "*Heterosexual* society. This gentle woman has had the courage to remove him from the home that would deny him that basic right. And we will attempt to prove to you, Your Honor, that Theo Bouvier is, indeed, an unfit mother, and that granting custody to Mary Hirsh is not only the right course for this boy, it will ensure that he suffer no future abuse."

Everyone sat deathly still. Claire swallowed hard, but I could tell from the blotches blooming on her neck that it wouldn't be long before rage lost out to tears. Just then, Grandma Doris jumped right out of her chair and said, "Claire is as much that boy's mother as Theo is, but if you want to leave out my daughter-in-law, and that's exactly what Roy and I, our family and the Good Lord consider her, then fine, leave her out. I'm the boy's natural grandmother and if anybody should have custody, it should be family. And I'll make sure he knows what that word means."

"Shut up, Mom," Theo said without any real rancor.

"You've been warned," said Judge Shapiro. "One more outburst and I will clear this room."

"Doris honey, gettin' all flustered like that isn't helping anybody, least of all you," hushed Roy.

Alice shot Doris a look and said to Theo, "She's out of here if she does that again." Then she stood up, smoothing her jacket, tottering a little on her high heels.

Judge Shapiro ignored Grandma Doris, who was still settling down, and looked directly at Alice. "Miss Coombs," he said mildly, adjusting his eyes to this new level of her insistence on formality, "I am sure you are just as eloquent a speaker as Mr. Darlington, but I would appreciate it if you would be a little less long-winded than your opponent. Otherwise William here will no longer be a minor by the time we move into the courtroom."

Alice smiled in the tight way women who know they have been put at a disadvantage signal their displeasure. She lowered her head and leaned in to the challenge.

"Your Honor, on behalf of my clients, Claire Hirsh *and* Theo Bouvier, *both* mothers of William Bouvier-Hirsh, one by nature of blood and the other by virtue of love, I am here to prove that they are responsible, fit, and proper guardians for their son, William, despite their sexual orientation. And, further, I will prove that Mary Hirsh does not have the best interests of William at heart, but rather her own sick need to transfer her unresolved grief for her elder son, Roland, who was killed in a tragic auto accident many years ago, and whose death she has never accepted, to this poor, unwitting child. Any child psychologist will tell you such a situation is certainly not in the boy's best interest."

Alice spoke like a machine gun spraying bullets into a crowd, and my grandma visibly flinched. As Alice talked, I got the feeling that Judge Shapiro was wincing, too, knowing it was his fault he hadn't left her any room to sugar-coat things. But I knew Alice would never have done that, even if she had all day.

"And finally," said Alice, thrusting her chin at the big desk, "I will prove that Mary Hirsh accepted her daughter's life-style and had even welcomed Miss Bouvier into the family. Only when there was some difficulty in the relationship between these two women, and she feared she might lose contact with her grandson, did she suddenly and maliciously take this boy from his parents and his rightful home under the pretext of her concern for his sexual orientation.

"Your Honor, these good women do not deserve to have their child taken away under any circumstances and it is certainly not in the best interests of this boy to be raised by an elderly woman who cannot distinguish between her dead son and her grandson, and whose motives for this sudden about-face after almost eleven years of accepting her daughter's life-style are questionable at best."

Alice paused to aim a dead smile at me.

"I will not only prove to you that these women are fit to raise their son, and *have* raised him with love, I will further submit proof that Mrs. Hirsh is unfit for such an important enterprise."

When Alice got to the part about Grandma not being able to tell the difference between Roland and me, there was a gasp, and just before the back of Mr. Darlington's navy chalk-stripe blocked my view, I saw my grandmother's trembling hand reach for her mouth. Her face, suddenly old, collapsed, its haughty bravado gone. She made a move to get up, but thought better of it and allowed Mr. Darlington, who leaned over her like a doctor, shielding her from view, to ease her back down.

At this, Judge Shapiro asked if there was anything further to discuss in chambers, if there was a way this case could be resolved to the satisfaction of all parties. Alice and Darlington each said, "No, Your Honor," and we moved through a side door into a cavernous courtroom. A man called Bailiff asked us to stand while he announced,

"The honorable Albert J. Shapiro," and another tapped at a machine taking down everything that was said. A juror's box stood empty and a handful of people settled into the farthest benches to watch the proceedings with the detachment of strangers on a bus.

One by one, people stood up and talked about my mothers. Aunt Suzie told about how when I was small Claire would bring me to the gallery in a papoose pouch and carefully turn her back on each picture and ask me what I thought of it. Suzie told everybody how Claire would look at the drawings I brought home from school and critique each one with the same care she gave to her photography students. She told them I never had a baby-sitter in my life because one of my mothers was always there, either at home or at the store, and most nights we all walked home through the park together.

Mr. Darlington stood up and called her Miss Weiner, which we all knew she hated. She was simply Suzie, Suze, or in my case, Aunt Suzie.

"Could you tell us how many times you've been married?" he asked kindly.

"Is she going to count Duane?" I whispered to Claire, who had told me she had been married to him for a week and always forgot to count him.

Claire shook her head at me, but kept her eyes on Suzie. I knew she'd say four or five times, depending on Duane, but when she narrowed her eyes, thought for a second and said, "Six," even Mom was surprised.

After that, he asked her if she had ever had a relationship with a woman, and she said yes so quietly, I almost missed it.

24

Right after Aunt Suzie said that being a lesbian a long time ago had nothing to do with her subsequent divorces and that heartache and betrayal was not exclusive to one group or another, as evidenced by these proceedings, Alice jumped up and said, "Objection!" Judge Shapiro tilted his head in Mr. Darlington's direction and asked him to get to the point, to which the lawyer replied with a terse "No further questions" and a triumphant smile at Grandma Hirsh. Aunt Suzie settled back into her chair, leaning forward as she sat to mumble "Sorry" to the back of Claire's head, and Judge Shapiro looked at me over plastic tortoiseshell drugstore glasses and motioned me up to his desk.

"William, will you come up here for a moment. I'd like to speak with you privately," he said in an I'm-pretending-to-treat-you-like-an-adult tone. I hesitated, fearing he would let Mr. Darlington speak to me the way he had to Suzie, first with respectful questions and then with accusations that did little to conceal his growing contempt for her and her long friendship with Claire, which he seemed to imply was criminal in some way I did not grasp. I looked to Theo and then to Claire for a signal. Claire shooed me to my feet and said, "Go ahead, he won't bite," and Theo bobbed nervously, saying, "He wouldn't dare," tugging at the back of my sweater as I scrambled up on shaky feet.

"William, I know that you wanted to be here today, but I would like your permission to ask you to sit outside while we ask these people some questions. We're going to talk about some things you may not understand and which may upset you and I think it would be better if I asked Mr. Darlington to take you outside for a while."

I knew I was supposed to do what the judge said, even if it was unfair, but I thought of Shorty's Purple Heart banging next to my own and swallowed hard. "But I want to be a witness, too," I said.

Judge Shapiro leaned toward me as though we were the only people in the room. "What if I promise to call you into a special session, just you and me? Then we can talk man to man and you can answer all my questions and tell me anything you'd like."

"Then nobody will hear what I want to say. Just you. And I *hate* Mr. Darlington," I said, loudly enough for everyone in the room to hear.

Judge Shapiro recoiled at this and shifted uncomfortably in his robe, but kept smiling, even though I knew he was cross with me. As I waited for his reprimand, I stood my ground and allowed the low murmur of approval and laughter from our side of the room to keep my wobbly legs from folding under me.

"Tell you what," said Judge Shapiro after the longest minute I ever spent in front of a room without speaking, even longer than the time I stood up in front of the whole assembly and held the flag while everyone sang "The Star Spangled Banner."

There was no teacher to pluck me out of this, to gently lead me to the wings with the swaying pole. I waited.

"When I call you back," he said finally, "I'll call everyone else back, too, so they can hear what you have to say. How's that?"

"Okay," I said without enthusiasm.

"Okay, what?" he said.

"Okay, Your Honor."

"Good," he said, as though we had just decided a critical point of law; then louder, in his droning judge voice, to everyone: "We're going to take a short, fifteen-minute recess during which I ask that young Mr. Hirsh be made comfortable out in the hall or in my chambers." Theo winced.

"Bouvier-Hirsh," Alice interrupted without looking up.

"Thank you, Miss Coombs," he replied obviously annoyed. "We will make note of that."

"You stood up to him, didn't you?" Claire said into my ear as she walked me to the door, Theo on my other side, gripping my arm the way sailors do when they help you up the gangplank, passing you hand over hand until you're safely on the moving deck.

"I guess."

I watched everybody gather their coats and bags and papers, a cardboard cup with tan liquid at the bottom, a half-eaten bagel discreetly tucked into Aunt Suzie's bag. Uncle Peter squeezed and twisted his tweed cap, jammed it into his raincoat pocket, and looked hunted. Uncle Baxter took Aunt Jessica's hand, snapped his trenchcoat over his shoulder like a pair of dueling gloves, and directed at my grandmother a hard stare, one that ran ice cold from the arch of his brow down the haughty incline of his nose, right to the upturned tips of his bristling handlebar. It made her shudder and turn away, such was its malevolence.

As we approached the door to the noisy hallway, Claire pressed her camera bag into my hand. "Hang on to this for me, okay? This will be over before you know it, and we'll all go celebrate over something disgusting and gooey at Serendipity."

Theo said nothing at all, just pressed me to her with such ferocity, I heard her stomach rumbling. In the borrowed black skirt and blouse, which didn't suit her at all, she seemed lost, diminished without all her bracelets whose jingling was as much a voice as any. Claire looked silly and awkward in the ruffly white blouse Alice had insisted would lessen her severity. Like Aunt Suzie in her simple brown pantsuit and white silk blouse, without her ropes of pearls and rhinestones, her black cigarettes, the shock of red lipstick in a face devoid of color, they both looked smaller, not like my mothers at all. They waved me off with forced smiles and worried eyes and disappeared back into the courtroom.

As I settled into my place on a bench in the stale corridor (I preferred not to wait in the enemy camp, as I considered Judge Shapiro's chambers to be), and felt a slight shift, a tiny thrust of power coursing through me, I sensed that it came from something I had said, from some ground I would not relinquish. The feeling was not altogether unfamiliar, but lighter than the one that moved through me when my mothers fought, Claire went away, and the eyes of my teachers and my classmates' parents would not meet my own. It did not sink down into my stomach, mixing with the food, turning into dread, but fluttered like a trapped bird in my chest, up through my throat, into my ears, to the very roots of my hair.

They took turns sitting with me after they were called to testify by the bored-looking man named Bailiff. Aunt Jessica, Uncle Baxter, Uncle Peter, Grandma Doris, and finally Grandpa Roy, who told me he gave the judge a piece of his mind. We drank Cokes from a machine that was supposed to pour ice into a cup, then shoot soda over it, but the ice didn't work the first time and the second time the soda missed the cup and Uncle Peter got so mad he kicked the machine and hurt his foot.

As I waited for my turn to talk to the judge, I thought about how I would stare straight at Grandma without blinking and would say my moms never did the things people said they did and sometimes we laughed about who I would marry when I grew up, how I promised Claire I would go anywhere for someone I loved, even to Brooklyn, but that I would go to college first. Without giving away their address, I'd tell Judge Shapiro about Shorty and Mr. Cosmopoulos and about how they took care of each other, checked on Thelma, and were a family, too, and that I would run away forever if he made me live with Grandma and Grandpa Barnaby.

I practiced how these words would feel when I said them, in order to get used to the fear that might make me stammer or forget, might make me sound like a baby. There were other people I didn't know. Aunt Suzie said the man with a stuffed tan leather schoolbag and enormous eyes behind thick glasses, who was sitting off to one side of the door to the chambers, was a shrink. The shrink was there to say I was showing signs of gender confusion.

"What's a shrink?" I asked.

"Somebody who can shrink an hour into forty-five minutes and charge you for two," she answered with a dramatic pull on her Nat Sherman, now out of its hiding place in her handbag. "Gender confusion is when you're a boy and think you're a girl and you grow up not knowing who to marry."

"I know I'm a boy," I said.

"I know that and you know that and your mothers know that, but that snake over there is going to tell the judge that because you have two mothers, you're not sure whether to wear an athletic cup or a training bra," she said, forcing more smoke into the noxious cloud hovering above our heads.

I decided I would ask Judge Shapiro why my grandmother should be allowed to raise me if she already raised her daughter to be a lesbian and that was a bad thing. Wasn't it her fault and not Claire's? Would I grow up to be bad, too? I would look him in the eye until he answered.

But I never got the chance.

The door opened and Claire said, "Alice will call when there is a decision. Let's go home."

"But I have to be a witness," I protested, digging my heels into the dirty floor. "I have to tell Grandma I don't want to live with her. I have to tell the judge I'm going to get married."

Theo slid an arm around my heaving shoulders. "He lied, honey. He just wanted you to wait outside."

"But it's my life!" I cried.

"I know, baby," she said.

IT HAD BEGUN to snow. While we slept, millions of thick flakes floated on brittle air and began the slow and steady work of wrapping the city in a soundless cocoon. Somewhere in the swirling white dawn something must have happened—a cold death witnessed only by the rattle of pipes; a waxy infant wrapped in newspaper, attended by no one but the mother who was a child herself; a knife, a gun, a gasp, followed by a blinding moment of blood billowing black and sticky on the silent snow—because the hand that had just offered the city its first hint of spring earlier that week suddenly changed its mind in the icy dawn and flung daggers of sleet over the soft white baffle blurring the line between pedestrians and cars, transforming Central Park West and the silver paths crisscrossing the park into treacherous veins pulsing with mercury as a frozen March sun slithered up the side of our building.

Needles of light, the peanut-brittle sound of ice giving way under heavy boots, the whine of tires spinning in place, the scrape of shovels and the hollow sound of empty garbage cans on slick pavement penetrated the thin membrane that had rolled down over the hours waiting for Judge Shapiro's decision and snapped it open like a broken shade.

Exhausted, fear gave way to sleep, but did not succumb and was never far from the edges of the dreams that troubled its course. Trapped in flannel, snared by the sheets and twitching furiously, my heavy sleeping legs failed me as they tried to run from Judge Shapiro, who wielded a giant gavel and wore the face of a hag, the leer of a clown, and the gap-toothed innocence of the killer in the newspaper who tore college co-eds apart with his bare hands. When it did not wear these disguises, fear sat coiled at the foot of my bed, rotting in its own desperate stench, waiting for me to wake up, so it could slide back into my gut like the pickles and the chili peppers and the spicy meatballs in the Alka-Seltzer commercial.

I dreamed there were twelve people arguing in a stale hotel room. Alice Coombs was there, scribbling furiously on her pale blue legal pad, but she did not speak in our defense. My grandmother, silent and cold, smiled, baring sharpened teeth and gums dripping with blood. A tall man with kind eyes and rusted hair stood behind a glass wall, watching, saying nothing. Recognizing him from other dreams, I ran to him, but the room stretched into a tunnel and the end of it, where he stood, became a flickering light I could not reach. A fat, heavily made-up Spanish woman, complaining bitterly of the cruelty of the others, would not cast her vote for my grandmother and each time she refused, the others nicked her skin with knives. The woman cried out in pain and in anger and wiped her face with a large blue-and-white terrycloth dish towel. With each pass of the soft material across the swarthy landscape of her features, the huge brown eyes, the proud Castillian nose, a little bit more of her face melted into the towel until all that was left of her face were greasy streaks of heavy makeup mixed with blood and bits of bone. Underneath the woman's sallow Mediterranean skin was another, paler and more fragile, a wash of peach coloring, a dusting of freckles rode high on delicate bones; under the heavy Spanish hair, a flash of flame, another of flax, under soulful eyes of olive black, one iris of cool gray, the other the color of moss under a cold, rushing stream.

Unmasked, standing before the shocked panel, begging them not to take me away, the melting woman had arisen and become half Claire and half Theo, four arms moving in unison, supplicating, dodging, four fists pounding the cheap Formica table and two mouths forming sentences together, one wide and sensuous and full of words tumbling over one another, the other finely drawn over a dazzling white fence of teeth that measures the weight of each utterance and keeps the heart from saying too much at one time.

Slowly, the dream faded. The faces of the twelve jurors became the face of the man who had promised to call me as a witness, but never did, and each stab of his knife became an urgent plea from my bladder. The flashing light dancing dangerously on its razor edge became the feeble sun, which, having limply risen from somewhere behind Fifth Avenue and blurred the outline of my grandmother's bleak gray building (where I prayed she lay dead), now tiptoed across my bedroom floor and peeled back the skin of sleep that had grown over the waiting and the sound of my mothers, pleading for me from one body.

Like vampires, my dream people lost their power in the gathering light, seeking a deeper, darker place in my brain as morning tugged at my bedclothes. One by one, they slipped under the troubled surface of my conscious mind, leaving nothing of themselves save the singular and shrill insistence of their telephone.

I listened to the pounding heart of our apartment. Somewhere, an intake of air, held beyond the normal rhythm of exhalation. The tape machine clicked on. "You have reached the Bouvier-Hirsh household. We'd love to—" A hand reached out in the dark. Whose?

"Yes?"

There was no sleep in Theo's voice, just the huskiness of too little, as her question implored the instrument to spare us its message.

"I'm sorry," whispered Alice Coombs, pouring heartache into a day that never had a chance. It was March 11, 1975.

Sole custody. Visitation. One of my mothers could visit at a time, but never could they see me together. Words tangled up in bedsheets and pumping adrenalin. Forty-eight hours. Bench warrant. Contempt. Precedent. I strained Theo's voice for meaning as she mouthed these unfamiliar terms in the direction of the bed, where Claire lay huddled in the duvet, flinching as each one found a fresh target on her sleep-bruised body, but they crashed over me as I vainly struggled to swim up through my confusion to understanding.

We staggered into the kitchen, more from habit than hunger, reeling from the news, seeking comfort in one another, still warm from bed. We went through the motions of breakfast like the zombies in *Invasion of the Body Snatchers.* I climbed into the chair and stared at the granola Theo had shaken into our bowls—yellow for me, red for her, blue for Claire; too bright for this day, too cheerful. We sat at the table for a long time without speaking, running our hands over the outlines of familiar objects, shooting suspicious glances at the phone as if it, too, had defected to my grandmother's camp.

Milk bubbled in a pitcher, a spoon stood unaided in the strawberry jam, forgotten overnight, a lone banana hemorrhaged under its mottled skin and no one moved to rescue the toast from the fire taking hold deep within the toaster's coils. Smoke drifted to the ceiling and stung our eyes as the toast curled and blackened.

Without thinking Theo had picked up Tweety Bird, forgetting this was not an ordinary day. She drew him out of a deep pocket in the old blue chenille robe that once seemed magical to me, with its moon rising on one shoulder, stars twinkling on the arms. She held its chipped metal body in her hand as though it were alive. Before she had a chance to wind it up and pretend life had not been unalterably changed, a gesture I could not bear to see, I swept my arm across the silver key in Tweety's back and sent him flying across the tiles. He lay on his back, impaled by his mechanical heart, a bright puddle of yellow on the black-and-white floor, and from that distance, he looked for all the world like the baby sparrows that fall out of trees and die at your feet.

"We'll appeal," Theo said finally, thrusting her chin at Claire, who was sifting through her cereal bowl for answers.

"We'll appeal and appeal and appeal again." Theo held me in a gaze so determined, so full of hope, I had to turn away.

"We won't let them take you away from us, honey, we won't," she said to my downcast head.

Claire did not believe these words either, and we both knew that they were Theo's way of fighting the devastation we were all feeling, but we said nothing, letting the numbness creep over us the way you do at the dentist, waiting for the tingling to vanish before you submit to the drill.

"*You* appeal to the court if you want," barked Claire suddenly, breaking the mournful silence that had settled over us like a fog, shocking us into sitting up straight in our chairs. She pushed her uneaten breakfast away, undid the top button of her pajamas, slammed back her chair so hard it wobbled for a second on its back legs before righting itself, and jabbed a finger at Mr. Kimsky as she strode past his picture, kitchen doors banging behind her.

"I'm going to start playing as dirty as my mother. And Peter is going to help whether he damn well wants to or not."

She was marching through the living room and down the hall toward their bedroom and we dumbly followed, not wanting to be out of her sight.

"I'm not running from this one," she said without turning around to look at us, knowing we were right behind her. "All my life I've let her defeat me. I really believed he was everything and I was nothing. And she made sure of it. Every time I detected the faintest whiff of a problem, I split, got out of there before the inevitable happened and I got left. Oh, I was taught by the expert. 'You are no good,' she said. 'You are second best,' she said. 'I loved *him,*' she said. 'I am stuck with *you,*' she said, with every condescending word, every all-suffering look, every judgmental sigh, every 'I wonder where he would be now, what he would have done with his life, who he would have married.' She can't do this."

Theo just nodded quietly as Claire let the anger take her wherever it would, accompanying her with a steady low murmur meant to let her know she was there, to soothe, without inhibiting the flow of words that had to be said. "I know," Theo hummed, nodding her encouragement, eyes dark with Claire's pain. "It hurts so much . . . Yes . . . I love you . . . We love you . . . Go ahead, let it out . . . It's okay."

Claire wrapped her slender arms around both of us, drawing us in with surprising strength. "I thought you would leave me and I couldn't bear that, losing both of you. So I ran. So I wouldn't have to be hurt again. I'm so sorry."

Theo squeezed her and said, simply, "I know."

I felt my chin quiver and pretended I was on the ceiling watching us clinging to one another, willing myself not to cry.

"Well, that's not going to happen again," Claire announced as she released us on a new burst of energy. She was inside her walk-in closet stripping clothes off hangers, slamming drawers, grabbing bright balls of cotton out of her sock basket. We watched her slide the baggy flannel pajama bottoms out from under the matching navy-blue top that had twisted around her lean torso, even thinner now, exposing collarbones delicate as bird wings. A flash of leg, well-muscled and athletic from years of walking the streets searching for pictures, disappeared into underpants with dopey pink flowers all over them, thick red sweat socks and the faded blue jeans she claimed she had on when she photographed Woodstock, which now just seemed worn.

She continued talking from inside the closet. The soft sound of flannel hitting the floor.

"Well, I'm going to pay old Uncle Peter a visit, because it's time for my baby brother to take a side. You know, he told me a long time ago, when I was so scared you'd leave, that you were just being a mother, that our fights didn't have anything to do with me. I didn't see it then, but now I do. And I see what I have to do and God help him if he doesn't get it." She yanked at the hangers.

"Roland is dead and gone, goddamnit, and I won't let her get away with pretending he's Willy. That's what this is about, you know, her dead son. All my life, she looked so hard for him, she never even saw me, now she's ruining my son's life." She softened for a second and said quietly to Theo, *"Our* son's life." Then, to me: "Your life, my precious darling." And, back to the closet: "And I'm not going to let her get away it. No way. I'm not running anymore."

I caught a glimpse of her bending over a drawer and counted the buttons of her spine, one, two, three, four, five, six, the last two bruised a bluish yellow from repeated collisions with the back of her chair at her light table and lately, I suspected, the hard backs of hotel chairs and the stiff vinyl of rental cars. I was surprised at how fragile she really was. She seemed so strong in her clothes, so capable.

"Dakota meant nothing to me," I overheard Claire say to Theo, who had stepped inside the mirrored doors. "She just reminded me of you, in a sleazy kind of way. I was scared. And angry. And horny."

"I know," Theo said, tracing Claire's cheek with a fingertip. "I know."

As Claire spoke, she touched the hard kernel of something that had been growing inside my chest for a long time, something that was calcifying into the belief that she had left us because I wasn't good enough, because she really didn't love me—love us—enough, because Theo drove her away. But as I listened to her getting ready to do battle, that hard something softened a little in the wake of words that were too raw, too naked to be lies, and I wondered how Mr. Cosmopoulos could have known her so well without ever having met her.

The plastic sound of a bra hooking in front, like a small toy breaking, tiny breasts shifting into place. Skin against silk, silk against cotton. I imagined the Hanes Beefy T shimmying down over the wisp of flesh-colored lace. She emerged again as an avalanche of snowy cables was poised to fall.

"Well, I'm going to beat my mother at her own game," Claire said, looking up at the thick white sweater she always wore when she was sick or "feeling small," which was her way of announcing her need for attention. When she let it drop down over her hair, we knew without being told that she was a lot more scared than she sounded.

Nodding at the ice-encrusted window still buzzing from the freezing rain, Theo reached up to a shelf and brought down another sweater, a fluffy mohair cardigan that looked more like a cloud of peach fuzz than a garment. She carefully undid its wooden buttons and held it over one arm until Claire was ready to put it on. Theo had knitted it for her before I was born, when no one could have imagined this, when things were simpler and the notion that love could be held between two knitting needles was not so ridiculous. When she held the sweater open for Claire's upraised arms, something passed between them that had nothing to do with me, and I was warmed by this exclusion.

"For luck," Theo had said when Claire smiled in recognition.

"Phone Peter, let him know I'm coming," called Claire from their bathroom, where we huddled in the doorway watching her slap water on her face, trying to contain the electricity in her sleep-creased hair by running a wet comb through it, then not succeeding, not caring, not seeing, just sweeping it all up into a rubber band.

"Tell him it's time to decide. No more Mr. Good Son trying to make nice. Okay?"

Theo nodded. "Okay."

We stood at the front door. Theo and I were still in our pajamas, robes drooping, mine dragging its sash on the floor. Claire rooted through the closet for a coat, car keys, wallet; she instinctively reached for her camera bag, then shook off this reflex and stuffed only what was necessary into her pockets.

"If I saw the Pulitzer Prize photograph today, I wouldn't have time to take it," she said, letting the satchel slump back to the floor.

"I love you very much," Theo said, placing herself in front of Claire's frenetic leavetaking, pressing her nose to Claire's the way Eskimos do, zipping up her parka to the plastic toggle that dangled a tiny thermometer.

"It's cold . . ." Theo said, and then, in a voice I had to strain to hear: "I could never have left you. I never will."

"I love you, too, Mommy," I said, waiting my turn. Claire wrapped her arms around me and tugged, trying to pry me off my feet.

"You're too big for this now," she grunted, but kept trying even though I didn't budge. I willed myself lighter so she could pick me up the way she did when I was small, so I could breathe the sleep in her hair, the soap-and-citrus smell of her that always reminded me of clean clothes.

"Never too big." Theo smiled at the door as it closed softly, not angrily this time, not indefinite, but reassuring and solid like the sound of a fighter who has found his second wind and wrestles his opponent to the mat.

THEO AND I were curiously lighthearted after that. We knew that something good had happened and that because of it, everything would change. We believed in Claire's determination to save us, and this carried us out to the snowy park, past the lake and Bethesda Fountain, and all the way over to The Latest Dish, which Theo had closed for a few days; no one would think of looking for us there. We decided to make apple and cinnamon muffins; my idea of helping was to eat one from each pan I drew out of the oven, finding the appetite I had learned to suppress with my friends underground.

Someone saw us moving in the kitchen and rang the bell. Theo pointed to the sign that said "Closed," but the sight of some poor soul out in that hissing ice softened her resolve and she let him in for a free muffin. We watched him eye his good fortune with a mixture of gratitude and suspicion only New Yorkers possess.

"We've got to get out of this town," Theo said, and I agreed.

We didn't talk about what Claire and Uncle Peter were doing, or how he was going to help her make Grandma let me stay with them. We just knew he would, so we discussed where I would go to school when I came home for good.

"Could I go to a school where there are other lesbians?" I asked as we nibbled the crunchy parts of the muffins where they had oozed over the tins and baked crisp.

Theo nuzzled my hair with her chin because her hands were sticky.

"If you want. But we'd have to do some homework, because schools don't exactly advertise that. Other parents might not send their kids there if they thought they'd be making friends with people who had two moms or two dads. You know, there are a lot of people like Mrs. Jacoby and your grandma who don't like us because we're not the same kind of family as theirs."

I had heard this explanation before, but it didn't help. I had even asked Grandma herself how she could love us without liking us, but all she said was that I would understand when I grew up.

"Are there kids with two dads?" I asked, much more interested in this new information.

"Sure," she said, "lots."

"Cool."

"Why is that cool?" she asked without turning away from the steaming water where she was soaking the batter-encrusted tins. Her arms were full of soap bubbles.

"Well, if I went to a school with people who had two dads and no moms, I could borrow one of theirs and they could borrow one of you and then everybody could have one of each when they wanted to," I reasoned, feeling a small shiver of hope take hold at the base of my spine at the thought of actually finding a school like that.

"What a good heart you have." Theo laughed. It was a good, solid sound that felt like sun on my face. I had not heard it for so long, had not realized how much I had missed it. Later, it would seem like the rare, untroubled light that bursts forth from the eye of a storm.

"Why don't you want to tell me where you were when you ran away from Grandma's? I was really worried." She did not look up from the sink, but let the question float in the steamy air above it.

"I don't know," I said.

"Sure you do," she answered, reaching for the sifter, which bobbed on the surface of the water.

"Because I don't want my friends to get in trouble. Because the police would think they kidnapped me and they'd get arrested. And because if the judge makes me live with Grandma, I'll go there again."

I didn't tell her why I didn't come home to her instead; I think she already knew I had blamed her for what happened. She didn't press me, even though she had a right to. I realized Mr. Cosmopoulos wasn't the only person who treated me like a grown-up.

When we got too close to the things that scared us, we talked about silly things like the time Aunt Suzie fell off the pony cart at the children's zoo and the day we all posed behind cutouts of Al Capone, Frank Nitti, and Elliott Ness and sent the picture out as our Valentine's card. We giggled about the time we hid Easter eggs in poor Andy's knapsack and he sat down hard, about last summer when we were sick of Theo making everything out of blueberries, about how Claire rolled up a ball of dryer lint from her bathrobe and stuck it in the toilet so Theo would think one of us made a blue poop and switch to another fruit and when I was two, how Theo groaned and stuck out her belly and pretended she was practically in labor so we didn't have to stand in line at St. Pat's to say good-bye to Bobby Kennedy.

We didn't pay much attention as the temperature plunged, as the afternoon moved across the small kitchen toward a dangerous night. We felt safe just knowing that Claire was back and was fixing things, so safe we spoke of things beyond the immediate future of my new school, to a house in the country, a new store for Theo, what I wanted to be when I grew up.

In the shuttered store, the news of that morning seemed far away; we both knew we had turned a corner. We were together again, really together and we weren't going to wait for other people to decide our future anymore; we were marching right out to meet it and God help anybody who got in our way.

Suddenly, we weren't afraid of Alice and her doomsday voice filling us with dread and dire predictions, of Judge Shapiro and his cruel decision or that horrible woman from Child Welfare. Even the telephone had lost its power to terrorize as it sang out from time to time, breaking the comfortable silence in the store. So when it rang and kept on ringing in the apartment as we fumbled with keys and locks and mufflers, heavy, fleece-lined gloves and snow jackets, our faces flushed from our icy walk across the park, our stomachs full of warm cinnamon muffins, our hearts full of hope, our heads cleared of all but optimistic thoughts, we ran to it willingly. And once again it proved, in a split second of shock and searing pain, that it still had the power to blow out the sun.

A gentle-sounding man named Antonelli, of the Suffolk County Highway Patrol, said the driver of the truck had lost control on the icy curve, jumped the guardrail, and skidded into the oncoming lane. He said the eighteen-wheeler hit our little Volkswagon head-on. He said it was over so fast, she never saw it coming. He said she could not have had time to feel pain. He said the paramedics did everything they could, but it was too late. In a voice thick with pity for the woman at the other end of a line still crackling from the fierce spring storm, he said she died instantly.

Theo's knees buckled underneath her and she slid down the wall to the floor, one painful inch at a time, her legs splayed out in front of her, the phone cord bobbing above her. Officer Antonelli pressed on, letting his words sink in, understanding the mute anguish on the other end, knowing he had to go on, wanting to stop. He carefully pronounced the name and the number of the hospital where she was taken, saying a Dr. Gwen Something would await the family's instructions. He said her things would be safe with him until the family could arrange to pick them up, knowing this was premature, but also knowing from bitter experience that he could not bear to do this twice. He had no idea it was I who had taken the phone from Theo's trembling hand.

He asked if there was something he could do. He wanted to know if she had anyone else, a husband. I hung up.

After that, I ran to the intercom and begged Andy to call the doctor and come quickly and help us because Theo's eyes had rolled back and her head had pitched forward on a neck that could no longer hold it up.

I don't remember throwing the phone out the window, just shivering in the frigid air that burst through the jagged hole it left in one of the massive panes in our living room. Nor do I know how I compressed my body into a smaller version of itself and curled into Theo's lap, where I reassured myself that she was not dead by listening to her heartbeat against my ear, patted her fingers, clutched the soft black leather of the camera bag that lay inches away from us, and waited for Andy, who would know what to do.

I don't remembering putting the film canister in my pocket, but when I found it days later in the coat I wore to the funeral, after Theo woke up, but while she still wasn't completely there, I put it in the secret place in my closet. I believed then, as I do now, that she is still alive inside.

25

Whenever I am faced with the sorrow of others, I do not offer the prospect of a happier day, as the etiquette books suggest. Instead, I wish them, simply, the passing of time. Because I know, through the bitter scorch of my own experience, that distance is the only goal in the battle with this, the most unspeakable of all pain, as I also know that at some point in the slow ticking of days, the cruel edge of grief begins to dull. The face that appears out of nowhere, the memories that flood into an unsuspecting moment, no longer cut as deeply or as permanently. Only time can make that happen. Not the gracious, rolling vowels of well-chosen words written in funereal black ink. Not phone calls undertaken in tones subdued by the enormity of the loss. Not a photograph taken in good times, given back as an act of kindness that shocks the heart with tangible proof that there will be no more.

I tell people I would carry them, on my shoulders if I could, over this jagged place, so they don't have to step down on the treacherous ground between death and memory, but I know they must walk every razored inch if they are ever to arrive. I know the journey is different for everyone, I know it is longer for people whose bags are light, who cannot stop along the way and lose themselves in the contents, who did not have the time to gather enough to sustain them, the way it is when a child or a lover is taken too soon—or, as it was for me, when a mother hasn't really had a chance to take hold, and lives in the shadowy recollections of a small boy caught in the onslaught of becoming a man, one who remembers that his heart broke long before his voice ever did, but I do not say this part. I never say this part.

* * *

AFTER THE ACCIDENT, Theo and I moved to the outer edges of the Incorporated Village of Amagansett, where the tidy lawns and white picket fences of its founders gave way to wild juniper, sea grass, scrub pine, and the looming empty ghosts that reared up like architectural driftwood on the windswept headlands, abandoned for the winter by people for whom they were merely a summer respite, people who had no idea what fury could lick at their foundations in the dead season of northeasters and flood tides. People who weren't very different from the way we used to be.

Theo enrolled me in a modern, sprawling public school with no stairs, whose floors smelled of ammonia and wax, and whose endless hallways were full of banging lockers and country boys who sneaked sidelong looks at me out from under caps emblazoned with exotic names like "Cauliflower League," "Potato Association," and "Future Farmers of America," who sniffed around for signs of "summer money," eyed my tan chinos and oxford-cloth shirts with the undisguised suspicion of people who didn't waste cloth napkins on family and clothes like mine on school. After a mercifully short period of cautious circling, during which I was analyzed, discussed, and dissected like the sentences on the dusty blackboard in English class, they welcomed me into their ranks with the pull-up-a-chair matter-of-factness of a Sunday supper on the firehouse lawn.

Theo found a big, sunny space on Main Street that had housed a short-lived but extremely messy T-shirt and bathing-suit store called the Ocean. In its salad days it boasted a wave machine, beach scenes projected on the back wall, and well over a ton of sand and clamshells on the floor; now it was an abandoned and very reasonable piece of real estate whose ill-advised owners had sunk a fortune on the future of shopping barefoot. Once we cleaned up all the sand, strained it for valuables—we found an American Express Card, one small diamond ring, and an ankle bracelet—and borrowed an old pickup to haul it over to the cement works on Montauk Highway, Theo began work on a bigger, sunnier version of The Latest Dish, complete with a sidewalk café that ended up earning in one summer what the little Second Avenue shop earned in a whole year of grueling eight-day weeks.

Our house was a modest two-story cedar-shingled cottage off the beaten path, weathered and substantial in an unprepossessing way, which made it all the more appealing. It was protected by a tall hedgerow and seemed even more snug by virtue of its nightly enclosure in a deep, swirling shawl of mist that drew around the house as though to cosset the sleeping tenants, hugging the angles of its frame, softening the sharply sloping shoulders of the roof, stirring our dreams in its dark soup, leaving a damp impression on the pane as though someone or something had pressed a wet nose to the window. The fog always seemed to burn off in the presence of one of my mother's breakfasts. In winter, there was very little snow, only a fine, frozen drizzle whose chill was softened by the vast, undulating Atlantic lapping at the dunes just beyond the town bridge, and the house held firm against the occasional gales that blew across the eaves. In summer, the same salt-blackened shingle that kept us warm bloomed with a tumble of roses and the fat hum of bees.

We were like people you hear about on the news, ordinary folk who quietly live down their pasts in small towns whose citizenry never have the slightest idea who is in their midst. If pressed, I spoke of a father I never knew, never saying that knowing him was a choice that was always mine. Theo hinted at heartbreak in terms both tragic and vague. Mr. Kimsky became a mystery uncle in the front hall between Uncle Baxter's housewarming present, a Victorian hall stand that dangled our coats and hats and mufflers from what looked like iron antlers, and a blue porcelain jardinière unearthed in some forgotten flea market that held our umbrellas and my autographed Mickey Mantle baseball bat. Neither of us could bear to reproduce the gauntlet of photographs that had graced the other foyer. No need for warnings, instructions, introductions, explanations. In the end, they could not save us. Instead, we scattered the photographs around the house as we did Claire's ashes in the garden, so we'd never again have to meet so much of her in one place.

Later, I learned that Theo had saved a thimbleful for the tiny silver heart locket she always wore, but I didn't know it then and I'm grateful for that, just as Theo must have been, spared the secrets in the shoebox I held firmly in my lap the day the movers carried our possessions and our hopes out the door, sadly diminished in their neatly labeled cartons. A solemn Andy gave me a faded picture of a

Theo so swollen she seemed to shine and who appeared to be trying to smile, hold her back, hang on to his arm, and stand up all at the same time.

"That was taken the night you were born. She ran in here like a house on fire," he said as he held the door for me one last time. I think he started to say "I'll always remember her," but the words caught in his throat. He just nodded, touched his cap, and pressed the snapshot into my hand.

We lingered in the empty rooms for only a moment, lost in our separate versions of this final parting, before the shutter clicked and the tall windows that offered us a vast, ever-changing view of a city forest moving from verdant to flame, becoming a stark etching above the wail of sirens and the slam-dance of cabs, from which we tossed our whispered hopes and deepest prayers, sleep curled and urgent, from its wide sill into the leafy silence, went dark. Just beyond our own soaring panes were the distant eyes of other buildings, which looked like stars when lamps were lit from inside, adding their glow to the Milky Way indigo of the New York night, and hovered over the pitch-black of the sleeping park, which never gave us a hint of what was waiting for us just over the hill in my grandmother's rooms on its eastern edge.

We closed the French doors that led to the soft center of our lives—Theo's Sunday afternoons, the scattering of homework, recipes, and contact sheets against the nightly news, the ease of being alone together (and later, the stilted words that tried to stitch my mothers back together), the laughter of friends, the flickering of candles—and finally to my grandfather Barnaby telling us in the measured words of his own grief that his wife would withdraw her petition for my custody and would never bother us again, telling us how ashamed he was that he did nothing to stop her, that he let her do this terrible thing to their own child, a broken man who would not cry until we told him it was all right.

We stood for a moment in the kitchen that had held us together in spite of ourselves, where the beams were empty of Theo's well-used gleaming copper, casseroles, kettles, stock pots, sauté pans, her beloved poissonère, and the walls were washed clean of us. But the weight of what had happened here was still outlined on the floor, the black-and-white tile darkened by the legs of the big worktable, still echoing with the familiar slap of long, slipperless feet on its cold surface, still redolent of the sharp smell of the cigarettes Claire begged from Suzie and thought she was smoking in secret, lost in thoughts we'd never know, rising in a tantalizing spiral up into the loft where I learned to float my dreams on the raft of my mothers' voices. The click of the shutter, the snap of the lock, and it all went to black.

After that, we held Claire at arm's length. Our new house was not so open to the world, not so trusting. Its deep windows let in the light in slivers, as much as we could allow, eventually taking the shape of new faces, new friends for Theo, always discreet, always hopeful, never understanding that it wasn't I who held the key that kept her locked away from them. New friends for me, more than a person who was accustomed to being scorned could handle in the beginning. Like too many chocolates on Christmas Day. These boys did not taunt, did not laugh, did not accuse me of having two to their one; they laid their lives open to me like gutted bags of potato chips and offered their fathers like second and third helpings of everything else we ate in those years of cracking voices, muscles that did not yet know their own strength, and unfamiliar hollows carved in the lunar landscape of boyish cheeks dotted with Clearasil.

Aunt Suzie drove out for weekends in the beginning, once in a London taxicab that had been painted red by its driver, a large Englishman who resembled Henry VIII in appetite only, which tickled the corners of Theo's mouth into the first traces of a smile. He told us wonderful stories of his days as a thespian and declared at least a dozen times that Aunt Suzie was "over the moon" about him; for a while we were filled with a noise we hadn't known was missing until we heard it again. But Theo preferred to visit Suzie in the city, where she could manage Claire's estate and they could continue the business of the photographer who, like so many, became even more important in the requiem of praise and public outpouring that follows an artist's death.

I eventually came to understand Theo's solitary trips to the city as her way to expunge the past, at first to mourn, to sift through the evidence of that part of their life that did not include me, to look for how it had begun and why it had ended, to search for the meaning it still held, and finally to heal, but this knowledge did not come all at once. These pilgrimages could have torn us apart at a time when my own needs were greater, or at least appeared greater by virtue of my status as the child, but Theo's solitary journey toward insight, which I suspect included sporadic visits to a kindly Gestalt psychotherapist named Mariah Davis, coincided with my messy and very private path to adolescence and seemed to inspire in me a fresh determination to hold back something of my own.

In the beginning, I did not ask why, I simply looked forward with a delicious sense of freedom to her absences and to my easy shuffling between Amagansett and the rest of my extended family in South Neck.

Uncle Peter, Aunt Molly, cousins Harry and Charlotte, and the faithful and enthusiastic Labs Bartie and Blisset were just a short drive across the island, but in the weeks right after Claire's death, Theo could not bear to see Peter, so blond, so serious, so slender, so talented in his own writerly way, so like Claire. Just looking at him was for her like walking on broken glass, but one day there was a phone call, then a softening and the letting go of tears, which finally released the understanding that memories can be shared and do not choose only the worthiest to whisper their comfort. Theo began to see that the burden carried by the one who suffers most can be eased by the sorrow of all. After that, they quietly resumed their places in our lives.

Baxter and Jessica drove out on a windy crystalline day that hinted at cotton sweaters and corn on the cob, and promised they'd be back soon, but their lives required more rigorous planning than ours, which favored unexpected tapping at the kitchen door and the coming and goings of teenagers given to sudden hormonal changes in plans. The day-to-day glue that held us together was gone; instead, our rare visits were filled with the past tenses of people who no longer share life, but rather hoard it against the next conversation.

Uncle Bax and I still had our Saturdays in the city—less frequent but all the sweeter and more sacred for that—during which men were men, girls were banished, and the bologna sandwich was, to Theo's feigned horror, held in the highest esteem. We talked about sex, mostly, in between polite questions from the public, who slipped quietly onto the squeaky uneven floorboards and tiptoed reverently among the expensive ball-and-claw feet, camelbacks, and cabriole legs of the store's ever-changing procession of treasures. As a result, the subject took on an illicit air we both enjoyed. Years later, this was the basis for a rude joke about my inexplicable and frequent urges to have sex at crowded antique shows and department store model rooms.

But in the quiet of the years that passed in term papers, baseball teams, broken bones, school, unfulfilling encounters with female flesh, and part-time jobs—a month as a willing, yet hopeless assistant at The Latest Dish; a summer spent helping Aunt Suzie catalog negatives and mount a retrospective, a job requiring that I make hourly runs for Nat Shermans and black coffee and which I loved because it meant being close to Claire again; another delivering Uncle Peter's paper, proudly announcing to every customer that my uncle was the editor—she was there. All through the inevitable progression of awkward dates plotted and shared with Harry, after which breasts and thighs and tongues were discussed in terms of inches gained like beachheads in our war against virginity; during the leap to independence in our narrow Princeton dorm, where this conflict could rage in more ideal circumstances and our friendship would be sealed in beer and widened, much to my surprise, to include the prodigal and repentant Carl, she was there, smiling at the posturing of boys aching to be men.

And in the final exhilarating terror of striking out on my own, the old shoebox on my lap, a U-Haul fishtailing on the hitch behind me all the way through the Holland Tunnel and over to West Houston Street, where Harry and I littered a shared loft with broken hearts, jugs of wine, and dirty socks, while I made the occasional serious attempt to become a writer, I heard the soft click of her camera every step of the way, seeing us as we did not always want to be seen, showing us another version of the story that could be had with a minor change of angle, the slightest tilt in a different direction, a little cropping.

"SHE'S BEAUTIFUL. But would you go to Brooklyn for her?" whispered Theo when she met Annie that first time. My mother had tiptoed up behind me on Molly and Peter's lawn and asked in perfect imitation of Claire, who would have demanded proof—subway tokens, Nathan's matches, a Klein's shopping bag, something—if she'd been there herself.

"I would go to the ends of the earth," I declared, like every lovesick fool before me, with absolute faith in my ability to find that place, having no map and not the merest glimmer of where it actually is and what it means to go there. "Good," said Theo, "you may have to."

As it turned out, I barely got out of Queens. It felt like 106 degrees, the hottest day in the hottest June ever recorded, a few scorching days into my twenty-sixth year, the kind of suffocating morning anyone with a functioning brain would spend in an icy bathtub with a willing friend and a cold beer. I was stuck in the Jeep Uncle Peter had passed down to Harry, on the Long Island Expressway near Queens College, in a traffic jam that was backed up for what looked like ten miles. I was on my way out to the farm for Charlotte's wedding, a garden affair that left all the family women, serious women, women we admired, highly competent women, women who wouldn't be caught dead at a Tupperware party, hollow-eyed and sleepless with decisions, torn between organdy and voile, tulips and tea roses, white chocolate ganache and coconut angel-food cake.

I was listening for the traffic report, thinking that the family craziness would be over after today, fiddling with the radio, smiling at the memory of Theo and Molly poring over magazines thick with glossy layouts of wedding parties frolicking on summer lawns. That year an unusual number of brides were pictured playing softball with their trains hoisted up; this, Aunt Jessica explained, was fashion's way of debunking the myth of the bride as untouchable princess, a bit of playfulness to assure the future Mrs. So-and-So III or IV that she could let her real self shine through on this special day, though that would naturally require a few extra accessories, like a pair of those white satin sneakers, the beaded baseball cap, or the peau-de-soie ballet slippers for that mandatory gambol on page whatever. Marketing.

In its own way, the wedding had filled the big noisy hole Harry and I left behind when we moved into the city; if it didn't make the breaking away easier, it certainly made it less noticeable. Harry and I and even Carl, who had moved uptown when his grandmother died, inheriting the apartment that never stopped haunting me because on some level I never stopped believing that what had transpired there was not our crime, but mine, were all pressed into service, delivering swatches, running errands, hunting down fluffy bits of things in grimy wholesale bridal shops just off Fifth Avenue in the Thirties, staying out of the way as much as possible.

During the last frenzied weeks before the wedding, we drove out to the farm only when we could assure ourselves of a good meal and a willing hand with the laundry that was piling up on our empty apartment floor. One night, the father of the bride showed up at the loft, looking haunted and desperate for masculine company, Chinese food, and conversation that did not include the word "train."

Even the bride—who had blazed an academic trail through Bennington the likes of which put Harry and me to shame in New Jersey, and whose courtship with the equally accomplished, well-born and somewhat dull Orson J. Potter, had led predictably to a decision of marriage—even she was out of her mind with wedding mania. Suddenly Charlotte was completely overwhelmed and dissolved into a puddle of insecurities, requiring hourly reassurance that she was not too fat, not too clumsy, not too ugly, begging anyone within earshot to tell her she would not look like a giant vanilla custard on the Big Day.

Poor Charlotte. She was a big, blond, open-hearted puppy who was much more at home on a soccer field or on a tennis court than in the thousand yards of tulle and Alençon lace that threatened to swallow her whole. But it was our responsibility to tell her she'd be the most beautiful bride in the world and hers to believe it, so she endured.

"Such is the price of public love," she muttered as the circus spun out of control toward its flowery, four-handkerchief conclusion.

At one point, Charlotte threatened to break off the engagement rather than let the bridegroom-to-be know that his mother's antique seed-pearl headdress was too tiny for her large, intelligent brow, made even more massive by the thickness of her hair, which seemed to spring out of anything that attempted to contain it.

"How could he even consider marrying someone who looks like an elephant balancing a peanut on her head?" she moaned, and fled, leaving Aunt Molly to explain her daughter's strange behavior to the groom's mother, who had driven all the way down from Boston to make the presentation of this treasured family heirloom to her ungrateful daughter-in-law to be.

Not even Claire was allowed to rest in peace.

"If Claire were here to take my wedding pictures," Charlotte moaned, "she wouldn't let me look grainy and artsy-fartsy like this pretentious fop who thinks he's the next Weegee."

Jess did her best to remind Charlotte that the man was fashion's latest darling and would be there as a favor; Charlotte, she said, ought to be grateful he even entertained the idea of shooting a wedding, much less hers. Jessica reminded the ungrateful girl that the only reason he agreed was Jessica's promise to get the pictures in "all the trades." The rest of us wondered what Claire would have done for her favorite niece, what witty idea she would have come up with and we played the caption game she loved so: "Two on the Aisle," "Hirshes Banned on Long Island," "Unsuspecting Groom Falls into Charlotte's Web." I know I wasn't the only one who missed her, who felt another sliver of glass working its way out of my heart just when I thought they were all gone, and I tried to keep these thoughts to myself.

The delay in traffic gave me more time to worry about how it would go between Grandma and Theo after so many bitter and silent years, and I reminded myself of the farm's ability to swallow small children and dogs in its rolling breadth. Grandma had become dangerously frail, requiring a wheelchair and a private nurse named Greta, who filled her days with injections of a foul-smelling copper compound, acupuncture, and brisk rides through the park. Grandma suffered from a painful form of osteoarthritis common to overly thin women, but I believed it was the weight of her deeds slowly crushing her spine. I wondered if Greta had a formal uniform for weddings.

"She's my grandmother," Charlotte had said to Theo hesitantly one afternoon as they shared an iced cappuccino in the store.

"And you will invite her to your wedding and not worry about a thing," answered Theo simply, never letting on what a toll they both knew this would take. "There are too many regrets in this family already," she said, drawing her cotton smock a little closer in response to the involuntary shudder at the thought of looking into those cruel eyes again. "I don't want to add to yours. I'm a big girl, but I love you for thinking I'm not."

Barnaby, of course, would keep Theo and Mary apart. Nevertheless, my mother would suffer at the sight of her; I knew I would, too.

I was just beginning to realize I'd have nothing to worry about if I couldn't figure out how to get out of the left lane to the next exit, then over to the Northern State Parkway via Northern Boulevard, when I noticed the Sting Ray; a '65, I guessed. It was impeccably restored—mint, navy blue, and silver, with a silver racing stripe rolling over its low-slung body. The rag top showed new ribs through its black canvas; the metal gleamed; I wondered if the retractable headlights still worked, opening like cat's eyes in the dark.

"It's my father's," said the girl behind the wheel, too fragile for so much car. "I'm really the MG type."

I followed the voice to a mass of rich chestnut hair, hazel eyes that glinted gold in the harsh glare, a full mouth that hinted of a wide-open smile and was set in a face that could have belonged to Hepburn or Grace Kelly. Tiny beads of moisture gathered on a high forehead and on her upper lip, darkening the hair she swept back with her hand. A lesser woman would have looked clammy and damp. On her, the dampness seemed like a fine English mist. She was wearing one of those demure linen dresses that seemed to suggest more than it actually said, and from my perspective, this one suggested a body both supple and lush as it moved around gentle curves, baring a shoulder, the swell of a breast, a brown arm lightly resting on the idling wheel, long tanned legs riding the clutch. A black straw hat with an enormous brim, the kind that reveals only the wearer's eyes, lay on the seat next to her.

As always, in the presence of such beauty—"such good bones," as Aunt Jessica always said when she found the right model for one of her fashion layouts—I became acutely aware of my size and garish coloring and wished for the millionth time that I was the square-jawed, Wall Street squash player she was probably engaged to, was probably on her way to meet right now at the family estate in Old Brookville or Southampton or on Georgica Pond. At that moment, I would have sold my soul to be someone with money and horses and a pedigree of my own, instead of six feet four inches of freckles with dubious lineage and hair the color of an overcooked carrot. The striped pants that had seemed so elegant this morning were sticking to the backs of my sweaty knees, and the gray morning coat I had folded across the backseat now seemed ridiculous, and did nothing to dispel my cruel opinion of myself.

"I'm a Volkswagen bus myself," I blurted, promptly wishing I hadn't. But I plunged on, attempting to distance myself from this inane opening. "Where are you heading? Or should I say, not heading?" I asked, nodding at the standstill traffic around us.

"To Remsenberg. My mother's getting married." She paused, frowned, then leaned a little farther in my direction as though to keep the other drivers from hearing. "Again."

"Me, too," I said, holding up the morning coat and shaking it at her as though she needed proof. "My cousin Charlotte in South Neck. Her first and, I sincerely hope, her last. I'm concerned about the long-term implications of protracted wedding plans. The women in the family could be irreparably damaged," I said, thinking, *Can't you do better than that? You sound like the biggest twit on the planet.*

She shifted into neutral, turned toward me, placed an elbow on the driver's door and her chin in an open palm, and she smiled with her entire face: eyes, mouth, teeth, dimples, brows. Even her hair seemed to shake loose the huskiness of a laugh that bubbled up from somewhere I'd like to see for myself.

"I think I'm overheating," she said slowly, letting the implication drift between our cars.

I leaned over my empty front seat, as close to the passenger door as I could without strangling myself on the shoulder harness, and responded with what I hoped would be something between a smolder and a smile.

"That's a very good start," I said.

I'M SURE I was after something considerably more temporary than this turned out to be, and although I can't say I ever consciously admitted it to myself at the time, after several heated and short-lived attempts at the mysteries of relationships, all I had come to hope for in the way of love was a few sticky months of passion. While I had every indication this would be much more exciting, my history said its conclusion would be no different. It was difficult to tell from the way I found myself stammering with her, but I was generally excellent at beginnings and, some would say, bordering on brilliant at endings. It was middles I was lousy at.

Inevitably, my girlfriends got too close, asked too many questions, expected too much, found a way to introduce me to their parents whose sincere hospitality expressed the expectation that I would soon follow suit. They slowly unfolded all the scars, triumphs, confessions, and peculiarities of childhoods that begged to hear the details of my own, which was my cue to slip quietly out of view, displaying a real gift for letting the other person down easily while admitting my shortcomings in a way that left no messy scenes, no guilt, no blame but my own. I'd be once again immobilized by the memory of the first time it was not so, of the time I held nothing back, fell hard—and she retreated without any warning into the safety of her parents' view, announcing, with unshakeable faith in what they said, that I would someday follow in my mother's footsteps and leave her for another man.

After that, it was easier to simply stay in the same place with different people.

Maybe it had something to do with the temperature or the exhaust fumes from that vast parking lot the highway had become, probably a combination of oxygen loss and tar from the road surface buckling in the heat. And maybe it had nothing to do with any of these things. But I held my breath, steadied my nerves, and jumped right past the beginning into the middle.

"Want to come to a wedding?"

"Shouldn't we get to know each other a little better before we consider this important step?" she flirted right back.

"If you come to Charlotte's, I'll come to your mother's," I offered, as though this were the only reasonable choice.

"And what shall I say when I call? 'Mother dear, I'm going to be just a teensy bit late, I met someone in a traffic jam on the Long Island Expressway'?"

"Sounds plausible," I said, over a noisy demand from the cars behind us that we fill up the three inches that had opened up in front of our bumpers.

She ignored the horns with a defiant smile, knitted luxuriant brows, and considered. "Well, this *is* number four. She'll probably do it again, and I can be on time for that."

"Four?" I asked, incredulous, thinking she might be worse at middles than even I.

"Four," she nodded, hunching shoulders to ears in a gesture that said "Go figure." I nosed the Jeep into the lane in front of her. Miraculously, she followed me off the expressway; as we snaked through the side streets with their endless rows of neat two-story houses with jalousie windows, corrugated porches, the same vase of artificial flowers centered in every prefabricated bay window, over to Northern Boulevard, down to the Grand Central Parkway winding around Flushing Bay and past the shuttered gas stations on the leafy Northern State, I checked the rearview mirror to make sure I hadn't been dreaming.

She took the turns beautifully, downshifting into them, accelerating just before coming out of the curve, smoothing out on the straights, back up into fourth gear, tailgating, teasing, coming alongside and smiling, dropping back again, not seeing my eyes on her the whole time, but smiling as if she knew they were. At every bend in the road, I expected her to disappear, to make a sharp right and follow whatever direction her life had been taking that morning, but she hung on. I got the feeling that she, like the secrets that had followed me at the same discreet distance for as long as I could remember, was about to overtake me.

Oh my God. I don't even know her name! I tapped my right turn signal and gravel flew up into the wheel wells as I pulled the Jeep into a convenience-store parking lot and braked just outside the town of Southold, where the Northern State Parkway had long since turned into the two-lane blacktop that ran past the farms and vineyards clinging to the cliffs along the Long Island Sound.

"If we're going to pretend we're old friends, I should probably know your name," I said, stretching the stiffness out of my spine, leaning down to open her door, noticing her legs were even longer unfolded, and that mine were not altogether steady.

"Anna Rose Winfield Carver Childs. It's quite a title, isn't it? Mother insisted on giving me her maiden name, her favorite husband's name, *and* my father's name. In that order. Rose was my grandmother."

I couldn't help wondering if Rose was like her, delicate yet hardy in the way climbers are, taking hold with soft strong arms. She could be sweet, I could see that, but just when you thought you had her wrapped around your finger, she would show you a thorn the size of a dagger.

"Call me Annie, everyone does."

She gathered her words in small mouthfuls and as they disappeared into a smile, she took my hand and shook it with a firmness that was matter-of-fact, sincere, and absolutely guileless, not girlish and tentative. Long fingers. Tapered nails with tiny moons of white. A wash of pearl at the tips. A bracelet thin as a wire around a slender wrist. Skin the color of sun. Fine blond hairs scattered along bone. She held my hand for a heartbeat longer than necessary, increasing the pressure slightly, then brought her free hand over mine for another in a gesture that promised everything, guaranteed nothing. It was the sexiest handshake ever recorded.

"William Bouvier-Hirsh," I said, reeling a little from the effect it had on me. "I prefer Will, but I'm afraid I'm Willy today," I said, wincing at Theo's inability to accept this current assertion of my individuality.

"Willy Today," she said, frowning in mock seriousness. "Now, that's a nice solid Native American name. Any relation to the Tomorrows? To the Yesterdays?" She grinned, softening the first of many revelatory moments that would not be as easy as I made them look.

"My uncle's farm is just down the road. Would you like a Coke or something cold before we take the plunge into my crazy family?"

"Let's wait for champagne," she said, as though she already knew we'd have something to celebrate.

26

She didn't tell me what was wrong the morning after Charlotte's wedding when she wandered pale and troubled into the kitchen and found me leaning against the back door watching the sunrise through the screen. I didn't ask what had torn her from her bed, or whose ghost, which private anguish had shaken her out of her slumber, nor did I ask what dream could have raised its voice loudly enough to steal her bear's capacity for sleep, only that she promptly dismiss these concerns to greet my own news of Annie with the reverence and wonder reserved for sons on such occasions.

She brewed a pot of strong, chicory-laced coffee, laid a tired cheek in her hand, and listened as I recounted the miracle of Annie and my night in the dunes. I told her how we leaned back against a cushion of sand and found the Big Dipper, and after that, the more elusive Little; I told her how we traced the constellations, our fingers entwined, and gave credit to stiff necks, tuna sandwiches, and all those school trips to the Hayden Planetarium. I rambled on about how we lost all sense of time, our shoes, and two glasses of champagne, about Annie's whispered phone call to her mother from Aunt Molly's sewing room to apologize for not having arrived, trying to sound sincere as she explained about traffic on the Expressway and a long circuitous detour. She wasn't really lying, just selectively telling the truth, promising to get there no matter how late; all of it was forgotten as we sat barefoot in easy chairs of beach grass and recounted the story of our lives in one long drink of history that did nothing to quench the need to know more, beginning the business of falling in love in the presence of skittering crabs and an ocean that slumbered quietly before us, having heard it all before.

As the sun warmed the memory of this night, not even two hours old, I told Theo how I knew this would happen the minute I saw Annie in the car next to mine, how she shook my hand and called me Willy Today. How I knew she'd always be my friend, even when she became my lover.

Theo smiled. "Your grandma Doris called you Willy Two Squaws. Remember?" I remembered very well.

"That's how it was with us," she said into the dark smell of the French roast that seemed to revive her. "We talked all night, your mother and I. The Bouvier-Hirshes don't just fall in love. They talk themselves into it. Of course, in our case, food was involved. It always was. Hot dogs. We ate so many, we got sick."

"I told her about Claire," I said. "I don't know why."

"I do," she said, smiling, rising stiffly to make us the omelettes only I would have the stomach for. My eyes followed her to the stove for the answer, seeing only my question and how much was at stake in her answer; not seeing how hard she worked at the simple act of stretching for the familiar oval pan dangling on its hook just over her head.

"You told her your secrets because you wanted her to fall in love with the right version of you. If she's going to break your heart and betray your trust, it's better now," Theo said, never once crying out or ruining my happiness with the sharp pain of her own mortality.

A YEAR LATER, I sold my first story and broke all speed records driving out to the cottage, bursting with confidence and my first advance check, dreams of Round Tables and Paris cafés and running bulls urging me on. Uncle Peter raced to Amagansett with a bottle of Dom Pérignon balanced on his lap. Again I did not comment on how thin my mother had become or ask why she placed her own portion of smoked-chicken salad on my plate and sipped the champagne instead.

"My son, the writer," she said, grinning, raising her glass to me through a fevered mist of maternal pride and skin drawn too tightly over her bones. I knew she wasn't well, but she offered nothing and I dragged out the old saw about never being too rich or too thin.

"I knew you could do it," boasted Uncle Peter, who had read every word I'd written since college, as well as the sizable collection of rejection slips I'd amassed with a certain masochistic swagger. He never once applied empty avuncular praise or missed an opportunity to show me how a piece could be better, or to explain why it should be, no matter how close to a deadline he was himself. I wondered if he secretly wished that I was Harry, whose affinity for words extended only to pretentious chunks of Latin legalese and the "net nets" and "bottom lines" of the business slang he preferred and Uncle Peter protested against vehemently.

"Why can't an executive conjugate the verb 'to speak' like everybody else? What the hell is 'interface'? 'To interface'!" Uncle Peter's thoughtful ways and love of the language were lost on the boisterous adults his children had become. Harry, with his steady stream of blond MBAs and schemes of killings in the corporate jungle, and Charlotte, with her horses, her Labs, and a cherubic baby, called Tyler, the first of what would be her own noisy brood, had no time for lingering over ideas.

"Claire would have been so proud," Peter added softly.

"Just working too hard," Theo said when I finally noticed the twin smudges that appeared not to be affected by any amount of sleep. Nor did she mention any need for our concern when, after months of promises to visit and excuses for not coming, Annie and I rushed to her back door with our decision to put an end to the senseless commuting between Annie's Gramercy Park studio and the West Houston loft where I had become Harry's occasional guest and could not be counted on for anything except my share of the rent. Theo simply threw herself into the wedding plans with the pride of a mother and the creativity of a caterer who has just been given the assignment of a lifetime.

"I WISH DORIS could have been here to see you get married," Theo said wistfully that spring, when I joked about how out of her element my grandmother would have been in the old clapboard church with its ancient wisteria vines thick as arms, its gravestones silent and smooth with salt and time. Our small cottage garden was overwhelmed by a striped tent; my mother's nervous staff bustled even more furiously than usual in the knowledge that they were working for the boss's son, circulating their trays to guests in picture hats and summer blazers. As always, a representative of the fashion press trailed behind Jessica and Baxter, who rode the fierce currents of their lives with a grace that few could carry off. Harry had selected a particularly stunning blonde for the occasion, and Charlotte had her hands full between Sarah, a bundle of white pique and daisies, and young Ty in short pants, deceptively angelic toddling across the lawn, dragging the ring bearer's pillow behind him.

"Not a love bead in sight," Theo said into the quiet of the last moments before the wedding.

"Grandma Doris would have loved the way Carl turned out, especially today—he's making a fool of himself over that Derrick guy. I suppose it's a kind of justice, isn't it? Carl turning out to be what his family feared most," I said, remembering the first time I heard the word "queer." Carl's voice had wavered the night he told me he was gay, fully expecting my revenge after so many years.

"How could I *not* understand?" I had said, more shocked and pleased at my easy acceptance than he.

"Being different was Doris's way of belonging. Roy always knew it. So did I," said Theo, lingering in the memories that brought her to this moment.

"I'm afraid of other women." Suddenly I felt ten again, able to tell her everything.

"Oh, honey, you'll be fine. I think every man is afraid he'll be unfaithful. That's what keeps things interesting."

"I don't mean me."

For as long as I could remember, I had looked over my shoulder, first at the pretty cheerleaders in high school, then at the beautiful seniors lounging in the sorority house, teasing their younger sisters with secrets they had yet to learn, and I couldn't imagine why other men didn't see fierce competition in the smug seductiveness of their ways. I couldn't imagine the object of my affection preferring my large, inhospitable body and its sweaty urgency to what was already familiar, the soft sensuality of women. I had never told anyone this. I lived in dread of the day Annie would meet her Claire.

"Annie likes men, sweetheart. And even better, she loves *you*,"

Theo said firmly, as she pulled me close and wrapped me in one last hug.

"You were married once," I mumbled, trying not to squeeze her too hard, reminding myself that I was now so much bigger than she. "What if she meets the right girl?"

"It doesn't happen that way, my darling boy. It doesn't matter who's attracted to Annie. It's Annie who has to be attracted back. And Annie is a man's woman, your woman, the woman you're marrying today. She loves you, Willy Wonka. She's not a lesbian."

"How do you know?" I wanted a solemn oath, a mother's guarantee.

She laughed. "Trust me. I just do."

IT WAS JUST before her sixtieth birthday. She and "a friend" (which was how we referred to the women with whom she occasionally spent time, with whom she shared the part of her that still cried out for Claire but could be quieted in the face of something less demanding), a pediatrician named Louisa who plainly adored her, were planning a week in London, and Theo was looking forward to her *cook's tour* of all the new brasseries and bistros and "hopelessly expensive places" that had sprung up in her favorite city's most recent restaurant renaissance.

We were all in the garden, lazy and full of one of Theo's more exceptional lunches, which even she seemed to enjoy more than usual, our torpor heightened by the delicious, sleep-inducing Merlot she had been saving for just this day. I sprawled on the grass, feeling the sun on my city face. Theo arranged herself on the English garden bench in the slightly eccentric half-lotus she'd inherited from Claire, a position she claimed was the only one that eased her stiff back, and we both smiled in utter contentment as we watched Annie, bare feet tucked up under her on the dark green wicker swing, dozing against the cotton quilt Theo had gently placed under her head, a tiny mouth on each breast as our twins took their lunch in the soft afternoon.

We were both drawn to the past in the presence of such a perfect moment. I left Theo's thoughts undisturbed, hoping I could make her smile with my own.

"What man can say he had a mother who could explain what fatherhood really feels like, this being so close and yet feeling so left out, who actually knew herself?" I remembered an afternoon in the darkroom when Claire told me stories of my infancy, the shock of being left out of my infant's need for Theo, and her warnings that I, too, would be the victim of nature's preference for the mother. I felt something sharp in the vicinity of my heart at the sight of Annie nursing our new babies and thought, *Is this how it was for her?*

"I'll never forget coming home the day she tried to nurse you," said Theo laughing quietly, not wanting to disturb the dozing family. "You were both crying. I didn't have time to get my coat off."

I wanted to blurt it right out. I wanted to say, "I'm afraid you're dying." But this was a moment for looking back and looking ahead; not for seeing the present danger. We both knew the truth would not be told that day. We spoke of other things.

After their feeding, Annie put the twins down in the study just off the garden on the shady side of the house, where we'd hear them if they woke up. When she returned, the talk moved again to London.

"Louisa's running around like a crazy person getting gallery schedules and theater tickets, but I said, 'Lou, don't ask me which museum has which Old Master. Ask me which restaurant does Dover sole and how, and now we're cooking!" She chattered on about the trip with such obvious relish, such anticipation, I couldn't bear to cloud her plans and this day with my growing concern. I said nothing.

ANNIE PUSHED. "She's too thin."

"She's waited all her life for someone to say that," I cracked, not wanting to acknowledge her meaning.

"I'm serious. I don't think she's well. Promise you'll talk to her, get her to go for a checkup."

"I promise," I said, but I felt something dark uncoil.

"If you don't, I will," warned Annie, who walked right into things with a courage I sometimes envied, sometimes resented.

Theo told me a few weeks later, when she could avoid it no more, when she was sure it had come back. She had returned from London with Louisa, flushed and full of presents and funny stories and long, knowing silences, after she had traveled to the private part of herself that needed to be in another city in order to say good-bye, when the chemo bared the first patch of skin in her scalp, when she could escape the truth no longer. She told me on that same garden bench and I will always remember it as the sound of a curled yellow leaf crackling against metal, dry and hollow.

"I wanted to tell you, but there was no right time," she whispered, her voice full of sadness, her eyes not meeting mine, when she could avoid it no longer. "Your wonderful new job. Annie. The twins. You were so happy, so busy with life. I thought it was gone. There was a good chance the radiation had gotten it all. I know I should have told you sooner."

At first, she insisted on overseeing what she still modestly called the store, although it had grown to supermarket size, rambling in and out of the adjoining buildings she had added over the years. Like good, brokenhearted friends, the staff kept their tears to themselves during her increasingly infrequent visits. Later, she stayed at home and worked on the cookbooks that gave her a certain celebrity, along with regular royalty checks. When she could no longer move freely between kitchen and study, she hired a chef to test her recipes while she sat in the kitchen, creating, directing, adjusting, tasting what the treatments would allow.

Like every family before us, we denied the presence of death with a gaiety that left us gasping. Theo wound silk around her smooth head, piled scrawny arms with bracelets, wore sweeping jewel-colored skirts, which never gave away the bones that had begun to jut beneath her clothes' deceptive fullness, and took her place in the heart of the family that had moved to Molly's kitchen from her own. Over the course of a few short months, she celebrated birthdays: a noisy cocktail party for Suzie, an endless stream of ice cream and cake for children, dolls, and all the family dogs, and an elegant gathering for Baxter and Jess, whose marriage had miraculously survived each other's curious habits for thirty years.

She did her best to sparkle at the family's annual Fourth of July picnic and badminton tournament; she dressed in billowing velvet and antique lace for the long, dark autumn brunches she loved best; and finally, she struggled, as determined as a field marshal, to sit up without assistance at a groaning Thanksgiving table that still echoed with those she served so long ago. No one who posed on the porch that day in the bright cold light of encroaching winter could shake off the feeling that this Thanksgiving would be her last, least of all the photographer, who fooled no one with his attempt to hide his grief behind his mother's old Leica.

When she could no longer muster the strength or the bravado to come to us, we came to her. Annie and I temporarily abandoned the sprawling rent-stabilized apartment we had found on Gramercy Park, with its lovely view, its key to the gated park, and the tiny rooftop terrace we envisioned a giant outdoor playpen for the twins. From there the magazine that had recently named me assistant arts editor was a purposeful stride across the lower reaches of Fifth Avenue, but I often returned on some pretext or another—forgotten notes, a change of shoes, a phone number, the yen to pass on the lunchtime gossip and chili at Max's—just to make sure that I still had a family, that they had not been spirited away while I was gone. It was a home we had been slowly filling up with treasures from Baxter's "sources," out-of-the-way auctions and antique markets in small towns as far from New York as their prices. Baxter would lead us to an old wedding quilt or an English umbrella stand or a Staffordshire something or other, a rare bullet-glass cabinet, bought for a song to keep Claire's antique toys out of harm's way until the girls were big enough to handle them. I knew it would never be the same when we got back.

We moved into the cottage the first week of December. Annie looked after Theo and the babies and the house with the generosity of spirit and tenderness usually reserved for blood mothers and daughters, and I drove the ninety miles to the city three times a week, having convinced my new boss that technology and the opportunity to spend this precious time with my mother would not hamper my productivity.

Relieved that I did not have to quit, a decision I was terrified of but was nevertheless prepared to make, we made a nursery out of my old room, took the larger one adjoining it as sleeping quarters and my temporary office, and carried Theo's bed downstairs, next to the window that looked out on the garden. We piled the bed high with needlepoint cushions, Victorian shawls, soft quilts, and snowy matelasse shams from the vast collection of antique linens Aunt Jess could not resisting adding to with every visit to her old friend. From this perch, Theo directed us in the planting of bulbs and the laying of mulch, and talked of the cutting of kitchen herbs come spring.

I shopped in the village and Annie baked, and we invited everyone to Amagansett for Christmas breakfast and the opening of presents as early as possible. We asked them to come in their pajamas because we knew that Theo would tire quickly if she tried to dress.

The night of Christmas Eve, like intruders who do not wish to arouse the slumbering tenants during a burglary, we decorated the blue spruce outside Theo's window. We filled its arms with angels and candy canes and the tiny fairy lights she always preferred to the garish multicolored bulbs that blinked from most of the neighborhood roofs. While she slept, we surrounded her with presents so she could wake up inside Christmas.

When she awoke the next morning, our small family was gathered around her. As usual, Suzie elicited one of Theo's rare smiles and took the prize for the most interesting interpretation of pajamas in a silver dressing gown à la Gloria Swanson in *Sunset Boulevard.* Thad wore fifties flannel rodeo cowboys, button flap and all, Peter and Molly were wrapped in Stewart plaid, and Jessica and Baxter were elegant in velvet slippers and silk foulard that could have just as easily gone out to dinner. Theo herself wore a bottle green silk nightgown and the matching kimono Annie had thoughtfully placed within reach the night before.

None of this halted the steady progress of pain across her features or the bodily wasting that threatened to engulf her spirit but never did. I wondered which is worse, the terrible shock of the telephone and the darkness that follows, or watching someone you love disappear, imperceptibly at first, then dramatically, as medicine does battle with death. Is it better to say good-bye or to wish you had, to know there was no pain or to see there is too much?

She drifted in and out of the narcotic haze that I came to see as the interlude between episodes of agony. Most of the time, she was somewhere else, her voice a steady stream of muttering, a running commentary on what only she could see, and I imagined that she stood on the earth with one foot while the other was already firmly planted in another place, not quite ready to make the leap. I saw Claire just as she was the day she left us, in her torn jeans and peach mohair sweater, patiently waiting, encouraging Theo to take her time, to leave nothing undone, so they could take up where they left off so long ago. Just as I thought Theo was drifting away, she surprised me with the clarity of someone who speaks of the weather after years in a coma.

"Your grandmother never saw what she had; only what she lost. Because of that, she lost everything," she whispered one morning, apropos of nothing, breaking the years of silence she had kept on this subject. Her voice was touched by regret and an understanding I never suspected was there.

"I used to wish Claire would turn into a man, so I'd have a father. I used to think the accident was God's way of punishing me," I said.

"I would have told you if you had asked," Theo said weakly.

"If I knew who he was, then I'd have to ask him why, why he chose not to see me grow up. I guess it was easier to be left by someone with no face."

It would serve no purpose to tell her how I had longed for this man, how much it hurt to see other boys take this luxury for granted. Theo motioned for me to prop up the pillow, and waved away my offer of the narcotics I had been shown how to give her in larger and more frequent doses; now she chose the pain over not being present for me. She sighed, remained still for a long moment, and gathered what little strength she had left.

"She wanted to have you so badly, she would have done anything, but she couldn't. When she suggested we have a baby, I thought she was crazy at first. But I knew it wasn't a request, it was a *term.* And I loved her, so I agreed—but only after we almost broke up over it and I did some soul-searching and decided I wanted you, too."

She smiled and looked beyond me. "I served her baby food for dessert, as a way of announcing my decision. Puréed apricots.

"It wasn't enough for her to be your adoptive mother, even if the court would let such an adoption take place, which was unheard of at that time. She wanted to be your real family, the next best thing to being your mother. Technically, I suppose, she was your aunt."

There was nothing in that room except Theo's voice, struggling back to me from where she was going. Although I wanted to speak, I did not dare, for fear of exhausting her before she finished.

"Peter and Molly hadn't moved to the farm yet. They were living in the Village, in a tiny apartment that was really too small for two people, much less three, one of whom was in the crawling stage. I don't think Harry was even an idea then. Or maybe he was inspired by the idea of you." She smiled weakly.

"I went with Claire because I knew they would reject her crazy plan and I wanted to be there to pick up the pieces. Molly and I sat in the kitchen—it wasn't even big enough to change your mind in—while Claire asked Peter to donate his sperm. She met every one of his objections with a good reason—why you should have two sets of grandparents, two sets of aunts and uncles and cousins, what steps we could take to make sure everyone was protected, who should know and who shouldn't, right down to your legal name. She wanted to see herself in you, and she wanted you to see yourself in her, and Uncle Peter was the closest she could come. In the end, he agreed. He even convinced Molly, who took a lot longer."

She closed her eyes and gathered the strength to go on.

"We decided only Molly and I and Claire and Peter could know the truth. Peter signed a document saying he would waive all legal rights to paternity and gave Claire his blessing and his authorization to adopt you, which she'd planned to do when you were older and could speak for yourself, but never . . . There was no time." Theo's voice wavered and she paused, shifting on the pillow before continuing.

"We celebrated with lunch in one of those charming little basement restaurants on Waverly Place. It's gone now."

"Why didn't he ever tell me?"

"He would have if you had asked. Any of us would have, but you didn't ask, and we respected that. While Peter was waiting, he answered your second question first by doing everything a father would do."

" 'Why weren't you there?' being that question," I said, and she nodded.

"He was always there. You know, your grandmother didn't just drop the case after Claire died. Peter forced her to. He threatened he would make his secret public, seek custody as the biological father, and turn you right back over to me. He warned she'd never see you again if she pursued it. He asked her if she wanted to add a grandson to a son and a daughter who were gone forever. I know. I went with him that day. She had no choice.

"He blames himself for not threatening her sooner, before Claire had to come to him on that terrible icy day. I told him you would have forgiven him, as I have, if you knew. No one is to blame for that. Except God."

"You know, when the twins were born, I thought it confirmed what I had always suspected," I said.

She nodded. "Baxter."

"I suppose I've always wanted him to be Baxter," I said.

"Claire and Roland weren't identical like Jennifer and Brooke. They were fraternal twins, even though they looked so much alike. Roland was carefree, a little reckless. Claire was his darker side, he was her light. When he died no one realized they had to coax her to live.

"She was in the car that day, with Roland. They were on their way to a party, laughing, singing with the radio. That's why it was so hard for her, why she rarely spoke of him." Theo said this as if she knew more about it than anyone else; I realized that she probably did.

"I've always believed labels were overrated. Brother, sister, husband, wife, mother, son, lover, friend, uncle, father, grandmother," she said finally, reaching for my hand. "He loves you very much, Willy."

IT WAS RAINING the next day, a steady sloshing rain unusual for January. The deep, earthy smell of it clung to the sill, promising something beyond the ice-bound cottage and the slow dying of my mother. I gently took her hand, nails waxen and crisscrossed with ridges, the skin papery, a sickly yellow against my own meaty pink, marked by the nicks and pings of a life that continued beyond this room, my gold wedding band loudly proclaiming all I had to live for. It was unfair that I looked so obscenely healthy in the presence of so much frailty, such bone-chilling cold. I began.

"One afternoon, on my way back to school after lunch, I met a man named Mr. Cosmopoulos just outside the shop. He was the most interesting person I'd ever met and he called me mister, even though I was only nine. When I told him my mothers were lesbians, he said he thought I was Greek, from the island of Lesbos. He lived with his friend Shorty, who had been injured in the Korean War and who loved your cooking, which is why Mr. C. was near the store the day I met him." I paused to remember that booming voice behind me, how frightened I was, how grown-up I felt.

"After we became friends, I realized he had no money and I got you to give me the food. I always got extra for Mr. Cosmopoulos—I pretended it was for me and some new school friend you wanted to believe I had.

"Mr. Cosmopoulos wasn't really homeless the way people are now. He and Shorty lived in an abandoned tunnel under Twenty-ninth Street with a lamp and a hot plate and a secondhand cot and pillowcases made of shirts with the arms tied. They had a neighbor named Thelma who pretended she had food and invited us to a make-believe dinner, which really annoyed Shorty. That's where I went when I ran away. That's why the police couldn't find me. I was underground."

"Did he give you the Purple Heart?" she asked.

I shook my head. "No, Shorty did. He pinned it to my jacket the day I left. Mr. C. said Shorty didn't need it anymore. Shorty told him to tell me I had earned it for knowing when to run away and when to fight. Shorty wasn't good at saying good-bye either."

She closed her eyes and I waited, willing myself not to fall apart before I was finished. When I felt a light touch on my arm, I continued. "Mr. C. had a son in Hoboken who hadn't seen him in years.

"He'd walked me all the way home the day poor Andy almost fainted at the sight of me in the lobby. He said he was going to go visit him, maybe pick up where they left off. I think he figured his son might have missed him as much as I missed not knowing my father.

"I looked for him many times, but I never saw him again. I like to think he's with his son in New Jersey somewhere and that I had something to do with it."

She leaned as close to me as she could. "I'm going to miss that good heart of yours" was all she said.

THAT NIGHT she said good-bye instead of her usual good night. Annie and I found her the next morning, sleeping on her right side, her left arm extended toward the window as if she were reaching for something, as if someone had said, "come take my hand." The faint smile at the corners of her mouth said there was no pain. I touched the pale skin of her eyelids and before drawing them closed, I held the brilliant, bottomless green gaze to the place in my brain that remembers such things as the color of a mother's eyes.

She was gone. The boy who had too many mothers is now the man who has none.

I SIT IN THEO'S CHAIR, where she invented the menus that would help people remember what certain moments in their lives tasted like, where she imagined combinations of foods and flavors unheard of until she suggested them. And I think of Claire. "Cropping," she reminds me; "what's left out is just as important as what's showing."

The Sunday paper is open to the obituaries as I look for important clues in the terse announcements. The house, still alive with her, pulses around me as I struggle to say everything and achieve nothing. I wonder why no one in this week's worth of bereaved strangers has had the pluck to tell the truth—"Dad just wasn't the same after Ma died," or "Our beloved son, Rocco, died cruelly of AIDS and left a lover who now questions the value of getting up in the morning"—instead of the utterances of family "spokespersons" and "undisclosed" causes of death and the long lists of "survived by"s I see before me. I wonder how people can bear to even use the word "survive." Isn't there something more accurate? Getting by. Still breathing. Coping.

I think of Mr. Kimsky and the shadow Claire left in, but didn't explain. I think of the words that cannot be spoken in the presence of strangers who pick up this particular edition on an abandoned subway seat or use it to wrap the good crystal for the movers, train the new puppy, stuff in the path of a draft. Suddenly I feel the comfort in the precise language of a *New York Times* obituary, the euphemisms of mourning, and I, too, choose familiar phrases that do not give away what they really feel. No need to rake the heart with an unexpected clipping tucked into a condolence note by a distant and well-meaning friend. No need to say the words that have the power to open the wound on a day that isn't as raw as this one. No need to say what cannot be said. No use trying.

I run my hand over the patina of her desk and feel that peculiar combination of grooves worn by the way Theo worried an idea, and I think of Claire's heel marks on the stool she used in her darkroom. I think of the maimed bodies of pencils, chewed victims of my struggle with a story; of how I love to cook; of how I am funniest when I feel pain; of how I *see* into pictures. And, no matter what I've heard to the contrary, when Annie and I go to a party and she is pursued by a new friend and they punctuate their courtship with the light touching of fingers, whispered talk, secrets, plans, laughter low and secretive, and the urgent chatter of people filling in their histories up to the happy juncture of their association, I am not entirely unaware of the possibilities and I still believe a woman could steal Annie away at any second.

Peter knocks quietly and approaches the desk, laying a gentle pressure on my shoulder. "It's time to go," he says. Everything I would expect from a father and far more than I would dare ask is in his eyes, sharing a place with his own sorrow. I run my finger around the cool surface of the Purple Heart in my pocket that I will place in Theo's casket, next to the tiny silver locket. Two hearts now one. I will do this for Claire as well as for me after every one else has whispered their good-byes. Peter fights his own grief for the sake of mine and I wonder how I could not have seen. He offers an arm and I accept, saying nothing of what I know.

As we walk out into a room that at first seems too sunny for this day, oddly neat, into the wave of sorrow that breaks over me in the faces of our family, her friends, in my wife who loved my mother with a fierce loyalty never inspired by her own and who now beams this strength to me, I see why.

My beautiful twin girls, born together from two different eggs dropped mysteriously and simultaneously into our lives, one pale and blond, reserved, even in play, the other showing all the signs of red, already reaching for the brightest colors, look up from their game and smile. One called Theo; the other, Claire.

"We'll be going home soon," I say to them, and they gurgle their fat content.